More advance praise for Stacy Robinson and *Surface*

"In her gripping debut, Stacy Robinson introduces a cast of complex characters facing tough choices—and even tougher consequences. With sharp, smart writing, and a palpable undercurrent of tension from start to finish, *Surface* will captivate readers and give book clubs plenty to talk about."

—Michelle Gable, author of *A Paris Apartment*

"Stacy Robinson has written a heart twisting story of modern family life told with compassion, keen insight, and a healthy dash of fun. *Surface* affirms that resilience can counter the most profound personal tragedy, and self-discovery is timeless."

—Carol Cassella, national bestselling author of *Gemini*

"I can't remember the last time I devoured a h̶
From the first page, readers will want to d̶
beneath the *Surface* to discover the se̶
family. Magr̶

—Elin Hilderbrand, *New Yo.̶ ̶ ̶ ̶ ̶.̶ ̶.̶ ̶.̶ ̶.̶ ̶ ̶.̶ ̶ ̶ ̶.̶*̶ .ıor

SURFACE

STACY ROBINSON

KENSINGTON BOOKS
www.kensingtonbooks.com

KENSINGTON BOOKS are published by

Kensington Publishing Corp.
119 West 40th Street
New York, NY 10018

All Kensington titles, imprints, and distributed lines are available at special quantity discounts for bulk purchases for sales promotion, premiums, fund-raising, and educational or institutional use.

Special book excerpts or customized printings can also be created to fit specific needs. For details, write or phone the office of the Kensington Special Sales Manager: Kensington Publishing Corp., 119 West 40th Street, New York, NY 10018. Attn. Special Sales Department. Phone: 1-800-221-2647.

eISBN-13: 978-1-61773-376-5
eISBN-10: 1-61773-376-8
First Kensington Electronic Edition: March 2015

ISBN-13: 978-1-61773-375-8
ISBN-10: 1-61773-375-X
First Kensington Trade Paperback Printing: March 2015

10 9 8 7 6 5 4 3 2

Printed in the United States of America

For my parents—
who have always encouraged,
believed, loved, and *kvelled*.
You are simply the greatest!

Please skip the sex scenes.

ACKNOWLEDGMENTS

Thank you, first and foremost, to my husband, Jeff—chief cheerleader, enthusiastic dance partner, best bad joke teller, extraordinary spouse, dad and step-dad—for sharing your beautiful heart with me, and for staying up late. . . . You are my perfect. A big thank-you and a million and one hugs to my kids, Joe, Anna, and Tucker. Watching you grow into the incredible people you are has been my greatest joy, and your support and patience throughout this process has meant the world.

To my fabulous agent, David Forrer, whose advice, tenacity and unwavering belief in *Surface* helped make this book a reality—I am forever indebted to you. Very special thanks also go to my wonderful editor, John Scognamiglio, for taking me on so enthusiastically, and for bringing out the best in my words. I am truly lucky to have worked with both of you, along with all of the great folks at Inkwell Management and Kensington.

I'd like to express my gratitude to the other talented people who read, offered support, comments, and critiques, and otherwise helped me polish early versions of the manuscript: Michael Mezzo, William Haywood Henderson, and all the fine instructors at Lighthouse Writers Workshop; my brilliant writer friends, Rachel Greenwald, Emily Sinclair, Lauren Sinclair, Melanie Buscher, Alexandra Hill, and Betsy Leighton; and to my Brutally Frank Sisters, Justyn Shwayder and Meghan Zucker, for your shoulders, your wisdom and humor, and most importantly, your love—with an extra added thank-you to Meghan for sharing your invaluable expertise in physical therapy and experience with TBI patients.

To my wonderful community of family and friends who managed to remain encouraging during this embarrassingly long "birthing" process: thank you for resisting the urge to roll your eyes when asking, for the hundredth time, how the book was coming along (Mom and Dad, Suzie, Ellen, Scott, Jolie, Robert, David, Lisa Searles, Hyla Feder, Ethel McGlynn, Josh Hanfling, my dear BFUs: Julie Kennedy, Mary Obana, Jeanne Arneson, Ann Banchoff, and Danielle Waples, and so many others).

And to all of the extraordinary teachers I've had, especially: David Arnold, Dawn Hood, and Maud Gleason—thank you for instilling a love of words and stories, and for all of your guidance and encouragement. Finally, a big shout-out to my very favorite bookstore, the Tattered Cover, along with the baristas there, for keeping me inspired and caffeinated while I wrote and rewrote, and rewrote in your balconies. I'll be back.

*The real voyage of discovery consists not in
seeking new landscapes, but in having new eyes.*

—Marcel Proust

PROLOGUE

Nicholas stood in the shadows of the Millers' pool house watching the familiar pack of girls—so blond and tan and Abercrombie-fresh—as they swayed with the music, their mouths glistening and drunk with the new freedom of summer. He had known most of them since grade school, some even before that. And now they ran their hands over their breasts and across the slow orbit of their hips, eyeing their audience nearby. An invitation to dance, to hook up? He swigged his beer and tucked farther into the darkness. A lot had changed in just one year away.

His buddies were drinking and tossing lacrosse balls from one end of the landscaped terrace to the other, checking out the view as they did. Nick leaned against the pool-house wall, safe from the lame comments about how chill boarding school must be without parents around to constantly harass you. The hip-hop bass vibrated through his heels and rolled up his legs and spine. A warm gust rippled the pool, dropping a cascade of leaves onto its surface. It was June, and the night air pulsed. Nick swallowed the last of his beer, the lip of the bottle knocking his front tooth hard as he did, and the image of what he'd seen in his parents' study flashed through his mind again. His mother standing there next to Bricker, the look of surprise in her eyes as he opened the door on their little meeting. The night went silent for him.

Nick felt the hair stand up on the back of his neck as the wind swelled and he strained to remember whether their fingers were touching on the desk, or if he had just imagined it. But all he could picture was the glimmer of her ring as her hand disappeared into her pocket like a hermit crab into its shell. He blinked hard, catching a glimpse of someone pumping the keg, a muscled arm thrusting to an inaudible beat. More leaves blanketed the pool. Why had she seemed so edgy, so totally . . . off? After the forced "dialogue" with his dad a couple nights earlier—which, more accurately, had been a pathetic, excuse-ridden monologue—all Nick wanted was for his parents to go back to being normal again. To not be like his friends' parents. He swallowed against the surge in his throat and chucked his Coors bottle at the cement.

Nick stepped forward into the light and felt the muted, satisfying crunch of glass beneath his rubber sole, as Barry Manilow's "Copacabana" pierced the silence. The party froze for an instant, and by the time someone corrected the aberration in the playlist, he had picked up the jagged neck of the bottle and was pushing through the side gate, while his friends resumed their grinding, and red plastic cups rolled across the grass.

He walked up the tree-lined parkway toward his home half a mile away. The moon had taken its own shelter in the dusty sky, and only the occasional streetlamp lit the large expanses of lawns and gardens along his path. As he approached his block, he heard the low rev of an engine and saw Bricker's Porsche emerge from the gates of his house and speed past him on the street. He ran to the center parkway median and fingered the sharp rim of the bottle before hurling it. It fell short and shattered as the car vanished. Concealed in the shadows, Nick circled his block and the one adjacent several times in a figure eight, while the storm lost its resolve and he recovered his own, before passing through the gates himself.

With a mounting sense of what had happened inside the house after he'd left for the party, he crouched in the darkness, mulling the possibilities and concocting scenarios to explain them away. A lone football straddled the divide between the peonies and freshly mowed lawn. He picked it up and tossed it from palm to palm. No way. Maybe. Maybe not. *The moon reappeared from behind a veil of clouds. On an inconclusive* probably, *he dropped the ball and headed up the long path to the front door.*

Nick entered the house quietly. *He heard the shower upstairs and looked both ways down the foyer, the light burning in the guest room catching his attention. He felt a familiar nervousness in his stomach as he approached the room—the same sick tug he tried to dismiss each time the nurse prepared to draw his blood, his own voice telling him that he wasn't a pussy, that he was seventeen for Chrissakes, and the glaring certainty that it was still going to hurt. From the doorway, Nicholas inspected the bedroom, searching for a sign that he was wrong, that they hadn't been in there together. But he knew. The room felt hot and close. The night table was off-center, the bedspread and sheets were sloppy. He moved toward the bed and noticed something on the floor not quite blending in with the pattern of the rug. The glint of glass and its contents. He picked up the small vial and stared at the white powder inside.*

Squeezing it in his palm, he began pacing the room. Rewinding time. Honey, I'd like you to meet Andrew Bricker. He just stopped by to drop off some papers for your father. *The surge crowded his throat again as he tried to reconcile all he had known to be true with the razor sharpness of this new reality. His mother— the one person who could rouse him from his bouts of frustration with her late-night cinnamon French toast and reassuring words, her protective arms holding him until two a.m. after his seizure, her always upbeat, thoughtful approach to life's curveballs—doing coke? No way. It had to belong to Bricker. Dicker. Still.*

His father was a keeper of secrets—that had become painfully clear over the last week. Nick sat down on the edge of the bed recalling the same look of nervous surprise in his dad's eyes when he told him he'd found out the truth, the tremble of that characteristically strong jaw when he'd asked him about the choices he made all those years ago, the serrated edge of his own voice when he called his father out for not being the do-the-right-thing good guy he had always believed him to be. And for holding Nick so tightly to that fiction. Where was that hero he'd always worshipped, his Atticus?

Clenching his jaw, Nicholas poured the entire contents of the vial onto the glass surface of the night table. He dipped his pinky into the powder and ran his tongue over his finger. Bitterness, numbness. There was enough there, he figured, to get really high. He took a bill out of his wallet and rolled it into a tight cylinder. Then he cut two lines with his credit card and snorted them. He'd done it once before, in spite of his diabetes, and he'd watched a couple buddies do it often enough.

It stung his nostrils. And then it didn't. His confusion and angst, so freighted with adolescence, splintered into a thousand shards of light. Nick cut two more lines, fatter this time, and inhaled them, feeling an exquisitely anaesthetizing rush through his body. And then, nothingness.

PART ONE

CHAPTER 1

Claire Montgomery took a long sip of chardonnay and arched her head back, savoring the cool liquid slide in her throat. Her eye twitched, and somewhere behind her closed lids a faint throbbing set in. She tried to shake it away and placed her glass on the mahogany partners' desk of the study. The throbbing traveled to her neck. She steadied her hands on the back of a chaise and looked out the window to see the crimson dusk wash over her garden and the distant mountains.

Her arms were tanned from hours planting impatiens and peonies despite Michael's insistence that Rigo, the gardener, lighter of winter fires and sous chef to his wife Maria's efforts in the kitchen, could manage it much better. Her watch read seven thirty, and the carats on her finger flickered in the descending sunlight. In the background Joni Mitchell lamented the paving of paradise. Claire tried humming along, averting her eyes from the clusters of family photos on the bookshelves. But there *was* no shaking it away. The whole thing was so ridiculous, so unlike her. She reached for the phone to tell him not to come after all.

The doorbell rang, and for a second Claire considered ducking under the desk and cupping her hands over her ears. He'd leave, she'd apologize later. Done. Forget the idea of one stolen hour of *Oh my God, I* **matter** again, forget the rush and tingle. But a persistent knocking followed the bell, and her thoughts ricocheted to the night at The Palm—to his voice, his scar. And she could hear the pounding in her chest amplified to full acoustic brilliance.

Taking a deep breath and, for good measure, another healthy slug of the Louis Latour, Claire backed away from the desk and walked out to the foyer. Her capri sandals clapped across the floor and the sweet fragrance of Casablanca lilies filled her nose as she fluffed the arrangement on the table before opening the door.

Andrew Bricker stood under the marble portico. Whistling. She reached out to shake his hand and he leaned in and kissed her cheek, admiring her through his glasses.

"Well, don't you look gorgeous," he said, the corners of his eyes creasing with his smile.

She concentrated on keeping her voice calm, her expression casual—donning all her armor to avoid revealing her inner teenager. "It's nice to see you, too. Been enjoying Denver, I hope?"

She smoothed her summer dress over her hips and showed Andrew into the study, offering him a chair at the desk. The remnants of daylight were still fading outside the windows, and the glow brought an eerie calm to the house. Andrew removed an envelope and fountain pen from his jacket pocket and sat down, grazing Claire's bare shoulder as he did.

"I watched *The Thomas Crown Affair* last night," he said, uncapping his pen and flashing her the same bedroom smile that had launched her into this unfamiliar territory. "Nice recommendation." He paused. "That staircase scene was a real showstopper."

Claire tried to ignore the reference in a desperate attempt to forestall a fantasy detour to three-alarm movie sex. Instead she focused on Andrew's hand as he began writing a note to Michael. She saw the blue-green of his veins roll with his script and heard the scratch of the pen's silver tip along the paper. Again she felt the peculiar sensation that he was also scratching awake something from deep inside her. As if overcome by an uninhibited and wholly incongruous spirit, Claire placed her fingers on top of Andrew's, and was instantly disrobed of what little armor she had left.

Chapter 2

Claire had met Andrew Bricker on a pink-sky night the previous week. She'd been downtown finalizing details for the Art Museum gala she was co-chairing—her nine-month, semi full-time, fully unpaid labor of love. And just a few weeks shy of term, all signs were pointing to a record-breaking event. Drawing on her New York and European art world connections, Claire had gathered the exquisite and the exotic for an auction that would be part of the evening's festivities. She'd secured underwriting and matching funds; Harry Connick Jr. would be performing. Denver's art patrons and boldfaced names were in for a spectacular night, and with a last-minute half-million-dollar gift from a certain NFL Hall of Famer and a late rush in table sales, Claire was in the mood for some early celebration.

She gave Maria and Rigo the evening off, then dialed Michael's cell as she paced the cluttered museum office, jotting notes for the volunteers and staff.

"Hell-o," Michael answered, with his usual emphasis on the first syllable.

"Hell-o, yourself. How do you feel about a festive night on the town with your wife?"

"Ah, your little project must be going well."

Claire kept her smile fixed. "Yes, my *little project* looks like it's going to be a huge success, and I'd love a celebratory cocktail." She punctuated a Post-it note with red exclamation points and placed it on a file folder as she continued. "And maybe a little something else. So whaddya say, honey? Can we sneak off for some fun tonight?"

Michael cleared his throat and laughed in his clipped Bostonian way. "Sounds interesting, but I'm in the middle of a meeting at The Palm, and I'm afraid I've put Mr. Bricker here through the wringer. And I'm not quite finished." He had mentioned Andrew Bricker before. A young VC player in from New York making the investment rounds. Michael's lighthearted tone betrayed a thinly veiled enthusiasm for his guest's business pitch. "Lemme call you back in a few minutes?"

Claire sat on the edge of a desk and massaged the arches of her bare feet, fighting off a sense of deflation, and wistfully contemplating her early days in New York with Michael and the white-hot passion they'd shared then. How he'd jump at the chance for an unexpected rendezvous, and how he had loved to show her off to his colleagues, bragging about her latest projects at Sotheby's and her expertise in a world they didn't understand. But the farther they'd traveled from that time, the more he seemed to have replaced those memories with the weightier issues of business and busy living. She slipped into her slingbacks again and paused to remind herself that there was nothing unique in such marital hills and valleys. She'd had countless conversations with girlfriends about absent, inattentive spouses—especially those whose names regularly appeared in the business section—and she always walked away from those female bonding fests thinking that she and Michael had done it far better than most.

Still, her mind wandered to a recent Sunday morning when they had been lounging in the sunroom, sipping their coffee and reading the *New York Times*. Michael had pulled out the crossword puzzle and uncapped his pen while she was still in the middle of the Book Review section. They always saved the puzzle for last to work on together, but he'd started without her, as if their history had been etched in her mind alone. She glanced up between reviews to see if he was making any progress. After a brief run, he appeared stymied.

"Italian Renaissance artist, six letters. That's your department, Clarabelle." Michael looked across the ottoman with an exhausted expression, pointing his pen in her direction. "Fourth letter's a *t,* I think."

"Giotto," she'd replied, swallowing her disappointment and reminding herself that he hadn't been sleeping well, that the snub was likely due to fatigue.

He filled in the boxes with staccato strokes and moved on to the next clue.

Claire watched him for several minutes, willing him to remember *them*. But his focus remained on the paper, his brow creased in exaggerated concentration. "You know," she offered in a buoyant voice, "it looks like we might bring in a new collection of de Koonings and some other incredible pieces next year."

Michael set the paper aside, appearing slightly less distracted. "What?"

"The gala, it's going to provide some important opportunities—"

Before she could finish he was standing beside her, one finger pressed to her lips while his other hand untied her robe. "You're doing great work, all of you gals at the museum." Artfully he slipped off his pajama bottoms. "Really great, babe. You should be proud."

Sunlight angled through the bamboo shades and jade-and-gold faille drapery, washing them in a warm glow. Michael hit play on the sound-system remote and Claire bolstered herself with the fact that enthusiasm *was* enthusiasm. She closed her eyes and propped her feet on the ottoman, curved her body into his, and they slipped into the rhythm of their years together, making silent love with her arms wrapped around the small of his back. The rustle of newspaper and the sting of Liza Minnelli's "Maybe This Time" bookended her *let's just let it slide* slide into sex. Just before Michael was ready to come, Claire grasped his thighs with both hands and pulled him deeper into her. He thrust faster, shuddered, and leaned back on his elbows, their bodies fashioning an unsteady X. She opened her eyes to see that his were still squeezed shut, his mouth frozen in a tight expression—reminding her of the grimacing Phoenician mask she had seen at the Louvre the previous summer. When they untangled, she waited for him to pull on his pajamas, which he did, as always, within seconds of finishing. She laughed silently at his fastidiousness. He sat back down in his chair and wiped at a phantom smear of newsprint from the knee of the paisley pajamas. Shards of violet and indigo bisected his face.

"I spoke to Nicholas yesterday," Claire said, leaning in toward him and pulling her hair away from her damp neck. "He may need you to go with him to Andrisen Morton to pick up a tux for the benefit when he gets back from Andover." She took his foot in her hands and began to massage it. "He's not exactly thrilled about it, but it should be a nice little outing for the two of you."

"Of course he's not thrilled. He's a teenager—seventeen already, *Jesus,*" he'd said with the same odd tinge of distress and disbelief that had been coloring similar oft-repeated remarks since Nick's October birthday. "And teenage boys don't want to attend boring black-tie benefits. Hell, I don't like to attend boring black-tie benefits. They're a waste of chicken." The light had shifted, and the rainbow had moved to the east wall. Michael slid his foot to the floor and stood. "I . . . didn't mean your deal, Claire. Just tell me the date and the time." He walked to the foyer muttering *seventeen,* his head canted and his mind somewhere else, not there.

"I already have."

A staff member peeked into the office and flashed Claire a check for a new Platinum Level table from Carolyn and Robert Spencer. She smiled gratefully, relocating her happy mood. Even with the economy in its dreadful state, her friends were stepping up and supporting the event. She made a few more notes for the auctioneer and telephoned Carolyn to thank her and make lunch plans, while she waited for Michael's call. It came fifteen minutes later.

"Sorry for the delay, babe. Everything okay on your end?"

"Well . . . things are good, but *could be* even better." She adjusted the straps of her shoes and ran her fingers slowly up her calf, waiting.

"Andrew and I were about to order some more drinks and a couple rib eyes," he said, sounding preoccupied.

"Then I guess my hopes for a little celebrating are dashed."

"You could join us if you want," Michael allowed after a short pause.

Claire hopped off the desk and stared out the window overlooking the skyline. "Is that the best you can do?"

"Okaay," he scrabbled. "How about some scintillating conversation and serious red meat to go with your cocktail? And Sabina's waiting on us. I'm sure she'd love to see you."

"Hmm. Two men for the price of one, a juicy steak, and Sabina? I guess that *is* my best offer of the day. I'll head over."

A fiery sunset hovered above the downtown high-rises, and a wind rustled the branches of the honey locust trees on the Sixteenth Street Mall. She walked to the restaurant, suppressing her chagrin that she'd had to goad her husband into an invitation that once would have come with enthusiasm, and arriving twenty minutes later focused on a triumphant bottom-line gala figure, and a taste for champagne.

As Claire navigated her way to their usual table just below Michael's autographed caricature on the wall, she raised her hand in a small wave to her husband. Michael nodded back and the man who sat beside him turned his head in her direction. His lips parted a fraction, and Claire watched him watch her approach. Behind his off-kilter smile, he appeared to be in his late thirties, a few years shy of her forty-three, and not at all like the rep tie, overgrown frat-boy types Michael often did business with. She noticed his eyes travel from her legs to her silk blouse that shifted over her lace camisole, before resting his gaze on her face. The gesture came as an almost satisfying, welcome surprise. Claire lowered her eyes and smiled toward a table of women coated with the glitz and hope of a girls' night out.

"Hi, babe," Michael said from his seat while craning his face upward to give her a kiss. "Don't you look elegantly exhausted. Busy day?"

She tucked her windblown hair back into place. "Fabulous day, actually." Claire extended her hand to Andrew. "So nice to meet you, Mr. Bricker. Michael's told me about you."

"Good reports, I hope?" Andrew stood with Claire's hand in his and pulled out a chair for her.

He was an inch or two taller than Michael's six feet, with the broad shoulders and slim torso of a swimmer—a butterflyer, Claire imagined. A faint scar rose from the center of his lip to the side of his nose, and his dark, wavy hair and tortoiseshell glasses reminded her of an enthralling Spanish artist she'd worked with in her first New York job. The young Spaniard had suffused his work with a complexity that belied his age, and Claire recalled for an electric instant the monumental self-control it had taken— despite the artist's best efforts—to keep their relationship professional. "Thank you, sir," she said to Andrew with the playful flirtatiousness Michael had once adored.

She ordered a glass of Veuve and surveyed both men. Michael wasn't wearing his usual poker face. He'd loosened his tie and was toasting Andrew, drawing him in. A platter of oysters arrived, a bottle of wine. They talked markets and interest rates, laughed knowingly over encounters with Trump and Larry Ellison, and made more toasts as Michael teased out inside figures and details on the biomedical company Andrew had come to pitch, and Andrew engaged them with a charismatic and cultured wit. The seduction was ramping up, and Claire could see there was an important deal in the offing. Andrew had something Michael wanted. She sipped her champagne appreciatively, enjoying how the evening was stacking up after all.

"So, where in New York did you say you live?" Claire asked Andrew over her petit filet.

"Soho. Just a quick walk to Balthazar." He smiled an intimate, reflective sort of smile. "I have several acquaintances with galleries in the area, which is also nice."

Claire pegged him as a sophisticated player. He was Tom Ford in a town whose tastes ran more toward mountain chic or, like Michael, Brioni suits and Hermes ties. She was amused by the contrast. Michael, always perfect and handsome in his French cuffs and sterling cuff links, his blond hair cut short and neatly groomed with pomade, was a man who took pride in his appearance. Andrew was more of an unmade bed—handsomely disheveled with a bit of scruff on his chin and maybe a tiny smear of lip gloss on his collar. As the wine and conversation flowed she tried to imagine what his acquaintances might look like.

"Do you know Arcadia Fine Arts?" she asked, picturing Greene Street's cobblestones and the exquisitely curated space where she'd first seen the Spaniard's work showcased.

"Sure. They bring in some interesting new artists. Great parties, too. I'm just around the corner."

"Ah. You must live in one of those wonderful cast iron buildings, then?"

Andrew gave her an intrigued nod, poised, it seemed, to walk with her through that neighborhood of her past.

"So," Michael interjected, reinserting himself into the conversation, "you're a big gallery aficionado, Andrew?"

Andrew turned his head toward Michael, but managed to keep his focus on Claire. "I am. Although I like to check in on the Met occasionally, too."

"Oh, *this* one," he said, glancing sideways at Claire, "is always trying to drag me to some new show or exhibit or some crazy event when we're in town." Michael had drunk enough wine to be careless with his casual mockery.

"Drag you?" Claire tried to remain good-natured about his comment as she slapped his elbow in mock outrage. The water in his glass jumped the rim and dribbled down his wrist, and she saw the controlled surprise of his expression mirror her own. "We've had some of our best afternoons in Manhattan at museums." She dabbed at the water stain with her napkin and tried to smile through her embarrassment.

"What I *meant,* my dear," Michael said in his most velvet tone, "is that you're the only woman I know who prefers the galleries and museums in New York to the boutiques." He cherry-topped the recovery with a kiss on her hand.

"So you think you're going to Cary Grant your way out of this one?" she asked, remembering they were a party of three, and laughing in Andrew's direction. "Art's always been a passion." She paused to gauge his earlier interest. His green eyes blinked slowly behind his glasses, his long lashes colliding softly, and he nodded for her to go on. In her peripheral vision Claire saw Michael checking his watch. She placed her hand on his wrist as she continued, one of a hundred involuntary gestures that had, over the years, become routine. "I'm involved in the local arts community, though not professionally anymore. I used to work at Sotheby's before Michael and I were married. Contemporary paintings and drawings mostly." Michael took his iPhone from his pocket with his free hand and began scrolling through messages. She felt the vibration of an incoming text message and gave his wrist a gentle squeeze, just as Michael eyed the screen and flipped it over. When he stood, Claire's fingers slid from his starched, wet cuff to the tablecloth.

"Michael," she whispered.

"I need to handle something," he said. He buttoned his suit coat and pushed his chair back into place. "I'm sure you two have a lot to chat about. Back in a few," he mouthed over his shoulder.

Claire laced her fingers tightly, feeling the patina of the evening start to crackle and fade like an out-of-range radio station.

"Asian markets on fire?" Andrew asked, filling the silence.

"There's always a deal burning somewhere." She took a sip of wine, washing away the prickly sensation in her chest. "I'm sorry for the disappearing act. These calls tend to take a while."

"He lives up to his reputation."

Claire's right eye began to twitch, as it often did when the headaches started. "You know, I'd really prefer to hear more about your interest in art," she said, clothes-pinning any further discussion of foreign markets and Wall Street reputations. "Talk to me about what's happening in New York now."

Andrew took off his glasses and set them beside Claire's hand, studying her face. "A much more enjoyable topic." Effortlessly he launched into details of recent shows at two of her favorite Tribeca galleries, the amusing provenance of a collector friend's rare Kandinsky, and his own modernist preferences at the MoMA. "I also saw an incredible artist in Montreal awhile back. I was at the 'Picasso Erotique' exhibit, and . . ."

Her eyes refocused. "I saw that exhibition the last time we were there. Amazing, wasn't it?"

"It was. But the real find was this guy I'd never heard of. Renato something. He did these pen-and-ink drawings of nudes. The images were unbelievably powerful."

"Renato Gaffarena?" Claire began pulling up the images in her mind, stunned. "Maltese artist?"

"Yeah, I think you may be right. Do you know him?"

"Years ago we oversaw the auction of a private collection that had about fifteen of his drawings. Right after he committed suicide."

"That would explain the darkness."

"I thought he was incredible. Those sensual, fluid lines. It was as if they poured from his pen." For an instant Claire was back in New York seeing the drawings for the first time, the artist's pathos and lust prompting a visceral response in her. "I desperately wanted one of his pieces at the time, but he was out of my price range. Especially after his death."

"Had you met him?"

"No, but I became a little obsessed with his work. I remember *feeling* the moods of his models, the frenzy in their worlds each time I looked at one of his pieces. And somehow he made these women seem, I don't know, almost chaste and erotic at the same time."

"Ah, but art is never chaste," Andrew said in the voice of a man who'd been a stranger to chastity for a good long while.

"I'm impressed. An entrepreneur who can quote Picasso." Her headache flitted away like a cocktail umbrella on a warm breeze. She pictured Gaffarena's nudes, and her thoughts wandered to *The Thomas Crown Affair.* And to two art lovers passionately tangled on a staircase.

Andrew slid his chair in closer to hers. "So, what else do you like, Claire?" His voice was plummy and smooth, decidedly more like Pierce Brosnan's Thomas Crown than Steve McQueen's.

She swallowed slowly and placed both of her hands on the table to steady them, but also for a bit of lighthearted emphasis. "The second floor of the MoMA is, hands down, my favorite place to spend an afternoon in Manhattan." Her rings caught the light from the nearby candles and reflected it onto Andrew's attentive face. "I would add Magritte and Klimt to your list, and just a bit of Dali for some fun, but I think we have very similar tastes."

"I think we do," Andrew said. A hush descended as they stared at each other over the flickering glow.

"Yes," Claire whispered.

"Maybe I could coax you into a professional tour of MoMA some day?"

She cradled her wine with both hands, looking down into the heavy redness, her head suddenly swimming a bit.

"See the future in there?" he asked after a moment.

"I was just thinking about a movie. *The Thomas Crown Affair.* I know it sounds corny, but I was watching the remake on TV last night, and it always gets me." A veil of wine slid down the inside of her glass as slow as honey.

"I saw the Steve McQueen version."

Claire looked up at him, into his deep-set soulful eyes, and she felt herself veering far enough from her comfort zone that she was afraid she'd missed a detour sign and stumbled onto some dodgy alternate route. She crossed and uncrossed her legs, smoothed her napkin over her skirt. She thought of the highly charged cat and mouse game the actors had played in both versions of the movie. "You should catch the remake," she said, tracing the rim of her glass. "The art and characters, the clothes. And the chase. It's all very . . ."

Andrew waited for her to find the right words. But she never did utter them. "Well, it sounds like a worthwhile evening," he finally said. "I'll be sure to take your advice."

Claire reached for her water glass.

"So," Andrew continued, his gaze still locked on her, "tell me about the little project Michael mentioned."

She worried a piece of ice with her tongue and waited for her pulse to slow its dervish spin through her chest. Easing back into less hazardous territory, Claire started with an overview of the museum benefit—thrilled, she realized, to actually have been asked. She described the décor, the commissioned bronze sculpture and the Villa in Cannes she'd wrangled for the auction, the new exhibits the museum would be able to mount with the gala revenue—her enthusiasm recovering, detail by detail, its luscious pre-headache ripeness. As Andrew listened, Claire saw in his face her father's interest and esteem, the Spaniard's smolder, and Michael's first glimmerings of attraction. And something else.

"Well, then"—Andrew raised his glass of Silver Oak to her—

"to Denver's own version of the Costume Institute Benefit. It's going to be a huge smash."

"You go to the Met party?" She took another small piece of ice into her mouth, fixing on the strong, un-manicured hand caressing the glass just inches from her face. "Seriously?" she said, swallowing the ice. "We're in New York for it every year. God, you probably recognized that I, uh, borrowed a few décor ideas—the apple tree hedges?" She watched him smiling wordlessly at her blabbering. "Anyway," she said, pausing for breath, "maybe we were even seated at nearby tables last year?"

"Intriguing thought, isn't it? Parallel lives?" His right eyebrow lifted in the center and he tapped her glass with his own, intersecting their parallels. "But I was the guy in the cheap seats and you, I'd hazard, were the stunning brunette seated near the dance floor with her husband."

"A lovely compliment, but five points off for inaccuracy. Michael hates those functions and usually finds a last-minute business engagement." She shrugged her shoulders. "I sat with one of the extra men."

"If I'd only known."

"Well, our son, Nicholas, is home for the summer now, so I'll have at least one terrific date for the benefit here. He's a very talented artist himself," she said with pride. "And if Michael *doesn't* show, he's a dead man."

Andrew rested his elbow on the table. "I admire your enthusiasm. It's great to have a passion that gives your world so much luster. Don't you think?"

Luster. Until then Claire had been unable to pinpoint what it was she had started to feel. But his words hit her with unexpected force. She nodded, open-mouthed, feeling as if he somehow understood something she had long ago forgotten. And in that dreamlike moment when the world exists in a narrow, slow motion frame, she reached out and touched the scar above his lip, letting her fingernail rest there for a second. His skin was warm and damp. "God, I'm so sorry," she said, quickly withdrawing from the intimacy of the gesture.

Andrew delicately brushed the inside of Claire's wrist before she'd completely pulled away. "It's all right. It was a skiing accident when I was a kid."

Sabina appeared at the table as Claire was collecting herself to offer coffee and dessert.

"I'll just have a cappuccino, thanks, Sabina," she said, twisting her napkin tightly around her offending finger. She felt heat in her cheeks and neck.

"Oh, come on. Live on the edge. Have some cheesecake in honor of New York, and its karmic possibilities." He ran a bent knuckle back and forth over the scar.

The dessert arrived on one plate, with two forks, and they relished it as little children would a last piece of birthday cake. Claire steered the conversation back to the safety of a certain Italian bakery on Mulberry Street, and to the city in general.

"So, what made you leave New York?" Andrew asked.

"Michael, actually. We met at the home of a mutual friend on Long Island. He was in from out of town, and he swept me right off my Charles Jourdan stilettos." She placed her fork on the edge of the plate and stared silently into the candlelight, recalling a dinner party nearly two decades earlier when a charming and brilliant new player had crashed her social whirl.

"And?"

"And after a few months of commuting, I found myself back in the Bay Area, engaged. It was the late eighties and Michael was just striking his semiconductor gold in Silicon Valley. Life was so . . . exciting." Her thoughts drifted, and she felt Andrew's leg skim hers under the table.

"Excuse me," he said with some embarrassment; whether it was feigned or real, Claire couldn't tell, and she didn't mind.

His eyes seemed a brighter green to her now with a hint of aqua, almost the same color as her own, and they burned with equal parts attraction and unbound desire. They picked up their forks. Claire wiped phantom crumbs from the tablecloth with her other hand. "Enough about me. Tell me what you do with *your* time when you're not attending museum galas or checking out the galleries." *Banter, I can do banter,* she reminded herself. "No, wait, let me guess. You like car racing. You definitely ski. And you paint animal portraiture on Thursdays."

"Very nice—ten points for originality and near-accuracy." Andrew swallowed the last of his wine. "I do actually enjoy car racing, and I like to heli-ski these days."

"Ah. I always seem to gravitate toward risk-takers."

Andrew raised both eyebrows this time.

"I mean, Michael's that way. The nature of his business and all."

As they stabbed at the crust of the cheesecake, Michael reappeared at the table and apologized to Andrew for his long absence. Issues in Hong Kong, he offered by way of excuse. "So, how long will you be in town, Andrew?" Michael asked, focusing in on his guest.

"I have meetings scheduled through the end of the week, and I'll be visiting friends in Aspen next week. But I'll be at the Hotel Monaco while I'm in Denver."

Claire ran her fingers through her hair, tucking one side behind her ear, leaving the other to fall over the corner of her eye and cheekbone.

"Fine. I'll be in touch with you before I leave for Europe." Michael handed his credit card to Sabina. "Excellent job as always, sweetheart," he said to the exotic server, who smiled demurely.

Andrew shook Michael's hand as they stood and walked out of the restaurant. "Thank you. It was a great evening. And you certainly have a lovely wife."

"So I've been told." Michael laughed and gave Claire's arm a squeeze before heading to the valet with his ticket.

Andrew stared at Claire for several seconds before speaking. "It was truly a pleasure."

"Yes . . . thank you. I enjoyed our conversation."

Andrew held the door open for her, and they parted at the valet.

In the days that followed, Claire wondered if Andrew had thought about the evening as much as she had. With Michael in London on business and Nicholas just home from boarding school and anxious to catch up with old friends, her dinner encounter with Andrew had taken up a cozy residence in her consciousness. During restless moments she paged through old Sotheby's catalogs and imagined the MoMA tour she might give. Alone in bed at night she tried to conjure Andrew's face and voice, and the competent, fascinating person she'd been with him, along with the dizzying chemistry she knew she hadn't invented. When she awoke from old familiar dreams, she felt the hot whisper of *querida* in her ear.

Feeling every inch the ridiculous schoolgirl, she telephoned Andrew's hotel three times before she actually had the nerve to be put through to his room. She hadn't planned any script beyond the "Hello, just checking to see how you're enjoying Denver" opener. But the words spilled out in rapid, ineloquent succession as she paced the wide perimeter of her bedroom. She found herself inviting him to the house to hear more about his deal. Michael mentioned there might be a diabetes application she said she'd like to hear about, maybe just a quick stop on his way to dinner if he had the time. And there was a painting she'd recently acquired at auction that she thought he might like to see as well. Similar impact to Renato's work, she explained.

"I'd love to," Andrew said, interrupting her description of the finer points of the artist's use of perspective. "Seven thirty?"

"What? Oh. That's . . . great," Claire spluttered. She clicked off and folded into her mohair reading chair, stunned by her own audacity. Closing her eyes, she whispered reassurances that there was nothing inappropriate about improving her grasp of technology, or showing a great piece of art to someone who genuinely shared her interest.

CHAPTER 3

Inside the library with Andrew, Claire imagined that she was someone else, that what was happening was somehow valid, even vital. She looked down at her hand on his. Their shared electricity seemed to course through her, and her breath came in shallow spurts. She felt heat, cold, fear, and restlessness—all the walls beginning to recede. Andrew let the pen fall and curled his thumb around her index finger, massaging it with a rhythmic and tender sensuality. She turned to him, about to speak, just as the library door swung open. Andrew inched to the left.

Nicholas stood framed in the doorway, and Claire saw Michael's blue-gray eyes staring back at her, saw the boy, the man, her son. She jerked her hand away from the desk and into her pocket, wondering what he had seen in that instant. "Nicky, honey, I thought you were at Reese's."

"Apparently," she heard him say under his breath.

Claire stepped forward and cleared her throat. "I'd like you to meet Andrew Bricker." Nicholas stared at her, unmoving, his eyes frozen wide. His light brown hair, a beautiful compromise between her chestnut and Michael's blond, fell in thick waves around his face, which now bore an expression of undisguised surprise. His arms hung at his sides, tan muscles peeking out from the sleeves of his Nantucket-red T-shirt. "He and your father have had a couple meetings. About a new biomedical software concept Mr. Bricker's company is funding." The room was deadly quiet, but for her voice. "And he just stopped by to drop off some papers." Claire turned back toward her guest. "Andrew, this is my son, Nicholas. He just finished his junior year at Andover and is home for the summer."

"Good to meet you, Nicholas." Andrew moved to shake his hand. "It must feel good to have a few months off from the grind."

"Yeah." Nicholas glanced down at Andrew's hand, then at the outline of Claire's in her pocket. He pulled away. "My dad won't be back from Europe for a week. You could've just dropped that off with his assistant downtown."

"Actually, your mom wanted to take a look at the prospectus. She was at our first dinner meeting and was very interested in the business."

Nicholas shot Claire one of his trademark sarcastic looks. "When did you get so into biomedical stuff?"

Claire walked over to Nicholas and sat down on the edge of the chair in front of the antique radio console Michael's parents had given them when Nick was born. "I'm interested in some of the applications, honey. There could be a diabetes connection," she said, guilt choking her words into a whisper.

Nick glanced at his Medic Alert bracelet, and then squinted back at her, and at Andrew. "Yeah, well. Cool, I guess." He splayed his fingers around the doorknob. "I've gotta go. Reese is picking me up and we're heading out."

"You're leaving?"

He nodded.

"O-kaay." She wasn't certain if what she felt was gratitude or dread, but she kept her gaze trained on Nicholas, trying to assure him he was the only person in the room who mattered. "Whose parents are out of town tonight?"

"Catherine Miller's," he said. "Just her dad. Don't stress."

Claire arranged her face into composure. "You know the rules, Nicky. And I don't want you getting into a car with anyone who's been drinking." She stood. "If you need a ride, you call me."

"Yeah."

"I'd like you home by midnight."

"I'm staying at Reese's tonight. He got the new *Call of Duty.*"

She wrapped her arm around her son's torso, squeezing him close to her. He smelled of soap and Axe spray. "Why don't you just call when you're leaving the party?"

"Sure." He twisted out from Claire's embrace. "I gotta roll. I'll see you in the morning." As he turned to leave he looked back over his shoulder. "Nice to meet you, Mr. Dicker."

"It's Bricker. But Andrew's fine."

Nicholas pulled the door shut behind him. A horn honked in the distance and the front door slammed.

Claire felt her stomach churn, and collapsed into the fringed toile pillows of her chaise. "Oh my God. I hope he didn't get the wrong idea." She reflected on the irony of her statement.

"Aw, he's just a kid dying to get to a party." Andrew sat down next to her. "The Dicker comment was clever, though." He placed his hand on Claire's clenched fist. "You okay?"

"No," she blurted out. Acid inched up her throat. "What must he be thinking? What if he—"

"Hey," Andrew said reassuringly, "we were just two people standing at a desk. It was nothing. He won't even remember this in an hour."

"But it was—"

"He'll be with his friends, flirting with all the girls. And between that and the new video game at his buddy's, he'll be *very* busy. Trust me. You know how teenage boys are. The goings-on in adult world don't hold much interest." He studied her intently. "How about a drink? You look a little pale."

Claire eyed the decanter on the shelf and moistened her dry lips, wanting to believe his logic. "I don't know." What would it matter now, she wondered? This whole thing, it was as if she was folding origami and none of the corners were matching up. She looked back at him, took him in, concerned expression and comforting hands. "Okay," she whispered. "Sure," she exhaled, as she struggled to bring her nerves under control.

Andrew poured two glasses of scotch and set them on the cocktail table next to Claire. "Whatever I can do to help." He smiled softly, brushing her hair from her cheek, and Claire closed her eyes, trying not to think of all the reasons she had wanted him to come. "In fact"—he lowered his voice—"I think I have something right here that might provide a little diversion."

She opened her eyes to see Andrew's hand resting on his pants pocket. Her initial irritation quickly turned to curiosity as he reached for something from deep inside the pocket. The small glass vial he pulled out caught the light of the chandelier above and glimmered.

Jesus. Claire did a double take at the powdery contents and heaved herself out of the chaise and away from him. Her mind spun. In her younger, mildly experimental days in New York, she'd tried a little coke, when everyone was doing coke. But it was a vague and distant memory from a lifetime away. What the hell had she been thinking at this stage in her life—the unlikely chemistry with this man she barely knew, her wild thoughts and desires? And now this. *This?* She had lived eighteen faithful years in the happy confines of her marriage to Michael. He was a good man. She loved her family. This was all a crazy, senseless mistake.

Andrew hastily shoved the vial back into his pocket and rushed to Claire before she'd pieced words together into a coherent response. "God, I'm sorry." He took her hands in his again, this time rubbing them as if to erase the memory of what he'd just offered. "I was trying—obviously in the most misguided, *idiotic* way—to distract you with a little party favor to take the edge off. And it was stupid. Mind-bogglingly stupid."

The hair of his forearm felt like tiny sparks along Claire's skin, and she retracted her hands.

"An old friend from Aspen, he dropped by and left it. I shouldn't have even—Forgive me? Please?"

With her edges frayed and about to unravel, she crossed her arms tightly over her chest and studied the crown molding through a haze of bewildering sensations.

"Let's start over—erase the last ten minutes." Tentatively, he wiped a smear of berry lipstick from just below her lip with his finger and turned her chin in his direction. "Please," he reiterated solemnly. "I'm an idiot, but you're extraordinary. Luminous. From the moment I saw you at the restaurant, I was bewitched."

Her shoulders descended an inch while her feet prepared to bolt.

"You're such a captivating, intelligent woman. And I'm fascinated by this buttoned-up sexiness you have about you. And that inner luster . . . I hope you know how attractive you are, Claire." He appeared to be replaying the memory of that evening in his mind with a zeal Claire was all too familiar with. "But"—he abruptly broke from his reverie and looked around the room— "you're living in a cage," he said. He stared squarely into her puzzled expression.

"What?" She felt her equilibrium ricochet like a pinball.

"It's a beautiful cage, no doubt. But let's be honest here. It could use a little . . . rattling, wouldn't you say?" His eyes were suddenly as penetrating and entrancing as the Spaniard's, his voice magnetic and certain. And Claire felt equal parts panicked and spellbound—panicked that she subconsciously might have been looking for a little disaster *and* that he could actually see this in her—and no less gripped by the force field that seemed to have enveloped them. She tried to back away, but tripped in the process. Andrew caught her shoulder and helped her regain her balance. He led her back toward the table and handed her the scotch.

She took a long drink, buying time. Her hand shook, the ice in the glass clattering as she tried to pull herself together. What else had he seen inside of her, she wondered? What did he know that she didn't? "Tell me . . . um . . . more about the software," she barely managed between more sips.

"Why don't we just relax for a minute?" He pointed toward the couch. A gust of wind kicked up outside and sent a faint whistle through the fireplace behind them. Neither of them moved.

Claire felt his gaze boring into her. "You know, I'm not comfortable with this," she said, finally finding her voice and setting down the empty glass. "I should never have called, and I think it would be best if you—"

Andrew stepped in closer to her. "I'm very glad you did call," he said before she could finish. "And, truly, I didn't mean to frighten you. I'm sorry for that. I came here for *you,* Claire." There was a hunger underlying the contrition in his voice. "Because you asked me to." He shifted his weight from one foot to the other. "Because I wanted to see you, to be with you again."

He was just inches from her and she could smell him, too— the scent of his soap and urgency, and some intoxicating quality that hindered her reason. It was a familiar, ambrosial essence that brought her back to a time when everything had seemed exciting and hopeful. She breathed it in, wanting him gone just as much as she didn't.

Just then, Andrew's cell phone breached the intense silence, startling them both. He checked his BlackBerry, looking distressed that the moment had been interrupted. And equally resolute that it would be continued. "I apologize," he said. "It's work and I unfortunately need to take this. Is there somewhere I could have just a minute?"

"There's the guest room." The words seemed to come from someone else as she indicated the doorway in the hall, instead of telling him to take the call in his car and leave. She watched him look back at her as he walked toward the door, his confidence and obvious desire for her rendering her paralyzed. She knew she should stop him and tell him to go, but she just stood there. Things like this did not happen to people like her. And yet. It was lopsided origami everywhere.

When she was finally able to unglue herself, Claire began to pace the long gallery-lit hallway outside the guest bedroom, punctuating her thoughts with the odd articulated word, and fighting to banish images of Michael and Nicholas. She stopped in front of a large oil painting by a still unknown modernist—the painting she'd wanted to show Andrew.

Lightly tracing the raised ochre curves of the nudes on the canvas, she listened to Andrew's muted voice as she tried to re-summon her strength. Turning away from the painting, she slid down the wall to the floor, still wanting and knowing that she shouldn't.

"This was a mistake," Claire said as she pushed open the bedroom door, "and you need to go." She squeezed the doorknob with one hand, and rubbed at her temple with the other. Her pulse hammered into her knuckles. "Please."

Andrew was just placing his phone into his pocket. "Claire," he said, moving toward her. "You can't tell me that's what you really want. You don't want me to leave now." He grasped her biceps. "I don't want to go," he said in a hoarse whisper.

Her arms dropped to her sides. They stood hip to hip and she felt the energy between them again, and sensed her fragile control slipping. "I'm sorry. I can't do this."

"Shh." He placed his fingers on her lips. "It's okay. Don't think so hard." His mouth grazed her earlobe and dotted a path down her shoulders.

"No." She didn't move.

He kissed the side of her neck. Her skin prickled as he circled around to her throat, his breath hot and then cold on her. She pulled away from him, and the unsettling sensation that had flooded her evaporated. There was a dreamlike instant of quiet in her head, a cessation of thought. She took his face in her hands and kissed his mouth deeply until it was no longer a kiss and they were devouring each other's lips and tongues. Andrew tugged her head back by the nape of her hair and caressed the hollow at the base of her neck. Then, winding her arms around his back, she yanked his shirt from his pants and ran her nails up the curve of his spine. Their clothing left a haphazard trail as they stumbled from the door to the bed.

Andrew laid her down and cupped her right breast in his hand and stroked her nipple, softly at first and then pinching it until Claire felt the reverberations between her thighs. She arched her head back and moaned as he flicked his tongue over her other nipple. It was a raw nerve, hard as a pebble. As she watched his face move rhythmically down her stomach, he whispered what he planned to do to each inch of her, what he had imagined doing since the night they'd met. "Do you want more?" he asked with a soul-seizing fervor that Michael had never displayed in their composed and quiet lovemaking.

"Yes," she panted.

Andrew leisurely alternated between her breasts and the small of her stomach, teasing open her thighs with his fingertips each time his mouth dipped to her belly button. She felt heat between her legs and a sudden, scorching desire for him to plunge his fingers inside her. As he caressed her nipples again, she reached down and his hand met hers. "Do you want me to touch you, Claire?" he asked, running his fingertips up the insides of her thighs.

"Yes," she whispered again.

"Where?"

She guided his hand between her legs, and he began to stroke her.

"Do you like it right here?" He ran his finger slowly over her clitoris, back and forth. "Or here?" He pushed his finger gently inside of her.

All she could do was gasp.

Andrew took a pillow and propped it under her hips and then slowly spread her legs apart, staring at her like a sculptor before soft clay. She froze, waiting. But he kept his hands immobile and his gaze fixed on her, even as she begged for his touch with her eyes. When she could no longer hold herself still, she ground her hips into the pillow in a slow arc, trying to replicate the sensation of him.

A look of glazed ecstasy washed over his face. Maintaining eye contact, he eased himself down onto his stomach and caressed the invisible line from her navel to her inner thighs, moving in with his tongue, licking and then sucking until she began to sigh.

After several moments, he lifted his chin above her hips. His hair glistened with sweat. "Do you like my mouth on you?

She parted her lips to speak, but couldn't bring herself to say anything.

"You taste so good."

Claire moaned, hoping he would continue.

"Or do you like my fingers?" He stroked her again, building up to a frenzied momentum, then slowed. "Tell me what you want." He stopped, waiting for her.

What she wanted was to cut free and swim in the deep murky waters of him. But she was paralyzed again, the torment both frustrating and exquisite. She sat up and tried to reach for his erection, but he guided her down to her back.

"Not yet," he whispered.

"What do you want from me," she finally whispered, desperate for him to touch her again.

"I want you to just let go," he said. "No one's looking, Claire. Tell me what you like."

"Please . . . I can't."

"Why can't you?"

The words rolled around in her head—his words, her own, things she hadn't said out loud in years—until finally, need trumped decorum. She closed her eyes. "Don't stop. Please." She was dizzy and panting, shedding her propriety like a coat. "Make me come," she moaned. "Please."

His mouth was on her again. It was as if he'd removed her skin and exposed every raw nerve ending. It was as if she were swimming in the infinite, exhilarating dark.

By the time Andrew came up for air, Claire had come two times. He slid up to her breasts and kissed her chin, and she rolled over onto him, feeling his heart pulsing under her chest. His body was slick, his sweat smelled of musk and sandalwood. She inhaled him—that smoldering scent of handsome bad boys and possibility—and she was a nineteen-year-old sophomore again, losing her virginity to the only boy who had ever moved her to be wild. She kissed her way down Andrew's stomach, running her tongue over him, biting him softly, lost in lustful time and space. Straddling his thighs, she heard her throaty voice ask for a condom, knowing he must have one, and afraid that if he didn't she wouldn't stop.

He slid from under her and reached for his pants. There was the sweet tearing sound of the packet, and he was on his knees in front of her, ready. "I was a boy scout," he said.

"Of course you were."

Andrew brushed the hair off her face and, taking her cheeks into his hands, kissed her deeply. Claire floated in his desire for her, a devouring kind of lust she realized in that moment that she'd never inspired in her husband, even in their erotically charged early years, and she grew hotter with each kiss. He traced her shoulders and torso, her waist, until finally his hands came to rest between her legs. Within seconds she was writhing and moaning atop her formerly pristine eight-hundred-thread-count sheets, her body on fire and spasming at his touch, her voice screaming, "fuck me, fuck me now," as if she had never wanted anything more in her life. He obliged, wrapping her legs around his neck and holding her hips tight. It was an electric jolt to her limbic system, a surrender that felt somehow safe and liberating.

"God, you're exquisite," Andrew said, his chest muscles contracting with their shared rhythm. She came again, this time a halo of exploding mirror flashing behind her closed eyes. Words of gratitude, even love, rattled around her head.

An hour had passed, maybe more, when they were finally able to pry themselves free from one another. They lay quiet and motionless as they waited for their bodies to calm. And as the hungry glow ebbed and the cool chill of reality blanketed the room, the passionate words Claire had imagined saying also slipped away. She rolled to the edge of the bed, suddenly nervous that Nicholas might actually come home instead of going to Reese's. The numbers on the clock flashed amber like a cat's eyes in the darkness. "We should . . . get moving."

They dressed in hurried silence. As they stepped into the hallway Andrew reached for her hand, and she shivered, feeling the sudden weight of her recklessness shroud her skin.

CHAPTER 4

Claire walked Andrew Bricker out into the June night, dazed. The temperature had dropped while they'd been in the house, and the scent of roses perfumed the gusty air. She inhaled and waited for the soothing effect of her garden to work its magic. Instead, like a weed, apprehension choked her.

"Incredible night," Andrew said, looking skyward, his voice gravelly and sated. Claire forced a nod and contemplated him from the side as they made their way to his car—his lingering smile and ruffled hair, the scar. But still she had no words for him, as if being clothed and vertical again had caused a shift in something more than her posture. Goose bumps flared on her bare arms and she hugged them to her chest, slowing her pace. When they reached the edge of the pathway, Claire watched him fold his body deep into the interior of his borrowed Porsche, his green eyes locked on her face. "When can I see you again?" he asked.

Her body tensed. *Never? Tomorrow?* She glanced up at the veiled moon for encouragement, as the wind whipped the branches of the Aspen trees along the circular drive and lifted dust into the air. She moved closer to the car, sensing the coming storm. Wiping cottonwood flecks from her lashes, Claire looked down at Andrew and then quickly away toward her house in the billowy moonlight, afraid to get caught in his gaze, afraid that if she spoke, regret would tumble from her mouth like rocks.

The chimneys and archways of the house cast wild shadows on the manicured lawn. Nicholas's lacrosse nets flapped in the gale. Interior lights glowed orange and comforting through the silk draperies. She ran her tongue across her upper lip, tasting Andrew and smarting at the rawness he'd left behind, wishing he were already gone. And in that split second, the possibility of escape and refuge was as bracing as the snap of a rubber band on skin. Claire gathered her windblown hair into her hand, looked back at Andrew, and shook her head as she closed his car door. Turning, she walked to the house still shaking her head in silent response, counting the steps to the front door. She heard him call her name over the wind several times, but she stayed her course. As the sound of the car finally faded beyond the gates, Claire prayed that Michael would not invest in Andrew's deal. She wanted to be free of anything that would tie their lives together any further. It was all such an incomprehensible lapse of everything that was at her core.

Claire shut the door behind her and leaned into it with all of her weight. She felt the curve of the carved mahogany between her shoulders, and exhaled like a woman who had just outrun the ghost in her dreams. She rushed to the guest room to survey the damage they'd left behind. It was as if the storm building outside had already passed inside. Pillows on the floor, sheets gnarled and tangled around the bedpost. She could smell him everywhere; she could smell *them*. She pulled up the bedclothes and opened a window, hoping the breeze would somehow suck out all traces of him. But the air outside had gone suddenly still and the moon had disappeared. Claire let go and watched the window slide back into place with a dull thud. She sank down onto the bed and, gathering a fistful of sheet, pulled it to her nose and closed her eyes.

In the darkness she imagined Andrew's hands on her body again, his lips on hers. She ran her fingers down her neck and over her breasts, reached her hand out to the empty space beside her. The sheet was cool and wrinkled under her palm. An unexpected beginning and an abrupt end. She knew this was how it had to be.

But still it weighed on her, the heaviness of knowing that she'd never be able to get this night out of her head.

She had tasted his compliments and his desire, and so satisfying were they in their intensity that she had nearly burst out with love for him as he was making her come, had nearly said something even more ridiculous. Thank God for small favors, she thought. Claire understood as she lay alone that she wasn't full of love for Andrew. He'd just shaken off the dust and drawn her in with some inexplicable sway. She had certainly never begged anyone to fuck her before. Not Michael, not anyone on the short list before him. At least not in that particular vernacular. *Fuck me.* Those words and the others he'd incredibly coaxed from her curdled in her mouth, the sharp tang of guilt coating her tongue.

She buried her face into a pillow and cried. "Damn it!" she screamed out to the empty room. "Damn you," she whispered, her mouth now dry as parchment. When she looked back at the clock a few minutes later, it was eleven. She wiped damp strands of hair from her eyes and headed upstairs. A shower first, and then she would change the bed, clean things up.

Claire removed her clothing for the second time that night, catching her reflection in the mirror. Her lips were puffy. Her eyes were swollen and red, the jagged crimson threads illuminating her irises to the brilliance of emeralds. Her hair was disheveled and matted like one of her mother's bouffants. As she was about to step into the shower, she noticed eight tiny pink half-moons on the small of her back—four on either side of her hips. She inched closer to the mirror, craning at the remnants of Andrew's grasp on her. How, she wondered, had the slice of his fingernails eluded her? Was pleasure that potent an anesthetic?

Dressed and marginally calmer, Claire toweled her hair dry as she walked downstairs. She thought of Michael's early morning kiss when he'd left for London, his car pulling away and the rush of sadness *and* excitement she'd felt in that moment. Eyeing the light still on in the guest room, she rubbed her hair until it stood on end and her scalp burned. *How did people do it? How did they sneak around without making themselves crazy with guilt?* Claire set the towel on the foyer table and rested her hands on the cool glass. She leaned in to smell the arrangement of lilies that nearly overflowed their vase.

Closing her eyes, she drew her face in closer to the cascading blooms. As the sweetness wrapped around her, Claire couldn't stop replaying the last few hours. The sound of the doorbell, the taste of her anxiety and ecstasy, the anvil oppressiveness of her remorse. She traced her jaw and neck with her finger, and she wondered if she would forever associate the flowers of her wedding bouquet with a man who was nothing like her husband. As if scalded by the thought, she flung her hands out, accidentally slapping a cluster of stems and knocking the vase. She caught the rim just before it crashed and shattered—the vintage Baccarat vase Michael had given her for their last anniversary. She assessed the near disaster, her shirt soaked and stained with pollen, her heart thudding in her throat. It took her a full minute to catch her breath.

Hydrangeas flashed through her brain. She would buy hydrangeas in the morning. And when Michael returned, they would sit down and finally discuss the distance that had grown between them. She would force him to acknowledge his distraction and withdrawal. She would apologize for her own. And they would work together at finding their way back to good.

But, Jesus, she thought, still straining for equilibrium, it was all so disturbing—this alien and now undeniably muddled picture of what had once felt perfect. How had they gone from such mutual fascination and desire to spend all their free moments together planning adventures, going, doing, living—to her falling into bed with a virtual stranger? She and Michael had it all, her mother had frequently pointed out. Of course that once prevailing sense of exhilaration and self-satisfaction had morphed into the real-life demands of managing a demanding business, raising a child, and the attendant missed dinners, cancelled vacations, guys' fishing trips, girls' spa escapes, and less than emotionally satisfying sunroom encounters. But not only was this real life, Claire had reminded herself on any one of those occasions, this was *midlife*. They were no longer lusty twenty-five-year-olds with wide eyes and boundless energy. Relationships, like people, necessarily evolved into more staid phases.

And yet. Standing there just yards from the place where she had trampled over her vows and moral principles, Claire struggled to pinpoint what it was about this last year in particular that felt different from run-of-the-mill midlife exhaustion and ennui. When once they had walked beside each other—in theory, if not in fact—now it seemed as if she was always running to catch up with her preoccupied husband and remind him she was there. A dull pain fanned across the space between her temples, and she wiped her eyes and stared at the bunched-up flowers in the vase. Despite the Bogie and Bacall fiction of it all—or maybe because of it—she wanted them to feel connected and foolish for each other again. Not tethered by some dusty license in a safe-deposit box. They needed to get back to that good and satisfying place.

Claire checked her watch. It was nearly midnight. She walked down the hallway to retrieve a fresh set of sheets from the linen closet, dizzied. As she stepped through the doorway of the guest bedroom ticking off in her mind the list of things she needed to do, something felt wrong. She peered over the stack of sheets and pillowcases and saw movement near the bed.

The linens fell from her arms.

Nicholas lay convulsing on the floor. An inky red trail trickled from his nose onto the rug.

"Oh my God, Nicky," she screamed, dropping beside him, her fingers instantly bathed in his blood and vomit. His eyes were open, but he didn't respond to her. She put her cheek to his mouth to feel for breath, to listen for obstruction, for something. His body suddenly stiffened and a strange, loud gasp popped from his throat. Claire fell back, terrified. She fumbled for the telephone on the night table as Nicholas's face began to twitch, his right arm and leg jerking in a violent one-sided dance. Afraid to let go of his body, Claire held his seizing hand and dialed 911. Then she saw the chalky trail on the night table, the vial and a rolled-up twenty below it on the floor, and she knew. She felt herself slipping sideways from reality. Fighting the urge to scream, she hit the speakerphone button with a sharp jab.

"There's been an accident. I think my son . . . overdosed on cocaine. He's having some kind of seizure." She could hear herself answering the operator's questions, could see her hands wiping Nicholas's mouth clean with a pillowcase and smoothing the hair from his face as he shook. Her head grew dizzy, as the operator's voice seemed to deepen and slow. *I was just trying to distract you with a little party favor.* Nick's face turned a purplish blue. "Please help us," she yelled, "he's turning blue!"

"An ambulance is on its way. His color should come back shortly. The muscles of respiration tighten during a seizure, then release."

Claire held her breath and waited for the convulsions to stop. The woman on the phone tried to keep her calm, and after another minute Nicholas's body relaxed and the blue in his lips and face receded like low tide, leaving paleness in its wake. "It stopped," she cried out through tears. She cupped her hands around his, careful not to jostle his body. "Nick, honey, can you hear me?" Mucus dribbled from the corner of his mouth and his breath grew thin and tortured. His fingers suddenly flexed, then released, and his eyes stared vacantly at Claire before rolling back. "Oh, God, no." She heard the front door crash open and yelled for the paramedics to hurry. "He's losing consciousness. And he's diabetic. Please, help him."

The paramedics swarmed around Nicholas, and Claire stood watching from behind. In what seemed like seconds, the technicians had intubated Nick, placed him on a gurney and tore out of the house and into the circular drive. She raced behind them and was swallowed into the back of the ambulance where she held his hand and whispered into his ear, trying to drown out the sirens and chaos around them.

By the time they arrived at the emergency room, Nicholas had fallen into a coma.

CHAPTER 5

As the darkness surrendered to the new day, Claire felt brittle as glass in the face of the "if-onlys" cycling through her head. Like the Salvador Dali clock painting she adored, her mind had begun playing tricks on her, toying with her terror and guilt as she grappled with the devastating reality of the situation. If only she hadn't showered, if she had found Nicholas earlier. Images oozed forward and back through her brain, flaccid and persistent, surreal as Dali's clocks. The neurologist telling her that Nick had suffered a subarachnoid hemorrhage. Her boy so shrunken and gray with the ventilator supporting his tenuous grip on life. The horror that her fleeting ecstasy came at the cost of her son's agony. If only she had never met Andrew Bricker. The Persistence of Memory, indeed.

She had called Michael in London at three a.m. when it became clear that Nicholas wouldn't be coming home anytime soon, her attempts at composed, hopeful language disintegrating under the punishing weight of her fear. Good things rarely happened at three a.m., and this was not a conversation she wanted to have over the telephone at any hour. She told him there'd been an accident with some drugs. That Nicholas was in the hospital, in a coma, and to get home right away. There would be time enough later to explain the awful chain of events. Time she needed to think. But Michael had naturally wanted more, and his voice, so far-off and garbled at times, conveyed as much alarm as she imagined her own did.

"Tell me what happened," he'd said. "What the hell's going on there?"

Claire could hear horns honking and shouting in the background, and she felt her anxiety balloon in her chest. "Andrew Bricker came to the house. He had some papers for you." She said the words cautiously.

"What do I care about that right now, Claire? *What* happened?"

"He had cocaine with him. He must have dropped it, and . . ."

"What?"

"And Nicholas found it." She broke into sobs.

"What are you saying?"

Claire lowered the phone to her chest for a second and took a deep breath against the anger in her husband's voice. "Michael, they might have to do surgery. Please just get here as fast as you can."

"He overdosed?"

"It caused a brain hemorrhage."

"Christ." There was a muffled silence before he spoke again. "Can they wait on the surgery?"

"For the time being. But I don't know for how long. They need to do more tests."

"Who's taking care of him there?"

"Dr. Sheldon, the neurologist. He seems excellent. And I'm waiting to see the head of neurosurgery."

"I don't know who they are, but I'm calling Bruce Hoffman. I want him to make sure they bring in the best people. I won't get there until late afternoon, and I want him overseeing this. If anything happens, you talk to Bruce."

She ran to the bathroom to throw up before returning to Nick's bedside.

With the new shift coming on and sunlight stretching into the corridors, Claire knew she couldn't hold things together much longer on her own, and called her big sister, Jackie—the only person she could tell the horrible truth to and still count on for comfort. She was her best friend, her trusted if often blunt confidante, her adviser on all things parental. As a preschool teacher, Jackie had the patience of Job and the energy of a Zumba instructor, with an iridescent style to match. To see the two women from a distance—a seemingly odd couple pairing of pressed monochromatic elegance and colorful hippie-chick spontaneity, one would never guess they'd been raised under the same roof. But beyond the Burberry and batik prints, under the sophistication and practicality, they were compassionate mothers who shared a profound desire to get it right with their children. And for the most part they had managed to raise three thoughtful, creative cousins—Allie (eighteen, an eager epicurean bound for culinary school), Miranda (fifteen, still shy but devoted to volleyball and piano) and Nicholas (sandwiched between, and their go-to consultant on all things in guy world). Three seemingly levelheaded kids who respected their mothers and aunts, and who actually seemed to enjoy family gatherings.

As Claire anxiously waited for her sister, she hoped against hope that they all would be together again for their annual Fourth of July barbeque bash on Martha's Vineyard. And when Jackie arrived in the otherwise empty visitor's lounge, her dark brown curls still damp from the shower, her bare face suntanned and freckled, she wrapped Claire in a secure embrace. Claire lay her head in the crook of her neck, feeling her body settle into Jackie's warmth and imagining what it would be like to fall asleep there, safe and not having to say anything.

"I'm here, honey," Jackie repeated, the tiny crystals on her blouse tinkling as Claire's body shook.

Claire rubbed at the outline of a folded-up paper towel square in her pocket and blinked tears from her eyes. She had used the towel hours before to wipe a crusty splotch of Nick's blood from her cheek while waiting for the doctor. She removed the secret totem from her pants. The white paper had turned a deep russet, and she held it to her nose and inhaled its rusty, metallic scent.

A blood vessel had burst, she explained to Jackie, and blood had washed over the surfaces of Nick's brain and into the ventricles, increasing pressure on his brain, which in turn caused part of his central nervous system to shut down. The doctor felt it could have been caused just as easily by one single snort as by an entire gram of cocaine. Claire recounted her first meeting with Dr. Sheldon, remembering how color had gone flat around her as she'd looked into the doctor's long, thin face and asked if Nick was going to come out of this.

"Cases like this are unpredictable, Mrs. Montgomery," he'd told her.

"But will he be all right? When will he wake up?" She squeezed the paper towel tightly. "Please tell me the truth."

Doctor Sheldon paused and looked into her eyes before speaking. "The data shows that patients in your son's situation have a thirty percent survival rate. And there is the possibility of neurologic disability if he does survive. But he absolutely could come through this. We just can't tell at this point." He tried to encourage Claire by reporting some of the positive signs that Nicholas was exhibiting, his good corneal and deep-tendon reflexes. But all she heard was that Nick stood a seventy percent chance of dying.

Nick's strong, he's an athlete. Those numbers can't apply. "What happens now?"

"The most important thing is preventing his brain from swelling. Then, once we've located the damaged blood vessel, we'll most likely need to go in and remove it surgically. The neurosurgeon will make that call."

"I need to see my son." Claire felt the immensity of her emotions pin her down as she attempted to stand. Dr. Sheldon took her hand and helped her to her feet, and they walked together to the ICU, his arm steadying her as they went.

Cumbersome beeping equipment overwhelmed the small curtained room. A window to the left of the bed cast slatted moonlight onto Nick's face. Dr. Sheldon advised her not to stimulate him with a lot of talking. "Contrary to what you see on television, it might agitate him and raise the pressure in his brain. Hold his hand and let him know you're here. But try and keep things as relaxed as possible."

Claire approached the bed, one hand pinching the damp square of paper in her pocket, the other skimming the sheet alongside Nick's motionless body. Fewer than twenty-four hours earlier she had made a reckless decision, and now that she stood before its consequences, she shuddered in disbelief. She tried to focus on Nicholas's closed eyelids, waiting for any movement. His matted hair looked an oily shade of brown, his puffy face distorted, his mouth propped wide with tubing. She could still see tiny flakes of blood caked under the surgical tape around his nose. Larger stains dotted the white-and-blue gown near his neck. She wondered if they'd had to slice off his T-shirt, if it was sitting on the floor of the trauma room like a discarded rag. Stroking his forehead, she silently begged for him to open his eyes. The decibels of her voice rose in her head. She railed at herself. She railed at Andrew and prayed. Then, changing tracks, she squeezed Nick's hand and whispered beautiful promises into his ear—promises of school in Denver, the family ski trip they missed that year, a river rafting week with his buddies—anything, and everything, if he would just squeeze back.

As the night wore on Claire felt the silent influence of Dr. Hoffman, their longtime physician and chief of staff, at work behind the scenes. She watched with muted hope the frequent brain-wave tests to check for improvements, and the neurosurgeon's physical assessments. A revolving crew of nurses checked intracranial pressure and blood pressure, tested blood glucose levels and suctioned the secretions from his mouth. By early morning, Dr. Sheldon informed Claire that the pressure on Nicholas's brain had stabilized to a safe level—good news she repeated into Michael's voice mail.

Claire unfolded from Jackie's embrace and wiped her face. "Nicky is going to come through this," she cried, spilling more tears. "He has to."

"Of course he will, honey. I know he will." Jackie combed Claire's hair with her graceful piano fingers as their breathing came into sync. "But," she finally said, breaking the silence, "I feel like there's something you're not telling me. Where did he get the coke?"

Claire studied a nub in the worn chair fabric, wondering how she could possibly explain the events of the previous eighteen hours, wondering how Jackie would respond to her utter failure in character. As sisters they didn't judge so much as measure themselves against each other. And despite being younger by two years, Claire had always been the responsible sister, the voice of reason in the days when frat guys had been the "morning after" topic of discussion. Steer away from the bad boys, she'd warned Jackie. The ones who stick around just long enough to tighten a vise around your heart and leave you breathless and sorry.

Amid her dread and delirium, Claire thought back to their high school days, and to the running tally of little rescues they'd performed for one another. She thought of the night Jackie, looking so effortlessly cool in her Dolphin shorts and tattered Cal sweatshirt, had convinced Claire to hide one of her boyfriends in the basement because a newer and cuter crush had come to ask her to a Grateful Dead concert. Point, Claire. And to the time Claire needed Jackie to run interference for her with their parents over a minor curfew violation. Point, Jackie. They'd calculate their points weekly, always winding up in Claire's bed giggling over the score and negotiating the "winner's" fee.

Claire chewed on her lip trying to construct an explanation for this most uncharacteristic transgression. But that first step across the threshold of truth froze her. What an idiot she'd been with her advice to Jackie all those years. Avoid the poets, the lusty artists, the hipsters. Go for the business-school guys with their intensity and promise—those were Claire's pearls to her sister, antiques handed down from their mother. But Jackie never listened and instead suffered her fair share of lover's asthma while accumulating a notable collection of memories along the way. And later marrying a successful engineer—a man whose groundedness and devotion bore a striking similarity to their father's—and who loved her with a passion matched only by her own desire for him. As Claire thought about their different paths, she felt reasonably certain that if she'd been less concerned with doing the right thing back then, she would have gotten the wrong thing out of her system when things didn't count so critically.

She looked up at her sister, feeling soreness in her jaws and teeth. She massaged the pressure points just below her ears and slowly began her story at The Palm. And detail by detail, she felt the burden of her secret lift slightly, as if in the telling she was un-clasping a necklace that weighed heavily around her neck.

"No one's ever kissed me the way he did, Jax. Or wanted me with such intensity." The tracks of saltiness on her cheeks and lips stung. "I felt like I wasn't me. Or I was this me that I've never let myself be." She closed her eyes and swallowed mouthfuls of air like she had just swam an entire pool length underwater. "I don't know how I let myself get so drawn in. It just felt so unbelievable. Until it was over."

"Oh, honey. I'm so sorry." She cupped her hands around Claire's. "These things sometimes—"

"The attraction was beyond intoxicating," she fought to ex-plain. "This guy, this total stranger somehow worked his way un-der my skin and deprived me of . . . my sanity."

"Like slow-acting poison," Jackie said under her breath.

"Do you think I should come completely clean with Michael?" Claire asked after a moment. "Tell him everything, and pray for the best?"

Jackie looked through concerned red eyes at her before an-swering. "I'm not sure he needs all of the details at this point." She dispensed a tissue from the band of her sleeve to Claire. "Eventu-ally, maybe, but men are different. They don't always crave the in-formation and minutiae we do. The broad facts, yes, but . . ."

"The fact is I did something neither of us could have ever imagined me doing. I *still* can't believe it. And I'd give anything to undo it all. For Nicky to just wake up and be okay." She looked in the direction of Nick's room and saw a trail of attendants, could hear the zip of curtains being drawn. "I don't know how I'm go-ing to face Michael."

Jackie inched in closer and lowered her voice. "How well do you know this Bricker character?"

Claire smirked, shaking her head.

"I mean, do you think he'll keep things quiet about the two of you if Michael tries to string him up for the drugs? It would cer-tainly be in his best interest."

"Maybe Andrew will just disappear. Maybe he's already on a plane back to New York."

"Right. And maybe the story just stops with the coke having accidentally fallen out of his pocket, Claire."

"But Nicky saw us together in the library. He saw the bedroom."

"I don't mean to be indelicate here, sweetie, but," she squeezed Claire's hands tightly again, "it's possible that Nick might be confused when he wakes up, right? What you and Michael need to focus on right now is Nicky's recovery. Help each other get through that. There will be plenty of time for the whys and wherefores later."

Claire stared into her sister's unwavering eyes, trying not to go down such a dark alley. "I'm a horrible liar, Jackie. You know that."

"That's a whole other Oprah," Jackie said, smiling softly and shaking her head. "And I can't believe I just gave you such Mother-like counsel. But occasionally Cora does come up with some winners. *Very* occasionally."

They both laughed through their tears over the harebrained advice their mother regularly bestowed over the years, the momentary distraction bringing a guilty levity to the otherwise grave scene. Claire wiped her eyes. "So what do I do then? What would you do?"

"Well, I don't think you should lie, Claire. I just don't think you should be generous with the truth either at this point. Omission isn't the worst thing under the circumstances."

"I don't expect Michael to forgive me. I don't know that I could forgive *him,* but maybe if he just understood that—"

"Do *you* understand, Claire?" Jackie asked, her confidently questioning expression hinting at an established theory of her own.

She rubbed Nicholas's paper towel square, searching. "I . . . I . . . no. I just lost my bearings. Or my mind. Jesus, I could never even color outside the lines, and the one time I'm impulsive in my entire appropriate, rule-following life, look what happens," she wept. "Look what I've done."

"Michael isn't going to care about that. He's my brother-in-law, and I love him to bits, but . . ." Jackie paused, looking around the long, mauve-flowered room, as if searching for her words on the walls. "He's definitely on the emotionally constipated end of the spectrum."

Claire slumped in her chair.

"I'm sorry, I don't mean to be harsh, but you know he's not going to get the emotional piece. Think about all the times we've joked"—Jackie placed the word in air quotes, emphasizing the not-so-funniness of their longstanding jibes—"about Michael's allergy to peoples' *feelings*. You just need to keep him focused on Nick's recovery right now. Go with the broadest of facts, and then let things fall where they will."

"Oh my God," Claire shrieked, jumping out of the chair. "I completely forgot about the guest room. It's a mess, and Michael—"

Jackie eased her back down. "I'll handle it."

Claire washed her face with cold water and pulled her hair into a ponytail with a rubber band from the nurses' station, and resumed her vigil at Nick's bedside. It was late afternoon when she finally saw Michael walk into the ICU. His blazer and starched shirt divulged nothing of his long trip; his hair was gelled into place, but his haggard, bloodshot eyes told her all she needed to know. Claire walked toward him and buried her face into his chest, feeling only slightly less brittle. He squeezed her tightly.

"I'm glad you're home," Claire said in a whisper. She could feel pounding in Michael's chest and she looked up to see him gazing at Nicholas, saw the tears in her husband's eyes. They pressed closer, twining together as if to insulate their hearts from everything around them.

Finally Michael released her and placed an unsteady hand onto Nicholas's wrist. "What's happening here?" he asked. "Why hasn't he regained consciousness?"

"There's been no change since my last message. No more hemorrhaging," she said, forcing a hopeful smile. "But they're not sure about the coma." She couldn't believe that she was speaking about their son. The words seemed to echo in the small room.

"They're not sure?"

"They just can't predict when he'll wake up." She moved toward Michael, feeling an awkward need to fill the silence around them.

"Dr. Sheldon can explain everything better. He's supposed to be here soon. But they're doing everything they can. Bruce has been great."

Michael ran both hands over his hair, leaving a molded cowlick in their wake. He walked around her to the other side of the bed. His skin had gone ashen, the color of old clay. "Tell me again," he said, looking directly into her eyes and speaking slowly, "how this happened. It doesn't make sense."

The saliva dissolved from Claire's mouth and her weedy composure vanished. She looked at Nicky's face, at his closed eyes. "I don't know exactly. I never thought, I mean I could never have—"

Visibly shaking, Michael grasped the bedrail. "*Why* was Bricker at our house?"

"I told you. He came by to drop off some paperwork for you." Claire fumbled for the paper towel totem in her pocket, which had worn thin like the knees of Nick's favorite blue jeans. "And to discuss the deal."

"He called *you* to discuss his deal?"

"No. I mean, I'd been interested and I wanted to hear more. So I invited him in."

With each word, Claire felt more helpless in her ability to keep things from collapsing. He studied her. She was like a child hoping she wouldn't be discovered, and wondering what the judgment would be if she were.

"So you asked him in and he just whipped out some coke?"

"No!" Claire tried to hold the muscles of her jaw and mouth in a calm line. "We just spent some time talking about the software he mentioned at dinner," she said, focusing on the gold buttons of his blazer as she spoke. "You know, the diabetes connection, and—"

"And what? He suddenly wanted to do drugs over your shared interest in software?"

Claire looked up and searched Michael's face, trying to read his thoughts, desperate to find some evidence of empathy, of a we'll-get-through-this-together spirit. But she couldn't meet his eyes.

"Help me out here, Claire. Help me understand this. Tell me

something to make me feel crazy for jumping to the conclusions I've been jumping to. Please."

The knot in her stomach tightened. She watched him pace, hugging the edge of the bed like a cat, his neck obscured by his arched shoulders. When he stopped and turned toward her, his eyes darted back and forth somewhere above her ponytail. And she was certain the truth she'd hoped to avoid had already dawned on him. "I—" she started.

Shaking his head, Michael stared through her.

She stepped back, nearly falling into the chair at Nick's bedside. "Why are you looking at me like that?"

"Because it stinks, Claire. And now . . ."

Claire saw Michael's lips tremble, saw his disbelief. She looked down at the floor tiles and the dulled path that marked the way from the entry to Nick's bed, then back up at their comatose son. And the explanation she sought to speak evaporated. She wished she could do the same. "You know I'd never do anything to endanger Nicholas," she said, her voice small with surrender.

Michael raised his eyebrows. The wretched sound of Nicholas's respirator reverberated around them.

Claire reached out for her husband's hands over the bed, but he stepped away. "Not intentionally, Michael. You know that."

The curtain drew open with zipper swiftness, startling Claire. Dr. Sheldon entered and introduced himself to Michael, shook his hand. Michael cleared his throat and looked sidelong at Claire, in what the doctor might have interpreted as an attempt to stifle his grief. Dr. Sheldon suggested they go to the lounge to talk. Claire followed, suddenly panicked that she'd allowed such an inappropriate conversation to take place in front of Nicholas. She hoped for any morsel of good news from the doctor, and wondered how she could possibly cool Michael's simmering anger.

As Dr. Sheldon explained Nick's condition in detail to Michael, Claire tried not to focus on the skepticism she read in the doctor's tired eyes. Those first twenty-four hours, already ticking away, were crucial, he explained. It was positive that there had been no more bleeds, and while Nicholas's hemorrhage was severe, he did not yet want to characterize it as massive. But the level of the coma was deep, even though Nicholas did exhibit some eye movement when his head was turned. Good always tempered with bad.

"What about surgery?" Michael asked.

"We've performed some tests to locate the damaged blood vessel, and Dr. Marks, the head of neurosurgery, will be making his evaluation based on the results. But it was critical we stabilized Nicholas before any surgical treatment."

"And you've done that, which seems to be good news. So how long do we wait for a decision?"

"Dr. Marks should be down to meet with you both when he gets out of the OR. But it's not really a question of *if* we'll do surgery in Nicholas's case, but when. We need to go in and drain the hemorrhaged blood. And we may need to remove the damaged area to prevent another hemorrhage, depending on what Dr. Marks finds. Really, it's the type of procedure that Dr. Marks needs to determine. He'll discuss all this with you."

"Will the removal of the vessel wake Nick from the coma?" Claire asked.

"It's possible the surgery could rouse him. That would be the optimal outcome, but unfortunately we just can't predict these things."

Claire looked from Michael, whose stoic veneer revealed nothing, back to Dr. Sheldon. "So would you recommend—?"

But Michael cut her off. "What are the risks of the surgery?"

"Dr. Marks is one of the finest neurosurgeons in the country. But I'll be frank. In a case like this, the potential risks are severe disability, vegetative survival, or death. But Nicholas could pull through this with little or no permanent disability, and that's what we hope for."

Michael stood and walked to the other side of the long empty lounge, his arms folded tightly over his chest. "When can we expect Dr. Marks?"

"He should be scrubbing out right now. I'd say another ten minutes."

When the doctor left, Claire crossed to Michael, who stood studying a print of hot air balloons floating in the mountain mist. "I think he should have the surgery as soon as possible," she said in a soft voice.

Michael closed his eyes for a long moment, then turned and walked out of the room.

They waited in Nicholas's room for the doctor, Claire on one side of the bed, Michael on the other, the alternating pings and sloshing noises from the monitors and ventilator punctuating the silence between them. A nurse poked her head in to tell them that Dr. Marks had been delayed for another half hour. Before Claire could respond, Michael stepped around the bed, placed his palm on the small of her back and steered her out of the room and down the corridor to the elevators. "C'mon," he said. Nothing more. They stepped into the crowded compartment, and Claire felt a split second of relief at seeing all the floors lit up. Five stops to think; five stops until the moment of reckoning. She thought of Jackie's advice, of full disclosure versus omission, but was unable to wrap her mind around anything more than vagaries.

They got out of the elevator at the lobby, and as the pressure of Michael's hand on Claire's back grew she quickened her pace. They walked through the sliding doors and out into the gardens where patients in drafty blue gowns, some hooked up to rolling IVs, were smoking in the designated area. Claire imagined joking with Michael about the irony, as they would have done under any other circumstance. He released his grip from her shirt. The hot afternoon sun blazed and the heat gyrated in waves off the cement in the distance.

"What the hell were you thinking, Claire? That you could screw some guy I was about to do a deal with, and we'd all live happily ever after?" He punched the Plexiglas smoking shelter on which she had been leaning. "Jesus Christ. Were you snorting coke off of each other's naked bodies?"

"What? God no!" she shouted through a flinch before regaining her equilibrium. Michael was not a violent man. He was proud, he could be arrogant, and he was hurt. But he would never physically harm her, she reminded herself. "It must have fallen out of his pocket. But I didn't . . ." She took a deep, slow breath, and turned away from him.

"Don't, Claire," he said. "Don't lie to me. It's not one of your strengths."

Claire's body went rigid, but her mind filled with the relief of not having to construct lies she knew she couldn't sustain. "I'm so sorry," she said, coming around to him. "I made a terrible mistake and I'd give anything to take it all back."

"Yeah," he replied, shaking his head. "In our home, for Christ's sake.

She squeezed her eyes shut, then open. "It wasn't a rational choice, Michael. I don't even know how I let it happen."

A woman pushed her husband past in his wheelchair, laughing with him as they moved toward the gardens.

"Our son is in a coma because of—" He stopped short, looking utterly riven. He took several deep breaths. "Because of . . . your recklessness."

Claire stood there—exposed, contemptible, small—and watched her husband take her in. The lines of his face filled his features with weariness. And there was a sense of nervousness, she noticed, a darting and twitching of his eyes that conveyed some other preoccupation, as if he, too, struggled under the weight of some fateful secret. But she quickly shook off such deflections, knowing that she alone bore responsibility for bringing them to this frightening place. After several more deep breaths, Claire saw Michael's face slacken, saw the hint of tears drying up before they could fall. The wheels were turning. She knew the look—business mode, spin. He moved away from her and paced the edge of the cactus garden with his arms folded, deep in tortured conversation with himself.

When he returned a few moments later, he was stony. He didn't ask if she still loved him, he didn't say that he still loved her or that they would work through this together, as Claire had imagined and hoped he might. Michael announced that for now they would keep things as quiet as possible and maintain the story of an accidental insulin overdose. "We'll deal with the rest of this mess after we get a handle on Nicholas's situation."

"I'm so sorry Michael. You know you and Nicky are the most important things in my life. Please, can we—"

A formation of jets roared overhead. They both glanced skyward. Claire placed her hands over her face and concentrated on her breathing, trying hard to silence her sobs. When she looked out, she saw Michael walking toward the hospital entrance, head bowed, shoulders slumped.

She returned to the ICU alone and found Michael already in conversation with Dr. Marks in the lounge. Claire listened as the doctor recommended a craniotomy and clip ligation of the aneurysm, whereby he would open a hole in Nick's skull and secure the damaged vessel. The other option was to wait and see if he would emerge from the coma on his own before reducing the pressure on his brain, which might put Nicholas at risk for further hemorrhaging. Dr. Marks left them to make a decision.

Back in Nick's room, Claire sat next to her son and stroked his arm as she considered the doctor's words. She touched his lips and eyelids with her fingertips. His mouth twitched, just a reflex—the nurses had explained this to Claire the first time she'd witnessed it. But she took it as a sign, as the response she'd been waiting for. And in that instant she knew that the surgery would work. She felt it as a mother senses the sex of a baby still in her womb, felt it etched in the grout beneath her feet and the soft hum in the air around them. Nicholas would wake up after his surgery.

"If he comes out of that surgery a vegetable, or if he . . ."

"Shut up," she hissed, seizing Michael's hand and yanking him through the curtain to the hallway. "Don't you ever speak like that in front of him again. Ever." She hit his chest with her fists, thud after thud like low drumbeats, and Michael grabbed her, pulling her to him as she began to shout. She felt his arms grow tighter around her, felt her anger peak and then tick slowly down like a blood pressure monitor with one final, muted scream into his chest.

"Calm down," he whispered, guiding her to the lounge and away from the eyes and ears in the corridor. "I'm sorry. I shouldn't have said that."

Claire yanked herself free and wiped her eyes, putting as much distance between them as the room would allow. "I think Nicky should have the surgery as soon as possible," she said.

"Why?" His tears were flowing freely now.

"Because I know it's going to work."

Michael moved into her line of sight. "And you think you can trust your instincts? They've served you well up until now?"

"Damn it, Michael," she said, the ticker soaring again, "I know I made a terrible choice, but don't ever question the choices I make about Nicky's health. Just remember who's been there for every doctor's appointment, and who's done all the middle-of-the-night blood tests. I *know* our son." She rested her arm on the wall. "Nicky's going to wake up."

"I want Bruce to get us a consult with one of his colleagues at Mayo. I could fly someone out tomorrow," he said, stiffening his body.

"The doctors here are excellent, Michael. Bruce has total confidence in them, and it's not like you can just snap your fingers and have someone here immediately. There's no time for that."

Michael cradled his face in his hands. A buzzer sounded in the distance. "I know," he finally said, his voice stained with grief. "I know."

Claire returned to Nicholas's room and took out the blood-glucose monitor she kept in her purse. Another test between the nurses' checks to give her some peace of mind. As she pricked the pad of his middle finger with the lancet and squeezed a droplet of blood onto the meter, she thought of Nick's diabetes diagnosis years earlier, of how traumatic and overwhelming it had been. And how manageable, in light of the present circumstances, it really was. What she wouldn't give for just diabetes now.

CHAPTER 6

She remembered the moon peeking through the shades over Nicholas's bed that night it all started, illuminating the silver stars on his ceiling and casting a strange glow on his then tiny nine-year-old face. His eyes were open and his brows were drawn tightly together in an angry V. Claire noticed a large, empty bottle of water on his night table as she sat down on the edge of his bed and stroked his hair.

"I can't sleep," he said, his voice unusually high, almost whiney.

"What's wrong?" Claire looked at his heavy lids and the hint of black circles beginning under his eyes.

"I've had to go to the bathroom like ten times tonight." Nicholas sat up, knocking Claire's hand away.

She picked up the water bottle and wiped off the sweat ring from the night table with her fingers. "Did you drink this whole bottle before you went to bed? If I'd have drunk that much water, I'd have had to go to the bathroom like eleven times." She poked his tickle spot and hoped for a smile, but the visible fatigue and irritability in his face worried her.

"I was having a bad dream and I woke up real thirsty, so I went downstairs and got the water." Nicholas sat up against the headboard.

"What was your dream about?"

"I was in the backseat of Dad's car and we were driving to soccer practice and I didn't have my ball because Dad threw it out the window." His jaw clenched and his watery eyes narrowed.

"You know Daddy would never really do that, don't you?" She took Nicholas in her arms and hugged him tightly. "You're going to be okay, buddy." After a few minutes, Claire went to his closet and rummaged through the shelves, returning to the bed with a short-handled net, its rim decorated with dangling superheroes and dinosaurs.

"What's that?"

"Your dream catcher. Remember?"

Nicholas sat up and took it from her hands. He turned it over and over, running his fingers across the netting, swatting it through the air in front of him. Claire asked if he'd like to hang it over his bed again, for old time's sake. Nicholas didn't speak for a while; he just gripped the worn handle tightly, and she wondered if he was coming down with some kind of virus. She knelt beside his bed, and after a few moments Nicholas put it down and interlaced his long fingers with hers.

"What does sublime mean?" he asked in that way that makes parents invoke words like *precocious*.

"Sublime?" Claire sat back on her heels, "Where'd you hear that?"

"On my radio, while I was trying to fall asleep."

"Sublime means something that's beautiful and perfect." She searched for more appropriate words. "Something . . . heavenly." She climbed into bed next to him and spread his blanket over the both of them.

The next morning Claire brought French toast sprinkled with powdered-sugar happy faces into the breakfast room where Nicholas was refilling his glass with orange juice. She placed their plates on the table and sat down across from him. He shoveled the French toast and some bacon into his mouth with unusual enthusiasm. After he plowed through a second helping and two more glasses of juice, Claire asked again if he felt all right, if he wanted to go to school—just to be sure.

Around lunchtime, Claire received a phone call from the

school nurse, telling her that Nicholas had been demonstrating some symptoms that concerned her, and had asked if there was a history of diabetes in the family. Claire grabbed her car keys and was out the door in a flash, grilling the nurse about other possibilities. She called Michael on his cell in Boston. And as she heard herself explain the nurse's theory to him, she somehow knew it was the truth, that Nicholas did have this frightening thing.

"Let's not jump to any conclusions before you see the pediatrician, Claire," he'd cautioned. "It could be any number of things. Right?"

She chewed at her upper lip and felt the sting of air and blood. "When can you be on the plane?"

There was a pause. "Why don't you call me when we have a definitive answer from Dr. Stevens? Nicholas is going to be fine, he's a tough kid." His voice broke slightly. "Just be strong for him."

"Strong? I'm not like your parents, Michael. I won't inflict that 'one must not display weakness' bullshit on him. This is a nine-year-old boy here, not a teenager with a sports injury he can suck up."

"Listen, this deal's on the wire, and I'm sure I can get just about everything wrapped up by the time you're finished at the doctor's. And that way we'll know for sure. Okay?" He spoke gently but convincingly. "Then I can be home within a few hours. I'll have the plane waiting. I'm sure it's just the flu, babe."

There was no point in arguing over a few hours, or anything for that matter, with him. When Michael made up his mind about something, he could convince anyone of the correctness of his decision. And mostly she admired that about him. Paused in traffic, Claire caught sight of a homeless man standing on the median, shirtless under the already raging midday sun. He held a sign that read, "ALL TAPED OUT. PLEASE HELP." *Taped,* she repeated to herself as she sped toward school.

When she and Nicholas arrived at the pediatrician's office, Nicky went straight for the unoccupied Nintendo set, while Claire relayed the morning's events to the nurse at the front desk. Nicholas continued battling Space Invaders as Claire sat across from him and drank in the image of her happy, carefree little boy—preserving this picture of childhood innocence in her memory.

"The good news is that we caught things early," Dr. Stevens told Claire after an interminable wait for the blood test results. "He's going to be fine just as soon as we start treatment." He explained that it was insulin dependent, or juvenile diabetes, and that they would give Nicholas an injection to bring his blood sugar down and get him feeling better.

Claire repeated the strange diagnosis and stared at the painted fish swimming across the walls. "How do I do this, Bob? How do I tell him he'll need shots every day for the rest of his life?"

"Why don't we get Michael on the phone and just get through today first?"

She followed Dr. Stevens into his office and perched herself on the side of his desk by the telephone, where she dialed Michael and allowed the doctor to fill in the information she couldn't convey.

"I'm on my way to the airport now. Have you told Nicholas yet?" he asked.

"Not yet. But he needs insulin." The thought bore down on her again. It would be one of those visceral images seared into memory—the moment before her boy's first shot as a diabetic, separating him from the afterward of a thousand more.

"Christ." Michael paused. "What does this mean for . . . his future? What about school and sports? Can he still be a normal kid?"

Claire waited for the answer to Michael's question.

"Nicholas can still be a normal kid. It just won't be easy, particularly in the beginning when you're all making adjustments. But this is a manageable disease."

Over the speaker came the sound of static and muffled voices.

"Who's there with you?" Claire asked, angry that he was so far away at such a crucial moment.

"What?"

"I thought I heard voices in the car."

"It's just a couple of the attorneys on the deal. They're flying back with me." More lowered voices. "Why don't we talk to Nicholas together now? I want him to know I'm here for him."

When the nurse brought Nicky in, his polo shirt was untucked and his hair stood up in sweaty tufts from his scalp. He plopped down onto the doctor's couch and announced that he was starving. Dr. Bob told him he'd be able to eat just as soon as they talked about what his blood test results meant, and after he got some special medicine. Claire rubbed his back while Dr. Stevens explained to him, and to his parents, what it meant to have a pancreas that decided it no longer wanted to work.

Nicholas listened quietly, his feet frozen throughout the doctor's G-rated description of the disease. But with the mention of daily shots and finger pokes, Nicholas's body tensed and the flush drained from his face. Claire held him tightly, watching the tears tremble on his eyelids.

Nicholas wriggled free from his mother's embrace, scooted off the edge of the couch and walked over to Dr. Bob's desk. "Daddy," Nicholas asked the telephone, "are you mad at me?"

Claire closed her eyes and turned her head away.

"Of course I'm not mad at you, pal. I'm just upset that this had to happen."

Claire bent down next to him. "You're gonna be fine, honey, just fine."

He looked at her, studying her face and nodding.

"Nick Montgomery, you're a champ and you're going to be good as new in no time. You'll be playing baseball and lacrosse all summer," Michael said through the static. "You just stay tough."

"When will you be home, Daddy?"

"Before dinner tonight, sport."

Nicholas smiled through his tears and squared his shoulders.

CHAPTER 7

The following afternoon, Claire waited in the corner of the hospital room as they shaved Nicholas's head and prepped him for brain surgery. His hair fell to the floor in thick clumps, forming a downy brown blanket over the attendant's feet. When it was done she wept at the pale scalp she hadn't seen since he was a baby and ran her palm over the moony surface from his crown to his nose. She kissed his forehead and fingers. "I love you, Nicky," she said, picking up a small handful of hair. "I love you."

As Claire stood there thinking about the ever-changing landscape of experience, this was not a picture she could have ever fathomed. Seeing her boy against such a backdrop of upended lives and frantic hope, she felt a vein open and begin to bleed somewhere inside her, just as she'd felt before his first insulin shot all those years before. Because as desperately as she wished, she couldn't trade places with him.

She rolled bits of Nick's shorn hair between her thumb and middle finger until they resembled a feather—wispy and supple. "I'll be waiting for you, honey," she whispered on her way out. In the corridor Claire propped herself up against the shiny white wall and let Michael have a moment before they wheeled Nicholas to the OR.

When the time came, she and Michael helped roll the gurney

as far as the double-door entrance to the operating room. They kept a two-foot distance between them on the side rail, making sure their hands didn't brush as they made the tense walk. The bars they gripped were no longer shiny and reflective, but dull and somber-edged—what remorse would feel like, Claire imagined, if she held it in her hands. She wiped a sweaty palm onto her pant leg and said a silent prayer.

The surgery would last nearly four hours. Four hours to insert a lumbar drain, drill open Nick's skull, dissect and retract the membranes, locate and expose the aneurysm, clip it, drain the excess blood, and close his skull with staples. Four swift hours of exacting precision in the operating room; four protracted hours of angst and uncertainty in the waiting room.

Claire and Michael didn't find comfort in anxious chatter or mutual reassurances. After the previous night's tense and blame-riddled vigil, they were both drained and barely spoke at all. She: chipped away the last remnants of her nail polish and feigned interest in Sudoku. He: text messaged and disappeared for longer than usual phone breaks, the food he brought back going cold and uneaten. Jackie sat with them briefly doing her best to encourage, but Claire had sent her home to be with her own family until the evening. And the room filled with the sound of two people breathing the heavy air of their guilt and resentment.

Claire thought about the last conversation she'd had with Nick, how he had twisted out of her arms to escape the library and all the awkwardness. How Andrew's presence would forever stain the memory of that brief hug and kiss. And how she hadn't realized in that moment that she might not have a thousand more chances at *I love you.* The silence bore down on her, pushing her deeper into a sinkhole. To speak or not to speak—such a strange question for two parents, she thought, as she listened to her own shallow breathing. The pungent warmth from the coffee urn in the corner suited the jittery mood of the room. From that day on, she knew she'd never be able to grab a latte to go without smelling June, hospital. Hyperventilation suddenly seemed likely on her list of waiting room possibilities.

"What did you and Nick talk about before you left for London?" Claire finally asked, well into the second hour. "You two seemed liked you were having a pretty intense conversation when I came by the study the night before you went."

Michael startled up from his phone with swollen eyes and stared at her, though really he appeared to be looking into the past. His lips were moving as if he were having a dialogue with someone in his head, and after a prolonged silence, his mumblings found voice in a distracted whisper. "I should never have tried to keep . . . It was all so—" He buried his face in his hands. "Christ. Kids do stupid things."

"Keep what?" she asked, confused, but recognizing the strangled remorse in his words. His last conversation with Nicholas had clearly not been a happy one either, their last memory together unpleasant as well.

Michael focused back in on her and winced. "Nothing." His voice splintered and he clamped his lips.

In the cheerless bubble of their new world, Claire had at last found common ground with her husband. She pulled a quarter-sized clump of Nick's hair from her pocket and held out her palm. Michael dipped a finger into it.

When Dr. Marks finally came in to speak with them, a lurid yellow sun was beginning its descent across the frame of the waiting-room window. He reported that the surgery had gone well. No intraoperative ruptures, no injury to the surrounding arteries. He'd had to remove a significant amount of blood from the hemorrhage, but with that, the pressure on Nicholas's brain was also reduced. "Things looked good in there," he told them.

Claire cried as she walked in small circles, her hands laced tightly under her chin. "Thank you," she repeated over and over.

"And what about his recovery?" Michael asked.

"I'm hopeful we've minimized any damage. But based on the location of the aneurysm, your son will likely need physical and cognitive therapy when he emerges from the coma. To what extent, I can't yet be certain."

Claire stopped. "So now what?"

"Now we wait."

CHAPTER 8

Four days after the surgery, as Claire uncoiled from the cot on which she'd sporadically dozed in Nick's room, Dr. Sheldon sat down opposite her. The early hopeful hours of watching Nicholas for any indication that he was emerging from the coma had given way to bleak, restless days. All the testing and monitoring were yielding no clear answers. Michael had developed an aversion to anything but the most brusque exchange of words with anyone—unless he was having one of his frequently distraught and unintelligible monologues en route to the elevator—while Claire had developed a constant twitch to her mouth and eyelids from lack of any real sleep.

With a fatherly voice, Dr. Sheldon encouraged her to go home. "You need to rest, Claire. You've been running on adrenaline and pretty soon you're going to crash."

"I'm fine," she said curtly.

"You need to take care of yourself and save your energy for what comes later. This isn't a sprint."

Michael and Jackie appeared in the doorway, and Claire wondered how long they'd been waiting outside, if they'd put him up to his speech. Michael looked only marginally better than Claire, still spending his nights at the house and coming in before and after work.

"You should go for a few hours," Michael said with the forced smile he reserved for the presence of the hospital staff. "Go home and get some rest." The gray rings under his eyes were growing more pronounced by the day, she noticed, and he seemed to look at Nick with as much regret as she did. But it *was* the first time since she'd set up camp that Michael had encouraged this, the first time since the waiting room that he'd truly engaged with her. The prospect gave her limited hope, even if he wasn't exactly asking her to join him. Still, how could she leave? Claire looked at Nicholas, hoping that he would wake up and resolve this ridiculous standoff. But the only sounds he made were the gurgling, labored breaths that the ventilator pumped through his lungs. He looked to her like a broken puppet, flimsier and paler by the day—not the vital boy who had skied circles around her and closed his e-mails to her with *I love ya*. She blinked her eyes at the sting.

"Come on," Jackie said, removing keys from her pocket, "let's get you out of here for a while."

When Jackie pulled her minivan into the long circular drive of her sister's home, the sight of pink peonies and roses immediately struck Claire. They were the first vibrant things she'd seen in days. She smiled and tried to banish the hospital images, and wondered if she had been wrong about Nick's surgery.

"You okay?" Jackie asked.

Claire nodded and followed her inside. The lilies in the foyer vase had been replaced with blooming yellow gladioli. She ran her fingers across the stems, rippling them like wind chimes, grateful for Maria's thoroughness, and even more grateful that she was off for the day. The thought of Maria's reaction to her beloved Nicky's condition would be too dramatic for her to handle. She followed Jackie up the stairs.

Walking into her bedroom, Claire counted backward the days that had passed since she'd last slept there. "I feel like I'm in a bad cable melodrama," she said after a long silence. She picked up a small leopard-print pillow and began to tug at it from both sides of its corded border as she spoke. "How did this get to be our story?" As Jackie approached, Claire chucked the pillow to the floor. "I've destroyed his life," she said, tears grazing her lips.

"Nicholas made a choice."

"No, I made the choice." Claire turned her head away.

"Look at me, honey. You can't take *all* the blame for this. Nick is seventeen, Claire. He's not a baby." Jackie wiped hair from Claire's mouth and eyes.

Claire stared at the ceiling, trapped in the bright moment of rushing emotions. "Please, just go back to the hospital and be with him."

Jackie wrapped Claire in her arms, and together they rocked, slowly and steadily as they had done when Claire had miscarried her first baby, and when their father had died during Jackie's breast cancer treatment, and on the countless other life-changing events they'd braced each other through—locking out the pain of the present, if only for a while. When the dance ended Claire urged her again to go.

"Claire, please lie down and get some rest, okay?"

"You'll call me, right?"

"I'll call you."

"Because Michael, well . . . you know. He can barely speak to me, and he seems so . . . off."

"Um, yeah," Jackie said, her stupefied expression communicating the unspoken obvious.

Claire sucked in a sharp lungful of air. "I mean, it's like there's something else other than Nicky and . . . what happened that's preoccupying him. Something's different about him now. You know?"

"Honey, you really look like hell."

"Nothing's making sense anymore." She rubbed circles on both of her temples, trying to erase the pressure between them.

Jackie paused, as if debating whether or not to say what she was thinking.

"What?" Claire finally asked. "What else?"

"Mother's been calling nonstop since yesterday."

"I've been ignoring it. It was hard enough going through the insulin overdose story with her before the surgery. And it's not helpful that I keep having to tell her there's been no change."

"She wants to come out here, Claire."

"Ugh." She flopped down into the pillows on the bed. "I can't face anyone now. Especially Cora."

"I've been trying to discourage her, but I thought I should check with you. Just in case."

"In case what? That after a few days of ministering to me, Mother would become a bit achy herself, and *I'd* want to take care of *her*?" She looked up at Jackie. "Please just hold her off for a little while longer."

"You got it, kiddo." She kissed Claire on the forehead. "Now be smart, and listen to your big sis. Just chill here for a while, please."

As the sound of Jackie's footsteps faded down the staircase, Claire pulled the sheets up over her face, grateful for her sister's steadiness, for all the phone calls and offers of help she fielded when Claire had decided to go radio silent and focus her energy on the only thing that really mattered. How could anyone help? And how could she talk to anyone without letting her guilt collapse the flimsy house of cards they'd had to erect? Guilt. It had become the defining precept of her days. And Michael's, it seemed, too, with his retreat into uncharacteristically remorseful moods and strange mumblings. Or maybe not. Who knew anymore? Thank God for Jackie, she thought, stretching out under the covers. The sheets were crisp and cool, the mattress firm and strangely foreign to her. She smelled Michael on the pillows, some new scent she couldn't pinpoint, but still unmistakably his, fresh and clean. She wondered if they would ever share a bed again. If he could ever want her.

Claire fidgeted and rolled between her side and Michael's, wanting badly to sleep for just a few dreamless hours. She turned on some music—Elvis Costello's "Almost Blue"—but still her mind wouldn't let her forget. Ultimately, her search for comfort proved more frustrating than therapeutic, and she stripped off her clothes for a quick shower. Her hair, she noticed, felt old, like fallen leaves. Everything about her needed some tending to, but it all seemed so pointless, she thought as she trudged into the bathroom. She flipped on the light, and the instant her toes hit the marble floor an ice-cold shiver shot through her. She hadn't been in there since the night of the accident, and the startling reminder sent her sliding backward from the present. Suddenly it was eleven o'clock, Saturday night. And the smell of Andrew seemed to wash over her again.

Claire turned and raced out of the room and into the hallway in a panic of blood and cocaine and flashing lights. Flinging open the door to the upstairs guest bathroom, she saw the cream-and-gold toile shower curtains shudder. She stepped, practically jumped, over the tub ledge and drew the curtains shut with both hands, crisscrossing her wrists so that nothing could slip past. She turned on the taps and stood under the showerhead as the water spouted shockingly cold and then hot on her body, letting it beat down on her shoulders. For ten minutes Claire stood there shaking, waiting for the spray to wash the emotional shock of her flashback down the drain.

Finally she reached for the soap and began lathering her body. One pass of the finely milled bar over her arms and legs turned to five, then ten before she moved on to the loofah. She washed her hair and shaved her legs with the never-used guest razor, reciting her litany of hatred for Andrew: his magnetism, his "party favor," his general existence. Because no matter how long she exfoliated and scoured, *it* would always be there—the unforgettable spark of their lust, and the damning shadow of its fallout. Because with every cat and mouse game, someone had to lose.

After, as she dressed, Claire tried hard to picture Michael and all the goodness of their life together. The breezy holidays, the lazy Sunday mornings following one of their fabulous dinner parties, the secrets and dreams and jokes they had shared. But all she could bring to mind were his words at the hospital. *You think you can trust your instincts?* And their now obvious lack of communion. When she and Andrew had fucked, they had kissed so passionately that she'd felt her entire body vibrate. But kissing had long since gone missing from her lovemaking with Michael; all that had remained was the act itself and a cool sense of release when it was done. Claire considered for a moment that perhaps she'd applied the wrong terminology to the wrong partner. She could hardly call the swift and occasional maneuverings with Michael *lovemaking* now, and she hated Andrew even more for magnifying this.

Before him, things had seemed decent in their sex life—not perfect, not like the days of their swoon-worthy make-out sessions on the stoop of her Park Slope brownstone, or the comfortable twice-weekly pattern they'd settled into the year after Nick went to preschool, or even the diversion they'd enjoyed with the "bunny" when Michael started doing all of his deals in Asia a few years back and coming to bed too exhausted to give more than ten minutes to the effort. A little more romance and eroticism would have been nice, sure, but their expectations and patterns had shifted. It was the same story she'd heard in countless marriages at that stage in life. *We don't have the energy; I just can't muster the interest; he needs Viagra; Every time he gets that edge to his voice it's like a gut-check to my libido.* Claire could relate to many of these complaints, but not with the degree of resentment or resignation that seemed to deflate so many women she knew. While theirs had never been a crazy, nails-digging-into-flesh kind of hunger for one another, at least she and Michael still had sex, and at least they didn't fight about it. Certainly this was a more ideal status quo than the majority of her friends' relationships.

But the old adage about not knowing what you've been missing until it shows up on your doorstep hit Claire with a force she couldn't ignore. Standing there half-naked in her dressing room and brushing her hand over the little half-moon scabs on her back, she acknowledged that their sex life, in fact, had been miles from perfect. Light-years. She tried to recall the last time she and Michael had made the fervent, passionate kind of love she knew she was capable of, and all she could come up with was a couple years' worth of lackluster-in-hindsight fucks that had become even more robotic since the fall—de rigueur quickies before a business trip or on the odd leisurely weekend, and then nothing for long stretches. And she also had to admit that she shared the blame for this loss of intimacy. It had probably been at least as long that she hadn't initiated sex. Why had she given up? she asked herself for the first time. Why had this not been important to her anymore? They'd stopped kissing good night when she started falling asleep before him a couple years ago, and then the inattention to any sort of real flame fanning seemed to have snow-balled into . . . what? Zipping up her jeans, Claire closed her eyes and thought, *desolation.* And she began to weep for all that they had lost, and all that she had allowed to go unspoken, and all that was broken. And through the blur of those fresh tears and the terrifying uncertainty of the future, she whispered an imploring prayer that she and Michael could somehow bridge their gap and find a route back to each other.

Back in the bedroom she looked for her cell phone to check voice mail, discovering it lodged under the bed where she must have kicked it during her mad dash from the bathroom. But there had been no calls or updates. Feeling even more unsettled and weary, Claire drifted around the house tilting artwork a few degrees up or down to levelness, sorting through unopened mail, rearranging magazine stacks. Stay home a bit longer, or go back to the hospital and let Michael's smoldering anger bloat around them—the choices were equally disheartening. Finding herself on the stairway landing, she got down on her knees to comb the fringe on the Persian rug with her fingers, and just stayed there.

When she woke up, her head felt heavy and dense. She rolled onto her back, scanning the balcony windows, wondering how long she'd been on the floor. Her cheek, she could feel, bore the indentation of fringe. She checked her watch, incredulous that she'd been asleep for six hours, and called Jackie.

"Hell-o."

Startled to hear Michael's voice, Claire immediately felt her body tense up. "Oh, you're still there."

"I just got back about an hour ago. Jackie is talking to one of the nurses."

"Has there been any change?"

"Don't you think we'd have called?"

"So, nothing?"

"No, Claire, there's been no miracle yet. Do you want your sister?"

"That's all right. I'm on my way."

Claire took her own car and returned to the hospital. Michael left when she arrived. Separate shifts, the new order.

CHAPTER 9

Around 10:00 the next morning, as Claire was discussing Nicholas's feeding tube with Dr. Sheldon, a nurse interrupted to tell her that there was someone to see her. "I explained to the gentleman several times," the nurse said, "that we only admit family members to the ICU. But he was insistent. A Mr. Bricker?"

Somehow, Claire managed to smile pleasantly and tell the nurse to let him know she'd be out shortly. She finished with the doctor and filed the notes she had taken into a loose-leaf binder with a trembling hand, alongside the bits information she'd started to gather about Nick's condition and treatment. Then she walked through the ICU door hearing her shallow breath echo in her ears.

Andrew Bricker stood behind a gray chair, leaning the weight of his body over its back and clutching the armrests. Claire watched him lift his head as the doors shut behind her. She had the sensation of sinking.

"What are you doing here?" she hissed, walking past him out of view of the ICU window, looking over her shoulder.

He followed her down a long corridor. "I called you."

She stopped short in front a stained glass wall that listed major donors to the hospital. Michael's corporation headed the Silver Benefactor list above their heads. "You what?"

"You seemed shaken up after I left. I called for two days. I knew Michael was gone. Finally I got your housekeeper."

"You called my house? You talked to Maria?"

He nodded and shoved his hands into his pockets. "I didn't have your cell. I told her I was an old friend, and she said you were at the hospital with Nicholas. Something about a diabetic coma?"

Around the corner, elevator bells rang, people filed out. More doors opened and closed. Claire thought she heard someone call her name, and she looked over her shoulder only to see Michael's $50,000 corporate gift acknowledgement confronting her from the stained glass wall. She stepped in closer to Andrew, trying to shut out the commotion round them. "So you just show up here? How would you explain this to Michael?"

"Relax. I made sure he wasn't here before I asked for you."

She stared into his eyes, which looked not exactly predatory, as she feared they might in the unsparing glare of the hospital, but no longer beautiful either. "Nicholas is *not* in a diabetic coma. Nick overdosed on your little stash of cocaine." She stabbed her fingers into his chest as she spoke in a muted shout, tears beginning to roll down her face. "It must have fallen out of your pocket, and he found it in the bedroom after you left, when I was taking a shower."

"Holy shit." Panic froze his features.

"And he snorted it and ended up with a brain hemorrhage. They had to do surgery, and he still hasn't woken up." Her body was shaking.

Andrew fumbled in a stunned silence and reached out for her shoulders. "I'm so deeply sorry. I never thought—"

She felt the warmth of his hands through her shirt and backed away. "Yeah. Neither did I." As she raised her hand to shove him away, she looked into his face and saw shock and fear and remorse. She dropped her arm and leaned against the wall next to him.

"What are the doctors saying? Is he going to be okay?"

"They don't know when he's going to wake up. They don't know if there's been any permanent damage." She turned to him.

"And I don't know when Michael's going to be back here, so you need to leave. Now."

"He knows about us?" His voice quavered.

"He pieced it together. So I'd go back to New York without any more phone calls. We're trying to keep things private for everyone's sake. And I'm trying to save my marriage."

"What's going to happen?"

Her stomach felt explosive and empty at the same time. *What's going to happen?* "We're going to get Nicholas through this and then, I don't know. Hopefully Michael will be able to forgive me some day."

"If there's anything I can do, Claire. Anything."

"You can pray for my son. I don't know if you pray, Andrew. I never really did, but I do now."

He nodded.

"And I'm going to have to live the rest of my life with this, so it would be much easier if you would just disappear. That's what you can do." She wiped her eyes. "Cut off your deals in Denver, and disappear. I think that would be in everyone's best interest." She stared into his eyes as she emphasized the *everyone,* making sure he understood exactly what he risked with his presence, before she turned to walk back to the ICU. "Good-bye," she said firmly, still holding onto the image of Andrew's mouth, his lips trembling under the scar. *Please, just be smart, and be gone.*

As Claire rounded the corner toward the ICU, she bumped into—and was practically smothered by—an enormous bouquet of orange-pink roses. She let out a yelp as both she and the person behind the flowers simultaneously jumped backward.

"Oh, Claire, here you are! I was just coming to see you," a woman said, lowering the flowers to reveal her face. It was Jeannie Chase, an old Junior League friend and member of the museum gala committee.

Claire swallowed her surprise and did her best to appear unruffled and gracious, checking behind her to be sure Andrew was, indeed, gone, while making small talk and cutting short this latest unexpected visit. "These are beautiful, and you are so kind to come," she managed, accepting the bouquet and Jeannie's sympathy over Nicholas's condition. "I was just on my way to a meeting

with one of the doctors, so I'm afraid I can't sit down with you
and—"

"Oh, please. No apologies," Jeannie said, nodding solemnly. "I
completely understand. You go do what you need to do." She
gave Claire a hasty embrace and retreated toward the elevator,
waving and wishing her and Nicholas her best.

Dazed, Claire made her way back to Nicholas's room, where
she crumpled into her chair and read and reread a flyer on rehabilitation facilities. A new shift nurse appeared, whom she didn't
recognize. Her nameplate read Anne Corbett. She stared at Anne
Corbett across the web of wires and tubes above Nicholas, trying
to quiet her brain. If Nicholas had been a girl, they would have
named her Anne, and called her Annie. But Claire knew that this
woman with her severe black bun and dry, down-turned lips had
never been called Annie. She was someone, Claire was certain,
who had witnessed all the pain and sadness life had to deliver, and
at some point became resigned to its unfairness with quiet re-
serve. Claire looked away until she heard the squeak of the nurse's
white rubber soles exit the room.

She walked to Nicholas's bed and softly rubbed the stubble
that had begun to grow back on his scalp. "Do you remember all
those trips we made to the ER, Nicky?" she asked. "The monkey
bar incident and your arm cast? Your chin stitches." He grunted
and ground his teeth—reflexive responses that she had grown
used to, but responses nonetheless. "At one point they knew you
by name downstairs, didn't they, kiddo?" She smiled, remembering how she would read from his favorite book, *The Phantom
Tollbooth,* to keep him calm and entertained as he was being
stitched up or wrapped in a cast, always the same chapter about
the Senses Taker, over and over, as his fear and pain disappeared
into the cleverness of the wordplay.

She rested her fingers on the zipper-like staples on Nick's
skull, and it occurred to her that maybe her little boy just needed
an old, familiar key to get back to them.

Claire ran her hands along the spines of the books on Nick's
bedroom shelves and bookcases, searched the drawers of his
desk. She worried if during one of her cleaning flurries she had

boxed up his childhood books and given them away. She looked in the closet, among the cubbies of old trophies and jerseys, computer games and art projects, taking in, as she did, the range of her son's young life. She pulled out a blue notebook with a squirrelly spiral binding. Eighth-grade history. Claire opened the worn cover and thumbed through the pages, tentatively at first, tracing her son's maturing script, the unexpected flourish around Dr. King's initials, the sharp angles of a Washington Monument rendering; and then faster, flipping through the pages like an animator trying to bring it all to life. Claire pressed her nose into its pages, but only smelled a faint staleness. As she went to replace the binder, a note fell to the carpet. *Meet me after school. xxoo P. P.,* it read in purple ink. *P. P.? Peyton Pierce?* She smiled and bent down to pick it up. *Nick and Peyton had a crush?* Neatly she folded the note and reinserted it into the middle of the binder, acknowledging that her son did have a life beyond what she knew.

Claire closed the closet door and returned to the bookcases, reading each title aloud this time, book by book, shelf by shelf, to be sure she hadn't missed it. Lodged between two yearbooks near the bottom, she finally found *The Phantom Tollbooth.* Clutching it, she went down to the kitchen to make a cup of tea before returning to the hospital.

As the water was heating, Claire's cell phone rang. Michael's private line glowed on the screen.

"Where are you?" he asked.

"Has something happened?" She was already grabbing her car keys from the counter.

"Yeah, something's happened. But not with Nick."

"What are you talking about?"

"I just got a call from Robert Spencer."

She could hear the agitation in his voice, but wasn't sure where he was going with it. Jackie had taken messages from Robert and Carolyn Spencer about Nicholas, but everyone was calling. "And?"

"And he wanted to let me know about a ridiculous story he'd just heard from Jim Chase and his wife about you and a younger man, and a cocaine overdose." His tone grew more hostile. "Who have you talked to, Claire?"

Claire lowered herself into the breakfast area banquette. "No one," she choked, replaying Jeannie Chase's polite willingness to cut short her visit, and trying to imagine just how much she might have overheard in the lobby.

"Cut the bullshit, Claire."

"Do you think I'd want anyone to know about this? Jesus, Michael." All along she had harbored a fantasy—Michael's fantasy—that they would get through this privately, that no one else would ever have to know what she'd done. She felt nauseous, as she looked at the bouquet she'd brought home from her "friend."

"Yeah. *Jesus*." Michael's words stung with a fury and sarcasm that seemed to be flourishing in him by the day.

She sank back into the cushions and closed her eyes, imagining her husband's angry face. "What did you say to Robert?" she asked in a barely audible voice.

"It doesn't matter what I said."

CHAPTER 10

Claire tried to focus on the road as she headed to the hospital, but the vision of Jeannie and her camouflage bouquet flashed in her head, imprinted in her mind's eye like the final image on a television screen the moment someone switches it off. When she batted at her calfskin bag on the passenger seat searching for a tissue, it tipped forward, spilling its contents onto the floor of the Mercedes. She swerved into the next lane trying to reach it. *Carolyn and Robert heard a ridiculous story.* Word leaks, the other shoe drops. And knowing that her darkest regret and God knows what other embellishments were now "Can you believe it?" lunchtime fodder, *that* knowledge seared. She had reduced her family to a story.

Cars were rapidly approaching in her rearview mirror, and Claire gripped the steering wheel tighter, locking her arms out in front of her. A pedestrian jumped back onto the curb as she hauled through a yellow light. From under the passenger seat, she heard her cell phone ring. She fished for it over the center console but decided not to make any more unwise moves. Not while she was navigating thousands of pounds of German steel through downtown. The ringing stopped.

As she continued east, she noticed a faded pickup truck in front of her, which, according to its bumper sticker, was powered by Jesus. She scoffed, thinking how confident and prepared that driver must be for the randomness life might hurl at him. She slowed for a red light, and a muffled shout suddenly filled the car. Claire looked at the silent radio and clock displays, puzzled, imagining her own dashboard Jesus calling her out for her sins.

Another muted shout emanated from the floor. She followed the angry voice to the base of the passenger seat and was able to grab her cell phone. "Hello?"

"Finally. I've been shouting for you for the last two minutes. What's going on, Claire?" the voice asked frantically.

"Mother?"

"Of course it's me. I'm calling you back. And why did you leave me hanging like that?"

"What? I didn't call. The speed dial must have—"

"That's not important. *What* is going on there for God's sake? I called Michael's phone by mistake before I called you, and he was very unpleasant and told me I should talk to you about the latest developments? Did Nicky take a turn for the worse?"

Claire exhaled loudly as the light turned green, and she pulled nervously into the intersection. "No, Mother. Nothing's changed with Nicky." She weighed the dreadfulness of admitting an infidelity to a spouse versus a parent. Either way it was a shitty proposition, but she didn't have much choice, considering it would all be out there soon enough. "I, um . . . you don't have the entire story, the reason Nicholas is in the coma."

"What? You said it was an insulin reaction."

"I know what we said, but there was more to it than that. The truth is—" The dreadfulness stabbed at her. "The truth is that he overdosed. On some cocaine."

"Cocaine? What kind of people is Nicholas around?" Cora's voice was frenetic, just like a blade on glass. "At Andover of all places."

"Mother, the drugs weren't Nicky's. They belonged to a man who came to the house. He left it behind accidentally."

"What kind of man? What are you talking about, Claire?"

"I'm just going to say this because people have found out certain things. I had something with him, a fling or whatever you want to call it, and—"

"You had a . . . a fling with some kind of drug fiend?"

"Mother, he isn't a drug fiend. He was just a person I thought I—" Claire heard honking horns and noticed a crush of traffic behind her in the mirror, and the wide-open space ahead. She gunned the gas. "I don't know. It was a colossal mistake and I'll regret it for the rest of my life. But it happened, and Nicky found the cocaine." As the frayed scenery of apartment buildings gave way to the traffic of Colorado Boulevard, she slowed to thirty-five. "It was a fluke that he had the reaction he did."

"Oh, good lord. And everyone knows about this now?"

Claire felt her sense of dread congeal like refrigerated pan drippings.

Pulling into the hospital parking lot, Claire wondered how they would get through this already untenable situation under a public magnifying glass. To think clearly about anything seemed so tricky, like trying to unzip a heavy fog. She rested her hand on Nicholas's book and imagined sitting down with him and reading in smooth, reassuring tones. And she imagined Nick coming back to her. Slowly opening his eyes, squeezing her fingers, waking with no memory of what had taken him away.

When she arrived at Nick's room, it was empty, his bed gone. And with her last nerve shattered, Claire heard herself cry out. A passing nurse rushed in to assist her.

"Mrs. Montgomery, Dr. Sheldon wanted to run another CAT scan. He saw some increased eye movement and responses during his rounds and thought it was worth a check. I thought your husband would be waiting here to tell you."

Adrenaline pumped through Claire's body. "He's coming out of it? Isn't he?"

"They should be bringing Nicholas back in twenty minutes or so, and Dr. Sheldon should be in to see you."

She asked to go to him, but the nurse indicated Claire's regular chair in the corner of Nicholas's suddenly cavernous-looking room. Instead she walked over to the window and placed the book on the ledge. Beyond the glass, life was in motion—birds, people, cars. Clouds made their animal shapes for those who stopped to notice. But from where she stood, time seemed suspended.

She opened *The Phantom Tollbooth* to a dog-eared page and began to read aloud.

"Dig in," said the king, poking Milo with his elbow and looking disapprovingly at his plate. "I can't say that I think much of your choice."

"I didn't know that I was going to have to eat my words," objected Milo.

"Of course, of course, everyone here does," the king grunted. "You should have made a tastier speech."

"Here, try some somersault," suggested the duke. "It improves the flavor."

"Have a rigmarole," offered the count, passing the breadbasket.

"Or a ragamuffin," seconded the minister.

"Perhaps you'd care for a synonym bun," suggested the duke.

"Why not wait for your just desserts?" mumbled the earl indistinctly, his mouth full of food.

The page morphed into a dancing jumble of words, and Nicholas's profile appeared to Claire in the black-and-white print, a lost boy in a surreal world, just like Milo. If he just knew how she would gladly swallow a thousand half-baked ideas and climb The Mountains of Ignorance to take back that night and have him whole again.

Pressing the book to her chest, Claire paced and sat, repeating her silent prayers of hope. She looked out at the gunmetal horizon. It seemed impossible to her that the sun had risen and set six times since Nicholas was last able to speak to her. And like the predictable but still surprising pop of an overblown balloon, it hit her just then—the date and time—and the fact that the art museum benefit would be starting in just a couple of hours. Earlier in the week in what seemed like an hallucinatory phone call, she'd given everything over to Peggy, her co-chair for the event, to handle, and had promptly hit the delete button in her mind.

How strange and awful it seemed, peoples' lives proceeding as usual. While the mere act of changing her shirt in the morning had become a distraction for Claire, women all over town were, at that very moment, having their hair done, removing their gowns from garment bags, trying to decide between the black or the red, the Oscar or the Valentino. She put down the book and checked her cell phone. No new calls. But her voice-mail box was already full of messages about auction items, centerpieces, and a hundred other last-minute details, in addition to all of the Nicholas calls. The act of ignoring them had, for those long days, fueled her delusion that her friends' declarations of concern and sympathy were premature and unnecessary.

Claire stared at the whiteboard near the door with its foreign language of medical abbreviations and dosages, at the hanging plastic bags and IV tubes, and she wished for normal life in color again. She shouldn't be waiting for Nicholas to be wheeled back to the ICU. She should be tying his bowtie, checking to see that he had a full set of studs and cufflinks for his tux, and that Michael would be home early from his meetings. Longingly she imagined standing with both of them in the ballroom, holding them tightly, her two handsome men. She imagined Michael smiling proudly, and Nick nudging them with an eye roll to the center of the dance floor.

Claire drummed her fingers on the windowsill, hoping for a miracle, knowing that something good had to be happening in that scan room. She tried distracting herself with the chaos she envisioned for the night ahead inside the museum doors. She could hear Peggy extending apologies for her absence during her welcome speech. "As many of you are aware," she'd say, "our friend Claire Montgomery and her husband Michael are by the side of their son tonight, and our thoughts and prayers are with them." Claire also could hear more than a few guests whispering to their spouses that the Montgomerys were certainly not *together* at the hospital, given the latest turn of events.

She could see the scene playing out against the backdrop of breathtaking floral displays and ice carvings that she had ordered, the butler-passed hors d'oeuvres and champagne. How ironic, she thought, that it would probably serve as the backdrop of her family's public undoing. The daisy chain of rumor and innuendo began to unfold in Claire's mind as she imagined the women comparing couture designs, and deconstructing and magnifying one of the sadder bits of scandal in Denver since the former Miss

America went public about her abusive childhood. Only this time, she'd be the one under the glass. A few friends would be vocal in her defense—Peggy certainly, and of course Carolyn. And Gail Harrold, if she were even in town. But on a night fueled by champagne and gossip, the air would be thick with conjecture. And she'd overheard enough games of telephone to know that the end message was generally far worse than the truth.

From the corridor came the sound of an approaching gurney. Claire ran out to greet her son, poised for the miracle. Grabbing on to the bed rail, she raced along as an orderly wheeled Nicholas back to his room. She held her breath and looked into his face, but his eyes remained closed. From down the hallway, Michael and Dr. Sheldon approached. She placed the book near Nicholas's hand. "I brought *The Phantom Tollbooth,* Nicky."

With everyone gathered, Dr. Sheldon explained that Nicholas had been showing increasing awareness of external stimuli all afternoon, and that the scan had shown improvement in his brainwave activity. He walked over to the bed and motioned Claire and Michael in closer. He pinched Nicholas just below his collarbone, and Nicholas reached toward the doctor's hand with his own. Claire gasped, transfixed as Nick's skin reddened then slowly faded back to pale. Michael remained standing with his arms folded. Dr. Sheldon then walked away from the bed and clapped his hands together loudly. Though his eyes remained closed, Nicholas turned his head toward the sound.

"Oh my God." Claire squeezed his hand softly, waiting for him to respond.

"Scratch his chin," Dr. Sheldon suggested.

Nicholas swiped at the spot Claire scratched, and she immediately began to cry with relief.

"Why don't we step outside and talk for a moment," Dr. Sheldon said.

He explained that there were many levels of coma, and that Nicholas seemed to be emerging from one of the lowest levels of generalized response to that of localized, if inconsistent responses. Claire beamed at Michael.

"Now I can't say with certainty that Nicholas is going to be fine, or that he isn't going to be fine." Dr. Sheldon chose his words carefully. "But I'm optimistic that we'll be seeing some changes for the better." He recommended that Claire and Michael look into getting a spot for Nick at a rehabilitation facility. It was entirely feasible that he could be moved in a week or two. The doctor asked one of the nurses to give them information on Craig Hospital.

"I've got some already." Claire pulled a packet labeled "Craig" from the file folder in her bag and handed it to Michael.

Michael reminded her that Nicholas still had not opened his eyes or spoken.

CHAPTER 11

Two days later, as if in defiance of his father's reminder, Nicholas began to flutter his eyelids rapidly. The following morning he opened them. Although he was still unable to recognize anyone or understand what was going on around him, Claire remained positive. There was life and movement behind his intense expression, she was certain. Her quiet prayers were being answered, their boy was fighting to come back to them.

Amid Nicholas's progress, Michael tried to make inroads at Craig Hospital, just a few miles from their home. But despite calls from hospital board members, even offers of financial donations, he was unable to move Nicholas through the crowded wait list. There were simply too many patients and too few beds, no matter who was asking.

"This is bullshit," he said as they stood facing each other in the visitors' lounge—the familiar scene for the brief exchanges that punctuated their overlapping visits. "There are no strings I can pull, not a fucking thing I can do to get him in there."

"A little patience, Michael." Claire knew he had none when it came to situations out of his control—business or otherwise. His perceived opponents always morphed into the great fuckers of the western world, Asia, or the planet. This, from a man otherwise known for his Murrow-esque eloquence and elegance. But it was always better to try and check his frustration early on than let it run. "A spot will open up eventually," she offered, as much for her own mollification as his. "People get better and move on."

Michael studied her mouth as if trying to lip-read a madwoman. "We can't keep him here for three months, Claire. He needs to start recovering in a rehab hospital. And no spot is going to magically open up in time if it hasn't already, with what I've been through."

"Have you talked to Teddy?"

"Yeah, I've talked to Teddy. He and practically every other doctor on staff at Cedars Sinai have called on our behalf. And nothing. It's ridiculous the way they run these places." He looked out the door toward Nick's room.

Claire reached her hand out across the two or so feet that always seemed to divide them, and rested it lightly on his forearm. Not an extravagant gesture, just the merest insinuation of what had been.

"How can I help him if no one will let me?" he asked.

"I know." Claire kept the space between them, but gripped his wrist, connecting them in the only way she could anymore. "I feel helpless, too. Every day."

They stood side-by-side and rigid like paper dolls, gazing in the direction of their truest connection. "Nick's the kid who always gets picked first," Michael whispered. "For every team." His voice dripped with pain and he closed his eyes. "He needs to know that I'm trying everything."

Claire slid her hand from his wrist and laced their fingers, hoping if they could hold each other up like this, they wouldn't both drown in their sorrow.

After a moment Michael's posture stiffened and he pulled his hand free. As he appeared to refocus, he fixed his attention on the magazine table and stepped away from her, the tenderness of the moment recalibrating in an instant. "You know, I've had it," he said, wiping his eyes, "dealing with all of the rumors and questions."

"What?" She still felt the warm weight of his fingers against hers.

Michael picked up *The Post* from the table and slapped it into her hand. The paper was already folded over to the Society column with its snapshots of the Art Museum Gala. Claire eyed him nervously. He was a looming building again, casting his long shadows. She skimmed through the account of the evening. *Most elegant soirée in recent memory ... enormous success ... fabulously attended.* All the bold-faced names. The compliments abounded, but Claire held her breath as she read on, her anxiety beginning to inch up her throat as she reached the third paragraph. *Gala cochairwoman Claire Montgomery did not attend because of the family crisis involving her son's tragic hospitalization. Many of the patrons in attendance expressed their best wishes to the Montgomerys as they persevere through this difficult time.* On the surface, it was adequately benign. But for those with keen enough vision to read between the lines, it dangled volumes.

"Damn it," Claire said, knowing Michael was dead-on in his assessment that the mere mention would only spawn further gossip.

"She might not have alluded to your *pal* in this *tragic* mess, but other people are. And I'm tired of the heads-up phone calls and the veiled sympathy from your friends' husbands. This whole thing, it's such an unmitigated, fucking, tragic—" He'd begun pacing, the muscles of his neck tensed, his hands fidgeting anxiously with some invisible object.

Claire flung the paper at his feet, the boundary between her hope and anger blurring. "Michael, I'm sorrier than I'll ever be able to express that I did this. And sorry the whole world apparently knows about it now, too. But I don't know what to do other than to just try and get through this together." She looked into his eyes. "Can't we please try to do that?"

Michael's cheeks were drawn in tightly, as if he were sucking an aspirin tablet. "Persevere like the paper said?" He slipped his cell phone from his sport coat pocket with a shaky hand. "I'm going to try Teddy again. Maybe there's something he can do for Nicholas out in LA."

"Michael," Claire shouted out after him as she watched him disappear, again, past the nurses' station. "LA?"

CHAPTER 12

The kids who could now freely come to see Nicholas were a wonderful boost—so upbeat in their brief but frequent appearances. They'd hug Claire hello, but their visits were focused on their friend, and Claire could blend into the background as they launched into one-sided conversations about concerts they'd go to or parties they'd have once he was better. The boys brought their iPods and played new downloads for Nick in the speakers they'd set up. The girls brought stuffed animals and balloons and filled the room with their hope. But many of the others who showed up—the not-so-close family friends—brought a more complicated vibe, and as the days lumbered past, Claire realized that the stigma of what she had done seemed to be taking on a life of its own. Jackie still stood in as best she could as a buffer against the phone calls and spontaneous hospital visits, but it was becoming obvious that more "facts" had begun to leak in certain circles, and the fabric of her insulation was wearing thin.

After seven or eight voice mail messages on her cell—all variations of "I don't mean to be indelicate here, sweetie, but I'm having a hard time believing what I'm hearing"—Claire just stopped listening to them. What good would it do to return the calls and try to deny what she knew she couldn't? Better, she thought, to go with a no-comment approach, and let Jackie update the sincerely concerned about Nick's progress. Claire thanked the few lucky stars she had for her sister's steadfast presence and unshrinking ability to play sentry. She needed her focus and energy for her son, and if she didn't confirm the rumors with answers, eventually, she rationalized, they'd lose their steam. She could crawl back out of her hole and reconnect with the world when Nicky was through the worst, and when the spotlight was no longer so harsh. Easier living through avoidance—she'd learned it from Michael, a champion at the game.

Of course sometimes there was just no avoiding reality. On her way home from the hospital the week following the society column flare-up, Claire stopped to pick up a late lunch for herself at Pasta Pasta Pasta—long past the midday social hour there. As the counter girl packed up her salad, Claire heard the door chimes ring. She turned to see a committee friend of many years walk into the small café. The woman stopped just a few feet away, her jaw tensing above her tightly wound scarf. She stared at Claire, as if Claire had just lost a limb and was out in public for the first time.

"Hello, Judy," Claire said, rolling the top of the paper bag down until the Styrofoam container belched from within. "It's good to see you."

"Oh. Claire. Yes, it's so nice. I didn't think I'd be seeing you out and about and . . ." she paused with her mouth open, seemingly balancing some unspoken words on her tongue. "Everyone feels so horrible, and I'm just meeting Renee here." Her eyes were focused on Claire's elbow. "I hope your son is coming through all right?"

"Thank you."

The woman stepped in closer to Claire. "So, where are you staying now?" she asked in a hushed voice.

"Staying?" She could feel the dampness of her palms transferring onto the paper bag. "When I'm not at the hospital? I go home. To my house."

"Oh! Really? I'd just heard that . . . well . . . Anyway, it's so nice you're out. I'll be sure and tell Renee I saw you." She continued past Claire to the counter.

Claire slogged to her car, her appetite lost.

Michael was pulling out of the driveway as she pulled in.

Soon enough the phone calls and visits began to taper. The looky-loos had grown nervous, Claire imagined, when she gave it any thought at all, that the scent of scandal might somehow cling to their own reputations if they commiserated with the *adulteress* who had made the worst possible choice in lovers. And she was relieved. The only person she wanted to hunker down with and be completely honest and ugly and raw about the whole awful mess was the only person she couldn't reach. Michael slept in the guest room on the nights she returned from the hospital, retreating into his isolation, guarding his resentment or vulnerability— or whatever it was that seemed to be propelling him ever deeper into a fugue-like state about their marriage—with fierce resolve. And with each milestone Nicholas reached—reestablishing cycles of sleeping and waking, focusing on objects—Michael expressed dismay at the slowness of the progress, gripping his half-empty glass. So she resigned herself to waiting for a breakthrough.

And at the end of the next week there was a shift. Late on a Friday afternoon Michael arrived at the hospital, appearing calmer to Claire, his edginess rounded out somehow. "It's nice out," he'd said to her with an actual smile. "Why don't we take a little walk in the gardens?" His cell phone was nowhere in sight and his tone was pleasant, almost buoyant. "We should talk."

Claire looked at him with surprise, seeing a spark of the old Michael, and feeling as if she'd been asked out on a second date. She ducked into the tiny bathroom near the nurse's station and looked at herself in the mirror. Things weren't looking good, she knew. And neither was she. But still. He wanted to talk, and the idea that he might finally be moving through his anger, remote as it was, was a beguiling beacon. Combing through her hair with her fingers, she noticed a bright strand of gray at her temple. She grabbed it between her thumb and index finger and plucked it from her scalp.

She met Michael in the hall and they walked outside. Bright mounds of impatiens rimmed the sculpture garden, and a sunset readied itself in the distance. She considered floating the idea of counseling as they made comfortable small talk, but she was also poised for whatever might help them to move forward.

They sat down on a wooden bench in the courtyard, their knees gently brushing. She looked at Michael's profile and saw a nick on his jaw where he always shaved too closely. Maybe this was what they needed to do first, feel their way back to the pace of just being side-by-side again. "Do a little blood-letting this morning?" she teased.

Michael let out a soft laugh and placed his hand on her thigh, causing Claire to fill up like a wind sock puppet, caught in a surprise gust of intimacy.

"Teddy got Nicholas in at Rancho Los Amigos," he said after a beat, beaming.

"What?"

"It's one of the best rehabilitation facilities in the country for traumatic brain injury."

"I know what it is, I've read all about it." She pulled her knee away and turned to face him. "But it's in LA."

"Teddy's tight with one of the neurologists there, and he was finally able to call in a favor. He's going to make sure Nicholas gets the best staff." Michael took his sunglasses from his pocket and put them on. "They can take him in a few days."

"What are you talking about? This sounds like a done deal."

"It *is* a done deal."

And just like that, Claire felt herself falling down the rabbit hole. "LA?" She pushed herself up and stood in front of him, squinting through the glare of the sun. "How could you do this without even discussing it? You can't just ship him away," she cried, ignoring the smattering of other visitors in the garden. "He needs his family around him."

"No one's *shipping* Nicholas away. You can stay out there with him until he's ready to come back."

The heat seemed to tighten around Claire's head, occluding her vision and leaving her woozy. She hated Michael in that moment, the way all women hate an irrationally behaving husband. "Oh. So that's why you show up here in such a pleasant mood—

because you've figured out a convenient way to get rid of me? Stash your problems a thousand miles away so you can continue avoiding them?"

"Claire," he said, his tone unwavering, "that's not what's happening here."

She blinked rapidly until her vision sharpened back into focus, leaving her instantly ashamed and surprised by her reaction. But the fact that he had not discussed such a major decision with her, that he hadn't even let her know it was on the table, was insensitive. And so typical. Her mouth hung slack as a short list of Michael's increasingly unilateral decisions came to mind: his declaration on Nicky's tenth birthday that their boy would be following the Montgomery family tradition of attending Andover, despite her reservations; his long-term rental of the Cape house two years later—which was lovely and wonderful, but which he hadn't once consulted her about; and his stunning announcement the previous year that he had scheduled a vasectomy. Any concern or disagreement she voiced, Michael had met with a persuasive, lawyerly response, a long list of pros that could sway even the most resistant opponent—followed by a forgiveness-inspiring bottle of wine and a shoulder rub. Sometimes she hated herself for acquiescing, especially on the boarding school issue, but mostly it was just more sensible to agree. Conflict was not something she enjoyed, and compromise was key to a good marriage. But there would be no Caymus this time. "Michael," she said, squaring her shoulders, "*Craig* is the right place for Nicky."

He shook his head deliberately. "This is for the best." No disdain, no rage.

"But he can't make that trip yet; he's not strong enough. He should be near his home, in a familiar setting. And how could you make this kind of decision without even talking to me first?"

"Teddy's got it all arranged, Claire."

"Nicholas is *our* son." Tumbling like Alice deeper into a place where nothing was how it should have been, she wondered when it would end, when she would land.

"Teddy pulled a lot of major strings. It's the best TBI program available. And Nicky needs to get started. You know this."

She waved her arms in front of his Ray-Ban-shaded eyes, feeling the sting of all those one-sided conversation she'd let slide, and all of the other little mayhems of their marriage. "Do you see me, Michael? Hello! Do I count at all? Do my opinions count?"

Michael removed his sunglasses. "Would you please—"

"Would I please *what?* Bite my tongue like I always do and cave to what *you* want?" Michael remained seated while Claire paced in front of him. All of her hopes and the white-hot accumulation of her frustration and guilt escaped like gas into air, fueling the inevitable explosion. "I'm so tired of being invisible to you, Michael. We used to be a team, you used to care about my opinions. But you started tuning me out and disappearing from this marriage long before Nicky's accident. You've been running 'the Michael show,' when it should have been 'the Michael and Claire show.'" She leaned in close to his face, her hands clasping the backrest on either side of his shoulders. "Is it really a surprise that I fucked him? At least he saw me." She hurled the words and hoped they'd shatter all around him.

Michael winced, but his voice remained controlled in his response. "It's the best solution for Nicholas right now, Claire."

Bells from a nearby church tolled.

"I asked you a question, Michael." She was on her knees in front of him now, crying. "DO YOU SEE ME?"

"Yes, I see you. And if you could for just one moment separate yourself from the situation, *you* would see that this is what's best for *our* son. A top facility with top doctors, available to us NOW."

She sat back on her feet and placed both hands on the ground, gathering her balance. Righting herself from the tumble.

PART TWO

Los Angeles

CHAPTER 13

The bedroom was still dim, with only faint shards of daylight piercing the skewed plastic mini-blinds. As her eyes focused, the headache set in. Claire took a moment to remind herself that the tiny apartment was home now. She felt sluggish, almost drugged. She had slept too long and now she was sorry. Too much sleep or too little, either way it drained the life right out of you, she thought. Her Swiss-efficient body clock, the one that woke her early and rushed her out the door to Rancho by eight every morning, had somehow failed. There was silence where there should have been a rush of mental lists and plans.

She called the nurses' station outside Nick's room. Lydia answered. She liked Lydia, who always had the name of a grocery store or restaurant near the facility written on a piece of paper before Claire could even ask. Lydia informed Claire that the therapist was on her way to take Nicholas to his mat class. All was well. Claire checked her watch. Nine o'clock. Mat class, followed by speech therapy, followed by rest time, followed by lunch. Thursdays. She tucked deeper into the warm sheets.

The flight out to Los Angeles the previous month in a chartered air ambulance Learjet had taken just over two hours. The plane carried Nicholas, the medical transport team, the critical care nurse, Michael, Claire, and the three bags she had assembled for a stay of undetermined length. Drs. Hoffman and Sheldon had added the convincing coda to Michael's argument for Rancho Los Amigos with their assurances that Nicholas was, indeed, strong enough to be transferred, and that timing was of the essence.

Michael returned to Denver just two days after their arrival in LA, after handling the registration at the hospital and meeting Nicholas's team. On that afternoon, Claire had watched in the pale yellow room, with its framed photos of jonquils, irises, and butterflies as Michael appeared to search for words of farewell that would not break his composure. She watched as he spoke to what he surely saw as the damaged, withered shadow of his son.

"I'll be back real soon, pal. You're gonna do just great here," he had said, his hands wrapped around Nicholas's clenched fist, his eyes focused somewhere far away.

The unspoken message was not from father to son, but from husband to wife. *You'll make sure they fix him.* She needed no reminder. She only had to look at Nicholas in the low, padded-wall-framed bed, with his left arm and leg propped up on a mound of pillows, his left foot relentlessly pointing down and inward, and the Frankenstein scar on his still patchy skull.

"Fuuckk," Nicholas responded in a loud, slow slur. "Fuuckk."

Claire stepped in next to Michael on Nicholas's right side—his "good" side—and bent down to stroke his spiky hair. She whispered that everything was going to be okay, that they would help him here.

"Fuuuuckkk," he moaned again, staring out the window over her shoulder.

Michael walked around to the left side of the bed where Nicholas had perceptual difficulties. He clutched the edge until his knuckles went white, and shook his head as if he were trying to shake loose the urge to throw something hard against the wall. Claire's cheek prickled. She wanted to remind him that Nick's behavior was to be expected at this stage, that he didn't even realize who they were or what he was saying. But there was no point. Nothing seemed to penetrate the barrier he'd erected around himself. After several moments of congested silence, Michael bent over and kissed Nicholas on the forehead and turned to walk out of the room, his gait no longer a confident swagger, but the lumbering of a shattered, struggling man. "I'll talk to you soon," he said in a distant voice.

I guess it's just the two of us now, Claire thought as she stood glancing around the forced lemon cheer of the room. The moment shouldn't have come as a shock. Still, she trembled. She wanted to crawl into bed next to her boy and hold him tightly, but the walls that kept him safely in also shut her out.

In her apartment bedroom, Claire flipped on the television with the remote and lingered in the cocoon of her sheets for another half hour. After the third weather report she made her way to the shower. By the time she'd dressed and finished breakfast it was already ten thirty, and she finally admitted the horrible truth to herself. *I can't go there now.*

Then the fantasies began. A day off, she caught herself thinking. A trip to the Getty, maybe a movie. A walk on the beach. The possibilities rolled like film credits through her mind, and before she'd even made a conscious decision, Claire was out the door of her adequately cheery abode in the Casa Del Sol Apartments in Downey, California—just ten miles southeast of downtown LA, a convenient half mile from Rancho Los Amigos Rehabilitation Hospital, and a million miles from anywhere she'd ever thought she'd be.

When she pulled off the Pacific Coast Highway, she saw the giant boardwalk carousel sitting motionless. She parked near the pier and removed her sunglasses uneasily, as if she'd just come from the eye doctor's. The sun should have been a vibrant presence overhead by then. The shoreline below should have been pocked with joggers' treads and gull prints, and surfers ought to have been clamoring for dominance on curling green swells. But the sky loomed gray, shrouding the Santa Monica foothills in fog. The air was damp and penetrating. Whitecaps dotted the coast and waves churned sand and spewed foam, leaving the appearance of frost on the surface. The gloom had done its steely best to discourage visitors.

Claire raised the collar of her sweater and moved toward the water, feeling comforted by the emptiness. No doctors, no wheelchairs, no stale antiseptic odor. No one. Only the rhythmic clapping of the waves and the salty mist glossing her cheeks. She hugged her body and inhaled deeply, feeling the sharp air travel from her nose down through her lungs. As she exhaled, the tightness in her chest released in subtle increments. She stretched her arms above her head, then let them fall to her sides and sat down on an incline at the edge of the shore. Her spine curved and her body loosened. Kicking off her shoes, Claire dug her feet into the sand until they found dampness. She noticed chipped ruby polish on her wandering toes, and smiled for the first time in days.

She and Nicholas had been in Los Angeles for over a month and this was her first visit to the beach, her first day away from him. Under other circumstances, nothing would have kept her from the water for so long. Its comforting rhythm always nourished the California native in her in a way the Rockies she so adored couldn't quite. But the thought of a trip to the beach had never occurred to Claire, not until that morning. The long string of days at the hospital with Nicholas, seeing him through his various tests, his appointments with the physical therapists, the doctors, the occupational therapists, and all the rest were finally starting to exact their toll. Nick's constellation of problems had seemed insurmountable from the moment they had arrived at Rancho, even though the doctors tried to prepare her and Michael for what their son would have to endure in the quest to increase his independence. But Claire was mostly alone with this new reality, and her inability to make some notable contribution to Nick's recovery had started to weigh on her like a two-ton block of ice. Jackie came out when she could, but her visits were short and almost painful in their savage reminder of just how different Nick was from that boy who'd taught Allie and Miranda to ski a few short years ago.

A gust of wind rang in Claire's ears. She closed her eyes to listen, and the ocean swelled inside her head, its strong briny perfume like liquid memory. She squeezed her eyes tighter, seeing herself at Monterey Bay with her eighth-grade science class, giggling at the sea otters at play in their kelp beds, secretly holding hands on the boat with a blue-eyed freckle-faced boy named Calum. She saw Nicholas wading in the tide pools on Cape Cod for hermit crabs; Nicholas running into the surf on Kaanapali at full adolescent throttle, his face tan and grinning.

The wind receded. Claire stood and walked down the short incline. The cold tide washed over her toes, and she jumped from one foot to the other until her ankles warmed to the temperature, remembering how Nicholas would mock her silly Indian dance just before leaping onto her back and sending them both headlong into the waves.

Though Nicholas had grown far more communicative as the days and weeks passed, he still experienced serious concentration problems, mood swings, and disorientation. The muscles of his left arm and leg, though not paralyzed, still failed to work properly, rendering him mobile only by wheelchair. Claire would watch helplessly during the long minutes it would take for him to assist in his own transfer from bed to wheelchair with the help of the therapist and the mechanical lift—minutes punctuated by the frustrated grunts and expletives she began to repeat silently in her own mind like a perverse cheer. She waited for him to call her "Mom," to respond to her as if she weren't just another nameless nurse, and she imagined how tightly he would hug her on that day. After a tense and discouraging visit by Michael at the two-week mark, punctuated by his own angry outbursts and inscrutability and complete avoidance of any of her attempts at addressing their relationship, Claire became convinced Michael would put off returning again until Nicholas showed signs of actually recognizing people. She still suspected he preferred the physical distance since it made his emotional distance easier to maintain. But she tried to reassure herself that people deal with tragedy in different ways and in different time frames, tried to maintain a clear vision as she concentrated on the daily routine.

She learned to place Nicholas's water cup, the TV remote, anything he needed on his good side, to approach him only from the right, to remind him to wipe the left side of his mouth after eating. She held his hand when his arm or leg would seize, and she read to him and played Go Fish with him, grateful for any small smile this would elicit.

But the lingering image that had sent Claire home shaken and depressed the previous night was the same image that haunted her as she walked the shoreline. She had been watching from the rear of the therapy gym as Nicholas's physical therapist stood several feet away from his wheelchair and served a beach ball to him. Earlier in the week he had been able to return five serves and seemed excited by his progress. There was even discussion of Nicholas playing in a group soon. "I'll ace 'em," he'd repeated for several hours. "I'll ace 'em."

What a cruel difference a few days made. The brightly striped ball floated and arced toward his knees, but Nicholas swung his arm too soon and missed swatting it back to her with his open palm. Amy moved closer and they tried several more times. Claire could see the frustration mounting on his face, and his familiar squint of determination. The ball bounced off his forehead and he flailed his arm, trying to catch it before it dropped to the floor. She smiled and nodded encouragingly at him from the back of the gym, her fingers laced tightly in prayer beneath her chin. Get this one, she chanted silently, get it, honey. *Please.* Then she felt an icy pain rise in her chest as Nicholas struggled and failed again to make contact with the large, inflatable ball—her boy who had played varsity hockey and lacrosse in ninth grade.

Nicholas, his face red and angry, wheeled his chair toward Amy with his right hand. Claire watched the young therapist kneel and place her hands on the frame to stop him. "No!" he screamed. "Fuuuck." Sweat dripped from his temples and tears streamed down his cheeks as he continued yelling expletives. Claire felt a wretchedness she'd never known.

Nicholas keened and grunted as they wheeled him back to his room, the seat belt around his torso the only barrier that prevented him from hurling himself face-first onto the floor. Claire's hands shook on the handle of the wheelchair.

"Please, do something. Please help him," she whispered.

Amy placed her hand over Claire's. "We'll try again tomorrow, Nicholas," Amy repeated in a soothing tone. "This takes a lot of practice, and some days are better than others. We'll try again."

"That's it, that's all you can do?"

"I know this is difficult to watch, Mrs. Montgomery, but it's all part of his recovery process." Nick dug his fingernails into the healing IV scab on his left arm until he began to bleed.

"But I want . . . to hit . . . the . . . ball," Claire heard him gasping from just outside the door to his room. Amy and an attendant hoisted Nicholas's thrashing body back into the bed and tried to redirect his energy. She walked over to a small cluster of chairs by the nurses' desk and sat down to cry.

Moments later Amy tapped her on the shoulder. "Mrs. Montgomery?"

Claire startled. "Why is this happening? What should I do?"

Amy pulled up a chair next to her. "That was a natural fight-or-flight reaction to his frustration. Patients in this stage are working from some of their most basic instincts. I know it may not seem like it, but he's gained so much strength since he started with me, and I'm confident we're going to see a lot more improvement. He's a fighter," she said, standing and glancing into Nick's room. "Look, he's already calming down. Why don't you just give him a few more minutes and then go in and be with him."

When Claire returned to Nicholas's room, she saw that his arm had been bandaged. His breath appeared calm and even, and he smiled vaguely at her as she approached the bed. She took his hand and held it.

"Where's . . . my toothbrush?" he asked her after several minutes.

"Do you want to brush your teeth, Nicholas?"

"Where's the . . . toothbrush. I want the toothbrush," he said, louder.

Claire retrieved his toothbrush from the bathroom sink and placed it in his right hand. He stared at it for several seconds and then tried to raise it with a shaking hand, but it fell from his grip. His eyebrows furrowed and his breath quickened. She quickly placed it back in his palm. Nicholas lifted the toothbrush once again and began to brush the right side of his cheek. Claire guided his hand and the toothbrush back toward his mouth, but he dropped it on his chest and looked away. She moved out of view and closed her eyes.

"Where's Mom?" he suddenly asked.

Claire spun around and saw that his gaze had returned to her face. She cupped his chin in her hand. "I'm right here, Nicholas. Your mom's right here. Do you remember?"

"Where's my toothbrush?"

"I'm your mom, Nicholas, can you remember now?" she asked slowly and calmly.

"I want . . . to hit the ball. Where's the ball?"

She felt defeat spread through her stomach.

"I want to hit the . . . volleyball," he repeated, slurring.

"Nicholas. Honey. I know this is frustrating, but you'll get there. I promise. It's just going to take a lot of baby steps."

"I'm not a baaaby," he screamed. Tears pooled in the corners of his eyes and he began punching the wall of the bed with his good hand. "Fuuckkk, I'm not a baby."

Claire tried to hold his raging arm as he thrust her wrist against the plastic edge. "Of course you're not a baby, Nicholas. You're seventeen years old and you're strong and smart and you're going to hit the ball again. I promise you will." *You're going to hit that damn beach ball.*

Claire walked the shoreline, the rolled-up cuffs of her jeans wet around her calves, the sand under her toes pulling back out to sea with the tide. She wondered if Nicholas would experience simple joys like this again. She kicked a soggy mound of sand and fractured shells into the surf with all the force of her body. It landed with a plop a few feet in front of her, swallowed into the retreating gray curtain.

She used to see the greatest joy of her life when she looked at Nicholas. Now she saw a reminder of her most hideous regret, and the stunted brilliance of young man trapped by a brain that might or might not have permanent deficits. The wind picked up, blowing sand and salty spray into her mouth. "Fuuuckk," came the cry from deep within her core. She grabbed rocks and threw them one after another until her arm ached. They flew in rapid succession, skipping and sinking into the waves. Then suddenly mindful of her surroundings, Claire turned to check if anyone had witnessed her outburst. But she was still alone in the gloom, embarrassed at her self-consciousness. She bent down and rinsed the sand from her fingers.

The penetrating chill rose to her ankles, then her knees, the crash of the waves a hypnotic song. She knew no deed went unrecognized, that there were consequences for every action or inaction, even consequences for acts of omission. A wave splashed onto her face. In the grand cosmic scheme, she questioned, why wasn't karma linear? Why was Nicholas made to suffer so greatly for her mistake? Things ricochet where we don't expect and life just gets messy, she remembered Jackie telling her more than once. The trick was figuring out how to repair the aftermath and move forward.

Claire felt the pull of the tide around her, its soothing ebb and flow. She noticed the graze of shells against her calves and the fluid eddy of kelp and sand. The wind calmed. Her shoulders relaxed and she dangled her fingertips in the water. It no longer felt cold. It just was. She was. She closed her eyes and let her mind float with the current. She listened to the crackle of the surf and sensed her heartbeat sync to its rhythm, feeling part of something whole and sustaining. After a minute or possibly several, she opened her eyes to the world around her—a world she endeavored not to see anchored in regret over the past or an increasingly distant partner, but simply in the sunrise and sunset of each day.

As Claire finally made her way to Nicholas's room, she bumped into one of the occupational therapists. "He's been asking for you, Mrs. Montgomery," the woman said with a wide smile.

"What?" Claire asked, yanking her sweater down over the rumpled sweatpants she'd found in her tote bag.

"Nicholas has been asking for his mother all morning."

She could feel the swell of anticipation but tried to keep her hopes in check. "Well, he's done that before, and still hasn't made the connection."

"He's had a very good day today, Mrs. Montgomery."

She rounded the corner near Nicholas's room, bracing herself for a reunion with her son, and also for the likelihood that today would be like all the others. Either way, she would take things as they came.

When Claire walked in, Nicholas lay staring out the window, the uneven patches of his hair standing up on end like the little bean sprouts they'd once planted in a Dixie cup in the kitchen. It was growing back in a darker shade of brown. Potato-peel brown.

"Where were you?" he asked slowly, his expression conveying neither recognition nor the contrary.

Claire pulled up a chair next to his bed, trying to temper her mounting hope. "Hi, honey. I'm sorry I wasn't here earlier."

"Where were you?" His words sounded deliberate and practiced.

"I was at the beach. Do you remember the last time we went to the beach, Nicholas?" She took his hand in hers, but he looked at her blankly, his eyes drooping as if fighting sleep. She tried a different approach. "Do you remember me?" she asked expectantly.

"What?"

Claire cleared her throat. "Do you know who I am, Nicholas?"

He grabbed the edge of the mattress and pushed himself up to a sitting position with his right hand. Claire could see his right leg digging for traction under the blanket. "You think I'm crazy?" he said, breathing hard from the exertion. "I'm not . . . crazy."

"No, honey, of course not. You had an accident, and it's been difficult for you to remember things." She blinked fast to keep her tears in check, still uncertain what Nicholas's words really meant, still wondering if he really *knew* who she was.

"I'm tired," he said, staring past her.

She nodded stoically. "Why don't you rest, and I'll be here when you wake up." She kissed his forehead as he closed his eyes, and Claire retreated to the small sofa near the door and rummaged through her tote for a book to read.

"Mom?" came his drowsy voice after two chapters of *The Goldfinch.* "Where's . . . where's Dad?"

Claire bolted to the bed. "Oh my God, Nicky, I'm here. *I'm* your mom," she cried, grasping his fingers and kissing them. The sweetness of the relief that washed over her was like nothing she had ever experienced. She felt dizziness and exhilaration crash together in her chest. And Nick simply looked back at her as if she were the one who had been having trouble comprehending things. On the verge of eye rolls, he looked at her like a teenager looks at a parent—and she couldn't have been more grateful. "Your dad's back home in Denver," Claire explained, marveling at the mysteries of the human brain, and still having a hard time

believing that the nurses' numerous experiences with sudden recall had actually occurred with Nicholas now, too. "And he's going to be so happy you asked for him. We love you so much,
honey."

"Okay." Nicholas closed his eyes again and drifted off, mumbling something—a name, Claire thought, but couldn't quite
make out.

CHAPTER 14

Michael finally answered his cell after her third call. In the background Claire heard the din of voices and cutlery on plates, but at the sound of his clipped tone, she could only clear her throat.

"Is that you, Claire? What is it, has something happened?"

She took a deep breath. "Nicholas asked for you. And he remembered me."

"What? When?"

"Today. He—"

"Wait, hold on a sec." Claire could make out a muffled "excuse me," and footsteps before Michael retuned to the line. "What happened?"

"He asked where you were and he called me 'Mom.' The doctors were right, Michael." She related the day's events, omitting her detour to the beach.

"Whoa, slow down, Claire. He's recovered his memory, is that what they're saying?"

"That's what they believe. He's still got retrograde amnesia from the night of—from that night. He may never remember the overdose, or even the days leading up to it. But he's been asking for you all day."

There was silence on the other end of the line. A long silence. And Claire braced herself for another round of the blame game.

She still hadn't figured out a way to share good news when it was really only camouflaged sad news in the bigger picture. But then she heard quiet, hiccup-like sobs.

"Thank God," Michael finally said, several times between loud breaths.

"Are you all right?"

He exhaled loudly. "I'm fine. I'm just—" his voice cracked, "I wasn't sure he'd ever—" he paused. "Did he say anything else? He really has no recollection of . . . of things before?"

"Not yet. He just asked where you were. And he really seemed to know me."

"What did you tell him?"

Claire walked in small circles around the kitchen, wanting to reach through the airwaves and touch him. She imagined them hugging and sharing the relief that two parents in their position should be sharing. "I told him you were in Denver, but that you'd be here again soon."

"I was planning on coming out next week, but I'll be there to-morrow."

"That's great." She studied a large gouge at the foot of her kitchen stool.

"Claire?"

"Yes?"

"I, uh . . . Jeez, this is such a relief. Thank you. I'll see you both tomorrow."

"Travel safe."

Gone was the sandpaper quality of their exchanges, replaced by a sense of joy and—she was almost afraid to think it—connec-tion. For once her fears had gone unfounded. Their child was get-ting better and Michael had accepted it without any caveats, had even exhibited a glimmer of warmth. Were these their first small steps toward détente? She thought of the plans they could start making to participate together in some of Nicky's therapy ses-sions, even outings they might take. She stared at the telephone, the conduit of such promise, and heard Michael's familiar *"whoa, slow down, Claire,"* echo in her mind. The clock on the oven rolled over to the new hour with a loud, achy grinding. Maybe she was reading far too much into a three-minute telephone conversation.

Her phone rang, and she immediately clicked back on with anticipation.

"Hello, dear."

"Oh." Claire looked at the phone screen, shaking her head. "Hello, Mother."

"I hadn't heard from you in a while. How've you been?"

"It's been hectic, but—"

"How's Nicholas doing?"

"He's had a breakthrough, actually." She walked over to the couch and, falling into the cushions, gave Cora the good news.

"My goodness, Claire, what . . . a . . . relief." Claire could hear her mother struggling with the words between her smoker's hack. "That's so . . . wonderful, sweetheart. What did Michael say? Is he warming up a little bit now?"

Claire winced at the idea that she had shared this same thought with her mother who, as always, managed to elicit and dissect the entire conversation.

"So, he seemed optimistic about Nicky's progress?"

"Sort of."

"And he didn't bring up the accident?"

"Not once." Claire doodled flowers on a magazine page, picturing Cora's Fanci-Tone White Minx curls and her soft, rouged cheeks pressed into the princess phone in the family room.

"Well, that's just the copper on the penny, dear. This is progress."

By the time Cora was finished, Claire found herself puffed up. She heard Cora's excitement mount with each nuance of intimacy she'd unearthed from the phone call. And against her better judgment, she was infected by Cora's optimism.

"You work on that boy of yours when he comes out there," Cora added. "You do what you need to do to get him back."

"Michael's not a boy."

"They're all boys. And they all have their childish ways of dealing with things. It sounds like he needs you. He misses you, even though he's too stubborn and proud to admit it. But he's given you an opening here, Claire. Now you take that and run with it. You fix this thing you did, for what reason I'll never be able to fathom"—she exhaled loudly—"and you put your family back together."

"Mother, I'm trying."

"And I'm so thrilled about Nicholas," Cora continued. "I was going to suggest a little visit, but I'll wait until after you and Michael have your time together. You just grab that ball he's offered you, honey, and you run with it."

The weather had shifted from gray to blue, and the first of the season's Santa Ana winds blew fast and hot through the night. Claire closed her bedroom window against the dust, and fell asleep to tree branches scratching at the glass, thinking that on a night like that anything could happen. Good things, or earthquakes.

CHAPTER 15

The next morning, one of the clearest in memory, Claire sat waiting for Michael outside Nicholas's room. She watched her husband approach from the elevator in a cornflower-blue dress shirt and dark suit pants, his face slimmer and with more than the usual amount of tired around his eyes. He carried a small gym bag over his shoulder. Claire ran her fingers through her hair and stood to greet him. She hoped Cora had been right. If Michael could keep this flicker of optimism lit, then there just might be room for some healing between them.

Claire reached out to him, and he stuck his hands in his pockets. "How've you been?" she asked, keeping her voice upbeat.

"I'm fine." He cleared his throat. "Better now."

"Good flight?"

"Yeah. I brought the plane."

"Oh? Just for you?" Claire looked away, unable to discourage the rush of nostalgia this news brought. The luxury of romantic birthday jaunts to New York or Aspen. Their privileged life as a couple. Their once beautiful life as a family. A patient with a walker approached, and Claire was forced to move in close to Michael to allow the man to make his arduous way past. A staleness lingered in the air behind him, and Claire smiled weakly. Their life now.

"I flew out some of the Manhattan Beach Fund investors, too."

They stared at each other in silence for a few seconds, nodding like colleagues.

Then Michael stepped forward, leaning in toward her, and Claire saw a softening of his body language, a warming in his eyes. Impulsively, she wrapped her arms around his waist, holding him and nestling her cheek into his neck in their old familiar way. She smelled Eau Sauvage and closed her eyes, waiting for him to return the embrace and celebrate their son's triumph. But what she felt instead were the muscles of Michael's neck tense against her just before he took her shoulders and gently eased her away. He stepped back and rubbed at the small damp spot where Claire's face had rested. "I was just looking for Nicholas," he said, indicating with his chin Nicholas's empty room behind her. "I see he's not there."

"Oh. I thought—" She pretended to wipe a stray lash from the corner of her eye, then smoothed the front of the pale jade sweater he had given her the previous Christmas, lost for a second in the collision of hope and reality. "They just took him to the therapy pool." She pulled the soft sleeves over her knuckles. "I'll walk you over," she said quietly.

When they arrived at the pool, Nicholas was finishing his balancing exercises with the therapist. Claire and Michael stood near the steps and watched him from behind. As the therapist held Nicholas's arm, he moved forward with her assistance and the natural support of the water.

"So he really is starting to walk again," Michael said with a half smile.

"Well, not yet on land. They're working on his balance here first." Claire watched the smile wane. "He's made so much progress, Michael. Really, it's amazing. Look at the difference since you were last here."

"Yeah." Michael started to pace along the side of the pool, with Claire following behind. "I'm glad to see he's out of bed and exercising. And not swearing at everyone in sight."

"He's been asking for you all morning. And his strength is getting better."

The therapist let go of Nicholas and he continued walking forward with his arms in floaties, and outstretched on the surface of the water. After several seconds he teetered to the side, but managed to regain his balance for another few seconds before breaking to rest. The therapist high-fived Nicholas as she helped him over to the steps. Michael knelt down at the edge of the pool, still out of Nick's line of sight, and Claire was afraid he was about to yell something to push Nicholas on, to keep him from quitting just yet. Little League, swim meets, and lacrosse matches flashed through her mind, and she cut Michael off before he could speak.

"The pool's been good for him, Michael. It's really helped with his confidence. And the great news is that they removed his catheter last week." Michael squinted at her and Claire struggled to make the words sound better. "I mean, he couldn't work out in the pool until he was fully, you know . . . continent."

His squint turned into a glare as he stood and walked toward her. "That's just *great.*"

"For God's sakes, Michael," Claire hissed through clenched teeth, the smell of chlorine filling her head. "Everyone here is working very hard to help Nicholas. Can't you see the positive?" She knew better than anyone how difficult that was, but she couldn't risk letting his irritation spoil the reunion. She watched Michael turn away, watched his fingers swiping at his eyes, pinching the bridge of his nose before he refocused on Nick. They waited until Nicholas was raised out of the water by the mechanical lift and then placed back into his wheelchair before greeting him. Claire nudged Michael forward, holding in the rest of her anger. Slowly he set down his gym bag, eyeing his son closely, warily, as if assessing his reaction to his arrival.

"Dad!" Nicholas shouted. "Dad!"

Michael moved in quickly then and wrapped his arms around Nick's torso. Nicholas hugged back with his right arm, his left still resting on the side of the wheelchair.

"I'm so glad to see you, pal." Michael was on his knees now, kissing Nick's cheek, clinging tightly to his son. "How're you doing?" he asked, pushing up to a squat and searching Nick's face for . . . something.

"Did you . . . see me out there?" Nicholas asked with wide-open eyes.

"I sure did. You're going to be doing the hundred fly by next year, sport."

Nicholas's expression wilted slightly.

"Well maybe not quite that soon," the therapist said as she finished toweling Nicholas off. "But your son is making some amazing strides, Mr. Montgomery."

"Did you see me . . . in . . . the water?" Nicholas asked again.

Michael looked over to Claire. She nodded at him to answer again. "Yeah, Nicholas, I sure did. You're doing a great job in the pool."

"So, Liz," Claire asked in the rosiest voice she could muster, "what's next on the schedule for today?"

"Nick has group mat class with Amy in fifteen minutes, and you're both welcome to watch."

Michael grasped Nicholas's shoulders and smiled a broad smile before kissing and then hugging him again. "You look wonderful, Nicky. And I'm looking forward to seeing what you can do in the gym. I know you're going to blow me away." As he stood, he clapped Nicholas on the arm. "You knock 'em dead in there, champ." Nick's elbow flopped from the armrest into his lap.

Claire dug her fingers into Michael's wrist and hurried him out of the pool room, gazing back at Nicholas. When she opened the door into the empty hallway, she felt the rush of cool air on her damp neck. She turned and abruptly stopped, nearly tripping Michael. "Damn it," she said, squaring herself to him, "I know you're frustrated, but you can't put pressure on him like that anymore. Some days are good and some aren't so good. It's a slow process, and he needs a lighter touch now. You've got to tone it down."

Michael pulled his hand free. "Don't tell me how to treat my own son. Especially now," he said, his voice thick with anger and, Claire was pretty sure, surprise at her reproach. "You think Nicholas got to be an all-star lacrosse and hockey player, or a nearly straight-A student with a light touch?" He ran both hands through his hair, tugging at the roots. "He needs the push. *That's* what's going to get him through this."

In her husband's sunken expression, Claire saw the distillation of a childhood's worth of disappointing Bs and *you can do better* backslaps. They stood staring at each other, numb with the venom of their words. After a moment the standoff abated with muted *sorrys,* and they continued on in silence to the therapy gym. As they passed patients with walkers or canes moving close to the railings on the wall, Claire watched Michael studying their strained efforts. Her stomach began to ache, and she worried that if Nicholas didn't have a successful mat class, there would be no conversation with Michael over dinner later about their own situation. There would be no dinner at all. When they reached the entrance to the observation area, Michael held the door open, cradling Claire's waist as she passed through, as had always been his habit. Claire turned to him and whispered her thanks.

Michael and Claire stood behind the gym's glass doors and watched a group of eight men, women, teenagers, and attendants assemble their wheelchairs into a circle. Nicholas was one of the youngest patients. He scanned the room until his eyes met Claire's. She elbowed Michael, and he gave him a thumbs-up, as they both smiled at their son. Nicholas raised his right thumb back. Amy led the group through some stretching exercises and then produced a balloon, to the apparent dismay of the group.

She tossed the balloon to a young man in a Mickey Mouse sweatshirt, who then swatted it over toward Nicholas's end of the circle. Claire held her breath. *Oh, God, please let him hit it.* Nicholas looked up at them and grinned. When the balloon came his way he began to rock his torso back and forth in his wheelchair and raise his arm, as if preparing for his moment to shine. He made perfect contact, tapping the balloon forward to a woman with long black braids.

Claire exhaled. "Look how much his coordination has improved." She reached into her pocket and pulled out a pack of gum, offering a stick in Michael's direction. "Remember those great picnics on the Vineyard, how much Nicky loved the sand volleyball games with all the kids?"

Michael remained focused on the gym. The balloon traveled straight to its target, but the woman opposite Nicholas made no effort to strike it. It drifted to the floor and came to rest in the center of the circle. Claire saw the subtle shift in Nicholas's face, the downward cast of his eyes and mouth. He looked back up at Michael, his lips pursed into the same frustrated expression he'd have after making a brilliant assist on the ice, and then failing to lead the team to victory. Nick's cheeks reddened and he glared at the braided woman who had decimated his moment. Amy set the balloon in motion again, and he began to flail his arm every time the balloon caught air. But he never made contact again.

Michael smacked the frame of the door. "This is what you were so excited for me to see?" He pointed to the group of patients now rolling indiscriminately in a dance of minor frenzy. *"This?"*

Claire tried to direct his attention to the weight room on their left. "I know it's disappointing, but he really is getting stronger, and he's meeting milestones."

Michael's eyes were red and glassy, the veins at his temples throbbing like boiling oatmeal.

"I mean, what did you expect after such a short time, relatively?" she continued. Nicholas's shouting drew their attention back to the gym, and they both looked on as an attendant wheeled his thrashing body away from the group.

Michael pressed his hands up against the glass and stared at the commotion. When he looked back at Claire, his face was wet with tears. He unzipped his gym bag and pulled out a football, turning it over and over in his hands. "Yeah, he's made progress, but I can't watch this." He walked into the hallway, shoving the ball back into the bag.

"Michael, I know it's hard to manage expectations, but—"

"I just wanted to toss a ball with him. I thought we'd at least be able to play catch, you know? He's just seventeen. He was just on the verge of . . . everything promising." He wiped his cheeks with the back of his free hand and repeated *seventeen* in his peculiarly anguished way. "I have so much to make up," he said, his voice trailing off. "And you've taken that away."

"Please," she shouted as she followed him to the elevator, "please don't go like this."

Michael raised his arm in a gesture of dismissal and quickened his pace. "And this so-called progress is costing a goddamn fortune." His voice had returned to full volume. "It's ludicrous."

"What?" Michael rarely complained about the cost of things. "Wait. Maybe we could talk to the staff psychologist together," Claire said, tripping as she tried to catch him. She was grabbing at straws, she knew, given his low esteem for the profession, but she was desperate to pin him down to some sort of meaningful dialogue, and to understand his progressively cryptic remarks.

But he did not turn back, and Claire stopped in the center of the yawning hallway and closed her eyes, listening to his footsteps fall heavily on the linoleum. And with each step, her sense of loss and bewilderment grew more acute. The elevator doors closed. She walked to the wall of windows near the elevator bank and looked down. Seconds later she saw Michael push through the double glass doors three floors below, his head cast toward the gray cement. This was not at all how the day was supposed to go. They were supposed to be reprising their role as a team. Supporting their child and becoming a family again. She watched him wander in the small visitor's garden near the exit, his lips moving as he paced circles around lush beds of begonias and birds of paradise. Finally he sat down on a bench and lurched forward, cradling his head in his palms. Claire saw his torso rise and fall in rapid, violent spasms. She felt her own body jerk against the window, tapping out their anguished beat.

When Michael headed toward the parking garage, Claire realized they had completely abandoned Nicholas, and she rushed to his room.

"Where's Dad?" he asked sullenly, eyes focused on the TV.

"He'll be back a little later, hon."

"Where is he?"

Claire handed him a water cup and straw. "He, um, had an appointment. But he was so proud of you today, Nicholas. Really proud."

Nick's jaw twitched. His eyes narrowed. "Sure," he mumbled.

"Honey, you did such a nice job in the pool." Claire watched as he took the straw into the corner of his mouth and sucked water until it began to dribble from his lips and spill onto his chest.

Saliva bubbled on his chin. She reached for a tissue, and Nick let the cup drop from his fingers like it was nothing, a scrap of paper.

"I'm retarded," he suddenly cried. A dark stain bled its way down to his legs. "Why . . . am I . . . retarded?"

Claire snatched the cup from his lap and, gathering wads of tissue, pressed them onto his sweatpants, dabbing at the wet stain, her voice caught somewhere between her throat and her shock. Wiping her eyes, she bent over him and rested her cheek on his temple. His skin was warm and sticky. "Nicky, don't ever think that. You're not retarded," she declared. "You had an accident with some drugs, which caused a blood vessel in your brain to burst. And it's made things difficult for you, just like Dr. Adamson has explained. Remember?" she anxiously added. "But you're recovering now. You are *not* retarded."

Nick stared at her, his face reddening with anger or possibly a struggle to parse her words. Or exhaustion. "Leave me . . . alone," he said, rolling away from her and looking out the window. "It's not true. None of that's . . . true."

She gazed helplessly at the muted TV screen and reiterated the doctor's explanation of brain injury and how it can make some memories difficult to access, how his brain had to heal and pathways had to regenerate—careful to balance Dr. Adamson's optimism for an excellent recovery with his mantra of "no certainties."

After what seemed like minutes of nonresponsiveness, Nick suddenly blurted, "Taylor."

"What, honey?"

"Who's Taylor?" he demanded, turning back to face Claire.

"I'm not sure who you're talking about, Nicky. Is that another patient here?"

Nicholas squeezed his eyebrows together, looking even more frustrated and perplexed than he had just moments before. "No," he shouted. "Tay-lor."

"I'm sorry, I don't know who that is," Claire said, trying to remember the names of some of the boys from Nick's dorm or on his lacrosse and hockey teams, and thinking that the name did ring some vague bell. "What made you think of Taylor?"

"I don't know," he said, his cheeks flushing again. "Just . . . I don't know." He rolled back toward the wall and pulled the sheet tentlike over his head. "I'm tired. Never mind."

The staff psychologist had also cautioned Claire about memories resurfacing in random order like pieces of a jigsaw puzzle, and about the amount of details Nicholas could process. And with traumatic brain injury, there was also that distinct possibility that he might never be able to fully recall certain people or comprehend the events leading up to his overdose. Amnesia as a coping mechanism. As Claire bent down and kissed the back of Nicky's head, she prayed that he might somehow be okay without *all* of the details and missing pieces. And she felt immediately ashamed.

Michael's coping mechanisms, however, were another story. "I just can't see him like this," he told her over the phone that evening. "And I can't see you. Not now."

"He needs you, Michael. I know it's hard, but we *both* need you," Claire said evenly. "And you just can't disappear when things are difficult or not up to your standards."

"Nicholas wouldn't be in this mess if"—he paused and exhaled a doleful-sounding breath—"if you'd thought about how much you needed me before hopping into bed with that pissant."

Claire slid into a chair, astonished by the raw, uncorked emotion in his voice—an articulation that finally revealed just how deeply her betrayal had wounded him. Not just Nicholas, but *him*. And in that knowledge she found unexpected comfort. It was evidence of his lingering love for her, which, until that moment, he had hidden so well behind his detachment and strange behavior. She allowed herself a slight smile. Now all she needed was an opportunity to make things right, a second chance.

"We have a lot to work out, you and I," she said, feeling hamfisted and uncertain. "Clearly. And I don't know how many times I can tell you how much I wish I could change the past, that I want to fix this. I'll do whatever it takes, Michael. Anything. But we have our son to take care of now. And you just can't opt out of the hard stuff. You can't just bail like that."

"God damn it, Claire, stop telling me what I can't do. I'll call Nick now, and I *will* go back to see him . . . later."

"But—"

"And I'll get updates on his progress from the doctors. But this isn't working."

"Michael?"

Silence.

Claire closed her eyes. She felt like she had stood at this precipice a hundred times before. When business deals became treacherous and convoluted, Michael was the first to jump in and get his hands dirty in the untangling, but when it came to difficult situations with an *emotional* price tag, it was full head-in-the-sand ostrich mode. *If we ignore our personal problems, they will go away.* Generations of Montgomerys had soldiered dysfunctionally onward with this motto. And so, apparently, had they.

"So you're just giving up?" she pushed, "because it's too painful? We have a history, Michael. A family that's worth fighting for."

"I'm not giving up on Nicholas. And I wish we *could* change the past. More than you know. More than anything." His voice broke—pressed, it seemed, between the rock and hard place of the situation.

"What about us, then? I think we—"

"Us? There is no us now." He clicked off.

Claire dropped her cell phone onto the floor. The little I-told-you-so she'd tried to banish from her consciousness, the desire to fight and the desire to curl up and cry rivers—they all bunched up inside of her.

Her heart ached. It was the same terrifying ache of uncertainty she felt those first few weeks in the hospital with Nick. Seemingly in an instant, though really it was a series of instants over eighteen happy, lonely, good and not so good years—all the shades of gray that constitute a marriage—it was done. Claire was incredulous that it could come to this without regard for any of the brightness. Because there *had been* brightness, she reminded herself. She thought of earthquakes and rubble. Of dusty piles of blissful moments frozen in picture frames, and jagged shards of fresh pain.

The still-live currents of sizzling emotion, and the dull whiteness of so much fossilized anger and regret. She scanned the walls of her apartment. The wreckage was everywhere, and nowhere.

But then from beneath the fallout she imagined a noise, too. The cry of something wounded yet still alive, and in her mind's eye she saw light. On and off it flickered like failing neon. Claire imagined digging her hands into the fallout, knowing if she could only reach it, she could save them. But might she be messing with the painful, natural order of things? The question weighed on her—breathe new life into something and give it a shot at survival, or walk away and let it sputter and fade to black? There were never any guarantees, no reliable odds. She heard the noise again, its pull so magnetic and strong, its history so much a part of her.

CHAPTER 16

Claire took off her clothes and threw them at the bedroom dresser, knocking over a lone bottle of perfume. A police siren wailed outside the window. She got into bed. Then she crawled back out and put the clothes in the hamper.

Lying in the semidarkness, she tried to assign significance to the faint patterns of streetlight and shadow on the walls. The curved silhouette of a rotund Henry Moore nude. The maroon and black portals of Rothko's Seagram panels. Rodin's *The Kiss. The Gates of Hell. Sometimes we see just what we want to see.* The words were Jackie's, just before they'd hung up from their nightly phone call. Claire closed her eyes. The room smelled of musty paper and loneliness. She rolled over, longing for something more fragrant. Those perfumed yesterdays, Cora would say. Those perfumed yesterdays that steal your troubles away.

She opened one eye. The damask print on the bedspread shimmered in the moonlight. She opened the other and ran her hands along the fabric, feeling a shiver as images and memories leapt out at her like ghosts. She dug herself deep into the covers, thinking of her wedding day, and the cold chill she had felt as she stood in front of the mirror in her suite at the San Francisco Fairmont. The walls, she remembered, were covered in shiny pink-and-green damask and bathed in soft light.

* * *

Inside the Bridal Suite, Claire steadied her clammy hands on the vanity and stared at her reflection with vague detachment. Then, moving her hands down her lace bustier to her thighs, she began to sway her hips. She danced slowly, sensually. Michael had had the lingerie sent from La Perla and delivered with her orange juice and coffee that morning. *Dreaming of you in this—see you at six,* the card read. A fit of cold perspiration seized her. She picked up the note card and read it again, looked for more evidence of their perfect union in the blue ink.

Claire moved closer to the mirror and loosened the stays of her bustier, trying to admire the intricate lace detailing. Maybe she should call Michael for a pre-wedding peek. Some reassurance. Anything to blot out the crazy nightmare that had awoken her before the sun, with its surreal images of Michael dancing away from her, ignoring her pleas for him to come back, to take her in his arms and not run.

With a mother's timing, Cora swept into the suite, a vision in pink chiffon. The menthol scent of cigarettes lurked just beneath a cloud of Norell. "Aren't these shoulder pads terrific," she said, eyeing herself in the mirror from behind Claire. "I feel like Joan Collins—very *Dynasty*. And I just love what your gal did with my hair." Her short platinum bob was teased and curled to its biggest and highest glory, orange silk flowers sprouting from behind her ears. "What do you think, honey? Très chic, no?"

"You look great, Mother," Claire said softly.

Cora placed her hands on her daughter's shoulders and looked closely at Claire for the first time since she entered the room. "And you look pale, honey. Let's put some makeup on you." She reached for Claire's cosmetic bag on the vanity, and began to apply powder to her own nose. "Didn't you sleep last night? That was quite a rehearsal dinner. I probably had a few too many glasses of champagne, but this only happens once, and I'm so proud and excited for you." She stopped to catch her breath.

"Actually, I had diarrhea all night after I came back."

Cora frowned. "Maybe it was that rich butter sauce. I'll call and have them send up something for your stomach."

"Don't bother, there's nothing left in there. I'm empty. And I had this horrible dream." Claire crossed her arms over her chest and could feel the perspiration inching its way across the fold of her breasts.

"Honey, that's perfectly normal. All brides are nervous; it's the biggest day of our lives. I was so panicked about my wedding night with Daddy, but I don't imagine you and Michael have to worry about that." She gave Claire an exaggerated wink. "Really, dear, don't get yourself so worked up over it. It will all be beautiful." She kissed Claire on her cheek and then pinched them both for color.

"Mother, did you ever wonder if you were doing the right thing. I mean, when you were getting ready to marry Dad?" Claire looked down into her lap.

"Nope. I knew he was the man for me, just like I know Michael's the man for you. You two are perfect together. Two peas in a very elegant pod."

"Yes, but I had this crazy—"

"You're marrying for all the right reasons, Claire. Security. Shared interests. I certainly don't know of another man who would spend as much time in a museum with you, or at the theater or jogging in the park. And he seems to positively bask in the light of your approval and admiration. Then"—she held up her fourth finger—"there's his family. They really do adore you, honey. And to marry into a family like that, well, the opportunities you'll have are beyond what I had ever dreamed." Cora took a deep breath, readying for her finish. "And of course, there's love, Claire. You two love each other. So I'd say you have quite a few wonderful reasons to marry Michael Montgomery, wouldn't you?" She placed her hands on Claire's shoulders and began rubbing. "Sometimes you just have to massage things a bit."

Claire smiled wanly as Cora's fingers worked to relax her apprehension about Michael and his occasional glimmers of—she wasn't sure what to call it—overachiever burnout, angst? He had confided toward the end of a recent and otherwise animated night of mai tais at the Tonga Room about feeling the constant weight of his family's expectations and standards, along with his own. And how this would sometimes make him want to just blow it all up and bolt, when he wasn't Type A-ing his way to a major pay-off on some deal. He was a relentless striver, a collector of accomplishments. But none of that seemed to make up for some haunting, unshakable failure he refused to name. The bar's theatrical thunderstorms underscored the drunk, desperate quality of his eyes as Claire assured him that he'd already surpassed the vast majority of the population with his many triumphs, and that she was so proud of him. Then she confided her own secret fear about living a life of ordinariness. "When my life flashes in front of my eyes," she had told him, her hands enclosing his balled fists, "I want it to be something authentic and worth watching." The next morning, hungover and laughing at the tiki umbrellas on the nightstand, they had sworn to cut a mutually fulfilling swath through life.

Now as Claire sat at the threshold of that life, she was having a minor panic attack about her future partner. Or maybe, she tried hard to rationalize, it was just the dichotomy between their two families that had brought on the nightmare, and not some veiled fear that she and Michael wouldn't be happy together. His parents were the very portrait of urbanity and culture in their East Coast sensibilities—in sharp contrast to her very salt-of-the-earth father. And peppery mother. Cora worked her way up Claire's neck, and she began to relax slightly. Maybe it wasn't Michael at all. Claire looked into the mirror at her mother and thought of the loud Norma Kamali number Cora had chosen for the rehearsal dinner, even louder alongside the quietly refined clothing of Margot Montgomery and her friends. It was Bill Blass versus the Macy's White Flower Day sale. Claire closed her eyes, trying to wrap her mind around the idea of another mother in her life.

"Paul and I are thrilled you'll be joining the family," Margot had said the night before in a voice that sounded three Dubonnet-and-sodas in, after all the toasts had been made. There, at the Top of the Mark and overlooking the sparkling city, she welcomed Claire into the fold in her own special way. "My dear, you're about to become a Montgomery. And as your mother-in-law to-be, I'd like to share a little secret with you." Margot slipped her arm around the tightly cinched waist of Claire's cocktail suit. "Relationships aren't always as pretty on the inside as they are on the outside," she slurred. "But we smile, because nothing ever truly is, darling, is it?" Margot smiled serenely in the direction of her husband, and then sharply turned her back on him. And in that gesture, Claire saw an entire marital history. "Your suit is gorgeous, as are you. And we are so happy that you will be at Michael's side now." She ran her palm across Claire's smooth cheek and looked into her eyes. "Lips up, darling," she said as she walked off to the bar.

Claire opened her eyes and stood. She made her way over to the window and pressed her forehead against the cool glass.

"Dear?" Cora whispered.

She gazed out at the bay and splayed her arms across the window like Dustin Hoffman in *The Graduate*. Margot was of a different generation, a different set, where marriages were permanent contracts in spite of the occasional dalliance or marked depreciation in affection. And Michael had made it clear that his parents' relationship was not one that he wanted to emulate. Claire turned her cheek and looked back at her mother, took in her pleading eyes and excited hands. Cora was Cora, all bottled-up hope and ambition for her daughters—Mama Rose with orange lilies in her hair. Pressing her body tighter against the chill of the window, Claire boxed away Margot's steely piece of advice along with Cora's dreams of vicarious privilege, *and* the silly nightmare. She wanted to be Michael's wife. Absolutely, she did.

"You're right, Mother," Claire said, peeling herself off the window. "I was just being the clichéd nervous bride." She checked the clock on the nightstand. "I'd better get moving." She walked back to the vanity table. "Would you help me with the dress?"

"Sweetheart, this is the moment I've been waiting for all your life. I'm so happy for you."

Claire got out of bed and looked into the dark mirror over her dresser. Her wedding—one of the most glorious days for a young girl raised on the fairy tale of a happy ending—and her strongest memories were of a nightmare and the nervous hours preceding the ceremony. She walked naked into her kitchen for a glass of water to wash away the bad taste in her mouth.

When she returned to the bedroom, she wondered what was really true in her life. Michael was running from her now, just as he had in the nightmare. Of course she had pushed him. And yet. Did intuition reside in a dream or a nervous gut? *Could that have been my one true moment? While all of these years have been . . . what? An accident of choice?* Claire glanced at her bed. A hunched silhouette with dark, gaping sockets on his face hung in the shadows above the headboard. *Blind Man's Meal,* she whispered into the darkness. She moved to the window and closed the mini-blinds, shutting out the Picasso patterns on the wall so they wouldn't plague her sleep.

And as she pressed her cheek to the pillow and drifted off, the name *Taylor* occupied her dreams instead.

CHAPTER 17

When Claire arrived at the hospital the next morning, Nicholas told her that his Dad had come back to say good-bye. That they watched some TV together, and that he would be returning for a visit soon. She could see the hope *and* disappointment in Nick's eyes. She recognized its resemblance to her own, the unalloyed hope of family. She played Scrabble with him after lunch and art class, and again after dinner, pondering questions for which there seemed to be no immediate answers and wrongs for which there might be no amends, as another sun-blasted day crept toward dusk.

"Did you remember who Taylor was?" she asked before saying good night, the puzzling reference having become an increasingly vexing earworm over the course of the day.

Nick looked at her like he'd completely forgotten the name, but then with it back out there and hanging between them, he became agitated again. Grinding his teeth, he breathed heavily and shook his head no. "No. Who is he?" he pleaded. "Who *is* Taylor?"

She could see him fighting hard, for whatever reason, to unearth the locus of this mystery, along with his frustration at his inability to succeed, and she felt like the worst kind of mother. "I'm sorry, honey, I didn't mean to upset you," she soothed. "Probably just someone you used to know. It's not important." Just another piece of the jigsaw that might never turn up. "Your memory still has some gaps, but that's okay now."

As he had before, Nick turned away and shielded himself inside his sheet, and Claire wondered if the name Andrew ever entered and, just as quickly, exited Nick's thoughts. She wondered, too, if Andrew still felt the hot sting of remorse. She kissed Nick good night and made a silent promise not to ask any more senseless questions. But she could most definitely not stop wondering what was going on in her husband's head.

As the week progressed without so much as a text from Michael, Claire focused her mounting intensity on Nicholas and all of his classes, and spending as little time in her apartment as possible. The busier she remained, the more distant her fears seemed, each day another bandage on her uncertainty. The exhaustion that arrived at night was her only hope for sleep. And as she lost herself in the routine, her uncertainty was displaced by the hope that somehow things might not really be as desperate as she had thought.

Nicholas had begun a rapid improvement in his communication and cognitive skills. A leap in word-finding ability fostered an increase in his thought-organization skills, which, in turn, bolstered his confidence. His burgeoning muscle strength and coordination allowed him to graduate from his wheelchair to a walker. And Claire saw his attitude shifting into positive terrain for the first time since they had been at Rancho. He was smiling and looking forward to his speech and art classes, and the Tourette's-like outbursts had become less frequent. The staff psychologist reported that Nicholas was making outstanding strides in their sessions. He had excellent recall of the events of his life leading up to the weeks before the accident, though his presence at Rancho still continued to confound him despite numerous discussions about the drug overdose.

Amy told her there were any number of reasons for Nick's sudden and impressive show of progress: the last bit of swelling in his brain going down; the computer-assisted programs he was working with; compensation by other parts of his brain; general healing. With traumatic brain injury, she saw mysteries and miracles every day. But Claire was convinced Nick's progress was partly the result of Michael's visit. She never discounted Michael's influence, and one thing Nick's rapid improvement told her was that he had been keenly aware of his father's disappointment in his progress. And now his body was going for gold. Subconsciously or not, Nick was always trying to grasp at Michael's brass rings.

She thought back to the start of Nicky's sophomore year at Andover. The moment they had arrived at Foxcroft Hall—the same dormitory that had housed former presidents, and Michael—she felt her son trying to hide the sense of duty he felt to measure up. Michael had arranged for Nicholas to have his old room there. With a nervous smile and both thumbs pointing skyward, Nick had posed for a photo with his dad in the quad before heading in to unpack. Claire remembered thinking it should somehow be easier the second time around, the setting up and the sending off. But depositing her child two thousand miles away from home for ten months was never the same pride-filled experience it was for Michael, who had been couch-jumpingly giddy when Nick's application to Andover had first arrived. Never mind her repeated misgivings about not having their son at home for first dates and dances and sporting events, never mind his diabetes and her belief that while it had been a good option for Michael and his brothers, *they* were a functional, loving family and Nick would be better off at home. In the end, though, she'd put aside her feelings and had caved to the soft-spoken wishes of her son, and to the sweetly narcotic but uncompromising *you'll come around since it's the only logical way* expression Michael had given her when he'd said, "You can't hover over him forever."

And so Claire found herself in the quad watching her son don his mask of confidence, and wondering if Michael's neck ever ached from carrying such conviction in the correctness of his choices. Then after the traditional dinner with Paul and Margot and the general family hoopla over the start of the school year, and after Michael had left for business in New York, Claire stayed in town for an extra day to help Nick get settled. As was *their* tradition.

She remembered Nick and his roommate, Charlie, constructing a pyramid of Ivy League shot glasses on the shelf over Charlie's desk, as Nick stopped to scan the room.

"Did you know a couple guys from the team painted the ceiling blue and white when my dad lived here? Kind of like in tribute," Nicholas had said with quiet pride in his voice. "Instead of this cracked gray crap?"

"Dude, everyone knows the story. We've all seen the trophy case. You're royalty, man. Son of the winningest QB at Andover," Charlie replied. They both stepped back to admire their handiwork while U2's "Beautiful Day" blasted from somewhere in the quad. "And we are going to have a fucking phenomenal year." When they went to high-five each other they caught Claire's eye from her spot in the corner. "Oh, I'm very sorry, Mrs. M.," Charlie said in his most Brahmin elocution.

"Yeah, sorry, Mom. It's just kind of cool, you know?"

"I know." Claire stood and went to level the top edge of a poster. "Your father was pretty hot shit in his day," she said, looking over her shoulder at them with a wink. She hoped Nick would find inspiration, not pressure, in the Montgomery history here. "But you never heard me say that." It really was inevitable, the whole setup, she thought.

Along the moldings Claire could see various shades of gray and blue crackling through the topcoat, the quiet force of history whispering not to be forgotten. And she wondered if the echoes of previous generations, of fathers and grandfathers, had already become a persistent whir in Nicholas's mind.

"So, can I take you boys to lunch?"

"Thanks, Mrs. M., but I'm meeting my brother in Boston later."

Nicholas was staring out of the window onto the quad below. "Let me just finish these boxes, and maybe we could walk into town?"

She tied her cardigan around her shoulders and sat down on Nick's bed, watching the boys get back to the business of unpacking. The rickety steel frame groaned. She looked around the room at the ancient pine desks, the too-small closet and drooping door frame—further reminders of the old-money tradition that permeated boarding school life out there. The prudent squeakiness of it all. But the squeaky people, Cora loved to remind, were the keepers of status and convention, the glory-makers of society. And if Nicholas continued on the prescribed Montgomery path to glory, Princeton would be next. Claire smiled and lay back into Nick's pillow, relishing their secret that he wanted to follow *her* path to Stanford instead, where there might just be a little more room to breathe. *That* kind of tradition she relished.

When Claire awoke from a brief catnap, she heard Nick and Charlie talking in the hallway. She rolled over onto her stomach and picked up a framed family photo from Nick's night table. The three of them, huddled together with open smiles and foggy breath at the base of Ruthie's Run in Aspen, just after Nicholas had raced Michael from the top and beat him for the first time.

"That asshole already took all of my Diet Coke from the refrigerator. I can't believe we're in the same freakin' dorm again." Claire heard the barely controlled anger in Nick's voice outside the door, and sat up to listen. "Last year it was my shampoo and towels. All year. Fucking Blake."

"Dude, don't let it bother you so much. Buy extra next time."

"Why do we have to put up with this shit? I'm sick of it."

"It's just, you know, how it's always been. We get hazed, and then we get to do the hazing."

"Yeah, right. I know all it about it." There was a long pause and Claire wasn't sure if Nick was holding back tears or about to punch the wall, though she couldn't imagine he'd cry in front of anyone else. "And Chaz," she heard him say quietly, "don't say anything again about my diabetes in front of everyone, okay?"

"Sorry, man. I didn't think it was a big deal anymore."

"It's not. But . . . whatever."

Dust particles floated in a halo of sunlight near the door frame, and Claire waited for Nicholas to reappear. Instead she heard his footsteps disappearing down the hall, and the bathroom door slamming shut. The sensitivity and stoicism, the masks of teenage boys. She tried to see Nicholas the way others did. Typical all-American boy, popular, a budding hockey and lacrosse star. The son of one of Andover's famous sons. But she knew he suffered the taunts and hazing of the upperclassmen with more sensitivity than he would have liked. Michael had shared his own stories with Nick of stolen towels and "swirlies" in the toilet. The many rites of passage and traditions to look back on. But how do you immunize your son against the constant specter of his father's greatness? She got up from the bed and began organizing his diabetes supplies into a storage box for under the bed. It was a lot of weight for a kid's shoulders.

As Claire was placing the last boxes of test strips into the container, Nicholas came into the room and sat down heavily on the bed. "Are you okay?" she asked, looking up into damp eyes.

Nick shifted his posture from hunched preoccupation to slouching indifference. It was a delicate balance, boys and their emotions. She placed her hand on his knee and waited.

"I just want to be normal, you know?"

Understanding normal was a tall order for anyone. Claire paused, trying to refrain from making it all better with a pat response. "I know, honey. And I know it's difficult to feel normal—whatever that means—living with all this. But I want you to remember that you can define yourself in the ways that *you* want to. You're the one who—"

"Yeah, but I'm still the son of the legend," he said, pronouncing the word slowly, "no matter how I want to define myself. And all these guys are harder on me because of that. It just sucks."

"Why do you think they're harder on you?"

The shy hunch of his shoulders returned. "It's like I'm under a magnifying glass, and they're watching to see if the legacy can measure up." He stared at the bulging container of supplies at Claire's feet. "And sometimes I think they feel sorry for me." His tears began to fall in earnest, and he didn't try to wipe them away. They dripped down his nose and rested in the hint of stubble on his upper lip. "I don't want anyone to feel sorry for me."

Claire saw Michael's blossoming features in her son's face. Similar looks, different nature. She understood why Nicholas played his medical condition so close to the vest. To admit a weakness was to invite unnecessary scrutiny, or worse yet, sympathy. Maybe that's why they were harder on him on the playing field, because they knew he wasn't fragile there.

She stood and wrapped her arms around him, feeling him

squeeze back with the last remnants of openness and fear and helplessness a boy on the verge of manhood reveals. The walls, she knew, would soon become increasingly impenetrable. She closed her eyes, savoring one of the final sweet embraces of his childhood.

"Nicky," she said, taking his hands in hers, "everyone here is just trying to figure out who they are. They measure themselves against the people around them, and sometimes if they don't believe in their own strengths, they put others down or make things difficult for them in order to make themselves feel bigger."

The mask of self-assurance and adolescent swagger, the I-can-conquer-it-all smirk—they were gone from Nick's face, eclipsed by the sensitivity she wished he wouldn't be punished for expressing. "Honey, I wish I could just tell you to ignore them, but I know you can't. And I know it sucks." He smiled slightly. "But what I will tell you is to have confidence in your *own* abilities. You're a wonderful, compassionate person, Nicholas. You're a talented artist and you're an athlete in your own right, who just happens to be quite handsome on top of everything else."

"All right, Mom, I get it." He wiped his lip and cheeks with the back of his hand, and rolled his drying eyes. "I get it." He tried to scoot off the bed. "Can we go for some lunch now?"

"Not just yet, buddy boy."

"I know, I know." He inched back and leaned his head against the wall, crossed his arms and cleared his throat. "Always do the right thing and live up to our own high standards, no matter what," he said in a robotic imitation of Michael. "Dad gave me his speech, too."

"Look, your dad and I are very proud of *you,* Nicky. Not the fact that you happen to go to Andover or live in the same room your dad did. We love you and want you to find the best in yourself here. The only thing you have to live up to is your own potential." Claire felt a thick layer of emotion coating her throat, and she was afraid she was dripping too much syrup for his taste. But she also wanted to stockpile the reserves, give him something to draw on in her absence.

Nicholas nodded silently, staring down at his plaid bedspread, uncrossing his arms.

"You don't have to be perfect, Nicholas. Okay?"

"Right." He turned his face to hers. The storminess in his eyes, though still there, had settled considerably.

Claire kissed his forehead and they walked out into the hallway. There was silence all around them. He slipped his hand into hers. "Thanks, Mom," he whispered.

"Was that a little too sappy?" Claire asked, understanding when he released her hand in the sunlight.

"I may need some extra insulin."

They circled back though the grove of maples behind the dorm, taking the long way into town. The weathered trees were old and enormous. The afternoon was shiny and clear. "So," she asked after a few minutes, "should we stop at the store on the way home and pick up some more Diet Coke?"

Nicholas nodded.

The gleaming spires of the clock tower and the main buildings rose above them in the distance. A squirrel scampered across the path into the high green grass, still damp and glistening from the sprinklers. The strong odor of wet concrete vied with the sweet smell of moist earth. It was a majestic place, she couldn't deny that.

Claire looked to the ground and saw imprints of footsteps on the cement. She turned back and saw that they had been marking their way for some distance. The prints were not the waffle soles of athletic shoes, but smooth like the penny loafers Nicholas was wearing. Were they an intentionally humorous attempt at posterity, a sly prank on the institution, she speculated? Or were they the oblivious wanderings of a young man lost in contemplation and wet concrete? The walkway had been created around the time of the post Depression-era renovations on the campus, she guessed from the stories of Nick's grandfather. She wondered why this hiccup in the beautification project hadn't been smoothed over. Maybe no one noticed. Probably it was just too expensive. She wondered, too, about the boy who left his footprints behind.

At that moment, Nicholas slowed and placed his own shoes in the boy's. Then he continued walking, loafer to loafer, and slightly off-center down the path. It was an almost perfect fit. Claire imagined that the boy of the footprints might have been a boy like

Nicholas, with the same worries and hopes. She pictured a teenager with a letter sweater and a book satchel. A boy who strove to maintain the appearance of normalcy, to be a regular kid and just blend in. Did he feel the pressure to live up to his father's ambition? Did he tire of that weight, too? Abruptly the footsteps disappeared from the edge of the path.

Claire watched as Nicholas stopped, visibly lost in thought, with one foot still on the concrete, the other in the grass. She felt certain his thoughts were not far from her own. A warm breeze blew her hair across her face, and she looked into the distance, envisioning the specter of the imaginary boy, hightailing it away from the confines of the expected, his satchel tossed to the wind, his body light and carefree. When she looked back at Nicholas, he was lying down in the damp grass and closing his eyes, spreading his arms above his head. She walked over and lay down beside him.

Grass tickled her cheek as she angled her face to the sun. She questioned whether Nicholas would continue to walk stoically down his prescribed road, or if he, too, would veer from the path and run toward his own destiny? Someone once said that the way to make God laugh was to tell Him your plans. Maybe, she thought, it was better to keep things quiet and avoid some huge cosmic joke. She kicked off her shoes and dug her feet into the grass, listening to the hum of passing bicycles. After a few moments, she felt Nick's hand squeeze her shoulder.

CHAPTER 18

"I'm here," Michael's voice said through the static.

Claire pulled her cell phone away from her ear and stared at it as she walked out of the hospital doors, looking around the visitors' gardens ahead and over her shoulders. Morning shadows still insulated the cluster of benches from the heat that was yet to come. It had been over two weeks since they'd last spoken, and she had almost gotten used to the absence of communication. "You're where?"

"I'm on my way to the hospital. I want to see if these progress reports I'm getting from Dr. Adamson are for real."

"Okaay." She sat down on a garden bench, trying to keep her cool, and focusing on the browning edges of the giant bird of paradise. "Yes, Nick's made some pretty remarkable improvements since you were last here."

"I talked to him. But it was difficult to tell anything over the phone."

"Well, I could have given you all the details."

"I'll be there in about an hour," he said in a voice so dispassionate Claire wondered if he would feel the slightest need to address their last conversation.

"Why didn't you call me back? I left messages."

"I needed some distance."

"So you drop a bombshell like that, and then just . . . drop out? There is still an 'us,' Michael, whether or not we like the state of it. And we need to deal with this." She felt the retaining wall she'd cobbled together with all of her affirmations and exertions starting to crumble again.

"Look, we can talk after I see Nick."

Her ear hurt from pressing the phone so tightly against it, and she walked back to the hospital entrance. The electric doors opened and then slid shut behind her, and she felt her body being pulled into a cold, tentative vacuum. She remained standing in the antechamber as the doors continued to open and close around her. A security guard approached the doors from the information desk, and Claire stepped out and cut a quick left toward the cafeteria. She bought a cup of coffee and took it to her usual table in the back corner. Forcing down a sip, she set the cup back on the Formica table. An hour was a long time to kill.

Claire put her phone beside the cup and stared out into the courtyard, missing her home, her family, and the predictability of their old life. The coffee was strong but only lukewarm, and she thought of the consequences of her subsistence diet of caffeine and stale cafeteria food as her mind drifted to Michael's parents, and to the pain and humiliation she had caused them. Their lack of communication since she'd been in LA conveyed all she needed to know about her current standing with them. She thought, too, of her incongruous soft spot for Paul Montgomery, a man who'd always seemed genuinely interested in her pursuits, despite his frigid approach to paternal affection. She had liked him far more than Margot, and now, with bittersweet irony, they were both lost to her. As for Michael, she could only hope for the best, hope that they always wouldn't be like storm clouds colliding and sparking their emotional lightning.

Claire took another long sip of her coffee and picked up one of the pink sweetener packets on the table and shook it, settling its contents and wondering why the memories she tried to muster of her family always turned out to be saccharine. So sweet at first, with a bitter aftertaste. She leaned back in her chair and saw a man seated at the table near the door, typing on a laptop. She hadn't noticed him before, but recognized him from other afternoon coffee breaks, from the gardens and hallways. Another regular. She studied his chiseled features, the gray sprouting from his temples. The tired slope of his shoulders. Even at a distance, there was an acquiescence to whatever had brought him to this place. That much she could tell. Was it his wife, or his mother, maybe? She tried to imagine someone else's story.

The man glanced up, catching her eye and smiling, and Claire reached too quickly for her phone, checking for a phantom message. She considered what Cora would think of her appearance—the circles under her eyes she no longer bothered to conceal, her untended hair now wavy and past her shoulders, her uniform of white jeans and whatever shirt wasn't dirty—but just as quickly dismissed all thoughts of clothing and makeup. It wasn't the kind of place where people cared. She stirred her near-empty cup with determination, and returned to her view of the courtyard gardens.

Several minutes later she heard the groan of a table leg, and turned to see that the man had abandoned his computer and was approaching her. He wore jeans and a faded Oxford shirt, and carried a plate. Claire looked around, but there was no one else behind her in the cafeteria.

"Cookie?" He stood across the table from her, smiling.

"Pardon me?"

"Would you care for a cookie?" He set a plateful of cookies in front of her, and stepped back. "I bought every one they had, hoping at least one wouldn't be stale."

Claire looked at the crumbling mound, laughing to herself at the threat of cookies. "Well that's very nice. Thank you." At close range his face whispered at the same fatigue she imagined hers shouted.

"I thought we might as well introduce ourselves officially since we seem to be leading parallel lives here. Name's Richard Elliot." He remained standing, waiting tentatively.

Parallel lives. Claire felt the sharp bite of the phrase, felt the hair on her neck stand on end, thinking of Andrew and where that phrase had taken her.

"I'm sorry, did I say something wrong?" he asked after too long a silence.

She shook her head slowly, squeezing the metal edging of the table, wanting to be anywhere but there, yet not wanting to appear rude. "I'm Claire," she replied. "It's nice to meet you. Officially."

"Do you mind if I sit?"

"All right." She forced a smile and took a bite of an oatmeal raison cookie, finding it difficult to swallow.

"What's the verdict?"

"I'm sorry?"

"What's the verdict on the cookie?"

"Oh." She wiped a crumb from the corner of her mouth. "Crunchy, I guess."

"Well, that's a good sign." He broke off a piece of a peanut butter cookie. "Now here's the real test," he said, holding it up between them. "If they can't get peanut butter right, then they need a new pastry chef in this joint." He put the cookie into his mouth, considering it like a rare cheese.

She watched his eyes. Large and brown, and flecked with amber. They didn't smolder or incite, but seemed direct. Safe. "And?"

"And it tastes like old socks."

Her guard eased and she allowed herself to laugh the warming-up laugh of strangers. As they small-talked in the drab light of the cafeteria, it dawned on her that she hadn't had a discussion that was tragedy-free in months. So even if it was only a short reprieve—a conversation about nothing with someone who knew nothing about her—Richard with his plate of cookies was a welcome distraction. She broke off chunks of chocolate chip and finished another oatmeal raisin over his reports on the farmer's market and the Getty Museum. And for just a few minutes, she forgot to worry.

"So, I'm visiting my sister," he finally said. "You?"

"My son."

"How old is he?"

"Seventeen." She hoped that would be enough. "And your sister, how is she doing?"

"Better." His eyebrows drew together. "We were in a car accident. She didn't fare as well as I did."

"I'm sorry."

"Yeah. I didn't mean to bring things—"

"I know." She knew exactly. "My son's improving, too."

Richard glanced at the clock on the wall, and then pushed his chair back and stood. "Well, it was very nice to meet you, Claire. I need to stop by the pool. But maybe we could share a meal here sometime?"

"I'm married," she blurted out, feeling broadsided and then immediately embarrassed.

"Then in that case, we could wear hair shirts and sit at separate tables."

"God, I'm sorry." She lowered her eyes, shaking her head. "You weren't asking me on a date."

"No."

"It's just that everything is so, I don't know—" She sank back in her chair and plastered her hands over her face.

"Fraught?"

She slid her fingers down. "Fraught. And far too complicated to understand. But I apologize for being an idiot."

Richard looked deliberately around the cafeteria, and out onto the courtyard where two patients in wheelchairs sat next to one another staring in opposite directions. "I'd say I'm uniquely qualified to understand."

She smiled without effort, lost in thought. There was another long silence between them. "Have you ever just veered away from your path, but didn't really know you were veering?" she suddenly asked, without really meaning to.

He contemplated her hands for a moment. "Unanticipated choices aren't the worst thing a person can make."

"Thank you for the cookies," she said after a few seconds. "A meal might be lovely sometime. Soup, maybe."

"The sky's the limit."

Claire watched him walk to his table. His hair was flattened against the back of his scalp, as if he had slept sitting up in a chair. His jeans hung loosely on his frame, though she could tell they had once fit more snuggly, and there was just the slightest limp in his gait. "Richard," she called out to him as he was closing his computer, "what are you writing?"

"It's sort of my *Tuesdays with Morrie.*" He slid the computer into his bag. "I'm a journalist most hours, but I'm also working on a book. About all this." He flared his palms outward toward the inpatient and therapy buildings, the cafeteria, her.

She finished the last cookie on the plate, and went to wait for Michael in the lobby.

CHAPTER 19

The conversation happened at a hot dog stand a block from Rancho. They walked there after their two hours together watching Nicholas perform his Wednesday best. Michael had been pleased with Nick's crisis-free accomplishments in the therapy gym after he'd arrived. Nicholas was talkative and happy after his gait class, the improvements in his strength and attitude on full display. The doctors were encouraging as they gave the go-ahead for a complete dismissal of his walker, and spoke to Claire and Michael of discharging Nicholas for outpatient therapy back home. It was a very good morning, Michael had said. Everything was looking so strangely positive and upbeat, so unlike their last meeting. When it was time for Nick to go to his art workshop, Michael had suggested a late lunch to Claire.

They sat in white plastic chairs near a small patch of grass behind the Gingham Dog. A few pillowy clouds drifted overhead as if just passing through on holiday as they set out their chili specials and sodas and reviewed Nick's performance. Michael looked almost relaxed in his button-down shirt and jeans, and Claire felt almost hopeful. They would be returning to Denver soon, to a life at home they would somehow finally have to navigate. It was such a welcome and long-awaited moment, this urban picnic on such a seductively sunny afternoon. The fuchsia-haired girl behind the order window turned on an ancient radio and spun the dial until it landed on the Violent Femmes. Claire whistled along to the angsty reminder of the eighties, and for a while they just sat listening to the music and tossing crumbs to the gathering pigeons, while diners of all stripes—businessmen, halter-topped skater chicks, and orderlies in scrubs—came and ate their hot dogs and went.

When the last of the lunch crowd had finally gone, Michael set his Pepsi can on the cement between them. The straw spun a couple revolutions with the breeze until its bent tip stopped and pointed in his direction, like the spinner on a board game. Michael's cheeks had reddened with the heat, Claire noticed, and perspiration had started to form at his sideburns. She could see he was about to speak, and she placed a hand on his knee, preempting him. "I think I'll talk to Amy about having a going-away party for Nick when we get back to the hospital. Just a little something with all of his specialists and docs to celebrate his progress and to thank them for all they've helped him—"

"We can't do this anymore, Claire," Michael said, cutting her off. There was a hint of remorse in his voice, the hint of some long-buried sadness, but only just. "This can't go on."

And just like that, amid the gravel and rush of a suburban LA hot dog stand, Claire's reedy hope blistered in the sun. She stared speechless as her head began its own slow spin.

"I've talked with the director," he continued. "They'll be sending Nick's chart out to Craig Hospital, and I'll bring him back to Denver next week. You can have your party and then fly out ahead of us. And then you should make some arrangements, get yourself set up somewhere near the house," he'd said, averting his eyes. "We just can't live there together now and pretend nothing happened. Not with Nick coming home. And obviously he needs to be in the house."

"What?" she gasped, still fighting to catch her breath from the sucker punch. "You're serious? You want me to move out of our house? But how do you expect—"

"Face it, we haven't been happy for a long time."

"But that's crazy." She grabbed both of his hands, his pale smooth knuckles, holding on for their life together. "Until last year, we were fine. I mean, things weren't perfect, and I know there's a lot to work through, but—" Bile inched up her throat. "You can't possibly mean this. Let's use this time to . . . to work on our issues. We *need* to make that choice."

He pulled away from her grip. "You already made a choice, Claire. Were you really happy and fine when you chose him? And did it feel *fine* to trash me in the process? No," he said, shaking his head, "there's just too much—"

"Michael, people do make stupid, reckless decisions. Mea culpa, a thousand times! But this one had nothing to do with trashing you. Please."

He seemed to bristle at her words as he was regrouping. "Then maybe you should take a little time to think about what it *did* have to do with. We need to be apart now, Claire. This"—he made a back-and-forth motion with his hand between their two hearts— "this won't be good for Nick. You know that. He needs calm, and the two of us together under one roof will not make for a healthy environment. I don't want to put him under any more stress than he's already under."

Claire's head bobbed mechanically, her guilt over everything she had done to bring them to this cliff subduing the anger and shock. All she could think of was how not to push Michael away any further, of not giving him any more reasons to blow it all up and run for good. She couldn't believe he was asking this of her. And yet, he *was* hurt, maybe in his own version of shock, and not at all himself. The possibility of life as a divorced, single parent washed over her with frightful potency. And it was a life she could not fathom, even if her husband was acting like an irrational ass. They were a family, and if there was to be any shot at mending their relationship, maybe a temporary separation *was* their only hope. A searing ache started to unfold across her brain as she weighed the untenability of her options. If Michael moved out, he might never return. But if she were to go, as he was telling her she should, for some short, temporary trial period where she could further demonstrate her contrition and he could feel like he'd doled out the appropriate penalty . . . She couldn't find any other trapdoor to the argument. And she had to stop moving her head, had to circumvent the pain before it could take over. She placed pressure on the nerve just below her eyebrow and fished in her bag for some aspirin.

"I can have Dana look into a nice rental for you at Park Gardens if you want," he'd said as she watched him crush the empty soda can and straw in his palm. His expression was one of numbness and detachment, a stranger's. The sun flashed overhead, klieg lights, it seemed, on their increasingly surreal tableau.

CHAPTER 20

Claire requested a table for one near the bar. The restaurant was the only decent spot within walking distance of the hospital. Its walls were painted a deep red and covered with small oil paintings of Parisian nightlife, the crowd noisy. She ordered a dirty martini with extra olives. When it arrived, milky with chill, she drank half of it in one big gulp and stared into the ruby candlelight, the inconceivable events of the afternoon only just beginning to penetrate.

She stabbed at an olive at the bottom of her glass with the plastic cocktail sword. The damage was done, Michael had said, even if Nick did make a complete recovery. They'd *both* done too much damage. She pictured Michael's eyes as he'd uttered those words, how his expression had gone from tortured to practically somnolent. The olive rolled around the glass, eluding capture. Her husband had finally pulled his head out of the sand, and she felt as if the man who had spoken those unfeeling words to her and then refused to engage any further was someone she'd never met. Claire emptied her glass.

"Waiter, another martini, please. Extra dirty."

She didn't know what to make of their history anymore. The candle flame glowed pink, and under it, rivulets of wax dribbled honey-like down its sides. Her eyes burned, and she hated that

Michael had brought her to this again. How absurd to doubt the validity of eighteen years of one's life. And how nearsighted to disregard so much goodness for one failure, massive though it was.

In the background Edith Piaf's tragic voice soared over the static of an ancient record. *Quand il me prend dans ses bras, il me parle tout bas, Je vois la vie en rose.* She mouthed the words and wondered how they could not have been happy when she had tried to make everything so beautiful. She had gladly given up her job and devoted herself to creating the kind of warm family life and home Michael had never had. *La vie en rose.*

The second drink went down more smoothly. As Claire chewed on an olive, it occurred to her that maybe she didn't really know her husband at all. When they should have been plowing the depths of their souls and working through their difficulties together, he drifts deeper into his own murky world. She thought of his eyes again, the remoteness in them, the absence of light. She remembered seeing the look before. There was some important truth buried there, Claire was certain, something he was keeping from her.

She ran a finger around the moist rim of the glass, thinking about her own secrets and failures. *Had* she been happy the night she met Andrew? Did it matter anymore? She signaled to the waiter for another.

"Claire?"

She turned around, wondering how he had found her. But she couldn't see him. There was a blur and a voice, but no Michael. Maybe he'd realized his mistake. She heard her name again and looked expectantly past the banquette. There, sitting at the bar, was Richard. She attempted to stand, and possibly run, but her head was too heavy and her knees missed the message. He came to her instead and sat down.

The waiter returned with her drink as Richard sat. "What, no cookies?" she asked.

"How about some peanuts? It looks like you could use something to eat."

She held on to the base of the glass, making a triangle with her hands. "I'm drunk."

"I can see that. But you don't strike me as the type of woman who gets drunk in restaurants by herself."

She took a long sip, swirling the thick saltiness around in her mouth. "It's been a day."

"I guess so."

Claire leaned in over the table, barely registering the heat of the candle beneath her chin. "But I'll tell you who I am, Richard. I'm go-with-the-flow Claire. I'm the gal whom roommates loved and boyfriends wanted back. Because I'm the perennial goodwill ambassador who never, God forbid, wants to ruffle feathers, and always makes nice, always smiles and fixes." Richard pushed a glass of water across the tablecloth to her hand. She traced a line in the condensation with her finger, feeling her head wobble on her neck. "I told myself this was the strength of my character." She stared at Richard, seeing a hazy kaleidoscope of faces. "But it didn't make me strong. It just got me lost. Good and goddamned lost." Tears rolled down her cheeks. Red tears, she imagined, like the candle wax. "Lost me my marriage."

He tore off a piece of bread from the loaf in the basket and offered it up to her.

Hammered on Stoli and sinking deeper into her despair, she pushed away the bread and told him that she wanted to go home to her house, that she just wanted her life and family back. The words tasted tart, like cheerless Starbursts of regret. He drove her to her apartment and made sure she got safely to the door.

CHAPTER 21

The incessant pounding could not have been in her head. Or maybe it was. In her head. The noise grew louder and she began to decipher a sort of rhythm to it, a tune. Sinatra? Snippets of "Fly Me to the Moon" rushed in. A convertible, stars tumbling across the sky, the night breeze on her face. She slowly got out of bed and heard her name muffled through the front door. She checked the peephole.

"Well, aren't you a vision," Richard said as she opened the apartment door. He held a Gatorade bottle and coffee. "Glad to see you dressed for the occasion."

Claire, in the same clothes she'd been wearing when she crawled into bed, ran her hand over her hair, trying to tame its vertical wildness. "What are you doing here?" Her scalp throbbed and she could smell the fermentation on her breath as she spoke. The memory of martinis and Richard's voice came back to her, making her wonder if there was anything more to the previous night's story. She surveyed her clothing again.

"You, my friend, were a perfect mess. But I," he said, holding up his Gatorade hand, "was a perfect gentleman. Scout's honor."

She exhaled a mixture of dread and relief.

"So, are you gonna invite me in? I bring a cure for what ails you."

"Richard, I don't really want any—"

"Oh, you *will*." He ran the coffee under her nose.

She turned around and walked into the kitchen. Richard followed her. "First, the cold stuff. Then coffee." He placed them on the counter in front of her.

She unscrewed the bottle top. "You're forever bearing bounty, aren't you?"

"That's quite lyrical for a hangover."

Claire gulped half the bottle. "God, that's magnificent. Thank you."

"I thought you might be in bad shape this morning."

"Can't imagine why." She closed her eyes, trying to remember more scraps of the previous evening. "It feels like someone put tiny mittens on my teeth." She finished the Gatorade and started on the coffee.

Richard sat down at the small dining table and leaned his head back into interlaced fingers. A tolerable amount of morning light peeked through the half-open curtains behind him.

"I'm sorry for rambling on like such an idiot last night. After a certain point, it was just my drinks having another drink. You were really kind to drive me home." Claire stared across the counter at him, grateful that someone was actually looking after *her*, and suddenly aware of the gaping lack of human infrastructure in her world. She'd shut out all friends and kept Cora at a three-state distance—Cora, whom she couldn't sever from her life with a chainsaw, though she'd had fantasies. It was to be all Nicholas and all Michael, all the time. Reparation through insulation.

"Lucky I had a taste for French onion soup."

"Yes." She opened the refrigerator and scanned the shelves. *Lucky.* After a moment she retrieved a plum and set it down on the table in front of Richard. "But you've gone above and beyond, coming back this morning. You're a good friend."

He placed his hand on her wrist. "Well, friend, I didn't want you stewing in your despair all day."

She sat down opposite him. "Oh, I was stewed, all right. And I'm sorry if I was a bit—inelegant."

"Even drunk and swearing, you were still elegant." He picked up the fruit and bit into its purple flesh.

She covered her eyes with her hands. "Ugh."

"How's the hangover?"

Claire did a brief physical inventory, avoiding her psyche. "Not horrendous, considering. I think the fog's starting to lift."

"Excellent. Then we can get going."

"Going?" She was starting to lose her vague enthusiasm for company.

"We're taking a little field trip to the Getty."

She stood, feeling an instant and clobbering head rush. "Richard, I have to get to the hospital. I'm sorry, I really need to see—"

"You *will* see Nicholas. But I'd recommend a couple hours of fresh air, some exquisite gardens, and Van Gogh's *Irises* first. Then we'll head back to the hospital. After you're sufficiently . . . aerated."

Richard looked up at her, and Claire felt his eyes assessing her rumpled clothes, her unwashed face and hair, her wooziness and fragile veneer. Not as Michael might have, but in the nonjudgmental, just-observing-the-state-of-things manner of a journalist. A pal. Her brain ached thinking about Michael, her heart ached for simple companionship. Life, she noted, was becoming more fraught by the day.

He pulled out an *LA Times* piece on the museum, and placed it on the table. Claire ran her finger over the photo of the grounds and thought about her day at the beach, knowing she was beat. In every sense of the word. "I don't know. I just feel so wrecked right now."

"You said you've been dying to see it. And you said Nicholas was doing great."

"Yes, but—"

"Hey, it'll do us good. Both of us."

She stared out the window over Richard's head.

"Hair shirts, pal." He caught her eye.

"I need to call Nicky. And I'll need to shower."

* * *

As they strolled the tree-lined walkways en route from the museum courtyard to the central gardens, Claire surveyed the color around her—the vivid pink bougainvillea arbors, the red flowering crape myrtle trees, yellow climbing roses. She breathed in verbena and exhaled her hangover in small puffs. The Technicolor brightness of California hit her, and she realized her steady diet of stark white walls and black moods had not been a healthy one. All black and white, all work and no play—they both had the same psychic effect. She buried thoughts of her marriage, and focused on her surroundings. The Pacific Ocean glimmered like a sapphire in the distance.

"I'm tired of hearing my own voice, Richard. Talk to me. Tell me about you."

They had reached the gardens, and sat down opposite a pool blanketed by a floating maze of deep orange azaleas.

"About me? I generally like to ask the questions." Richard rolled up the sleeves of his denim shirt and looked out toward the Santa Monica Mountains. "I'm forty-nine, but think I look a sprightly forty-seven. I love my job at the paper, but it's just a job, something to keep me in steaks and skis and able to pay tuition." He paused and ruffled his wavy salt-and-pepper hair. "Though my ski season was cut a bit short this year. I've been divorced for three years, and my gorgeous daughter is at Berkeley." He shifted his gaze to Claire's face, a question forming on his lips. Just then a group of stilt dancers appeared on the museum terrace above the garden, and Richard directed her attention to the wildly costumed giant human puppets.

Claire watched them move with the awkward, slow motion gait of giraffes, and listened to the giggles of children at the terrace café, their boisterous squeals of delight as the puppet men dipped and danced for the crowd. She grabbed Richard's arm as a young boy tugged at one of the striped stilt legs, sending the puppet into an unanticipated lurch and totter, and sending the boy's mother into a wild-armed scolding.

"And in one fell swoop, the circus came to a swift and staggering stop," Claire said with a dramatic laugh.

Richard raised his eyebrows. "You're a real wordsmith, eh? That's supposed to be my department."

She gazed out at the sea, the city and the museum grounds. "It's been a week of firsts."

"What are you talking about, Smitty?"

"Are you giving me a nickname?" she asked, nudging him playfully, and liking the warm familiarity of a sobriquet, since she'd never had one. "You do seem to bring out the hungover poet in me." She stood and motioned for Richard to follow her around the pool. The sun was behind them, giving the water a honeyed glow. A young woman in large white-rimmed sunglasses and tailored jeans and heels stood behind an easel on the opposite side of the pool, painting, her long blond hair brushing the tops of sculpted breasts with each brushstroke. Claire wondered at her golden, photo-like quality.

"I'd say you don't see *that* every day," Richard said under his voice as they passed the painter. "Except that you do. In LA."

"This place is a bit unreal, don't you think? A bit perfect?"

He nodded.

"You didn't grow up here, did you?"

"Nope. San Francisco. Lived in Boston, Atlanta, and London."

"I'm a Burlingame girl, myself. Although Mother always tried to pass it off as the City. And we live in Denver. Nicky, Michael, and I. When we're home, I mean."

"You told me last night."

"Sorry." Claire cringed and quickened her pace.

"Do you miss it?"

"My life is there." She looked out at the pool, with its ribbons of orange.

"Even if it doesn't include your husband?"

Claire halted mid-stride, gravel lodging in her sandals. "Jesus. Did I say that, too?"

"No, but given what you did tell me, it seems not unlikely."

"Everything doesn't always have to be so black and white." Her voice hardened. "Things shift."

"I'm sorry. I was just restating the facts, ma'am."

"Well, don't be so quick to write the obituary on my marriage. In fact, just forget what I said last night. Apparently I already have." They began walking again, silently, through a cactus garden, stopping for pretzels at a refreshment cart. For a second

Claire imagined Michael plastered up against the prickly pins of a saguaro, like Wile E. Coyote, realizing his colossal misjudgment and giving her a second chance at making things right.

"I just don't want to find you face-first in another martini glass, Smitty."

"That's really not my style. I was kind of an accidental drunk last night."

He smiled softly, his eyes crinkling at the corners. "So, when do you go home?"

"It looks like they'll be discharging Nicky next week. He'll move back into the house and do outpatient at Craig."

"And you?"

"It seems I'll be getting an apartment." She turned to him and looked squarely into his face. "Michael's not mistaken about inflicting our difficulties and stress on Nicholas twenty-four seven. I'll make it work somehow, and then . . . well, we'll see," this last declaration as much a balm on her wavering conviction as it was a promise to herself.

He smiled a sort of placating half smile. "Shall we go see some irises?"

"Yes. And I could use about a gallon of water."

For two hours Claire was just another tourist in a museum, appreciating the brilliant rendering of flowers and light, the charged glances between two subjects on canvas, and the power and nobility of painting. And for those two sweet hours, the reassuring permanence of art displaced the not-so-beautiful chaos of her world.

"It was spectacular," Claire said as they approached the nurses' station on Nicholas's floor. "Thank you for such a perfect day. And I'm remarkably hangover-free now." They lingered for a moment at the sitting area, Claire placing her sunglasses in their case as Richard held her bag from the gift shop.

"Transformative, wasn't it?"

"Didn't I tell you it would be?" she said, winking. "You look forty-six, by the way."

Richard handed back her bag. "See you in the cafeteria,

Smitty. I still owe you a dinner." He turned and walked to the elevator.

A framed print of a sunlit wheat field caught her attention, and she took note of her complete lack of stress.

"Claire, where on earth have you been?"

Startled, Claire spun around to see a green pantsuited woman behind her at the nurses' station. "Good lord, Mother, where did you come from?"

"Why, the City, of course. And who on earth is Smitty?"

In an instant, the heartening powers of an art-filled morning were neutralized. "Why didn't you tell me you were coming?"

"Because I knew how busy you've been. So I made my own arrangements to see my grandson."

"How long have you been here?" Claire noticed a wrist brace on Cora's right hand, similar to the one Nicky wore.

"An hour or so. And I can only stay until tomorrow. I'm meeting Carol Morgenstern in Del Mar. But I've already had a lovely visit with Nicholas. He tells me he's going home soon." She looked over her shoulder and gave a broad smile to the nurses behind the desk. "And Nicky said Michael was already here?"

Claire felt her stomach pitch. "Have you hurt your wrist, Mother?"

"My bag was quite heavy, and all the carrying seemed to inflame it. I asked one of the girls"—again she smiled over toward the nurses' station—"if she could find some solution for me." Cora held out her hand, admiring her latest accessory, as Claire tried not to think about what that scene must have entailed. "Just remind me to return it before I leave." Cora shifted her gaze back to Claire. "Who was that man you were with, Claire? And why did he call you Smitty?"

"His sister's a patient here."

"And?"

"And what? We took a little break from the hospital this morning."

Cora eyed Claire's museum gift bag. "Now, I understand how difficult this is, dear, and how you might need a break. But you can't just go off with some man to a museum. Really, Claire, under the circumstances I would think that would be obvious to you."

"Mother, Richard is a friend. You don't need to complicate things. Our paths just happened to have crossed."

"Crossed paths or not, Claire, your only focus right now should be on Nicholas, and trying to repair your marriage. What would Michael think of you spending your morning with this Richard person, after everything that's happened?"

What would Michael think? "Mother, have you ever felt like you've been bitten by a vampire and are walking among the living dead?"

"Of course not, Claire. What a ghastly thought." Cora's lips drew tightly downward.

"Then I'm not going to have this conversation with you right now. But rest assured that I know exactly what my focus is." She spaced her words out deliberately.

Cora stepped forward and wrapped Claire in a hug. "I'm sorry, I know you do, sweetheart. I know you're doing all the right things to put your life back in order. And I'm so happy to be here." As they disengaged, Cora eyed Claire's hair, then reached both hands to Claire's head and fluffed it and tucked it behind her ears. "Really, dear, if you're going out . . ."

Claire flicked Cora's hands away from her face. "Hear this, Mother: I don't give a shit about my hair. No one in this place does. My hair is irrelevant."

"Well, at least you might put on some lipstick, dear. You are hardly irrelevant."

"Why don't we go see Nicholas? I was just on my way to his room, and I'd like to show him the posters I got for him."

Claire could hear Cora mumbling *irrelevant* and *Smitty* as they walked down the corridor. And she wondered how she was going to muster twenty-four hours' worth of patience.

"When will you and Michael be taking Nicholas home?" Cora asked as they watched Nick in his afternoon session with the gait specialist.

"About that." Claire rose from her folding chair and paced the length of the glass partition separating the observation area from the gym, wondering if she was destined to have only unpleasant conversations in this space. "Things didn't exactly go well with Michael while he was here."

"What do you mean, *not exactly well*?"

"He's flying Nicky home next week."

"That's wonderful. And?"

"And Nicky will be doing outpatient therapy at Craig Hospital."

"Claire, I'm not following—"

"And the living arrangements don't *exactly* include me at the moment," she snapped with the filter-free annoyance of a non-divorceable daughter. "He wants me to get an apartment."

"What? How on earth does Michael expect to—"

"Just hold off on the tirade. Please." Claire sank into the chair farthest away from Cora, imagining how gratifying it would be to show her that all of her advice about marital repair had been complete crap. But she knew there would be no victory in that kind of *I told you so.* Because a small part of her still wanted to believe. And what do you do when you want to hold on to crap, when the crap is your last handful of hope? She stared up at the ceiling trying to stem the tide of her tears. "Here's the deal, Mother. Michael said that too much damage has been done, that he can't face that, or me, night after night. And that it would be damaging to Nicky, too." As she spoke, all of the emotions she'd shoved behind the *Irises* and Rembrandts found their way out—slowly at first, and then emphatically like an angry case of food poisoning.

Cora scooted next to Claire and hooked an arm around her.

"I thought we'd have a chance at starting over when Nicky went home," Claire sobbed into her Mother's restrained bosom. Cora held Claire in her arms and listened quietly as she unleashed months of grief in between scraps of Michael's hot dog stand salvo and her disbelief that she would soon be *visiting* her child at her own house. "I never thought it would come down to this. Even with . . . what I did." Curling up on Cora's lap and the two adjacent chairs like a small girl, she fought the image of Andrew's face. "But the sad truth is that the tension between us really wouldn't be good for Nicky, and I guess I just need to remove it—remove myself—until I can make some sense of what I've done. And until Michael calms down. I don't want to risk pushing him away any farther."

"You know, dear," Cora weighed in after a contemplative pause, her voice soft but deliberate, "if that's how he needs things to be right now, a temporary separation really might not be the worst thing. Timing is everything, dear, and it would appear that your husband needs some time. I can understand that." She handed Claire a handkerchief from the sleeve of her pantsuit and propped her back up to sitting. "Time has a way of diminishing pain and anger. And then you'll be able to work on reuniting your family after Michael has had a chance to"—she paused again—"maybe recover a little of his pride? He's wounded and afraid. And putting everything with Nicky aside, I'm sure his self-respect has taken a beating too. This separation may be the only way that he can see coming through this with you. A public penance, as it were." She raised her eyebrows into a perfectly arched schoolteacher's directive. "You'll both get there, honey. The interim may just look a little different than you imagined."

Claire blew her nose, still terrified about the whole scenario, but willing herself toward cautious agreement with her mother. "Yes, but I'm worried about how Nicky will take this. If I'm in the house, it will be awful, and if I'm not, it could be just as bad for him." She watched Cora shift into strategy mode, index and middle fingers tapping her lips, her eyes focused on the future.

"You'll be taking Nicky to his outpatient classes and appointments—it's not as if you won't be there with him all the time. Breakfasts, activities, dinners. He'll hardly have a chance to notice your absence. And as for your husband, a man can't easily walk away from the comfort and habits of eighteen years, dear. This is only a temporary move. I give it a month at the outside. You'll see. You just need patience and perseverance." Cora was smiling now, clearly pleased with her strategy. "I'll speak to Jackie and ask her to find something for you near the house. There's that lovely building by the country club. We don't need Michael's assistance for that."

"BUT THE MAN CAN BARELY FUCKING LOOK AT ME."

Cora sucked in a wide mouthful of air. "Language, dear."

"The only language I'm interested in now is how to make this manageable for Nicky."

CHAPTER 22

As the preparations for Nicholas's departure were winding down, Claire found herself increasingly wound up. The prospect of explaining the new living arrangements to him had filled her with a creeping sense of dread. And while the staff psychologist reassured her that the nuances of the circumstances were less important than preparing him with the general facts, she found it difficult to rally the courage and the explanation.

But amid her apprehension and the chaos of getting Nicholas ready for the transition, there was one bright light: the party. The day arrived with a flourish of window-framed sunshine and a small mountain of parting gifts. Nick had grinned for the entire hour of his cake and high five–filled farewell with his favorite staff members. "I can totally . . . handle this," he kept telling each of them. "I'll handle it by . . . myself now," he'd said, hugging them all tightly, both grateful for and tired of the numerous hands invading his life. There would be more hands at home, more strange adjustments, but for that happy hour at least, there was no need to talk about it. And so Claire celebrated the moment, too, putting off for another day the conversation she dreaded.

Until time caught up with them, and she could no longer wait.

"Nicky, your father and I both love you very much," Claire began over lunch in his room two days before she was to leave for Denver.

Nicholas raised his sandwich from the plate, ready to take a bite. "I just want to get out here—get out of here," he said, shoving the sandwich into the corner of his mouth. "I'm over this."

"I know, honey. And we're so excited you're coming home. But I need to talk to you about how things are going to be back in Denver."

"Amy said I'll do some outpatient classes at a . . . place near the house. Craig."

"That's right. Sometimes I'll take you there, and some therapists will come to the house too." She took inventory of the surroundings that had once seemed so frightening and impersonal, and the thought of adjusting to a new equilibrium accelerated her anxiety. "You'll be back in your old room at home, but"—she wiped the jelly from his chin with a napkin—"but I'm not going to be staying at the house. I'll be visiting you every day, like I do here."

"What?" Dark circles underlined the one weepy and one dry eye staring up at her.

"I'll be very close by."

"Why?"

Why. "Well, your dad, um . . . your dad and I think this is best for now. It's just something we need to work out for a little bit," she said robotically.

He nodded, to Claire's surprise, almost as if he had been expecting this announcement. "Because of what . . . happened to me?"

"No, Nicky, no. This has nothing to do with you, honey. We just need some time to, uh, settle some things, and then we'll—"

"Because of something that . . . that happened before?" His eyes started blinking rapidly, his facial muscles tensed, the shift in his demeanor like quicksilver. "What did you do?" he suddenly shouted, mashing his sandwich into his tray. "What did *Dad* do?" Nicholas grabbed the tray and flung it like a Frisbee. "What . . . *did . . . HE . . . do?*"

Claire dodged the tray, but tripped over her chair and cut her leg. As the nurse rushed in, Claire pushed down on the bleeding flap of skin at her ankle until the gash merely stung. One hour later, after a trip to the art studio with Amy, Nicholas seemed to have no recollection of his outburst.

"Richard, I can't leave him like this," Claire said as she crumbled crackers into the bowl of soup she had no intention of eating. The cafeteria had emptied out over the course of the hour they'd been sitting together.

"Shouldn't you be home finishing that packing you've been complaining about? You're getting the hell out of this joint. This is good news."

"I'm afraid Nick might think I'm abandoning him instead of just flying out early. The short-term stuff doesn't seem to stick, but I think he's starting to remember things from . . . before." She couldn't stop replaying the questions he'd bellowed at her—so similar in their confused, beseeching quality to his questions about Taylor—and yet so much more fraught and unnerving.

"Look, yesterday was one blowup, Claire. But you just had a productive session with his social worker, and he seems much better with everything, right?"

"I suppose."

"He knows you would never abandon him. You should be used to all the unpredictability by now." Richard took her wrist. "The anger evaporates just as quickly as it rears up. Nicholas will adjust, and then there will be questions and confusion and all manner of volatility and things that don't make any sense. That's the only thing we can count on in TBI world. But we all have to adjust in life, don't we? Take things day by day."

Claire set down her spoon but let her hand remain in Richard's grip. Her thoughts flashed to Nicholas that night in the library assaying the scene with Andrew, his discomfort apparent but controlled. And she began to well up, feeling the nauseating certainty that there might never be enough flying trays or effective therapy sessions to make all these new adjustments manageable for him. "How do you deal with the guilt?" she asked in a flimsy voice. "How do you talk to Sandy about what happened?"

"Ah. That." Richard paused for a moment, looking out the window. "Maybe if I'd stopped sooner, that car would have missed Sandy and me. And maybe not. The point is, Claire, accidents happen in life. You made choices, and Nicholas made choices." Richard pulled his chair around to face her. "Believe me, I know what you're feeling. But the sooner you get past your guilt, the easier it'll be for you to deal with the situation if Nick really does start to remember details of that night. But, like they always tell us, he may not."

"And that terrifies me, too. I struggle with what's best for him to know." Claire wished the *getting past* part were as easy for all of them as Richard made it seem. She crinkled the plastic cracker wrapper in her palm. "Then there's Michael. He just can't seem to get past *his* anger and move forward. I'm hoping that with some more time he will, but . . ." Her voice trailed off.

"Well," he paused, pondering Claire, "life does march on. Even if it's not according to plan."

"You don't wrestle with your ghosts?"

Richard tilted his chair back onto two legs. "You've been married eighteen years?"

"Why are you changing the subject?"

"Tell me about the happiest time in your marriage."

"What?"

"Just humor me."

"Why?"

"Curious minds want to know."

Claire tried to pull up memories, but everything seemed slightly out of focus and distorted, like the pressed-flower center of a glycerin soap bar. She mentally scrolled backward, until gradually some images grew sharper. There was the King Cole room at the St. Regis in New York, and the afternoon she and Michael had gone for Bloody Marys, and left at midnight with a pair of art deco–style table lamps under their coats—a wink and a nod gift from the waiter they'd befriended. They'd been dating for three months, Michael flying in on business from the Bay Area every other week or so. Life was beautiful then; both of their careers were on the upswing, their love was blossoming. Each date, she recounted, was a three-day affair of important cocktail parties, runs in the park, romantic dinners, closing the Rainbow Room after a night of dancing. On that particular day Claire had taken Michael to the MoMA for an Andy Warhol retrospective. And then on to the St. Regis, where they'd sat in the banquette under the Maxfield Parrish mural of Old King Cole and drank and conspired for seven hours, giddily mapping out their future together. They barely made it to her apartment with their clothes intact, stopping under streetlights to kiss, and groping in shadowed corners. Claire got pregnant that night, she explained, and miscarried two months later just after Michael had proposed. But still, it was a magical time. She told Richard about extraordinary trips they had taken, about the beautiful home and family they had created.

"You know, Smitty, we guys are simple creatures—far less complicated than you of the fairer sex. We get clubbed over the head, we get pissed, we stew for a while. And then sometimes we go have a beer at the game with our clubber and talk about fastballs again."

She smiled a little. "I don't know. Those memories seem like a hundred years ago now. I hadn't realized how much we drifted apart until I—" She looked away. "What if I can't make him see the value of . . . going back to the game with me? He's different somehow. Darker. I just can't figure out what's going on inside his head."

"What about marriage counseling?"

"He has an issue with shrinks. It's *not* how his family operates, letting outsiders into private matters. Besides, all of his decisions are like business decisions, and why would some interloper know better about his marriage than he would?" Claire recited Michael's words with weary resignation.

"That's not a totally unusual male perspective, Smitty. But look, I made some bad choices in my marriage, too. And I had to deal with the fallout—"

"I'll do whatever it takes," Claire said. "I have to."

"What I'm trying to say is that I wasn't prepared to be punished forever. Would you want to stay with someone who can't forgive you?"

"I don't know how *not* to stay with him. We've been together practically my whole adult life."

Richard reached out for both of her hands this time, and held them firmly like a parent explaining the importance of looking both ways to a young child. "Is that guilt and habit talking, or love?"

"We made a commitment to each other, in spite of my lapse of reason. And I need to make this right."

"Sometimes, Claire, there are truths we try hard not to see."

She grimaced, recalling her sister's analogous observation.

"Just some food for thought, Smitty," he said, shrugging his shoulders. "And I'm sorry if I'm overstepping here. It's a tough thing, this separating business. But sometimes good can come of it. Happiness even."

They sky was darkening to a grapey twilight outside the window, and the garden below had emptied of its last visitors. They pushed their chairs back into place under the table that had, over the week, become their usual spot, and headed toward the cafeteria exit.

"Wait," Richard said, making a sudden detour to the cash register. A moment later he returned with a large cellophane-wrapped cookie.

"Peanut butter?" Claire asked.

"Specialty of the house."

Inside the parking garage Richard handed her his business card. "It's got my cell and e-mail on it. I want updates on Nicky's progress."

"Thank you." She gave him hers, sincerely hoping their paths would cross again. "For everything."

"I want updates on you, too, Smitty. And I'm great with all crises of the newly separated. Home Depot trips, insomnia, cable issues—although I'm a bit weak in the cuisine for one department, and generally defer to the deli Gods. But I *am* a good listener."

"Yes, Mr. Elliot, you are."

"Occasionally I even give decent advice." They hugged each other like college pals on graduation day, warmly and poignantly, sharers of a unique history. "You're going to be okay."

PART THREE

CHAPTER 23

Claire sidled into her cramped window seat and took a parting glance at exile city. Smog hung low on the runway. The hint of a golden red ball hovered to the west, and beyond the wingtip stood the restaurant tower, a groovy homage to the Space Age where tourists sipped their Electric Barbarellas and watched 747s disappear into the LA smog.

She remembered visiting the restaurant as a child with her parents and Jackie, on one of her first visits to Los Angeles. A "cultural foray," Mother had called the trip. Cora had laid out their traveling ensembles the night before in preparation for the trip: their best dresses, matching pea coats, and patent leather Mary Janes. She remembered Shirley Temples at the restaurant bar as the platform on which they sat rotated slowly around, and the thrill of the grand panorama beyond the windows. Although other details had faded with time, she did recall being happy then, a happy, wide-eyed girl poised on the edge of promise.

Across the aisle Claire heard a mother arguing with her teenage son in shrill whispers, but couldn't bring herself to look at the boy's face. Instead she thumbed through the latest *Vanity Fair*, trying to ignore the boarding chaos around her. As the engines screamed shrill during takeoff, she grasped the armrests at her sides and clicked her heels together. She propped her head against the window with a pillow, and wondered what it would be like for Nicholas boarding the plane with Michael for home.

As they reached cruising altitude, Claire closed her eyes and thought of grandparents' weekend at Andover the previous year. Nick emerging from the hooting, stick-waving throng on the lacrosse field, his jersey grass stained and dotted with sweat. She, watching from the bleachers with Cora amid a sea of blue-sweatered spectators, her voice hoarse from cheering, and the smell of popcorn and freshly cut grass filling the spring air along with the electric rush of victory. The players pulling off their helmets and saluting grandparents, parents, and alumni; and there against the waning afternoon sun, her father's lazy grin and Michael's patrician nose in beautiful concert on her son's face. Nicholas waves her down to the field. He has filled out since the start of the term and stands nearly a head taller than her. She wraps her arm around his waist and kisses his cheek. They high-five and whoop. She has never seen his eyes brighter or more fully alive, and her body warms with a sense of peace and gratitude.

Claire retrieved her baggage and drove into town in a rented Hertz Jeep. The lease on the Mercedes had expired while she'd been gone, and replacing it had clearly not been high on Michael's to-do list. A few lenticular clouds punctuated the crisp sky as she headed west toward the downtown skyline, the brown landscape along I-70 sparkling with ice, and the expansive plains rolling into the distance. As she exited the freeway, a school bus pulled into the lane beside her. The children waved and pressed their noses into the windows, fogging the glass as they made faces at Claire. She smiled and waved back. At the first traffic light she checked her cell phone for missed calls, but there were none. She imagined calling Michael at work. *I'm in, the flight was fine. How about a leg of lamb tonight? I'll roast a leg of lamb and we'll celebrate.*

Weaving from boulevard to parkway to side streets, Claire took a circuitous route to the apartment Jackie had arranged. In her long absence she had missed autumn, and the holidays, too, in their red and gold flourishes, and she focused on the canvas in front of her—bare tree branches, the breath of joggers floating white in the air. She opened the window and let the wind blow cold onto her cheeks.

As she made her way through the old-guard enclave of the Country Club neighborhood, the homes grew in size and luster. She surveyed the colorful mosaic of architectural styles from an outsider's perspective, as if recounting the neighborhood of her past to the specter of her future. Stuccoed Spanish Colonials with wrought iron balconettes rubbed hedgerows with gable-roofed Tudors and red brick Georgians. She missed the charm of this little world where the neighborhood children decorated bicycles and wagons with pinwheels each Fourth of July and paraded through the streets behind an antique fire truck; where block parties and Halloween haunted mansions were still traditions.

She rolled on, approaching a gated drive guarded by two enormous reclining lion statues with security cameras perched behind their haunches. Slowing the Jeep again, she gazed through the vine-covered gates, unable to avoid looking. Her smile collapsed. Only two summers before, the Wrightsmans had set tongues abuzz like swarming hornets. When everyone thought Nicola Wrightsman would retreat in humiliation over catching her husband and her sister screwing in the bathroom at Campo de' Fiori in Aspen, Nicola appeared the next day at the club in a thong bikini and ordered a bottle of Cristal. Cell phones burned and men left the driving range for a quick drink by the pool to glimpse her unblushing fuck-you to Roger Wrightsman and the joyful gossipers. Claire and Michael had been there together, watching the spectacle.

She maneuvered past Lionsgate and thought surely *Le Scandal Wrightsman's* expiration date had passed. Good news for Roger. But had theirs become the story that eclipsed it, she wondered? It was hard to know what people might be saying now, hard to know what Michael wouldn't discuss. Claire readjusted her posture and placed both hands on the steering wheel, hating the idea of people talking about her family when they drove by their home. She didn't wish ill upon anyone else, but still, a little something to focus the spotlight elsewhere wouldn't be so horrible either. A renovation disaster in the neighborhood, or maybe a minor "nannygate" of some sort. For a moment she wondered if it would be easier for Michael—the whole getting-over-the-past part—if they'd still been in New York, where yesterday's humiliations tended to go on to ballsy, even happy second acts.

Claire rounded the corner onto her block and pulled just past their house. She sat for a moment, then twisted around in the seat to see her gate, made a U-turn, and drove into the driveway. She watched the property unfold, chimneys and tiled roof first, her anxiety thinning as the rest of the Spanish-Mediterranean came into sight. Automatically she reached her hand up to the visor for the garage door opener, rubbing the barren fabric there.

She turned off the engine and stepped out. There was no wind, but still Claire felt a smarting in her lungs. She crossed her arms against the chill and walked across the gravel to the lawn, carrying all the weight of the past months with her.

When she reached the grass, her feet sank softly into the mud beneath, and she looked up at her home. The large Palladian windows seemed to gape at her, and in the reflection of the glass she imagined the sheen of tears. She approached one of the Italian stone planters and plucked a frozen pansy from the border, squishing the faded bloom between her fingers and glancing toward the side of the house. Brown vines hung from the pergola, dripping droplets onto the patio below. She squinted and stepped back, remembering the thirtieth birthday celebration Michael had thrown for her, and the long kisses they had stolen under the pergola that night. Why hadn't she come up with that story for Richard? she wondered. Stage fright, probably.

It had been a "Farewell to the Twenties" theme, with guests attired in Gatsby-esque finery. From the tented buffets and badminton court, to the orchestra surrounded by claw-footed bathtubs of gin and champagne, Michael had given her the most sparkling birthday party she'd ever had. "To my ever-beautiful bride," he had whispered into her ear as they glided across the dance floor to "Yes! We Have No Bananas," "you still drive me wild." The stars were lavish, like everything that night, and seemed to bathe them in an ethereal glow. She had been crazy about him, and her cheeks ached from smiling, her feet from dancing. And in the midst of one particularly passionate kiss, she had overheard a woman comment that Claire and Michael looked so beautiful together, just like Jay Gatsby and Daisy Buchanan.

Claire hadn't thought about that comment since the party, but as she blinked away tears, she wondered now at the sad irony of the reference. Somewhere along the way, had she and Michael also gotten caught up in the vitality of the illusion like the doomed characters? She backed away toward the Jeep, seeing no beauty in the beautiful house, no warmth in the warm colors. She checked her watch. She needed to retrieve some things from inside, but she just didn't have the stomach for it. Not right then. And she didn't want to risk being there when Michael returned from work. No, she thought, feeling the sting of their last encounter, if she was going to adjust to this crazy new chapter, it would be far easier to keep a forward momentum. At least for the time being. She got into the car and drove away, speeding past the country club, and south to her apartment building. She hoped Jackie had picked out something a little better than the LA apartment. Amid the haze and confusion of that first week in Los Angeles, surroundings hadn't seemed all that important. But now they were a bit more so.

When she pulled up to the handsome brick building, she was greeted by a row of sculpted junipers that stood at attention like soldiers. They were the same style she had once considered for her own garden. Claire killed the motor, took the key from the envelope in her purse, and glanced up to the building's roof garden some twenty floors up.

Unlocking the door to her furnished rental number 611, she dropped her bags in the center of the spacious living-dining-kitchen area, thinking it wasn't bad. She had almost grown used to living in other people's spaces. The off-white walls, the beige pile carpeting, the tan plastic blinds. They were all alike in their lack of charm and distinction, these mini-dwellings of the itinerant. Bland palettes where one could create a home if one so desired.

"Hey, Jax, I'm back," Claire said, sitting down on the queen bed's peach floral spread.

"What?"

"In Denver. I'm at the apartment. You did great, sis." She scanned the walls, which sported several hotel-quality landscapes, and the ceiling, which reminded her of large curds of cottage cheese. "It's nice. Thanks."

"You're not supposed to be here until Saturday. I would have met you at the airport." Claire could hear the concern in her sister's voice.

"I know. It was a last-minute thing. Michael will be leaving for LA to get ready to bring Nicky back. And Nick's therapist thought it would be better if we didn't overlap. He needs a little time to regroup before the changing of the guard, and blah blah blah. So, here I am."

"Why are you letting him do this to you?"

She stood and began pacing at the foot of the bed. "No one's doing anything *to* me, Jackie. It's just . . . the best solution at the moment.

"You're sure about this?"

"I'm not sure about anything, other than that it'll be good for Michael to spend some alone time with Nicholas at the hospital before he brings him home." Claire said this as convincingly as she could, stopping in front of the closet and pulling open the bi-fold doors. "And it'll give me some time to get things together on this end."

"You're being awfully brave about such a sucky situation."

"Look, I know you don't approve. I don't approve. But given everything, my options were limited. So just keep your fingers crossed that I won't be here for too long."

"I could come down and help if Steve can get home in time to give the girls dinner."

"I'd rather take it easy tonight and just get used to the place."

"It's okay, isn't it? The apartment, I mean. I liked the building, but my taste is a little more Asti than Dom."

She pictured Jackie's crinkled nose on the other end of the line. "The apartment's great, Jax. Really. Thank you." She unzipped her garment bag with one hand, fished out a kimono-print robe, and set it on the bedspread in a screaming pattern clash.

"Are you still planning on dinner with us Saturday? It's lasagna."

"I'll be there around five." She hung up, smelling the faint remnants of someone else's life all around her.

It had already grown dark, and though still on LA time, Claire felt the heaviness of the day closing in on her. She drew the blinds against the twinkle of the downtown lights, and dragged her garment bag and suitcase over to the tiny closet. One bulb hung naked from the ceiling, and she wiped down the shelves and bowed hanging rods as four empty wire hangers clanged together.

Sleep came fast that night, with dreams of Nicholas as a playful eight-year-old tickling her on a beach blanket on Martha's Vineyard, his hair smelling of watermelon shampoo.

Although she promised herself she'd give him his space, Claire called Nick the next morning, hoping he'd be the happy Nicholas who'd kissed her good-bye with a smile, and not the angry, tray-hurling Nicholas.

"Hey, honey, how are you?"

"Okay, I guess. Where are you?"

"I'm back in Denver, remember? And I can't wait for you to be here."

"I'm sick of this place. It sucks." His voice sounded tired and stressed. "The OT classes suck."

"I know, babe. But just hang in there. It won't be much longer."

"They're making me . . . do all these extra . . . classes and interviews. I supposedly had . . . a drug overdose? And that's why I'm here?"

Same shirt, different day. She could hear the sound of plastic pounding on a hard surface—Nicky's hand, she knew, gripped tightly around his cup and smacking his tray table. And she wondered if Michael's presence, the shift in the routine, had put him on edge.

Patience and perseverance, dear. "Yes, Nicky, that's right. But you're going to be home soon," she said, keeping her tone upbeat. "And Aunt Jackie and Uncle Steve and the girls are really excited to see you." She didn't mention his friends, whom he alternately missed and dismissed out of apprehension and embarrassment. She would let him dictate the terms of inviting his old life back in when he was ready. That part, she completely related to. They didn't discuss her new apartment or his outpatient therapy.

"Dad says he's bringing the plane. So that's . . . cool. I guess."

Claire thought of Michael's obsession with details, his thrill and expertise at closing a deal. And she hoped that he would keep things together just as perfectly when he walked their son out of those hospital doors forever. "I love you, Nicky."

Chapter 24

As she counted down the days to Nick's return, Claire devoted her time to meeting with the doctors and therapists at Craig and getting all the paperwork handled. She discussed with the new social worker her concern about the times when she would not be at the house with Nick to monitor all the issues that had been handled while he was at Rancho, and got a referral for a retired behavioral therapist who might help them out. He could augment the work they'd do at Craig, while keeping a trained eye on Nick at the house. It was overkill, and Claire knew Nick wouldn't be thrilled, but until she was confident that he was comfortably readjusted to living at home again, she was more than prepared to risk overkill. On this topic, Michael concurred. By text.

She filled her remaining hours setting up the apartment and making it feel homey enough. Not wishing to get distracted (depressed, deflated) by all that her real home represented, she hadn't returned. Removing anything from there and bringing it back with her would only make the temporary seem more permanent, she rationalized. She also didn't trust her ability to be dispassionate enough to walk into her closet for some extra shoes and not stay. So she pledged to keep her needs basic—which wasn't so hard. The requisite lightening of her load over the past months had actually felt liberating. And until she was certain how the situation with Michael would eventually play out, she wanted to be careful to maintain her checking account balance at a comfortable level. While she was grateful for the lump sum that continued to arrive there each month from Michael—they'd never shared a joint account, a Montgomery family tradition dating back to the Pilgrims, she was certain—said lump didn't quite compare to its pre-Andrew heft. But considering everything, she was hardly ready to discuss money with a husband who might, as Cora suggested, really miss her full presence at the house when Nicky got home, and might actually grow to miss *her*. The idea of contacting a lawyer had crossed her mind, but she worried more about what kind of message that would send if he were to find out. Besides, there would be plenty of time for lawyers later, if the *merde* really hit.

After a long morning of errands as Claire headed back toward the apartment, an unexpected splash of red caught her eye on Sixth Avenue. She slowed to take in the bright new awnings and window bays that had popped up at Lillian's shop. The consignment business, she noted, must be doing well. Given the state of the economy, it ought to have been. And Claire thought of the countless times she'd been in the little boutique over the years. Lillian's was an elegant and discreet business. Her old friend took only the finest designer clothing on consignment and paid her clients fifteen percent of the original purchase price on their previous season's Chanels, Armanis, and the like. Claire had been making quarterly trips there since Nick was born, providing a healthy pipeline of luncheon suits and evening couture as she thinned her closets for newer purchases. She and her friends never bought there, but they quietly reaped the fifteen percent reward for their fine taste.

Tired of the silence that seemed to have shrouded her world, Claire was tempted to stop in to say hello. Like a trusted hairstylist, Lillian knew all the little dramas of her clients—the vacation sagas, the romantic highs and woes, the divorces. But unlike some of the stylists Claire had dealt with, Lillian always put a positive spin on things, always had a kind word. It might be a good place, she thought, to stick her toes back in the water of her old life and test the temperature.

"Dah-rrling, is that you?" Lillian purred in her Hungarian accent, rushing over to Claire from behind a rack of evening gowns. "How wonderful to see you. When did you come?" As always she concealed her large frame in a simple black suit, and her eyeglasses dangled from the gold-and-pearl chain around her neck. She spoke with the measured dignity of one trying to conceal the remoteness of her origins.

"Just this week. You hadn't heard I've moved back?" Claire asked casually.

"No, no." Claire watched as Lillian looked her over for signs of something. Wear, perhaps. "Everyone was in with their collections at the beginning of the month, but it's been quiet now."

"I just thought I'd drop in to say hello."

"I'm glad you did. It's been too long." She wrapped her arm around Claire's shoulder and led her to the sofa where they used to share tea after their business was done. "And your Nicholas, how is he doing?"

Although she expected the question, facing her old friend under the shadow of tragedy was harder than she'd expected. She sank back and willed her eyes to stay dry. When they didn't cooperate, Claire dabbed at them with her knuckle and looked sheepishly through the hair that had fallen over her face. "I'm sorry. We're all doing much better. And Nicholas will be home soon."

"Oh, my dear." Lillian pulled a linen handkerchief from her pocket and placed it in Claire's lap. "You take this and I'll get us some tea." She let her hand linger gently on Claire's leg as she stared into her face with her dark, sympathetic eyes. Then she stood and walked to the back room of the shop, the swish of her slip and hose beneath her skirt the only sound Claire could hear. Moments later she returned with two porcelain cups, steaming and frothy with milk. They sipped in silence.

"Ah," Lillian said, suddenly placing her cup on the table, then clapping her hands, "I have something you will adore." She gave Claire a sidelong smile. From one of the small racks by the mirror, she removed a suit and held it out for inspection. "Yes," she said to the hanger.

Claire looked at it with curiosity. It was a lightweight cobalt blue wool Chanel with the signature double-C buttons and a satin camellia brooch.

"Come." Lillian motioned for Claire.

"It's exquisite," Claire said as she approached the mirror, still uncertain what Lillian wanted from her.

"This came in while I was on vacation. I just noticed it this morning." She held it up in front of Claire. "The color brings out the green in your eyes."

"But Lillian, I don't—"

"Shh. Try it. I want to see it on someone, and it's your size." She slipped the jacket off the hanger and guided Claire into the dressing room, handing her the garments. "I'm waiting outside," she said as she closed the slatted door behind Claire.

Claire looked around, bemused and equally embarrassed at the thought of trying on someone else's clothing. She pushed open the door and stepped back out, voicing her apologies, but Lillian would have none of her noncompliance.

"Just for fun, my dear. No one's here."

So Claire did the only polite thing she could and a moment later walked out, zipping the skirt and feeling as if she'd been thrust lampless into an unexpected fog.

"What did I tell you, my dear? It's divine, no?"

She fussed with the jacket hem and tugged at the waist of the skirt in front of the three-way mirror, despite the flawless fit. It was lovely, she had to admit. But maybe it just seemed so lovely in contrast to her functionally drab uniform since the accident, or because it accentuated the slim sway of her hips and rounded her out, instead of hanging lifelessly on her as most of her clothes now did. She'd given so little thought to clothing and appearance since the accident, and the shock of *seeing* herself again filled her with an odd wistfulness.

She removed the flower brooch from the lapel and placed it on a pocket, then arched her shoulders back and stood high on her stockinged toes, unsure what else to do. "Well, that was fun," she said, flat-footed again, "but I really need to be going, Lillian." Claire laughed awkwardly and started for the fitting room, but Lillian handed her a pair of high satin heels.

"Now try."

Claire glanced around the empty store, only to be met with Lillian's persistent eyebrows. She stepped into the shoes, and when she looked in the mirror she was surprised to see not exactly her old self, but a refreshed version of her new self. The lifelessness had gone from her demeanor. She felt almost . . . good.

"My dear, sometimes it just takes the most surprising little something." Lillian beamed behind her.

"Oh, Lillian. I'm not shopping. I just came to say hello." She hurried back into the dressing room and as she started to unbutton the jacket, Claire caught her reflection again and hesitated. She fluffed her hair, checking herself from the side. When she took the jacket off, the price tag dangled in front of her, revealing the amazing discount of "gently worn."

"It will be good for you," came the husky voice from behind the door. "A little pick-me-up, my dear. Trust me."

Claire pulled on her sweater thinking that Lillian, in all her good grace and tact, could sell a ball gown to a plumber. She carried the suit to the front of the store and draped it on the counter. She ran her fingers over the fabric, shaking her head, still feeling the awkwardness of the whole situation. "It was lovely to see you, Lillian," she said as she pulled her car keys from her purse. "Thank you for the little diversion."

Lillian snatched up the suit, placed it in a hanging bag and put the bag in Claire's free hand as she was walking out the door. "You can pay later, after you get settled."

Pulling into the driveway with her recycled couture and a hatchback full of household supplies and groceries, Claire ran through a list of other tasks for the week: the "I'm back" phone calls Lillian had encouraged her to make, an appointment with her own doctors, a haircut and color. And only when she reached for the phantom garage door opener again did she realize her navigational blunder. She stared out at the impenetrable garage doors and dark windows of her house, and put the car in park. The goddamned route was imprinted. She hit the steering wheel with both hands. The horn blared and the reality of her refugee status hit with blunt force. She rested her forehead on the wheel and tried to remind herself that home was where she made it.

After a few deep breaths, she glanced back up at the house and thought she saw movement in one of the upstairs windows. She stepped out of the car and watched the draperies being drawn shut. Maria had Thursdays off, Michael had gone to LA, and someone was in the house. Watching her. Claire turned off the ignition and walked to the front door. She rang the doorbell and waited, not having the faintest idea what she planned to do if someone answered. But no one came. She rang again and knocked loudly, growing uneasy with the whole situation. She peered through the foyer window and pounded on the glass, questioning whether she had just imagined the motion. Then she remembered her house keys in her purse.

Claire went back to the car and fished them from the zippered pocket they'd lived in since she'd been gone, and returned to the front door. She inserted the key into the lock. One way or another she would get an answer. The lock didn't move, wouldn't turn left or right. She tried another key while holding down the doorbell. Still the lock refused. She banged on the door with the heels of her palms. Finally, the door opened. A sturdy woman in a gray maid's uniform stood on the other side of the threshold.

"Who are you?" Claire demanded, stunned at the sight of this stranger in her house.

"Mrs. Montgomery?"

"Yes, I'm Mrs. Montgomery. But who are you, and where is Maria?"

"I am Mr. Montgomery's housekeeper."

Mr. Montgomery's housekeeper? "I'm sorry, I didn't get your name."

"Berna."

"Well, Berna, I was clearly having difficulty getting in. What's happened with the doors?"

"I couldn't say, Mrs. Montgomery, but I'm afraid—"

Claire pushed the door and attempted to step in, but Berna had it blocked with her body. "I'd like to come in and get some of my clothing upstairs, if you don't mind." She didn't have room for much more clothing in the apartment's small closet, never mind her earlier pledge. But suddenly that forsaken apparel seemed vital. It was vital she get into her house. Her eyes wandered over Berna's taut gray bun.

"Mr. Montgomery has instructed me not to allow anyone into the house while he is away."

"What are you talking about? This is my house, too, and my things are inside."

"I apologize for the confusion, Mrs. Montgomery. I'll let Mr. Montgomery know you came." Berna closed the door before Claire had the presence of mind to stick her foot in. The deadbolt clicked with a swift and final lock.

"You can't do this," Claire shouted. She raised her palm to pound at the door again, but her arm froze midair. A sharp pain ricocheted behind her eyes. Dumbfounded, she turned and ran to the car.

As she swerved out of the driveway, the wheels of the Jeep spewed fierce contrails of gravel.

CHAPTER 25

*Calm down before reaming him. Don't do anything rash. Clean
something.* Claire repeated Jackie's telephone advice as she carted
her bags into the apartment and unpacked them. She looked
around the kitchen, still fuming. There were drawers to be lined,
counters to scrub, and a hundred other mindless tasks to check
off her list. But, Oh. My. God. Was this for real? She shoved her
hands into the yellow rubber dish gloves she'd bought and wiped
down the sink. Then she uncorked her only bottle of wine and
poured a hefty glass. The apartment felt stuffy and the pungent
aroma of Indian food floated somewhere outside the door.

Dazed, Claire picked up the cocktail suit and walked it to the
closet, hooking it on the upper rack. Errant flecks of dust floated
down onto its sleeve. *What the hell am I doing with this,* she wondered, rebuking herself, the suit, Lillian, the whole goddamned
ridiculous scenario. She didn't need someone else's things. She
just needed her own. Unable to fathom this latest turn of events,
Claire speculated what other madness might be going on inside
her house. Had Michael moved her clothing and personal effects
to the off-season closet so as not to be reminded of her? Was that
it? Or more likely he'd donated them to the Eastern European
training camp where Berna had clearly honed her domestic skills.
"This is so not right," Jackie had admonished. The thought

plagued her as she lay down on the bed and sipped at her cabernet, her glove squeaking against the sides of the juice glass. She
wondered at her husband's motives, and what else he might be
doing in his efforts to discard what no longer seemed to fit in his
world, before grabbing the telephone.

"Michael, who is this Berna woman, and WHY THE HELL
HAVE YOU LOCKED ME OUT OF THE HOUSE?"

"Whoa, Claire. I understand that you wanted to get some
clothes from—"

"Answer my question, Michael." Her hands had begun to
sweat inside the gloves.

"I had to let Maria go. Scheduling issues. But I gave her and
Rigo a handsome severance."

"How could you? They worked for us for almost ten years."

"And now they're happily retired. Taking a well-deserved vacation in Miami, I think."

"Why didn't you tell me?"

"It just happened last week. Frankly I've had more important
issues to—"

"Like locking me out?"

"No. There were too many old keys floating around, and
there've been some break-ins in the neighborhood. The Law-
rences got cleaned out. But I'm sorry about the confusion."

She yanked at the pinky of the left glove, pulling and twisting
the tip. "So this is how it's going to be?" This was not at all how
it was supposed to be.

"You can get anything you need when I get back. Berna has
left for the week, so you'll just have to wait until Nicky and I get
home. I'm sorry."

"I don't understand why you're doing this. This was just a . . .
a temporary . . . I don't know what it was. I thought we could at
least—"

"We discussed all of this in LA. We'll formalize a schedule for
you to be with Nicholas at the house, and for my time with him.
Separately. I thought you understood that."

She struggled to bring into focus the dreamlike quality of the
last hour. Her pulse raced and saliva pooled in her mouth. What
a colossal fool she'd been cleaving to Cora's pipe dreams, and her

own. It had been yet another titanic miscalculation, in a long line of them. And as she weighed the consequences of saying the words she'd promised herself she wouldn't for the sake of the future, she took a deep breath. "Maybe I better talk to a lawyer."

There was a loud scoff as Michael responded, his voice stripped of calm. "So you really want to throw down the gauntlet? After everything that's happened?"

"Throw down the gauntlet? You're the one locking me out of our house. And you're telling me I shouldn't see a lawyer?"

"I'm telling you that we should keep things—" He paused, renegotiating. "Friendly. For Nick's sake."

"I'm hardly the one making things unfriendly here, Michael. I've been trying to salvage what I thought was left of our marriage. For everyone's sake. And by the way, we *are* still married and that's still *my* house too. So if you can—"

"You're right," he said, preempting further tirade. "But this isn't the time, Claire. Not on the telephone." His voice had curiously lost its threatening edge. "I hear you, though. And we'll deal with the situation when—"

"The situation? Our life isn't a *situation*." She pulled off the gloves, tossed them onto the floor.

"Look, we'll work it all out when I get back. I don't think there's any need to get a bunch of lawyers involved at this point. The episode with Berna was just an unfortunate . . . mistake. She was overzealous. And I'm sorry. Really. Let's get Nick settled, and then we'll figure out how to go forward."

Claire couldn't tell whether his contrition was bogus or sincere, but she did have the sudden realization that after a certain point the ambient heat in your world becomes cozy, so soothing you don't even notice the wallpaper peeling. She hung up the phone, utterly numb, and more uncertain than ever about the future. Was Jackie right in wondering whether this was more than just an unfortunate miscommunication? From her balcony Claire could see Washington Park and the jogging trails she hadn't stepped foot on for six months. She took off her clothes and changed into running shoes and tights. False hope, she noted, was terribly suffocating. She could wait a little longer to talk to a lawyer in order to keep Michael happy and amicable while she contemplated her options. But there was no point in making too many adjustments to this newest version of normal.

Outside, the air was crisp and the bruised sky prepared for dusk. She stretched her legs, ready to run fast and hard, away from the *merde*.

CHAPTER 26

In this foreign world of separation—permanent, reversible, or whatever it was to be—friends would be crucial, Claire knew. She would need the support and allies. Problem was, she had done such a bang-up job of keeping everyone at bay after the accident. And this, combined with her early focus shift from the art world to the art of cultivating a home—along with her devotion to Nicholas, her thirty-, then sixty-, and then one-hundred-fifty-pound object of attention—had served to consign most women with the exception of Jackie and just a few close girlfriends to the periphery of her life. She had been a well-respected organizer for important causes, a steadfast and generous member of the community, but not a collector of acquaintances. And this new loneliness would only grow. She knew that, too.

So Claire sat down to the task of reconnecting with those she'd let fall away. Her self-imposed isolation may have been efficacious, but she was not cut out to be a recluse forever. What Richard was able to supply in those final days in Los Angeles had reawakened her openness to fellowship. Now it was just a matter of conjuring the courage to step up and trust that people had short memories and big hearts.

Carolyn Spencer was at the top of her list. She'd called Claire persistently after the accident, and had briefly visited with her at the hospital during that first week, but like all the others, Carolyn's unreturned messages of concern grew sparser. Claire hoped she hadn't thought her evasiveness unforgivable. More likely it was Robert who'd find fault with her voyage underground, given his long history with Michael dating back to their Andover days. But she and Carolyn had their own history, too, as mothers and girlfriends and philanthropists. And Carolyn was an arbiter of sorts, the Katharine Graham of that well-heeled Denver circle. Kay Graham with a cocktail or three.

As Claire dialed the number, she felt a pinch of apprehension. What if Michael already had managed to freeze her out with her old friend? What if he'd gone beyond talking to locksmiths? She really had no idea now what he was thinking or capable of doing.

A maid answered swiftly.

"Is Carolyn in? This is Claire Montgomery."

"Just one moment please, Mrs. Montgomery. I'll see if she is available."

Claire waited as the seconds ticked away, the silence gnawing at her confidence. She twisted a strand of hair around her index finger and wondered what kind of excuse she'd be met with.

The voice returned to the line. "Mrs. Spencer asked if you would leave a number where you can be reached."

With a sinking feeling that Carolyn would not call back, Claire left her number and wondered if resurrecting her old life might require a little more heavy lifting than she'd anticipated. She thought of telephoning Richard for a boost of confidence, but the idea of recounting the latest Michael development was less than inspirational. Not that he'd say *I told you so*. But still. She decided to unpack the last bag she'd left sitting in the living room since her arrival, rather than continuing with any more phone calls.

She took two framed photos of Nicholas from the small carry-on, along with the collection of Edna St. Vincent Millay poetry he had sent for her last birthday, barely a month before the accident. She eyed the inscription inside the dust jacket: *Happy B-day, Mom May 15 Love ya, XO Nick.* Even in his absence Nicholas was present. And there were moments, just like this, when the thought of her faraway boy sent her imagination into a flurry of smashing dishes and shattering glasses—and the reassuring noise that such a hurling fit might bring.

As Claire walked toward the kitchen and its supply of breakables, her phone rang.

"Claire, hello, it's Carolyn. How *are* you, sweetie? I'm so happy you called."

A wave of gratitude roused her as she gathered her thoughts. "Well, I, um, I've just moved back to town. How are you?" She closed the cabinet, feeling as if some unknown anesthesia was beginning to wear off.

"Same as always. Busy as Brangelina and planning a dinner party for forty in between. You know, I left you about a hundred messages after we last spoke and . . ." There was a long pause in which Claire imagined all that her old pal was leaving unsaid.

"I know, and I'm so sorry I didn't—"

"Oh, please don't apologize. You must have needed an assistant to handle all the calls. But I'm so glad to hear your voice. How are you coping, honey?"

"It's been . . . bottomless, and so very scary. But things will be better when Nicky gets back this weekend. I hope." She was beginning to panic that things really might not be better, and she desperately didn't want to give in to that anxiety. "Maybe we could meet for lunch before then and catch up?"

"I'm so relieved to hear how well Nicky's doing and that he's coming home. Robert's been getting updates from Michael. And you know I'd *love* to see you for lunch, but I'm busy with the Malawi benefit and the Heart Ball, and I've got houseguests in from New York over the next week."

"I understand." Wondering what kind of updates Carolyn had really gotten, and wondering if she was politely fudging her way out of anything more than a phone call, Claire tried to keep her tone positive. "Why don't you just give me a call when you have some free time, then?"

"We'll never see each other in that case. Hold on for a sec, would you? . . . a bone-dry, nonfat . . . extra hot . . . You know, Claire, I'm having this little party tonight. . . . Be a dear . . . two pumps . . . sugar-free vanilla? Why don't you come?"

"Are you talking to me?"

"Yes. Sorry. Trouble with my earpiece. But you really should come to the party."

"Tonight?" Claire felt her throat tighten. "I'm not really in the right space for a party at the moment. And I'm sure you've planned everything down to the last detail."

"Don't worry about a thing. It'll be good for you, Claire."

"I don't think that's the best idea right now. You know, everyone all at once, after—" Claire found herself in the bathroom and she sat down on the cover of the toilet seat. "I appreciate the invitation, but I really can't."

"Don't be ridiculous. You have to come. I haven't seen you in five months."

"Almost six, actually."

"That long? Oh, good lord, then, it's settled. I'll see you around seven o'clock. Cocktail attire. God, did I say that out loud? I'm such a twit. You always look gorgeous. And I miss you."

Just then Claire's call waiting beeped and she saw that it was Michael. "Carolyn," she said, relieved by the interruption, "Michael's calling from LA. Can we chat tomorrow?"

"Or tonight, sweetie. Your choice. Either way, I'm *thrilled* you're home."

Claire hung up one call and answered the other.

"Listen, there's been a slight change in plans," came Michael's harried voice on the other end of a choppy connection.

"What are you talking about?"

"The guys were doing routine maintenance on the plane before the return flight. Turns out they need to replace the windshield, of all damned things. And they can't get one in until Monday morning."

"But you're supposed to be home this weekend. That's all Nicky's been talking about." No point in mentioning that it was all she'd been looking forward to. "I've arranged his first appointments at Craig for Monday morning, and we've got our meeting with Ray, the behavioral therapist." *And this sounds like some kind of bullshit excuse.*

"So we should get on a plane that needs a new windshield?" he asked indignantly. "We'll be home Monday afternoon. And

Nick, he's . . . he's fine with it. The appointments can wait a day, for God's sake."

Her posture stiffened, the armor of her mistrust galvanized. "This isn't just another client lunch you're trying to squeeze in, or a round of golf with Teddy at Riviera?" She rarely balked at the inevitable excuses for meetings tacked on to their vacations, or last-minute side trips. But not this time, not when she was dealing with multiple practitioners and a byzantine web of scheduling. And missing her son.

"The new windshield is ordered, Claire. But I *am* meeting with the Manhattan Beach fund group, for your information, not playing golf. The real estate market isn't exactly performing, in case you haven't noticed, and I've got fires to put out. Someone has to pay these insane medical bills. We blew through the insurance allowance months ago."

Michael's continued exasperation over finances surprised Claire, and she scrambled for a retort, something that could magically change the circumstances. But nothing emerged. He was clearly in salvage mode and stressed about a deal. There would be no rerouting him. She exhaled audibly. "Then I guess that's that, and I'll see you both at the house Monday afternoon."

"Where you'll be graciously let in," he added before clicking off.

Claire wandered around the small apartment looking for an outlet for her frustration. She went back to emptying the contents of the carry-on bag. Which took another full three minutes. After putting the bag away, she stood in the living-dining area and turned clockwise in a slow circle, looking for something else that needed doing. But there was nothing. Impulsively, she texted Carolyn.

Tonight would be lovely. Thank you.

She placed the phone on the counter and pinched her lips between her fingers, squeezing and releasing them. Several minutes later it rang again, and Claire slid slow-motion into the dining chair. "Hello, Mother."

"Why on earth didn't you tell me you were already in Denver? I just got off the phone with Jackie and she told me you're having dinner together on Saturday night. She assumed I knew you were back."

"It was a last-minute decision. But I was going to call just as soon as I finished unpacking."

"When will Nicholas be home?"

"Monday. Afternoon."

"That's just wonderful, dear. Everything is going to start falling back into place when the three of you are together again. You'll"—*cough*—"see"—*cough*—"dear."

No, you'll see, Mother. "Right."

"Now, why aren't you going to Jackie's tonight? You shouldn't be alone in that apartment."

"I won't be." The response slipped out before she even realized.

"You have plans?" Cora asked, a deep note of skepticism in her voice.

"Yes, I actually have plans." It dawned on Claire that this really was an unlikely turn of events, given the recent state of her social life. "There's a party this evening."

"You're going to a party?"

"Carolyn Spencer is having a small cocktail party."

"That's wonderful!" Claire heard the long sucking on a Kool Lite. "This will be so good for you, finally getting back into your life and friends, dear. It's just what you need."

"I wasn't going to go, but . . . I don't know. I hope it won't be a disaster."

"What are you talking about? This woman invites you to a party. That *means* something. You are still a beautiful, elegant, and intelligent person, and everyone deserves a second chance. I told you, this is all coming back together for you."

"But—" Claire held her breath, feeling the ache of having believed in all of Cora's maneuverings and rationalizing. The ache inflated like a gas bubble and she stood, hoping to release the blockage. "Michael had me locked out of the house—intentionally or by mistake, I can't be sure—but the point is, we aren't exactly coasting toward the reconciliation I had been hoping for. In fact, it looks like we're heading in the opposite direction." She gave Cora the abridged version of her run-in with Berna, Michael's telephone tirade and the mystifying sense of decisiveness to his words, and her own mounting sense that he might have been resigned to this direction for some time. And after it was out there—the truth, exposed in all its pathetic awfulness—Claire waited for some expression of shock and outrage at her "surrender," waited for Cora to ask why she didn't sound more devastated by this news. But nothing came. No outburst. Not even a cough. She felt the pressure under her ribs begin to ease like cured indigestion. In the twisted world where she now lived, she felt almost happy that Cora was finally seeing the situation for what it was. An irreparable disaster. And that not repairing things might be—she was still trying to wrap her mind and heart around this—the best course.

"Mother, are you still there?"

"Yes, Claire, I'm here. I'm just trying to come up with the right approach to this. I have to say I'm a little thrown."

"How about no approach, Mother? How about, 'Gee, Claire, I'm so sorry for what you're going through'? How about just being a mother and not a strategist for once in my life?"

"Of course I'm sorry, dear. You know I only want what's best for you and Nicky." The tenor of her voice hinted at remorse, but mostly it sounded smoke-stained and anxious as ever to bandage things up. "I just want you to be happy."

"I need to go now, Mother."

"Wait, dear. Maybe you better rethink this party tonight. It might not be such a great idea after all."

"Oh, this just keeps getting better."

"Honey, given what you've told me, maybe you should wait to go out socially. I don't want this to be an unnecessary debacle for you. That's all I'm saying."

"What happened to all the respect I was going to win by going in there with my head high?"

"Yes, but—"

"Listen, my friend invited me to a party. I haven't been in the company of friends for months, and it's pretty clear I'm going to need some other people to lean on." It felt like someone had switched on a jackhammer inside her chest, and it suddenly dawned on Claire why her father had dropped dead of a heart attack at fifty-nine. "You know, Mother, I've religiously followed your advice and believed in your harebrained fantasies about my life since I was a little girl. But I have, as of this moment, officially lost my religion."

"But dear, it might appear a bit unseemly for you to be out on the town, as it were, with your husband contemplating a divorce that others may see as . . . well, as something you may have caused, I'm sorry to say."

Claire held the receiver away from her face and stared at it like Dorothy seeing the little man behind the wizard's curtain for the first time. She gripped it tighter as she brought it back to her face. "Let me get this straight. It's acceptable for me to go to the party as *Separated, but working on the marriage* Claire, but not as *Looks like my husband wants to divorce me* Claire? Because being Mrs. Michael Montgomery somehow makes me okay, and the opposite makes me an outcast?" She uncorked the cabernet bottle with her free hand, poured herself a glass. "Well, I'm not about to let you, or Michael for that matter, make me feel like every step I take now is a step off the bridge to some kind of social suicide. This isn't Truman Capote or Dominick Dunne, despite what you'd like to believe, Mother. I've got a son to take care of and a life to live—husband or no husband—and I need to stay distracted until they get here. I need to get out of this damn apartment. I'll talk to you later." She hung up and drank the glass of wine in one mouthful.

It had seemed so empowering, her brief act of defiance. But as the high faded Claire found herself even more unsettled at the prospect of Carolyn's party than she'd been before Cora had called. What had she cornered herself into, and who was really right? The fact that Cora had her questioning herself all over again was the most infuriating part. Right or wrong, Claire knew she couldn't go on hiding under her rock. How to get out from under that rock without losing too much blood, though, *that* would be the real challenge.

"Why are the wealthy so fascinating, Mom?" Claire pressed her feet against the wall of the bathtub and remembered asking Cora that question eons ago. She had been twelve then, a precocious, long-limbed, waifish girl with a hunger for answers. She'd swung her ribboned pigtails from side to side as she waited for her mother to respond. But there had been no reply, nothing except the sound of the old Zenith echoing through the warm living room. Still waiting for her explanation, Claire stared at Cora and hummed "Bohemian Rhapsody," her fingers conducting an imaginary opera. Cora's eyes remained focused on the television set all the while.

Moments before, they had been laughing and eating deviled-egg sandwiches from TV trays in their Burlingame, California, pine-paneled A-frame. It had been a run-of-the-mill summer afternoon until a news report about a New York socialite and the recent scandal that had befallen her sparked serious, almost sisterly concern for the rich stranger on the part of Claire's mother. The beautiful woman on the screen squared her shoulders and smiled confidently, defiantly, it seemed, beneath her dark Jackie O. glasses in the direction of the cameras, and Claire again asked, "Why, Mom?" Her voice was louder this time, yearning to be acknowledged, but still tempered with the cultivated tolerance of a docile second child.

Cora adjusted a hairpin under her peach floral scarf and stubbed out her cigarette. Smoke sidled up into Claire's face from the chipped Fairmont Hotel ashtray. Cora turned to her and looked squarely into her eyes without blinking.

"Call me Mother, please, dear, it's much more dignified. And I'll tell you why they're so fascinating. The well-bred know just what to say and how to appear competent and elegant in any situation. They are always impeccably made up, no matter what the circumstances." She stood Claire up and twirled her around in her new school dress they had spent hours, it seemed, picking out at Bullock's. "They attend the right parties and know the right people. You believe they wake up looking perfect and prepared for what the day has in store for them. Appearances are crucial, Claire. Physical and otherwise. They can make or break your chances at so many things in life, influence so many outcomes." Cora glanced back at the woman on the screen. "You mark my words."

Claire sloughed her shoulders with a loofah and turned on the hot water to reheat the bath. Memories, it seemed, weren't always the cozy, protective coat of childhood. She tried to laugh at

Cora but couldn't find the mirth. Maybe it would be easier just to ignore her. What she did know for sure, though, was that she couldn't swallow anymore of her Kool-Aid.

She added some lavender oil to the tub and switched her focus to the more pressing issue of getting through the night ahead. As she leaned back and the calming scent rose to her nose, she was struck with another piece of maternal advice. This gem, however—one of Cora's most oft repeated—was actually helpful: Act like you've been there before.

The good news was that she *had* been there before, hundreds of times, to parties like Carolyn's. And having been raised to be prepared and to project the cool grace and sophistication of the swans of Cora's books and TV shows, Claire made a mental list of who she thought would be there, who might still be in her corner (if people actually were paying attention to such geometry), and who was already in Michael's. It was difficult to say, having been out of the loop for so long, but from a vague estimate, the balance seemed not unreasonable. If she managed to hold it all together, it might just be all right. These would be people sipping fabulous champagne at the home of a respected hostess, not jurors in a courtroom. And Carolyn had invited her back in.

After applying her makeup to appear more natural than dramatic, and spraying her hair back off of her face, she began to dress. Claire paid a silent debt of thanks to Lillian and took the suit from the closet, laughing at the irony of it all. She had nothing else appropriate to wear with her at the apartment, so it had all worked out delightfully. She stepped into some well-worn but well-preserved Ferragamos that had lingered at the bottom of her suitcase in LA. There was no substitute for a good pair of expensive shoes. More sage advice from Mother. She put on what jewelry she had with her and studied her appearance in the bathroom mirror. The pearl earrings were enough, and she abandoned the necklace next to the sink, less always being more. Spritzing a small amount of Coco into the air, she stepped through the mist, braced herself, and looked into the mirror again.

CHAPTER 27

Claire stood outside the enormous lacquered doors of the Spencer home. She switched her envelope purse from under her right arm to her left, and back again, and looked over her shoulder at the coterie of familiar Range Rovers, Mercedes, and Suburbans valet-parked along the street. Some were meticulous and glossy in the moonlight, others duller and unabashedly winter-worn. Denying the urge to cut and run back to the safety of the tub, she forced a broad smile and said a quick prayer to the gods of understanding and acceptance. She pushed the bell. Curtain time.

The butler opened the door with dramatic pomp and Claire was swallowed into the play. Inside the perfectly pink-lit foyer, she was met with strains of Gershwin on the piano and the aroma of rosemary and lamb. The lamb would be French-trimmed with an herb pesto, and passed on silver trays—that much she could expect. Her stomach rumbled as she walked down the long art-filled corridor in search of her hostess.

The Spencers had one of the finest abstract expressionist collections in the country, and Claire looked to see if any new pieces had been added. There was a small Motherwell she didn't recognize, a very nice acquisition, she noted, and next to it was her favorite Jackson Pollock. She paused in front of the canvas, an early drip painting, and drank it in to steel herself. Just ahead she could see that the drawing room was already crowded. Like most things in Carolyn's world, it was a showpiece of a space with crème velvet drapery and warm plum and brown accents against her Mies Van der Rohe and Lalique pieces. Claire had always appreciated the clean and sophisticated deference to the artwork on the walls. What she would appreciate now, though, had very little to do with Carolyn's décor. Slowly she approached the entry, hoping to give off the appearance of poise and calm. But inwardly she began to lose faith.

It reminded her of her terrifying debut so many years before. The unsteady walk to the center of the ballroom, the high heels and crinolines beneath her borrowed gown intensifying her awkwardness. Then the curtsy as she held on to her father's arm for dear life. She was certain the audience would laugh as Miss Claire Elizabeth Dunn, daughter of Mr. and Mrs. Gerry Dunn of San Francisco, California, was formally presented to society. Claire was also certain they were scoffing at her mother's herculean efforts with the Women's Board to get her daughter invited to be a deb. But the years of cotillion and etiquette classes had achieved Cora's desired effect, and the audience applauded resoundingly for Claire that night, as they did for all the debutantes.

Claire eyed Carolyn walking toward her from the drawing room, and she speculated how she would appear to her old friend. Would her eyes give away the cool façade she'd cobbled together? It was the first time she was self-conscious of what her private heartache and the passage of time may have done to her appearance. Carolyn glided over in an opalescent Valentino cocktail suit and her trademark emerald and diamond choker, her blond hair pulled perfectly into a cheekbone-highlighting chignon.

"Claire, sweetie, I'm *so* happy to see you. Welcome home." Carolyn embraced Claire and air-kissed her cheek. The familiar scent of Shalimar wafted up into the space between them. "I'm so sorry for all you've had to . . . deal with. But things are looking up now, aren't they?"

Claire forced a smile. "Thank you for having me. You look gorgeous as always."

"I have a new plastic surgeon," Carolyn said with a wink. "I'll get you in if you'd like, although you most definitely don't need her yet." She held Claire's shoulders and stepped back to look her over. "Your suit is just perfect on you, Claire. Perfection." She hugged her again, tightly, before continuing. "You know, I took a nice little collection over to Lillian's last month with an identical Chanel. I had a bit of an accident with some Port on my sleeve, so I only got to wear the damn thing once. But Lillian's assistant said no one would notice." She touched the camellia brooch on Claire's pocket.

Claire glanced nervously at the inside of her left sleeve and noticed the hint of a kidney-shaped stain. *Unfuckingbelievable.* Carolyn's eye traveled to the sleeve. They both gaped at it. Claire had two choices. She could either lie or laugh it off. The women looked into each other's eyes.

"I'm secondhand Claire now," Claire said when nothing else came to her. "Look what it's come to. I'm wearing your castoff. Can you believe it?"

There was an awkward pause, as Carolyn appeared to search for a response. Then she took Claire's hand in hers. "Well, it just shows what lovely taste we both have," she finally said. "I won't tell a soul. I promise. Let's just get you inside, hmm?"

"Maybe this wasn't such a great idea, Carolyn. Maybe I should just go," Claire said, wishing she had stayed in the bath with some cabernet.

Carolyn turned to her. "You look divine, and you can't stay in hiding now that you're back, Claire. Let's get you a drink and go."

The butler offered Claire a glass of champagne, and Carolyn led her into the party.

Claire recognized most of the faces in the room, and she could hear the buzz grow louder as she began circulating with her hostess. The laughter she'd heard from the foyer was now peppered with audible snippets of her name, and Michael's. And Nicholas's. She saw the president of the country club and his wife look up at her in mid-conversation with the Bal de Ballet chair emeritus, then turn and drift toward the terrace. There were a few nods of acknowledgement from afar and several smiles, but no one made any move to approach Claire. The look of distress on Robert Spencer's face when he noticed her made it clear that Carolyn had not prepped him for her appearance. Claire watched him shoot daggers at his wife across the room. She looked over her shoulder toward the door, but Carolyn urged her forward into the center of the room. "Ignore him, he's being an ass," she whispered through a ventriloquist's smile.

"Elaine and Bill, you remember Claire. She's just back in town this week. And of course you know Pamela and Diane, Claire. I'll be back to chat in a bit, sweetie, I promise," Carolyn said, depositing her with the small group standing by the fireplace, and reluctantly excusing herself to greet another arrival.

"Yes of course, Claire, how've you been?" Elaine asked tentatively. Bill and Elaine had been acquaintances of Claire and Michael's. Mixed doubles in a charity tennis tournament. Claire recalled his meager serve along with his weak handshake.

"I'm . . . well. Thanks. And you two? Playing much tennis?" She smiled as charmingly as she could manage.

"Of course we are. When we're down in West Palm or in Palm Springs. Or on Little Palm," Elaine added, erupting into laughter. "Palms and tennis just seem to go hand in hand, don't they, honey?" she said with a nudge to Bill's shoulder.

"I bumped into Michael last week at the Four Seasons," Bill announced, in an apparent attempt to quell his wife's enthusiasm for racquet resorts. But his lips tightened into a cringe. "I'm sorry about your . . . situation." He grasped Elaine's solidly jeweled hand. "We were just on our way to freshen our drinks. Do you need one?" He didn't even bother to look at her glass as he led Elaine away. "It was so great to catch up, Claire." As they were making their hasty evacuation to the bar, Houston Holland— serial dater of widows and divorcées, and a man who, with his highlighted hair, was not going gentle into that good night of middle age—was making a rapid approach. Claire turned her back too late.

"Claire Montgomery, how wonderful to see you, doll." Houston wore his customary striped monogrammed shirt and ascot, and half-mast vodka eyes. "I heard you're back in town, and you look gorgeous. Doesn't she, Diane?" he said, placing his hand on Claire's arm.

Diane gave a noncommittal nod as Claire turned her head to

substitute cheek for mouth in light of Houston's approaching lips. "It's nice to see you, Houston," she said. Claire felt the moist imprint of his urgency land on her face. "Still doing your coffee table books?" She rubbed her cheek and casually stepped back, trying to put a few feet between them. Diane and Pamela had already given them some distance, and were now confiding in low tones.

"I'm working on a gorgeous book about water right now. Leo thinks the idea is fabulous." Houston refilled the space with his sturdy frame.

"Leo Metzger? The doctor?"

"No, doll. DiCaprio. I was just out in LA pitching a documentary on it. The Zeta-Jones-Douglases loved it too, even if they might or might not be splitting. Who knows with those two."

"That's very . . . exciting. So, it's about oceans and lakes?"

"No, bottled water." He pulled out a small notepad and pen. "I'd love to show it to you. Maybe over drinks? Why don't you give me your number?"

"Well, I'm a little busy at the moment, and I just don't think it's a—"

A waiter appeared and offered them baby lamb chops, with herb pesto. Claire gratefully accepted one from the tray and took a bite.

"Divorce can be a lonely planet, doll." Houston wrote his number down and ripped it from the pad. "You call me when you're ready," he said, handing her a striped, monogrammed piece of paper.

"Wait, who said anything to you about divorce?" she asked, trying to swallow at the same time.

"It, uh, just stands to reason. You know, under the circumstances." He backed away slightly. "But I love a juicy story, and yours doesn't turn me off in the slightest." Houston made a swiping motion at his lip. "You've got a piece of rosemary there." He picked up a martini glass from the passing butler's tray and raised it to Claire before making his way to the piano, where Bill and Elaine now stood.

Claire wiped away the offending herb as she watched him shuffle off. Elaine, it seemed, was chuckling now with Robert Spencer, who was alternately giving Carolyn irritated looks again from the doorway. All around her, Claire saw the flicker of diamonds against crystal and waxy smiles, while the pianist launched into a snappy rendition of "Don't Get Around Much Anymore." *Good lord,* she thought, setting her plate of bones down on a tortoise-shell inlaid console. *This is the trifecta I've been missing? Palms, pompous cowards, and playboys?* She wondered if the entire room really had heard all the gory details about Andrew along with the apparently impending demise of her marriage. She searched the faces of her two remaining companions, quite certain at least that she was one of the few people in the room who could express emotion with her forehead muscles, Houston included. She spotted a friendlier figure near the sunroom and excused herself.

"Gail, how *are* you?" Claire said, placing her hand on her old friend's shoulder.

Gail spun around, startled. "Jeez, is that really you, hon?" She enveloped Claire in a tight embrace. "I'm so glad you're back. I only just got home myself a couple days ago, and Carolyn filled me in on all that's happened since I left. I can hardly believe it," she said, waving her hands, her multitude of bangles clanging like tubular bells. "And I hope you can forgive me for not being there for you."

Claire managed a small laugh. "It's all right, I know you've been out of the country with Ashton, and I don't blame—"

"It's Austin, actually. But Ashton seems much more apropos, given our demographics. It's a good thing he didn't call me Demi, though," she said, winking her lavish lash extensions. "We hit four continents before I sent him home to Miami." She paused to catch her breath and take a sip of champagne. "But I should have called you this week, and I'm a shit."

"No, you're not. I'm just grateful to find someone whose company is actually pleasant." She took an inventory of the room, finding most of the eyes on her, and just as quickly, off. "So," Claire asked, only half-kidding, "do you think my presence is causing another scandal?"

"In this group? Please. These people don't have enough closet space for all their skeletons." She downed the rest of her champagne. "Myself included." Gail motioned her chin over Claire's shoulder. "But you'd better brace yourself, hon. Here comes trouble."

An overly made-up woman with a tight face and cashmere sweater to match approached them. Lynn Wexler sat on nearly every major foundation board in the city and was known to adore her cocktails far more than her husband. She slid between Claire and Gail, fixing her nose about four inches from Claire's. "I'm surprised to see you here after all that . . . sordidness," she slurred, her breath bitter with scotch. "I've merely come over to inquire about your son." Before Claire could respond, Lynn proceeded to spill her entire drink on Claire's shoes.

"Oh, wait, let me check my watch," Gail said, raising her Harry Winston chrono under Lynn's chin, and passing Claire a napkin with her other hand. "Nope. Didn't think so. It's definitely not 1952, Lynn, so maybe tone down the Bette Davis a bit."

Carolyn swooped over and escorted the redoubtable Mrs. Wexler to the bar, mouthing a mortified *sorry* over her shoulder. Claire glanced around the room again. Amid the buzz of a dozen different conversations she was positive she heard mentions of cocaine and affairs—as if her ears had suddenly sprouted high-powered hearing aids. Several people turned away, and she wasn't sure if their collective head-shaking was aimed at her or at drunk Lynn. She prayed that the flames in her stomach hadn't risen to her cheeks. "That went well, don't you think?" she said, dabbing her shoes dry with the cocktail napkin. *Cora was proving to be prophetic after all, damn her.*

Gail rolled her eyes at the rigid backside of Lynn's departing figure. "Ugh, that horrible woman. But she has even more money than I do, so people tolerate her." She handed Claire another glass of champagne from a passing tray.

Another waiter appeared with hors d'oeuvres. "Canapés? Or lamb chops with—"

"No," Claire said a bit louder than she meant to. "Thank you."

Gail took one of each before the waiter left. "So, how are you really doing, honey?"

"Well, the situation with Nicholas has been emotional and scary, to say the least. He's doing much, much better, but . . ." She closed her eyes for a moment. "Michael and I are not in a good place, Houston Holland just hit on me, and it seems a lot of people know more about my personal life than I do." She opened her eyes and saw stars, as well as Houston Holland crawling along the border of the rug in search of something. "God, what is that man doing now?"

They both stared at what looked like a blind camel nosing through sand. "Um, looking for his glass eye?" Gail laughed.

"Actually, he's probably trying to pick up all those names he's dropped tonight."

Gail fixed the kindest smile Claire had seen in months on her, and hugged her a second time. "Aw, welcome home, honey. *You* are the Febreze this stale, overstuffed den needs. Seriously. I don't know why Carolyn entertains these people. And I don't know why we keep coming."

Claire was beginning to feel light-headed as she pondered the same question, and wished she'd taken one of the canapés. "The whole thing is just so surreal. I mean all of it, not just this party. Honestly, I feel like I'm just spinning."

"Ooh, did I just hear y'all talking about spinning?" A tall, slender woman in a leopard slip dress and spike-heeled Manolos paused to survey who she'd interrupted. Helenn Hamilton-Hayes, of Fort Worth. Via Beaver Dam, Kentucky. "Oh, hello, Claire, what a surprise to find you here. I haven't seen you since, what? The Met Ball?" Her chandelier earrings dangled like drumsticks as she spoke. "You just look so fantastically skinny. What's your secret?"

Claire tried to smile through her urge to spit. "I guess you could say I've been busy."

"Well, you look great. Considering."

"The body lies," she replied under her breath.

"Hmm?" Helenn looked Claire up and down. "Anyway, y'all were talking spinning, and as I started to say, I have found the most fabulous Yoga Spin instructor, and you just can't believe what he has done for my glutes." She gave her rear end an affectionate tap.

Claire stared incredulously at the scene, wishing somehow to bolster her resolve, but it was like trying to nail Jell-O to the wall. The more she smiled and tried to play the game, the farther floor-ward her composure slid. For a split second she imagined tossing her own drink at Helenn's perfectly spun derrière. Instead she set her glass down on the mantle and made a hasty retreat to the powder room.

Locking the door behind her, Claire walked over to the sink and splashed cool water onto her face. A stabbing pain hit her between the eyes. And there, in the candlelit glow of the Spencers' bathroom, she finally, mercifully, lost it.

Chapter 28

Claire sat curled up on the floor like a frightened caterpillar, fat black tears coursing down her cheeks. She opened her mouth to let out the muffled roar she felt building in her stomach, but nothing emerged. She longed to scream and hit the walls, to pound her fists into Andrew's chest, and Michael's and Cora's. She pictured herself bursting through the door of the bathroom to tell all the finger-waggers that she didn't give a damn about them, but instead she cupped her face in her hands and pictured the Edvard Munch *Scream* painting, the grotesque distortion of the screamer and his hellish world, and she felt hollow and powerless. Coming to this party was another colossal mistake, that much she now knew. *I know these people. I was one of these people.*

A gentle knock came at the door. "Claire, honey, it's Gail. Are you all right? You've been in there for a while," she stage-whispered.

Claire lifted her head from her knees and raised her eyes to the ceiling, but the attempt at tear stoppage proved futile. She held her breath and pulled herself up to her feet, holding on to the painted porcelain doorknob, and opened the door just enough to allow Gail to pass through. "Oh, God, Gail, the last thing I need is to cause a scene here, but I'm a mess. Look at me." She reached for a tissue. "I don't know what the hell I was thinking, coming here tonight," she said, wiping her nose and eyes. "I thought it would help me, but everything's such a convoluted disaster."

"Honey, you'll be fine," Gail said, parting Claire's hair out of her face with her fingers, and assessing the damage. "*I'm* going to help you, but it's going to take some work to get you out of here looking unscathed." She opened her bag and pulled out a silk makeup tote. "Here we are," she said as she unzipped the bulging case, revealing concealer, powder, foundation, and every other Laura Mercier product imaginable. "What I've got in here could make a raccoon look glamorous. Or a woman look like a raccoon." She sat Claire down on the toilet. "Now, let's forget about Lynn and batshit Helenn, and get to work. I'm sure that woman prays for the flu each winter to get in a couple extra days of weight loss on the can."

Claire snorted back the tears that clogged her sinuses. "Oh, God, I'm so pathetic," she said, covering her eyes again with her hands.

"Yes, hon, you are." Gail wiped the snot from Claire's lip with another tissue and placed the makeup case in her lap. "But we can fix you."

Claire held the case tightly. "Do you always carry the store with you?"

Gail reached in for a Q-tip. "Just the basics, hon. I have an entire room at home devoted solely to skin- and hair-care products, shelved and alphabetized. It used to be the second husband's closet, but I took it over before he even knew what hit him." Gail winked and walked over to the sink and dampened her tools. "Actually," she said, waving a Q-tip, "that may have been one of the reasons the marriage ended. But he was a hapless bastard."

Claire was surprised at the cavalier brush-off. "Why did you break up with Max? He seemed like such a great guy."

"Honey, I wasn't talking about Max. I adored Max. Except for that little legal issue. I was referring to Warren. He came before Max, before I knew you. And I just couldn't live for another day with that toupee under my roof. Besides, the man was the sexual equivalent of Valium *and* a clitourist."

"A what?"

"A clitourist, honey. In the bedroom. He would not ask for,

much less take, directions. He was just lost and wandering down there." Her voice dipped. "A stranger in a strange land."

"God, I've missed you."

"And I've missed you, too, my sweet mess of a friend. But we need to wipe all that mascara off of your face before it runs down your cleavage."

"I don't know what happened to me out there. I guess I just wasn't ready for . . . people," Claire said while her friend erased the evidence of her breakdown. She thought for a second of Cora's confounding prescience, and began tearing up again. "Oh, jeez, here we go again."

"Shh," Gail put her fingers on Claire's lips.

"But I . . ."

"I'm serious. Not another word out of you. You're not ready to talk about this without the necessary hysterics, and this isn't the place. Besides I've almost got you looking perfect again, and I do *not* want to start over. We'll have lunch at my house. No makeup, lots of Kleenex and champagne. It'll be good therapy. But in the meantime, we've got to get you out of here with minimum fallout."

"I'll need to say good-bye to Carolyn."

"Right. They'll be serving dinner shortly. I'll go tell Carolyn that you're not quite up to the rest of the evening. She'll understand, and we'll get one of her minions to remove your place card and seat from your table so you won't be so conspicuous in your absence. Then we'll walk you out together in deep, animated female conversation so no more of those gimlet-eyed assholes can bother you."

Claire felt skeptical, but no other options rushed to mind. "I guess it sounds like a good plan," she said as she checked her makeover in the mirror. "You're a lifesaver, Gail. You know, if you ever had to go back to work, you could always have a career as a makeup artist."

"Ugh, I couldn't stand being in women's faces all day long. I much prefer being up close and personal with men." She smoothed her long black hair and retouched her lips in scarlet. "In fact, we should get moving. There could be someone fabulous out there just waiting to meet me."

"Are you seriously looking for number four?"

"Honey, if I wanted to play mommy to a twenty-nine-year-old man any longer—fabulous as Austin is—I'd be on Craigslist. Besides, you never know where the next future Mr. Gail Harrold will appear. And one must always be prepared. He'll just be signing a more airtight prenup this time." Gail foraged at the bottom of the makeup bag and pulled out a small, jeweled atomizer, and, bending over, repositioned her breasts in her low-cut blouse and sprayed a fine mist between them. "Although tonight my chances really don't look so terrific. Carolyn has me seated next to her very gay hairdresser from New York. We're practically wearing matching outfits, and his ass looks better in the Galliano pants than mine does." She held her hand out to Claire. "So, you ready, hon?"

"I suppose," Claire said. As she straightened her suit jacket, a crumbled piece of pinstriped notepaper fell from her pocket.

Gail picked it up and unfolded it. *"Call me, dollface,"* she read in disbelief. "God, that man is about as ridiculous as overalls."

"Welcome to my new life."

"Well, I have just the place for this charming invitation."

"Where?"

"Lynn Wexler's purse. I'm sure it'll make for fabulous conversation with her husband."

Gail left a strong trail of Flowerbomb behind in the powder room, and Claire felt somehow calmed by her crazy savior in purple and red. She adjusted her hair and looked into the mirror again for any obvious signs of distress. She looked tired, but not as dreadful as she might have. Moments later there was a tap at the door.

"The coast is clear. Come on out, sweetheart," Gail said in an awful Humphrey Bogart imitation. Claire slipped out into the quiet foyer and Gail walked her toward the front door where Carolyn was waiting with a soft smile. "Carolyn's got everything covered, and she's coming to lunch with us tomorrow."

Claire moved as quickly as she could through the door, then stopped in her tracks. "Oh, God, I totally forgot, I'm supposed to meet my sister tomorrow."

"Great, bring her along. I need to work my chef a little more these days. He's getting bored with me."

Carolyn placed her arm around Claire's shoulder and gave her a squeeze. "Claire, I'm sorry this was not the greatest homecoming for you. Really sorry. Especially about Robert and Lynn. I'd like to wring both of their necks. Are you going to be all right?"

"I'm sure I will be. Eventually." She smiled over her shoulder and walked down the steps to the street.

She left her shoes pigeon-toed where she had stepped out of them at the door of the bedroom and undressed, flinging her suit and lingerie across the chair in the corner. Naked but for her jewelry, she climbed into bed and turned out the light. The mattress felt lumpy under her back. Her legs were restless, and the bed seemed emptier and colder to her than any bed had in years. She closed her eyes and lay there waiting for sleep to come while her mind wandered to the aloofness and hypocrisy of old "friends." And husbands. Propping herself onto her pillows, Claire stared blankly into the darkness, kicking the sheets loose from their hospital corners.

When sleep did not come, as was becoming more customary, she switched on the light, washed her face in the yellow dimness of the bathroom mirror, and took off the pearl earrings and the wedding band she couldn't imagine ditching. The subtle indentation and tan line on her finger would be more painful to glimpse throughout the day than the ring itself. She returned to the bedroom and prayed for just a few good hours of rest. And by some lovely miracle she fell into the security blanket of her dreams of Nicholas.

Padding drowsily down the hall and into his blue-and-yellow nursery, she looks into her infant's crib with nervous anticipation. Assured that he is alive and breathing, Claire stares at the beautiful sandy-haired boy lying there with the contented smile on his face and the hint of breast milk crusted on his cheek. She sits down in the rocking chair next to the crib. In the filminess of the predawn light, she peers through the slats, watching and listening to each breath he takes.

CHAPTER 29

"Hey," Claire said as she reached out to relieve her sister's arms of their Starbucks cargo. "Look at you." She stood back and took in Jackie's transformation. "More to the point, who are you?" The unruly brown curls that usually hid her eyes were pulled back into a sleek ponytail. Her freckles were subdued under well-applied makeup; her athletic frame accentuated in a slim skirt and kitten heels. "And when was the last time you wore a skirt?" Claire asked with mock disbelief. "It's Ralph Lauren, isn't it?"

"Two years ago. And yes, it's Ralph." She twirled through the door. "You gave it to me, remember? I just haven't had the right occasion for it since our anniversary trip to San Fran with you and the jerk. Ooh, sorry, I mean your husband."

Claire looked pathetically at her sister. "Don't, Jax. I don't want to get sucked into that vortex."

"Just sayin' . . ."

"That was a fun trip, wasn't it," Claire said, lost for a second in memories of the Clift Hotel and Tadiches and toasts to many more years of wedded bliss for all of them.

"I *am* sorry he's being such a prick now." Jackie gave her one of Cora's vintage "Oh my God can you believe the nerve" harrumphs, followed by a kiss on the cheek.

"Yeah, well . . . Anyway, you look très, très chic."

"I actually got worked up about having lunch with the *ladies,* and changed three times before I was feeling the vibe. And Steve pinched my ass as I was walking out the door. I think he'd forgotten how well I clean up when I want to." Jackie looked around the apartment. "I bet I get lucky tonight."

"You always get lucky." Claire gave Jackie a pinch with her free hand.

"The place looks nice."

"Thanks, I'm getting there." Claire set the tray on the kitchen table. "I told you I was making coffee, why'd you go to Starbucks?"

"Because you told me you were making coffee."

"Funny." She put out napkins and placemats, and peeled the wrapper away from a muffin. "I never even had dinner last night."

"Yeah, so what happened? You weren't very forthcoming on the phone."

"Ugh, I'll give you the abbreviated version. We should probably leave for Gail's soon."

Jackie listened as Claire recounted the evening, from the call to Carolyn, to the call from Cora, to her deflating odyssey from drawing room to powder room.

"I like Carolyn," Jackie said as they closed up the apartment and headed to the elevator. "She was very pleasant to me the two times we were together at your place, but I can't believe you wandered back into that wasp's nest thinking there'd be no buzz. It was dumb, Claire. Cosmic dumb."

Claire pressed the down button, wondering how Cora could still manage to be right, in the middle of being wrong on so many other counts.

The elevator arrived, and Jackie continued her monologue. "The people in that world you lived in obviously don't give a damn about what you've had to manage. Tell me again what, exactly, you were trying to accomplish?"

"I don't know. I guess I was just hoping that with the time and distance, people would be willing to see me the way they used to—you know, as a human being—and I could try to start my life again. And I needed to not sit around and stew." They stepped out of the elevator and walked to the Jeep. "But obviously I made another error in judgment."

"Oh, and there wasn't some small part of you trying to prove a point to Mother and Michael?"

She turned and looked into Jackie's big brown don't-bullshit-me eyes. "Maybe. But at least Gail and Carolyn are willing to give me another shot."

"Why do you need them to?"

"I need for someone other than you to know I'm not a monster. And I'm tired of living in Siberia. I need friends!"

"They can't give you absolution, you know."

"I know, but they're here for me. They were part of my world, and I want them to understand." Claire shifted in her seat, trying to make her chafing discomfort disappear.

Jackie shook her head, her ponytail wagging like the pendulum tail of the Felix clock they had in their kitchen when they were kids. "Okay, kiddo. Whatever you say."

As they made their way down Gail's cobblestone drive, Jackie's running commentary about the vast grounds and the evergreen bushes that were fashioned into a maze reminded Claire of the summer they'd cruised the mansions of Piedmont with their mother on weekends—Cora pointing out to them the finer details of moneyed landscape architecture and, best of all, not minding how loud they played the radio with the windows open. While Claire had been more intrigued by the design of the homes themselves, Jackie actually appreciated the garden tour and cultivated a prodigious green thumb by the time school had started in the fall, along with a small crop of pot plants in their bedroom closet.

Claire gazed at her sister's profile and clung for a moment to that leafy Pat Benatar summer. She parked the car and led Jackie to the entrance of the sculpted hedgerow labyrinth. She started to hum "Love is a Battlefield," and they walked with their arms linked and Jackie laughing under her breath. The temperature had drifted into the sixties, and any remnants from the frost earlier that week had vanished into the thirsty earth.

"I'm hardly a rube, but wow. Just . . . wow! Gail lives here alone?"

"Oh, God, no."

Jackie cocked her head as they climbed the steps, sniffing the plump pine twig she'd snipped from a maze bush. "I thought you said she was divorced."

"She is. Times three. She just has several live-in staff to keep her company."

"My life is so plebeian."

"Well, we all have our little trade-offs," Claire said.

They stepped up to the front door and a uniformed house-keeper showed them in before they had a chance to ring the bell. "Ms. Harrold will be down momentarily. Please make yourselves comfortable in the sunroom." She led them through the terrazzo marble gallery and into a sunlit room overlooking the backyard terrace and garden. Palm trees arched from celadon fishbowls, and the room's golden walls gave an illusion of tropical warmth. Floor-to-ceiling windows were draped in cerise satin, and striped pillows in black, white, and crimson dotted nearly every lounge-able piece of furniture.

Claire wandered over to several overstuffed chairs grouped around a leopard-print ottoman, while Jackie continued to soak up the surroundings. "She doesn't do anything small, this one, does she?"

"Oh, you have no idea," Gail said, striding into the room in skin-tight black leather pants that evoked visions of a sleek quar-ter horse. "Hello, ladies. Have a seat." Gail gathered her long hair into a twist and secured it with a red lacquer comb. "How're you feeling today, Claire?"

"A little less train-wreck-ish than I did last night. Thank you again for rescuing me."

Gail kissed her on the forehead. "It was my great pleasure."

"Do you know my sister, Jackie?"

"Lovely to meet you, Jackie." Gail picked up a tray of iced tea that had materialized seemingly from nowhere, and handed the drinks to her guests. "Carolyn's running a few minutes late, so I can tell you that the twenty minutes we spent together in the powder room last night, hon, were the highlight of my evening. It really was not one of her better soirées." As she spoke, Gail plopped down onto the satin love seat across from Claire and Jackie, and kicked off her velvet flats and tucked her feet under her thighs. "Usually she seats me with some fabulously eligible bachelor, but instead I got Mr. and Mrs. Nigel Boring from London, and of course, Francois the hairdresser. Five minutes into his assessment of my current cut and color, we both realized we'd met about ten years ago at my mother's house in Montauk, when he was Frank the dog groomer. Needless to say, he was *not* as charming and entertaining as he might have been."

"Oh my God," Jackie said, unable to stop laughing, "I'd love to have seen the look on his face when he was outed."

"It was fairly priceless. But other than that, no real gossip to report from the front, girls."

Claire studied the Tabriz rug at her feet. "Did anyone wonder why I left early?"

"Not so much," Gail replied before deftly turning the focus back to her mother. "Zibby, by the way, sends you her very best, Claire. I spoke to her this morning."

"That's sweet. How is my favorite Boston Grande dame?"

"Feisty and wacky as ever. She's taken to wearing caftans and eating only on paper plates. But still in full jewels."

"Ah," Jackie said to Gail, piecing together the puzzle, "so it's *your* mother who's made Claire's visits with Michael's parents so entertaining."

"Yes, and thank God for Zibby." Claire sighed. "She's the only person at their club who blows the mustiness off all of that old money on a regular basis."

As the three women chatted, another housekeeper showed a very pale-faced Carolyn into the sunroom.

"Bit of the cocktail flu?" Gail said under her breath.

Offering apologies for arriving late, Carolyn pecked the air near Claire's cheek, and then Jackie's. "It looks like there was a Versace explosion in here. When did you redecorate?"

"Honey, I'm always redecorating." Gail turned to Jackie. "I'll give you a little tour of the casa after lunch, if you'd like. And if you think this is over the top, wait till you see my boudoir."

Jackie's enthusiastic appraisal of Gail's home and gardens continued through more pleasantries, and only subsided when Carolyn asked about her children and her teaching job. Claire enjoyed watching her perfectly clad confidante acclimate to the alien surroundings and to her rather alien friends, without judgment. She eyed her sister gratefully. But now she had a job opening for equally nonjudgmental divorce nurses. She surveyed her two candidates, just as Carolyn announced a desperate need for some painkillers to ease a migraine. She also noted Jackie's poorly concealed shock at their hostess's quickness to supply a Percodan among a disturbingly varied supply of pharmaceuticals—which she arrayed on the ottoman. Claire huddled deep into the love seat, her mind flashing to Nicky unconscious on the floor.

With fortuitous timing, Lucy arrived with a tray of beluga, smoked salmon, and champagne, alleviating the mounting edginess. "Blinis, anyone?" Gail exclaimed, dipping a mother of pearl caviar spoon into the crème fraîche. Carolyn picked up a flute of the Perrier Jouët, swallowed her Percodan and raised her glass in a toast. "To feeling fabulous—all of us."

"Didn't I tell you you'd love it here?" Claire said to her sister with equal amounts of doubt and hope, as they all touched glasses.

Finally, after a lull in the chitchat about farm-raised versus wild salmon and outrageous mothers, Carolyn apologized for the previous evening's debacle. As she fumbled for the words to express her regret, Gail rescued her with her typical forwardness and turned to Claire.

"Hon," she said, liberating her enviable hair from the comb, "so what's the *real* story with you and Michael? What happened?"

What indeed. Claire smiled the grim smile of a defendant on the witness stand. And knowing that what she had come to this house for would require serious mettle, she downed her champagne and considered where to start and how to make them understand what she was still wrestling with. Jackie raised a skeptical eyebrow.

"I had this friend at the hospital in LA ask me about the happiest times in my marriage," she started. "And the odd thing was, the question kind of stumped me in that moment. I'd always thought Michael and I had a good marriage. In fact, I never thought we had anything even resembling *bad* until there was suddenly no marriage at all." She acknowledged the beauty of their life together while trying to convey that her early sense of feeling connected and vital and exceptional in that life had somehow vanished along the way.

"Oh, sweetie, we all were exceptional," Carolyn interjected while looking vacantly at her wedding ring. "And then we married men with the need to be even more exceptional, and we disappeared. Welcome to marriage."

Jackie shot Claire a not so subtle "WTF?" look. But Claire just kept talking, hoping that all of the unexamined feelings that were bubbling up would somehow begin to make sense, at least to her. "I guess I wasn't prepared for that. And then before I knew it, Nicholas was a teenager and Michael was ready to send him off to Andover. I was so nervous about Nicky's diabetes and, well, that's a whole other story. I'm just sort of thinking out loud here, and—"

"That's exactly what you should be doing, hon," Gail said, her voice full of froth and encouragement. "Talk therapy is fabulous. And *we're* much cheaper than my shrink."

"Snacks aren't bad either." Carolyn refilled Claire's champagne glass and pushed the caviar and a box of tissues toward her. "We want to help, sweetie. We do."

Claire took a sip, and bit by bit let flow the gilded emptiness of weeks at a time after Nick had gone and when Michael would be in Asia or off fishing with investors, and she would immerse herself in projects that seemed to need her or take her own jaunts—their once frequent getaways à deux all but a memory in the last couple years. And the way life would sail on as they ran their separate little fiefdoms within their seamlessly decorated world. "I thought we'd avoided the inevitable slow fade because we were busy. But apparently," she said, looking around the room at her eccentric support group, "it was happening right in front of my closed eyes."

Carolyn clenched her jaw in what seemed like woeful recognition. Gail looked as if she'd eaten a bad mouthful of caviar. And Jackie, who maintained perfect posture as she clasped Claire's hand, managed to appear both uptight and regally hopeful. For a second, Claire found herself reflecting on the absurdity of this scene that she never could have written. She also found herself surging with emotion.

"And that's just it," she continued, snapping everyone from their suspended animation. "I think my eyes *were* closed. All those years I assumed that because Michael and I didn't really argue, and because we enjoyed each other's company when we *were* together, and of course because of Nicky, that we'd created this solid, happy family. You keep telling yourself that things are fine, even when they're not *great* because something lovely will happen that allows you to erase a month or a year of whatever's been prickly or not so perfect."

"Ah, yes," Gail said meaningfully. "The little white lies we tell ourselves. It's much nicer that way."

Claire nodded for a moment, digesting this. "And when that sense of loneliness or invisibility would sneak in, I'd feel like a jerk for having negative thoughts. I mean, you can't unroll your yoga mat without hitting some other privileged midlifer mourning the loss of her bliss these days, right? It's such an embarrassing cliché."

"But if it helps, midlife *is* the new thirty, hon."

"I don't feel old," Claire struggled. "Looking back, I feel like I was . . . disappearing. Along with whatever intimacy we'd had." She was as surprised by her choice of description as by its feeling of accuracy.

Jackie turned to her with her authoritative teacher's look. "You know, Claire, people can't maintain intimacy if they're not present or engaged in their spouse's—"

"Oh, I can totally relate to that, sweetie," Carolyn cut in. "Robert's a little light on the 'tell me your thoughts on the lack of equality for Muslim women' comments and the 'you look gorgeous's these days, too. We become shadows of who we were. Afterthoughts. And I can see how you might have needed some *presence* or validation from another man," she added, clearly trying to cut to the chase on the Andrew portion of the story.

Claire let the napkin she'd been twisting in her hands fall to the couch, and walked over to the patio door to marshal her thoughts. The winter sun sparkled on the leaded panes, and she leaned into the door frame thinking about how hard she'd worked to make things so comfortable over the years, and wondering how she'd allowed herself to believe the *everything is fine* fiction of it all. The women waited as she watched a squirrel nibble at something small and green, rolling it round and around in its paws. Jackie's words about being present echoed in her head. Michael hadn't been present, not *emotionally* present, for over a year—since around the time of Nicky's birthday, which, as she really thought about it, marked the beginnings of the subtle shifts from normal, pleasant Michael, to edgy and detached Michael—and which seemed to have intensified after the accident. She hadn't spent much time considering this, or her own lack of presence within their marriage. Probably because the little white lies were much easier to fall asleep to. The squirrel, now watching *her* with a cocked head, stashed its bounty in his cheek, widened its eyes as if to say *Wake up!* and scampered off. She exhaled heavily.

When she returned to her circle, Carolyn was literally balancing on the edge of her chair, and Claire knew she couldn't get her friends' insights about Michael and what to make of their situation until she'd satisfied their curiosity about Andrew. And so, standing with the dignified bearing her mother had always commanded for important occasions, she recounted the story of the man who'd set her into the shoals, and her ceaseless regret over her failure to right herself. "It was all so . . . alluring," she whispered. "He made me feel substantial. And sexy, and valuable, and all those ridiculous things I wanted to be. And I just let myself get sucked in."

"Fucker," Gail said.

Jackie nodded.

"It was the wrongest, worst thing I've ever done," Claire continued, cautiously tiptoeing over the torrid interlude in the guest room, and hoping Gail wouldn't ask her to describe the sex.

"Claire, you're the last person in the world I'd imagine doing something like that!" Carolyn suddenly blurted, sounding like a tamped-down and tipsy Cora. "And unfortunately, when you play," she went on, flat-eyed, "you pay."

Stunned, Claire slunk into the chair next to Jackie, her sense of feeling embraced and empowered, all but eviscerated.

"Okay, this isn't helpful," Jackie said, her protective instincts clearly on tilt, as she grabbed Claire's wrist to stand. "And I think it's time to go."

"Oh my gosh!" Carolyn yelped, the harshness of her words only then appearing to register on her face. "I'm so sorry, please don't go. That was my husband talking, one of his stupid golf analogies. And it was uncalled for. I know how awful it can be, sweetie. Really, I do."

"Ladies," Gail said, easing everyone back into place, "we all have a need to be desired. Men included. *Right,* Carolyn?" she added between clenched teeth, leaning in and grasping Carolyn's knee, as if to keep her from raising foot to mouth again.

Carolyn gave her a pleading don't-go-there glance, the gloss on her lips bleeding from their tight, pinched lines. And Claire wondered if she had missed some unfortunate development in Carolyn's world while she'd been away, which was just the incongruous little shot of camaraderie she needed to keep her from decamping.

"It's all right," Claire said. "I know the whole thing seems so incomprehensible. I get it. It's not that I was itchy. I was just lost and . . ." Her voice trailed off. "And I didn't know it."

Resuming her role as distracter, Gail poured the last of the champagne into their glasses and lit scented candles around the room.

"Are you okay?" Carolyn asked sheepishly.

"I hate myself for being so impulsive. And I hate *him,*" she murmured. "It's hard to even say his name."

Jackie fixed her raised eyebrows on Carolyn and Gail. "Well, then let's not. From now on he's . . . Voldemort."

"That's perfect. And I think we can all agree that we hate Voldemort, too, honey. But you know," Gail said, coming to kneel beside Claire, "finding the right person is what life's all about. And I think it's a downright miracle that anyone can marry in their twenties and still love the person their spouse has become in their forties. We're not the same people anymore, we grow, we change. So sometimes we delude ourselves. And sometimes we do these crazy, inexplicable things when we haven't gotten it right." There were faint murmurs all around. "Take one part distracted husband, two parts intelligent, unfulfilled wife, add dazzling, passionate stranger, and stir—it's a surefire recipe for fireworks, wouldn't you say?"

Claire smiled awkwardly and readjusted the pillows behind her, remembering the good and bad of having outspoken girlfriends, and thinking about delusion and denial, and rattled cages. And when she looked back into their empathetic faces she felt them moving solidly into her corner, which gave her the resolve to finish her saga and get it out of their way for good. "Fireworks, yes," she replied after a beat. "That's an understatement. I remember catching myself in the mirror after . . . he left the house," she said, recalling that oddly visceral moment in the bathroom. "My lips looked bee-stung and my hair was wild. I'd never felt like that in my life."

"God, I love that look," Gail said in an obvious attempt to pierce the intensity that stretched around them. "It's especially great if you can achieve it just before going out in the evening. Hell, who needs Juvederm when you've got that!"

"Well, for those of us who don't get regularly screwed before dinner parties and charity events, Juvederm is *not* such a bad thing," Carolyn slurred.

"Oh my God, hon, you really should get in better touch with your lower chakras!"

"Ugh. My lower chakras are all about batteries these days. Double-A sized."

Claire turned to see Jackie trying to contain the champagne in her mouth, just as Carolyn speculated that the Percodan must have kicked in.

"You really *are* something when you're medicated, honey."

"I'm something? What about you, *Mrs. Robinson*? Tell me again how many times twenty-nine goes into forty-four," Carolyn said to Gail with a woozy grin.

"Ah, yes, young Austin of the six-pack abs and insatiable drive. Boys do have their benefits. But that's another story for another cocktail hour."

After a welcome digression into the topic of Gail's boy toys, Carolyn asked Claire about Nicholas, which caused the lightness that had briefly reclaimed the room to vanish. Claire heaved herself up once again, and though her legs taunted her with their unsteadiness, the scent of ylang ylang reminded her that all was not so bleak, and that there was, at long last, warmth around her.

"C'mon," Gail said, walking them all out to the terrace for lunch.

The four women sat shielded from the midday sun by a magnificent awning with an Italian-inspired trompe l'oeil mural painted on the underside. Claire leaned back to admire the craftsmanship, and was reminded of Botticelli's "Birth of Venus." The woman above her stood naked with outstretched hands and pleading eyes behind her smile. Lucy appeared on the terrace with a lunch of poached Mahi.

"You don't have to talk anymore if you don't want to," Jackie said.

"But I do." Claire placed her napkin in her lap, feeling as if the situation called for a new language—but all she had was her truth. And so she continued, feeling the frazzling months at Nick's bedside and her failed attempts at rescuing her marriage come alive like a vivid post-traumatic dream.

They all sat silently when she had finished—just short of the lockout fiasco and their current domestic arrangement (for which she had no remaining energy or courage)—and listened to the soft whisper of a fountain somewhere below them. The last remaining paperwhites of the season shivered with the gentle breeze in their cachepots, and warm tears rolled down Claire's cheeks as Lucy arrived to serve the dessert no one wanted. Gail's eyes brimmed with tenderness, and Claire noticed that Carolyn's eyes, too, shared her pain.

"I look at Nicky now, at what my selfishness did to him, and it's so hard to accept," she said in a voice overcome with remorse and shame. "Michael certainly can't. He's so . . . irritable and out of reach."

Carolyn stood, taking a moment to catch her balance, and walked over to Claire and entwined their hands. "You've been through more than I knew, and I'm so sorry." She kissed Claire on the cheek. "I think you've had enough for one day. Maybe we could all get together at my house again next week? And if there's anything I can do to help with Nicholas when he comes home, I'll be there."

They all waited for Claire to signal something.

Finally she took a small bite of the dessert in front of her but then pushed it away. "You know, maybe next week's a good idea," she said as exhaustion put her on final lockdown.

CHAPTER 30

Claire pushed the up button in her lobby as she ran through a list of adjectives to summarize the previous three hours. *Wrenching. Thorny. Helpful?* But as depleted as she felt, she also had to acknowledge that the emotional toll was bearable if the process would lead toward some sense of normalcy and connection again, to some perspective. Surely it had to. That, and she hadn't come up with a Plan B.

When she stepped out of the elevator on six, Claire looked out through her uncertainty and saw an enormous cellophane-wrapped basket sitting in front of her door. Upon closer examination, she saw that it was a cookie bouquet. Peanut butter, no doubt. The envelope on the cellophane simply read, "Smitty." She opened the door and brought the package inside, removing the enclosure card. *Saw one of these at Mrs. Fields and thought, what the hell?! Hope they don't taste like socks. Hope you're settling in. Call if I can help. R.*

The man's timing was impeccable. And she felt guilty for the meager e-mail she had sent him with only a brief hello and her new contact information. But an evening alone with a mountain of cookies seemed like the perfect analgesic postscript to the afternoon at Gail's, especially since she opted out of the lasagna party at Jackie's. She sliced open the wrapping and inhaled the luscious, buttery fragrance of her bouquet, and pondered her decision to open herself up so honestly to Gail and Carolyn. And something about sharing the trauma aloud with the support of friends felt useful. Like she was beginning to unearth small clumps of subterranean truth. She bit into one of the chewy cookies, and noticed, too, that her feelings of isolation were beginning to crumble.

In the country of denial, life had been comfortable and beautifully adorned, so easily navigable. Claire closed her eyes, pondering the *truths* she'd tried hard not to see and all those little white lies she'd wrapped them in. There had been too much neglect on *both* of their parts. Too many missed opportunities to make their relationship the source of fulfillment they'd pledged. She wondered what slights Michael had felt from her over the years before her deepest cut. What could have changed him from the thoughtful guy who, unsolicited, would take care of a parking ticket she'd left sitting on the counter, to someone who failed to even acknowledge the greeting card in the bathroom telling him "the best thing to hold on to in life is each other," or the other missives she'd scribbled on Post-its? Once attentive and buoyant, Michael had become remote and overgrown with dark vines long before Andrew. Yet righting her compass now, when that once-shiny picture with Michael had for so long been her north, was daunting.

She licked crumbs from her fingers and squinted at her bedside table. And for all her desire to stop bedazzling the past and accept the truth in all its screwed-up bleakness, she did the only thing her brain and eighteen years of habit knew to do. Because some habits, in spite of their glaring badness, are hard to break. And because she was still raw and drawn to the irresistible glimmer of reassurance. Much like a bug to a zapper.

Shoving another bite into her mouth, Claire picked up her phone and pressed his name on her Favorites screen, cursing her obvious need for some kind of intervention even as she waited for him to answer.

"Michael?"

"Yeah?"

"It wasn't always a lie, was it?" she asked, choking a little on all that she was swallowing.

"What? What wasn't a lie?"

"We had true moments in our marriage, didn't we?"

"Claire, why are you doing this?"

"I just need you to tell me that most of it *was* good. That over the years you felt it, too." She hated herself for her weakness.

She could hear annoyance and impatience in his voice, and she inched deeper into the covers, wondering if whatever he was feeling for her now had also distorted *his* perceptions.

"Of course there was happiness along the way. A lot of it. No one's saying there wasn't. But things obviously shift. And when you play, Claire"—he paused, sounding utterly worn down—"since you keep questioning everything that seems so obvious, I'll say it more clearly: You pay. I don't know why you can't see that."

She sat bolt upright against the headboard.

"So there's really no point in doing this again," he continued. "It's just not helpful, you know?"

An unintelligible tangle of *shit* and *right* and *okay* spilled from her mouth as she absorbed the impact of his words.

"Look, Nicky and I are set to leave at noon on Monday. He's dying for a Larkburger, so if you want to take him to dinner after we get in, that would be good. I have a late business meeting."

Claire hung up, picturing a golf course conversation between Michael and Robert Spencer, the two of them playing judge and jury to her crimes and misdemeanors. She had been responsible for this catastrophe, so she should remedy the mess and suffer appropriately—that was the penance Michael had levied upon her. And it was a penance she was prepared to do a million times over for Nicholas to be well again. But with that bargain, Claire also had to accept the gobsmacking truth that she could no longer live in a world—obviously of her own creation, and Cora's—where surface and subtext did not jibe.

She texted Richard an effusive thank-you for the cookies, then flipped on the TV remote and stretched her arms and legs across the sheets like snow angels. A little less stuck in the amber of what was.

CHAPTER 31

"The ghosts of better days are hard to banish," came Al Roker's response to the bleak Monday morning *Today Show* segment about a Louisiana shrimp-boat captain's woes.

No kidding. Claire switched off the television and tried to focus instead on the future. Her anticipation over seeing Nicky later that afternoon was nearly trumping her unease over the "family reunion" that would come with his arrival. How would she stay positive in the face of what was clearly going to be a confusing welcome home for Nicholas? His social worker at Rancho had done some more "home life integration" prep work with them after the tray-hurling episode, and Nick had responded surprisingly well, if abstractedly, to these sessions about the new living arrangements. But that was there, and Denver was miles and days away from the comfort of the therapist's office, and she couldn't predict how Michael would handle her presence at the house now. A little buttressing of the whole plan, she felt, wouldn't hurt.

Outside, the early gasps of a sudden cold front had left a light dusting of snow on the streets, and just a smear of yellow peeked from behind the clouds as Claire drove to the Tattered Cover. She ordered an Earl Grey with steamed milk from the bookstore's café, and browsed her way around the main floor of what was once a grand old theater, until she found the Relationships section. She had never seen herself as the gal in the self-help aisle, but there she was, looking for answers to the surprising circumstances she'd thrust herself into, searching for some strange magic in a book.

Passing the shelves on tantric sex, Mars & Venus, and finding husbands, Claire slowed at the section on divorce and parenting. The titles there—*Joint Custody with a Jerk, Co-Parenting Through a Difficult Divorce*—seemed so harsh and final. All she really needed was advice on reiterating the concept of a separation to a teenager who happened to have special needs, some words and phrases that would tell her exactly how not to shatter his world any further. She ran her fingers along the spines of several books, but none of them seemed right. She sat down on the floor, leaning against the step-families stack, still scanning for something that resonated and didn't shout *This Is Not Your Beautiful Life* quite so loudly. Taking a sip of her tea, Claire found herself staring at the red-lettered title directly in front of her: *Your Denial Called and Said It's Worn Out and in No Shape to Carry On.* She slid the book from the shelf and began to read.

And there, in authoritative Arial font, Claire found her resonance.

Your marriage is in trouble for any number of reasons (infidelity, lack of connection/intimacy/fulfillment, financial challenges)—this much you know. But are you optimistic things might still work out despite the fact that your spouse:

Has become distant and/or hostile?

Refuses to go to marriage counseling?

Is making other living arrangements?

Has mentioned divorce/contacted a lawyer?

Is taking money from your bank accounts?

And having experienced 3 or more of the above, are you still under the impression that:

Your separation (impending or current) is only temporary?

Your spouse really isn't serious about divorce?

If you don't hire a lawyer, you'll have a better shot at rescuing your relationship?

Your marriage can be saved?

The signs are unmistakable, but you are unable to face the fact that your marriage is over. To this we say, **Get off the hamster wheel of denial now!**

"Jesus," Claire whispered to the picture of an exhausted hamster, wanting to laugh and cry at the same time. But all she could do was read on, thinking that if the authors had asked, "Is Your Mother's Name Cora?" instead of the money-siphoning question, she'd have had a full-bingo blackout over the last several months. "Denial is a powerful compulsion," the chapter continued. She crossed her legs Indian-style, and settled in for a deeper examination of the material. And in the examples of women who thought it indulgent to fret over some niggling ennui in their marriages, or who were afraid to face hard relationship truths because the idea of divorcing and starting over was even harder, Claire saw herself. The more window dressing she had put up, the more paralyzed she had become. She pictured herself running on an endless, though attractively appointed treadmill, eyes closed, feet blistered. And it occurred to her that she was the one, and not her husband, who'd had her head in the sand for far too long. Hunched over the book, she felt like a feeble parenthesis to Michael's exclamation point about the state of their marriage.

Sudden laughter erupted in the stacks, and Claire straightened up to see two teenagers—a boy and a girl—sharing an overstuffed chair with a pile of books between them. The boy was writing on the girl's bare calf in blue pen, tattooing her, Claire imagined, with his adolescent messages of love. The girl giggled louder, then whispered something into his ear, and Claire's thoughts turned to Nicholas and to how lovely it would be for him to be like them one day again, so joyful and carefree.

"Have a ball, guys," she said to the teenagers as she made her way to the cash register. They looked up at her with quizzical moon faces. Claire pressed the book to her chest. It wasn't exactly the magic she'd set out for, or even wanted. But sometimes, she reminded herself, you find that you get what you need.

It was 4:00 when Claire pulled up to the house, just in time to see Michael helping Nicholas out of the front seat of the Range

Rover. She watched as the fading sunlight got tangled in his hair. It looked luminous and healthy, not the dull shade she'd remembered from the hospital. He appeared taller too, less impaired. She studied him, noticing that it was his posture that was making the difference. Nick had swayed slightly as he'd gotten his footing in the gravel, but then stood erect and took in his surroundings. Gratitude filled Claire's heart, and reflexively, she put on some lipstick and girded herself for her no-net leap into this strange new world.

Nick turned toward Claire's car and waved. She cut the engine and dashed out to him. "Welcome home, Nicky," she said, wrapping him tightly in her arms.

"Mom!" Nicholas hugged her back and held her extra long, just as she had imagined he would during their hospital days. His body felt soft under his Andover sweatshirt, his muscles only hinting at their pre-accident definition. But he was no longer the frail-looking kid he'd been for so many months. "We're back," he repeated several times as she clung to the perfection of the moment.

Michael said hello through her embrace with Nicky, and they locked eyes, yielding to the sudden crush of answered prayers, or even joy. And in that moment, Claire made an unspoken pledge that she would do her best not to let Nicholas feel as if were being hot-potatoed between two angry parents. And in the surprising softness of Michael's expression, it seemed to Claire that they were on the same page. Maybe they *could* get through this without too much carnage, she thought, as Nicholas released her.

"Yeah, welcome home, sport," Michael echoed.

"How long am I gone?" Nicholas asked, looking to Claire.

The social worker and speech therapist had prepared them for the likelihood that Nick would exhibit some increased aphasia and confusion upon his return home, but they'd given them tools to work through this tricky phase. Though Claire had failed to review *that* particular information at the bookstore as she'd planned, she did recall the basics of focusing on short-term goals, repetition, and above all, patience.

"You've been gone almost six months, honey."

"But now you're home to finish getting better," Michael added.

"I am better."

"Yes, sport, but there are still a lot of things—"

She signaled to Michael to head inside before things escalated, wondering if he would ever learn to modulate, or if she would forever be cuing him. The thought frustrated her, but he was being kinder than she'd expected, so she let it go. Michael retrieved Nick's bag from the car, and together they walked into the house.

"*See* how much better I'm doing?" Nick said with elation, moving doggedly between them. They held his hands and encouraged his progress up the steps and through the mudroom. The sheer delight of the moment overshadowed Claire's dread about returning home to the tattered remains of their old life. But it wasn't until they stepped into the kitchen and she saw Berna watering *her* English lavender plant on the center island—which had been completely rearranged—that Claire found herself crashing headlong into a personalized version of *The Far Side*.

"Oh," she said, in the perturbed manner that often accompanies the discovery of cracker crumbs in bed.

"Good afternoon, Mrs. Montgomery. It's nice to see you again." Berna put down the watering can and approached them. "Hello, Nicholas," she said, reaching out a fleshy hand to him. "My name is Berna, and I'll be here during the week doing the housekeeping."

Nicholas stared at her, rocking from left foot to right.

Claire's protective instincts fired, and she shot Michael an irritated glance. How could he not have considered how this change might affect Nicholas, especially at such an important juncture? Maria should have been there with her bountiful embrace and Nick's favorite carrot cake.

"Dad told you about me," Nick said to Berna, interrupting Claire's silent tirade. "Dad told *me* about *you*," he corrected after a brief stutter. He ran his hand across his chin, where a light shadow of stubble had grown. "He said you moved my room downstairs, but I want . . . to be in my old room, with my things. I can . . . handle the stairs." Nick looked from Berna to Michael to Claire with pleading eyes.

Claire's irritation intensified to fury. The image of Nick convulsing on the floor of the downstairs guest bedroom looped through her head, and she was astonished that Michael could be so thoughtless as to move him there—her own guilt and responsibility and lack of any seeming authority in the house be damned. "Nicky," she said, trying to keep her voice flat, "your dad and I need to discuss some things before—"

"Yes," Berna said, taking a large container out of the refrigerator. "Why don't you sit down here, Nicholas, and have some carrot cake. I made it this morning. Your father says it's your favorite."

Within seconds Nick and Berna were in pleasant getting-to-know-you conversation mode over the cake, and Claire was marshaling Michael into the foyer, looking over her shoulder at the maddening scene playing out in her own kitchen.

"We can't have him living in that room, Michael," she whisper-shouted, unable to contain the tornado of emotion inside her. "What kind of awful flashbacks could that bring up for him? No matter how much you blame me for everything that happened in there, you've got to just . . . ugh, I don't know." She dug her fists into her temples. "Think things out responsibly. There's a science to this, every little thing needs to be carefully orchestrated."

"Are you finished?" he asked, gently taking her wrist and guiding her down the hall. "Of course I wouldn't put him in there. We've set up the space behind the study for him. Amy recommended not tackling the stairs for another month or so. So I had a medical bed brought in, and Berna brought down all the important things from his bedroom." He looked at her calmly and opened the door to the room. "Okay?"

Inside were Nick's denim linens on the new bed, his framed Joe Sakic jersey hanging on the wall above it, his CD collection and art supplies, even his computer and photos on the desk. There was the picture of her with Nicky from Parents' Day on the night table, next to a vase of freshly cut flowers.

"Oh," she said again, this time annoyed at herself and feeling small for jumping to conclusions, which seemed to be the only exercise she'd been getting recently. She sat down on the bed and buried her face in her palms, trying to reconcile this weird place where happy photos and displaced mothers would coexist. She felt the weight of Michael's stare and reminded herself of her earlier pledge to remain calm. She would bide her time and try to get a better read on him before rushing into any demands about the future.

"I just don't know how to do this," she said, looking up.

"We'll all get through it. Nicky's been great these last few days, really tough and determined. He's been checking his own blood sugar without reminders. And he seems to be dealing well with the new arrangement." Michael pulled up a chair and sat down opposite the bed.

He smiled, but his eyes, which Claire had once found to be spirited, had no light in them. Even the blue of his shirt failed to bring out their life. And the circles beneath them were more pronounced than they had been in LA. Clearly he wasn't sleeping well—the old insomnia gremlin back for a visit, she thought—which gave her a modicum of satisfaction. "Well, you can pretend that's true all you like. But how could Nick really be okay with all of this?"

"I think he somehow knows he has to be."

She felt her stomach twist. "God. That's another couple years on the therapy couch."

Michael raised his eyebrows at her, conveying better than words the "Whose fault is that?" sentiment that would have been too much, even for him. She was grateful at least for his silence.

"So, how do you see this working?" Claire asked, regaining her focus. "This new *arrangement*?" A little roadmap into his psyche would be helpful as she lined up her ducks. "You know, this is still *my* house too. *Our* house." Even though moving back in now seemed as untenable as living away from them. The house felt foreign to her, angry and bleak, and not at all like the place she had so desperately missed. The pain in her stomach turned to a kind of nausea, as if she had eaten something bad.

"I know, Claire. Until we arrange something formally, why don't you plan to be here during the week to take him to Craig or other activities—whatever you guys want. And then I'll handle evenings and the weekends." He spoke logically, without disdain, and with the convincing charm that had made him so successful over the years. The charm, she noted, that he had lacked for the last six months. "How does that sound?"

Claire bit down on her lip, still furious that she'd allowed her guilt and naïve hope to back her into this corner. She subtly pressed Michael on other plans, but he eluded any further discussion, insisting their only concern for the present should be Nick's comfort and routine. She would wait, then, if that's how he was going to play. "So, you've talked to your lawyers about this?" she tried.

He looked at his watch and shifted in his seat. "This is just standard shared custody stuff. Nothing official. In fact, Nicky can stay at your place whenever you want after he gets settled."

"I only have one bedroom, Michael. I didn't anticipate any sort of permanence to this arrangement. You know this is *not* how it's going to be in perpetuity, right?"

"Look," Michael said, standing. "I have a dinner in a half hour, and we don't have the time to get into a discussion about major issues right now. Let's just see how things go for a while. There's no hurry. No rush." He held his palms out as if to say, "I don't have the final answer here. See, my hands are empty."

"Right," she said, maintaining her calm, and wondering what his game was. Clearly, though, the game would require patience and perseverance, too. "Then I guess I'll just get a few things from upstairs, and we'll discuss the future . . . sometime in the near future." She stood, feeling strangely grateful for the reprieve.

"I, uh, forgot to mention that my father is in town and he wants to spend some time with Nicky tomorrow. So it would be best if you came by later in the day."

"How long will he be here?" she asked, wondering if she'd have to spend the week avoiding a man who used to think she hung the moon.

"I'm having dinner with him tonight," he said, fumbling with something in his pocket and looking suddenly preoccupied and tense. It was his key chain, which he dropped and then scrambled to pick up. "He flies out tomorrow afternoon."

"You need to get me a new set of keys, by the way."

Footsteps echoed in the hall, and Nicholas appeared in the doorway. Claire could hear Berna retreating to the kitchen. She held her breath, still feeling the roiling in her gut.

"So, what do you think, pal?" Michael asked, ushering Nick

into the room with a generous smile. "Is there anything else you want in here?"

Nick looked around, checking out every corner and surface. He made his way to the bed and picked up the control and raised and lowered the mattress. With some strain he sat down in front of his computer and stared at the sleeping screen. After what seemed like minutes, his hands shakily skimmed the keyboard, but he didn't attempt to type anything. "I'm hungry," he said, turning to them with a frustrated frown, caught, it seemed, in the margins of what he had yet to overcome.

They helped him to stand, each holding an arm.

"Larkburger?" Claire asked.

"Your mom will take you wherever you want tonight."

Nicholas wriggled free and fumbled to open a CD from the stack on the desk. After a tense wrestling match with the case, he placed the disc in his computer. Wiping his eyes, he returned to where they stood. "Can I just have soup . . . Mom, can you just make me some soup here? I'm tired."

Claire looked to Michael for something she wasn't entirely sure of—permission or reassurance, some gesture to rescue her from the somber uncertainty of the moment. He nodded okay.

"Sure, honey," she said, squeezing Nick's fingers. "I'll make you soup tonight, and we can get burgers another time."

An acoustic harmonica wailed the intro to "Thunder Road," followed by Springsteen's gravelly launch into the lyrics they'd so often sung on drives up to Aspen. The three of them stood gazing out the window toward the backyard and the horizon in the distance. And through the lens of those dusky browns and reds, and the beginnings of the moon, Claire imagined Nicholas as the beautiful but weathered lighthouse around which she and Michael would occasionally gather for mooring. As the tempo and intensity of the song ramped up, she could see Michael mouthing the words, his features weary but somehow calmed.

"Who's Taylor?" Nick blurted at the coda, shifting his gaze to his computer, and then squarely onto his father.

Almost imperceptibly, Michael's body stiffened. "Taylor? I'm . . . not sure, pal."

"Really?" Nicholas raked his hair with his hands and rubbed

at his temples. "Damn it," he grunted, brushing past them to lie down on the bed.

Claire studied her husband closely as she related the previous incidents surrounding Nick's mention of Taylor. She had meant to ask him before, but his moods had always gotten in the way. Michael merely shrugged his shoulders and expressed equal bewilderment, unable to shed any more light on the mystery than she could. They both looked back to Nicholas, who had closed his eyes and was murmuring his way to sleep.

And in that moment Claire remembered why the name had sounded vaguely familiar the first time Nick had asked about Taylor. It was the same name, she was certain, that he had mumbled into his pillow the afternoon she'd returned from the beach—the afternoon he'd recognized her and wondered where his dad was. The name, which he continued to murmur into his pillow here, until the murmuring faded to a light snoring.

CHAPTER 32

"So, what's your plan for the day, girlfriend? I thought we might do a bit of retail therapy to lift your spirits. Neiman's is having a Burberry trunk show, and I feel the need for something British." Gail launched into her speech the moment Claire answered her cell.

"Funny you should mention therapy. I think I could actually use some of the non-retail kind."

"Sounds serious. Are you okay?"

"Well. Yes and no." She sunk into her couch with the phone and took a deep breath. "Okay. I was embarrassed to mention this at lunch, but I agreed to a kind of . . . separate living arrangement with Michael after some flare-ups, thinking it would be better to soft-pedal everything for a bit, you know, to see if we could still somehow work things out under separate roofs. But then he had me locked out of the house while he was in LA with Nicky, though he said it was unintentional, and then I got angry and pushed until it sounded like he was about to drop the divorce bomb. And now"—she paused, catching her breath and stepping officially off the hamster wheel—"it looks like I'll be eating my meals in the company of a novel for the foreseeable future."

"What's the new address? I'm coming right over."

* * *

Gail arrived shortly after 10:00 with a bag full of homemade croissants, fresh-squeezed OJ, and a platter of beautifully prepared tropical fruit.

"My God, this is gorgeous. You shouldn't have gone to so much trouble."

"No trouble at all, since I had Eric do it. Honey, I couldn't prepare a pineapple if I tried." Gail set her things down and scanned the apartment. "This is cozy."

"Thank you for being kind," Claire said, giving her the two-minute tour.

"Okay, so, spill. You two are actually talking the *d*-word?"

Claire spread their picnic out on the Formica table and proceeded to recount Cora's ludicrous-in-hindsight plan, and just how much she'd been willing to resign herself to out of the desire for reconciliation. Over a second round of juice—newly spiked with vodka—she segued into the catalog of Michael's increasingly enigmatic behavior and Nicky's ever-stoic response to the hurdles of coming home.

"Oh, Claire," Gail said, wiping crumbs from her chin. "For someone so smart, how can you be so obtuse? A scheduled visitor at your own house? You don't need a therapist, though it certainly wouldn't hurt. What you need is a lawyer."

Claire took a measured sip from her glass. "I know the setup sounds hard to swallow. But I stupidly thought it would be temporary, a way for us both to get some perspective. I was blinded by hope, and fear. And it seemed somehow . . . appropriate for the short term." She grazed on Gail's croissant remains. "If I hadn't invited Andrew in, none of this would have—"

"Yeah. And if my aunt had balls, she'd be my uncle." Gail leapt up with dramatic fanfare and began to dance around the table, waving her hands over Claire's head and shaking her hips and shoulders briskly, like a shaman. The sleeves of her Valentino tunic billowed and her bangles chimed as she chanted nonsensically, and with great fervor.

"What on earth are you doing?" Claire practically snorted.

"I am absolving you."

"Huh?"

"I've dispelled the evil. You may now officially remove that scarlet A from your psyche, hon."

Claire hung her head back and rested it on the chair. "Ugh. *I know*. But tell me, oh, Mystic One," she said, sitting back up. "How do I do this? How the *hell* do I do this?"

Gail poured them each a cup of coffee. "Good thing I have a little experience in this area. First thing you need to do is call Jack Kaufman. He handled two of my divorces like Tyson on Holyfield, God love him."

"I'm not looking for blood and carnage. I'm hoping we can do it somewhat amicably. And I don't know if I want to get that ball rolling just yet." She thought about Taylor, but didn't want to share her—what were they, concerns, suspicions?—until she could determine whether they might be somehow relevant, or if the mysterious outbursts were just another side effect of Nick's TBI.

"Sweetie. Divorce is a tough business, and you need someone tougher and smarter than whomever your husband is going to hire. And I guarantee he's already choosing his team." Gail paused and looked around the small apartment again, clearly weighing something troubling.

"What?" Claire asked.

"Are you sure about staying here? You have every right to march right back into your house and unpack, you know. In fact, it might be a good—"

"No," Claire said, lowering her eyes. "I can't. It made me feel . . . sick. Being there inside those walls with him felt wrong. It's crazy, but—" She swallowed another mouthful of the juice, searching for the words and the nerve to say aloud what she had been thinking all night and all morning. "I don't want to live there anymore," she finally said, meeting Gail's eyes. "I want to live with my son, but not there."

Gail clasped her hand. "That's okay, honey. I completely understand. So I doubly suggest getting Jack on retainer before Michael does. He will be a great asset. And besides, he's really a doll to work with."

"Well, I've got Nicky to consider in the way I handle everything, too. And civil would be best. It's just that"—she pushed slices of pineapple and kiwi around her plate with the edge of her fork—"the thought of spilling all the, um, unpleasant details to some stranger who I need to go out and advocate for me is so humiliating. For all of us."

"I know this is difficult to process at the moment. But trust me, yours isn't the first marriage to have gone south because of an affair brought on by"—Gail rolled her eyes and blew out what sounded like some long pent-up disdain for Michael—"well, a host of issues. Not to trivialize your situation, but Jack's seen it all, and your circumstances aren't unusual. Think of it like a gyno visit. Yours is just another vagina, hon, over the course of a busy day."

"Yeah," she sighed. "At least I won't have to take off my underwear."

"But Jack *will* get Michael to bend over."

"Gail, that's not my goal. I know he's hurt and angry with me. But he was acting reasonably pleasant when we were together yesterday. And I'd like to keep it that way."

Gail looked skeptically down her perfect nose at Claire. "And do you find that interesting?"

"What do you mean?"

"Maybe nothing at all. But you said he's been mercurial and emotionally distant, and now he's suddenly pleasant? I wouldn't call an hour of *allowing* you back into your house and acting polite in front of your son pleasant. Good parenting, yes. An understanding of marital property laws, most definitely. But it's been my experience that a cigar isn't always just a cigar."

Claire leaned across the table. "Do you know something I don't?"

"Of course not, hon. I don't mean to stir the pot. I'm just saying you need to be hyperaware and focused on your best interests right now."

"I've definitely been having a hard time being objective. When I look back on the last year or two, I can't tell if I'm reading too much into certain comments or behaviors because of where we are now. Or too little. I clearly wasn't paying close enough attention when I needed to be."

"Well," Gail said pointedly, "those distressed comments of his about Nicky's age strike me as someone who's feeling old. That's more of a female vanity thing, but in my not-so-humble opinion, your husband has always been a little too concerned about what people think of him."

Claire considered this surprising appraisal, doubting its accuracy even as she asked Gail whether she thought Michael could be having his own midlife crisis.

"I'm saying he's one of those Master of the Universe types who, in spite of his success, is insecure. I've watched him at enough cocktail parties, jockeying for praise and respect—in the most charismatic sort of way, mind you—but always setting up the story or the joke to pay off in kudos." She went on to describe dating someone just like Michael, how he'd subtly swayed her priorities until she'd practically lost herself in the job of making him feel good. Then she reached into her Birkin and pulled out a business card, and pushed it across the table to Claire. "This will be a healthy move for you, Claire. Jack helped me navigate my way through multiple crises."

"Hmm," Claire mumbled, convinced that Gail had inserted a little too much of her own baggage into the pile she'd just unloaded. "I'm not sure your assessment is right."

"Didn't you tell us yesterday how hard you worked to put such a pretty polish on everything, only to disappear into your role as not-so-happy homemaker?"

Claire nodded slowly.

"Well, our formerly vivacious, *happy,* unflappable Claire hasn't come out to play in a helluva long time. And I miss that friend." Gail lasered in on her with judiciousness reminiscent of Jackie. "You did disappear into that role you were playing. And it didn't seem to make your husband or your marriage any happier. Did it?"

"No," she whispered, closing her eyes.

"Look at me, honey," Gail said, framing her face with jazz hands. "Three divorces, and I'm still optimistic. Don't panic. Splittsville's no picnic, but you'll be okay."

"I just never imagined giving up, you know? I'm not a giver upper."

"Hey—letting go and moving forward is not giving up. It's being strong."

Claire forced a smile and picked up the business card. Then she entered Jack's number into her phone.

"You *will* get through this." Gail stood and pulled her into a calming hug. "I promise. But in the meantime, you could most definitely do with a diversion. And I could do with several new pieces for spring."

Claire tried begging off with her plans to see Jackie and Nicholas in the afternoon, along with the unwise nature of a shopping spree given the path she was headed down. But there was no deflecting her friend's insistence on a couple hours of mindless entertainment, which she was only too happy to supply.

"Hell, this is exactly what you need," Gail said, pointing a Rouge Noir fingernail right between Claire's eyes. "Your self-imposed penalty phase is officially over. It's field-trip time."

Claire's thoughts veered to Richard, and what perfect drinking buddies her two persistent pals would make.

Reaching over to the backseat of Gail's red Jaguar, Claire handed her sister a croissant still neatly wrapped in a napkin, the butter just beginning to seep through the fine linen. "Eat up. You're going to need sustenance."

"Thank you for dragging my sister out *and* for the chauffeured diversion," Jackie said to Gail. "I'm feeling very civilized back here." She ran her hand over the Burr walnut trim and the supple leather. "God, I really need to get rid of my minivan."

Gail eyed her in the rearview mirror. "You don't strike me as a minivan gal."

Jackie grimaced. "Yeah, well. One day you're driving around in a VW Bug with the top down, singing 'Satisfaction' at the top of your lungs, and the next thing you know you're scraping fish sticks out of the car seat, then you're hauling soccer gear and girl scouts, and then you're in the Chrysler showroom."

"Aren't life adjustments strange?" Claire said, not ironically.

"I know, honey. Keep your chin up." Gail rolled into the valet circle of the Cherry Creek shopping center at about forty and skidded to a stop. "Just last night I was contemplating the pathetically unhip state of my Walgreen's purchases. In my twenties it was breath mints, condoms, and a *Vogue*. And now, it's iron supplements and Monistat."

Claire gathered her purse from the floor, bracing for the hurricane of spending her pal was about to unleash. "So you're saying that you're not still buying condoms?"

Inside Neiman's, the women gravitated to the Etro scarf display in the accessories area. A purple-and-navy silk paisley stopped them in their tracks, and Gail asked the saleswoman to take it out. She draped it in a loose cowl around Claire's neck.

"Oh, honey, it just lights up your face."

"I told you," Claire said, glancing into the mirror as she unwrapped it. "I'm only here for the entertainment value, with the possible exception of something for Nicky. No goodies for me."

"But can't you hear it speaking to you," Gail asked, putting the scarf up to her ear. "Oh, yes. She says that she eez perfetto for you."

"Play nicely, Gail. I'm trying to exercise some willpower here."

"Fiiiine. Have it your way." Gail waved good-bye to the scarf and their sales associate and motioned toward the escalator. "But this shindig's just starting, ladies."

They ascended to the second floor couture department, where an immaculately coiffed woman of about fifty approached them with an enormous smile on her face and an undeniable skip in her step. Claire saw her coming before the others and whispered into Jackie's ear. "Watch this."

"Ms. Harrold, it's so *wonderful* to see you. You're here for the trunk show, I presume?" She turned in the direction of a small group of women sipping champagne and nibbling on tea sandwiches near the Chanel department. "I'm so glad you got my message, and I see you've brought some guests. I'm just *thrilled* you're all here."

"Wouldn't miss it, Sid," Gail replied. "How're sales holding up? I imagine it's been tough getting the crowds in."

She sighed and leaned in close to Gail. "It's certainly a blessing to have my regular clients."

"Hello, Sidney," Claire said in a measured voice.

The woman had been so busy fawning over Gail that she had failed to really take in Claire and Jackie. "Oh, Mrs. Montgomery, is that you? I'm so sorry, I didn't expect you, but I'm just *thrilled.*"

"It's nice to see you, too. This is my sister, Jackie Morgan."

"Yes, welcome, welcome. Are you visiting from out of state?"

"Nearly," Jackie replied. "Just outside of Boulder."

"Well, it's *thrilling* you're all here."

"If we have any more thrills here, Sid, we just might faint. What we really need is some bubbly and the large fitting room. And could you bring in the usual staples, the best of the trunk show, and an evening gown or three? But in the next size," she whispered. "And for my friend here," she added, indicating Jackie, "we'll need something fabulously slinky in Cavalli, and"— she paused again to size Jackie up—"also some Stella and Etro."

"Certainly. And for Mrs. Montgomery? Is there anything I can bring you?"

"Oh, I'm just browsing today, Sidney," Claire said with a non-committal smile.

"Ah, yes, of course." She lowered her voice. "If you'd like, I could bring in pieces from some of the Bridge collections?"

The implication stung Claire, though she pretended not to hear the comment. She imagined Sidney had gotten wind of her marital "situation" from one of her clients and surmised a down-turn in her financial wherewithal, among other things.

"That won't be necessary, Sidney," Gail broke in. "Bring her something fabulous. And don't skimp on the champagne."

The three women headed to the trunk show to browse the full collection, Claire's already weak enthusiasm for the outing on a rapid wane. When they made their way back to the fitting room, they found a small table set with flutes of champagne, mini cup-cakes, and truffles. Checking out the finery arrayed on the rolling rack, Gail picked up a flute and commanded Claire to take off her clothes and put on the Escada evening gown that grazed the floor in a puddle of dazzling velvet and crystals. "The red will be divine on you," she said with Wintour-ian authority.

"Yes, it'll go beautifully with the red in my eyes."

"Oh, c'mon," Jackie urged. "Let's have a fashion show. We did come here for some fun."

"Fine," Claire relented between sips of champagne. "Why don't *you* start with this crazy Cavalli number?" She held a scarf-print slip dress in front of her sister.

"Absolutely," Gail added. "I see that inner wild child just dying to step out of her minivan and say *ciao.*"

Jackie licked her lips wickedly until she noticed the label. "Size six? Are you kidding me? That's not going to work. I keep walking around feeling like someone's following me, but it's just my behind."

"You look amazing," Gail said, refilling her champagne glass with one hand, and biting into a red velvet cupcake with her other. "But I swear, *I'm* just one more cupcake away from a 'before' picture. Would you look at this bra fat?" She slipped off her tunic and examined her back in the mirror. "I was at the Children's Hospital Ball in this garnet Dolce number that I hadn't worn for a while. It was sort of a last-minute effort, and I just squeezed into as best I could. But it was like a tube of toothpaste, and I had to keep my wrap draped around me all night like the Dalai Lama so my tits wouldn't fall out."

Claire erupted into laughter, a deep frantic laughter that devolved after several gasps into the crying jag she had badly wanted to avoid. But there was no containing the tears. A failed marriage, Nicky's encumbered potential, a future of lawyers and forensic accountants and uncertainty, a saleswoman's careless barb—they were all there, embellished with wild flourishes like the Etro and Cavalli pieces on the rack, and taunting her with their siren call to abandon hope. Gail handed her a wad of tissues and eased her into the love seat in the corner. "I'm sorry," Claire sniffled. "It's all just hitting me, AGAIN. And I'm . . . I'm kind of at a loss here." She imagined Michael's father assessing Nick's limitations over their lunch together, and being unable to suppress his disappointment.

"It's *okay,*" Jackie soothed, "you're entitled. You've had a lot to deal with, and it's probably going to get harder before it gets better."

"It's karma, is what it is, Jax. I fucked up, and I deserve all this, I know. *I'll* get through it. But Nicky doesn't deserve any of this, the damn injustice of it all."

The uncharacteristic rawness of Claire's speech stunned everyone into momentary silence, until Jackie knelt down and looked Claire right in her third eye. "You did *not* consign Nick to some fate. Bad things can sometimes happen to open our eyes to possibility. Try looking at it that way, okay?"

Claire blinked the tears from her lashes. "I just lost sight of so much."

"Honey, you couldn't be the person you want or need to be the way things were. That's pretty apparent. And I'd venture the same is true for Michael, and Nicky, too," Jackie continued. "Of course, no one's saying this had to happen in order for things to change. But it did happen, and something good can come of it. The quicker you can accept that, the quicker you'll be able to heal and realize whatever possibilities are out there for all of you."

Staring up at the ceiling, Claire wanted with all her heart to believe the uplifting adage.

"What about you, Dalai," Jackie said, turning to Gail who was biting into another cupcake. "What's your take?"

"I ate a bad piece of karma once. Broke a tooth."

"Okay, okay." Claire stood, trying to shake off the embers of her flare-up. "I get it. You've both had to put up with enough of my hysteria, so let me just apologize and thank you for keeping me in check and cheering me up. And now I'll shut up."

"Any time, any place," Gail said, kissing her cheek. "You just remember what your sister said when there's some crappy development with the lawyers, and especially when Nicky takes more steps forward. Because he will. There *is* goodness around the corner, my dear. But for now," she said, handing the Cavalli dress to Jackie along with a pair of four-inch Louboutins, "let's get back to business."

Claire nodded, and Jackie took off her clothes, eased the dress up and the shoes on, and gazed into the mirror with an enormous grin. "Boy, would Steve love to see me in this." She winked at Claire.

"Bet it wouldn't stay on long, hon. That dress just oozes sex."

As Gail slipped in and out of lacy pencils skirts and graphic floral silk caban coats, her black hair electrified and standing on end, and Jackie moved on to a Dolce & Gabbana corset dress,

Claire observed the colorful show from the comfort of the love seat. Gail's "yes" pile grew more substantial by the moment, while Jackie got lost in the sheer joy of playing dress-up.

"Oh my God, Claire, we haven't done this together in ages. I'd forgotten how much fun we used to have tormenting Mother with my less-than-modest prom dress choices," Jackie said, standing only in her cotton bikini underwear and looking slightly tipsy.

Seeing her sister's amused face filled Claire with a blissful sort of satisfaction. She recalled earlier days in that same fitting room when her selections nearly rivaled those of Gail's. When she needed something for an event, she simply bought it. Just like groceries or towels or soap—stocking her closets like her pantry, with what had over the years become essentials. In her post-college days as a working girl in New York, she'd favored Macy's and Bloomies, plucking her classics from the sale racks. But with her marriage to Michael, bargains were something for which she no longer needed to hunt, though they still did inspire satisfaction. She knew what she liked and what suited her, and she knew where to find it. And Michael always took great pride in her taste. It had been such a quick transition to the life of moneyed ease, and as she sat there calculating the outrageous values assigned to the sublime articles strewn about, she wondered how the financial piece would play out with Michael. While Gail had guaranteed Jack's ability to assure Michael's "fairness," Claire knew there were no guarantees when it came to her husband's astute financial provisions and shelters. And the possible return to more moderate circumstances, while poetic—even prophetic in her karmic thinking—still left her feeling slightly anxious. She considered how marketable her skills as a fundraiser or a gallerist might be back in the real world. Because it was always easier to live in oblivion to the fineries of life, than to have enjoyed their six-ply lusciousness and be left with a lingering desire for what many would find absurd.

Sidney tapped on the door to inquire how everything was going, and Gail informed her they were just about finished and asked if she would she ring up her items and take her order from the trunk show. Claire excused herself while the damage was being assessed. As she approached the Ladies Lounge she noticed a young man outside the business office, small in stature, with a mop and bucket in one hand. His other arm dangled just above his waist and ended in a rounded stump with only a thumb and two tiny fingers. The warm, open expression on his face moved Claire. She smiled at him, a larger, more determined smile than she normally would have given a stranger, and said hello, averting her eyes from his disfigurement. She heard him humming as she turned into the ladies room, and it dawned on her that this might be the way people would look at Nicholas now: uncertain what to do except to force a smile and pretend nothing was wrong with him. But then she thought again of the man's demeanor, and something about his dignity encouraged her.

When she returned to the dressing room, she found Jackie putting on her jeans and staring at the pieces that remained.

"You got the bug, didn't you?" Claire said with a grin.

"I had a ball. It's never a bad idea to walk for a while in someone else's shoes—designer or otherwise," she kidded. "Gail's a hoot, and I can see how much she adores you."

At that moment the door flew open and Gail walked in with Carolyn. "All right, ladies, hand over the chocolate, and no one gets hurt." Gail grabbed two truffles from the tray and passed one to Carolyn, who declined it. "Look who I found in the handbag boutique."

"Double points today," Carolyn replied, indicating her bulging shopping bag. "But it's like high school out there, with money and fake boobs. I swear to God, that Shelly Garrison and her platinum helmet pals are a bunch of all hat and no cattle."

"Couldn't sell them a table at the Heart Ball?" Claire asked, recalling Carolyn's single-mindedness when it came to charity benefits.

"Table? Not even a seat. All they had time for was Fendi and Roger Vivier and who's the latest cougar to have slept with some Broncos player, and whose husband's been running around with some hot redheaded lawyer."

"That woman sucks up gossip like a vacuum cleaner. You know that." Gail patted Carolyn on the shoulder.

"I'm sure we can get her husband to buy a table. His firm is pretty good about underwriting," Claire said, feeling suddenly useful. "I could make a call and—" She stopped, feeling just as suddenly foolish for thinking she had any remaining cachet at said law firm, which Michael often used, and was possibly consulting with on *standard custody stuff.*

"God, I'm sorry for the tirade, sweetie. How are you? Hello, Jackie." Carolyn dropped her bags and kissed both Claire's and Jackie's cheeks and poured herself a glass of champagne. "Looks like you ladies have been having a grand time in here. Are you all finished?"

"I'd like to pick up a few things for Nicholas."

"Some welcome-home items—perfect idea," Carolyn said. "I'll help."

Downstairs they chose polo shirts and a hoodie. Nicholas had worn the same few pieces of clothing during his rehab, and Claire hoped a small change in his wardrobe would somehow symbolize the beginning of a new chapter for him. The purchases also made her feel like a regular mother again.

Claire handed her Neiman's card to Trevor, their sales associate, and waited for him to ring them up while they all contemplated an espresso stop.

"Pardon me, Mrs. Montgomery, but there seems to be a problem with your card."

"Really? Could you run it again? I haven't used it in ages, so it might just be a little dusty," Claire replied with a puzzled laugh.

"I'm sorry, but it's no longer . . . valid."

She looked from Gail to Jackie to Carolyn, once again reproaching herself for her naïveté about her husband's intentions. He may have been acting friendly and in no rush to formalize a divorce, but Gail had obviously been right about cigars. Gradually, and without her even noticing, had he been shifting her to the margins of their life? "Unbelievable," she whispered under her breath, just as Carolyn pushed her own card across the counter to Trevor.

"Oh, no, Carolyn, please. I'll just use a different card." She pulled out her American Express. When the transaction went through she started to breathe again.

CHAPTER 33

The four women made a hasty departure from the store and headed to an old coffeehouse haunt of Jackie's where hipsters in ironic T-shirts read Kierkegaard and Ray Bradbury through dark-rimmed glasses. In short, the sort of place they'd have no chance of bumping into anyone they knew. Over lattes, they caught Carolyn up on the recent Michael developments. Claire contributed with vague detachment, concentrating instead on what she was going to say to her husband later that evening, and how she was going to say it.

But after a round of strategizing about the launch of her new life as shrewd guardian of her future and Nicky's, she felt a sense of calm wash over her. As if in the tales of Gail's savvy financial detective work and relentless quest to emerge intact from her divorces, and Jackie's insistence that it would be easier to push through the emotional and nostalgic traps while Michael was behaving like a jerk, and Carolyn's (surprising) assertion that some marriages were like velvet prisons—comfortable enough until you're sprung, and better off terminated—Claire found added permission to be the staunch warrior she needed to be. She also felt a glimmer of hope.

"How are you all so smart about this?" she asked, taking a decadent bite into a brownie.

"It's easy to see other people's lives clearly," Jackie reminded her. "Except, of course, for our mother, who, by the way, has never met a scab she hasn't picked off. So please don't let her dig at your plans anymore. Just move forward with determination. In fact, the sooner you're able to resolve all this, the better off Nicholas will be."

"And it's crucial to show that you have the strength to deal with the situation moving forward. Don't let this just *happen* to you, Claire," Carolyn said, knocking over her coffee with the strength of her own convictions. The mug clattered to the floor and shattered. "Damn it!" She threw napkins on the spill, then dabbed at the corners of her eyes, looking less than her usual soignée. "Sorry."

"Um, what am I missing, Carolyn? Are you okay?" Claire asked. She thought she saw Carolyn flash Gail a loaded ix-nay glance just as the tattooed barista appeared with a towel and cleaned up the mess.

"This isn't about me, sweetie. I just want you to get prepared, and then you can move on with your life again," she said in the upbeat but firm voice of someone trying to believe her own advice.

"Seriously, what's going on here?" Claire asked.

"Let's just say that Carolyn and Robert hit a rough patch a while back, but they've put things back together again," Gail answered, ignoring Carolyn's now obvious attempts to shut her up with her eyes.

"God, I'm so sorry, Carolyn. I'm rambling on like—"

Carolyn pushed up the sleeves of her creamy sweater and held her hand up. "Look, I didn't want to get into to it because it's over and you've got more important things to focus on. But since Gail can't seem to help herself . . ."

"Hon, holding things in makes the moving-on part that much harder. Remember our little confab with your yoga instructor?"

"Fine. I'll give you the abridged version as long as we all can promise not to dwell on it." And with the succinct eloquence of a tabloid reporter, Carolyn proceeded to explain how on the night of the museum benefit, she took home the exquisite bronze sculpture of two lovers from the live auction, while Robert, not one week later, took home the *luvully* blond assistant who had processed the transaction. Carolyn had discovered the affair two months after via an untimely text message while Robert was standing naked in the bathroom brushing his teeth. But she had chosen to forgive him and stay for the sake of their privacy and their businesses and their nearly grown kids. And because he had reasoned with her, and retitled their entire art collection in her name. And because when you play you pay. "I didn't have it in me to start a legal battle and then start my life all over, so I just sucked it up and tried to put it behind us. And I apologize for being a little prickly when we were at Gail's. The scar tissue's still forming."

Claire cringed, imagining the raw nerve her breach of the marriage contract had clearly struck with Carolyn. And she thought about the multitude of disappointments and poor choices that had piled up over the last months like so much black snow, wishing they could somehow shovel it into the sun and let it all melt away. "I'm so sorry."

"Well, just don't be paralyzed by inertia and fear like I was, Claire. Get out there and dust off your 'take-no-prisoners hat,' and turn this into something good for yourself and for Nicholas."

"She will," Gail said, leaning in and squeezing Claire's knee.

The strong fragrance of Gail's perfume fanned out around her. Claire closed her eyes and breathed in the night in Carolyn's powder room and, going farther back, the heady days with Jules, her mentor at Sotheby's. It was the scent of bold women in high heels who knew where they were going. And for an instant Claire reveled in the exquisite solidarity of these smart women who had her back. "I just hope I can be as resolute as you think I can."

"Sweetie, hope is not a strategy," Carolyn said, fishing through the various pockets of her purse. "At least, not in my experience. You need to establish control of the situation, like I've seen you do so beautifully on all the projects we've worked on."

Claire sat up straight, threw her shoulders back, and saluted Carolyn, who was now trying to whiten her eyes with Visine.

"And another little piece of advice about the Neiman's account?" Carolyn asked, as if gauging Claire's mood for more.

"Yes?"

"Keep your words sweet just in case you have to eat them. It's *possible* that was not directed at you. And you don't want to give Michael any ammunition in the 'she's being irrational' department. Trust me."

"Sara Lee on the front lines and Hillary Clinton behind the scenes. Got it." Claire paused, pondering the other item that had been tugging at her. There was no point in holding anything back now. "Can any of you think of someone named Taylor, who Nicholas might have known?" She gave the girls a brief background.

"Taylor Swift? Taylor Momsen? Taylor Lautner? The teen celebrity options are endless," Jackie said, clarifying the *Gossip Girl* and *Twilight* references, with which she expressed embarrassing familiarity thanks to her daughters.

"Or," Carolyn said pointedly, "Taylor could be an *adult* woman. A 'friend' of Michael's?"

Claire laughed nervously at the idea, which she had, up to that point, refused to contemplate. "I had thought it was someone Nicky went to school with. But Michael might have seemed uneasy—just for a second—when Nicky asked him who Taylor was. And then he was himself again. And I had jumped to other stupid conclusions—"

"You can't afford to think any of your conclusions are stupid, hon," Gail said, pushing away her biscotti and discreetly releasing the top button of her skinny jeans. "If something isn't sitting well with you, you need to listen to your gut. Keep your eyes and ears *wide* open under that sweet smile. All Hillary and Sara Lee, all the time."

Claire took a long sip of her cappuccino, finally allowing herself to consider the possibility that Taylor might be a woman with whom Michael had more than a passing acquaintance, and what that would say about the way he'd dealt with her own indiscretion—all of which became too much to swallow after the day's already full menu. She checked her watch, anxious that she would be late for her appointment with Nick's behavioral therapist.

"And may I also suggest," Gail said, eyeing Claire as they walked to the parking lot, "that we wear black tomorrow to officially mourn the death of your self-reproach?"

On the way back to the apartment with her head feeling as if it was on the verge of exploding, Claire noticed a small item tucked away in separate tissue paper among Nicky's new clothes. She pulled it out of the Neiman's bag to inspect it, and discovered the Etro scarf.

"Happy birthday, hon," Gail said without missing a beat.

"My birthday's not until May."

"Consider it early. The colors were just too perfect on you to pass up."

"Is that Cavalli dress hiding in there, too?" Jackie asked from the backseat.

"No. But you might have a little delivery later this afternoon."

Claire kissed her friend's cheek just as Gail pulled up to the building's entrance. "You're too much. Thank you," she said. "More than you know."

"I wasn't there when I should have been, but I am now. And I plan to share all the fruits and nuts of my hard-won decoupling labors with you."

"Speaking of food, what's with all the desserts? You hardly ever eat like this."

Gail pulled her Gucci sunglasses down her nose and peered up at her. "I must be premenopausal. That, or pregnant."

CHAPTER 34

Ray greeted Jackie and Claire at the house later that afternoon. For a hulking man of six three, two hundred sixty or so, he had a gentle demeanor and warm smile that reminded Claire of Michael Clarke Duncan. And despite Nicky's insistence that he didn't need any help showering or getting dressed, it was clear from the fluidity of their communication and Nick's relaxed body language that they had already established a good rapport.

They had been making sandwiches when Claire and Jackie had arrived, and after the requisite reacquainting with his aunt, and sizing-up of his new clothes for fit and cool factor—all of which won thumbs-up—Nick led them back into the kitchen.

"I wanted to make grilled cheese, but Berna said no . . ." He paused, his face concentrating on his search for words.

"No?" Claire bristled.

"No cheese," he finally managed. "She had to go to the store. But, I rolled with it." The hint of a grin spread across his clean-shaven face, and in that rare smile, Claire saw the spark of life and the boy she remembered. His eyes looked vibrant, and while his skin remained pale, the weariness had begun to vanish. Nick pointed to the butcher block. There were six peanut butter and jelly sandwiches, some cut into triangles and some into rectangles, some with lined-up edges, some less artfully constructed. He handed them each a half from the group with matching edges. Ray grabbed one of the "misfits" from the other cluster before Nicholas threw its cubist mates into the sink.

"I told you I *like* the Picassos," Ray said, rescuing one from the water.

"This is perfect, Nicky. I'm starving," Jackie said with enthusiasm.

Claire kissed Nick on his forehead and wiped a splotch of peanut butter from his chin. "Well done."

They ate their sandwiches while Ray gave Claire a brief rundown on his work with patients in Nick's situation. He loved the highly motivated patients, kids mostly, who worked hard to be normal again. The hardest part was *choosing* to recover from injury, and Nick, he emphasized, had the fight and the desire.

After they finished, Claire watched Nick pick up the lid to the jelly jar and try to screw it back on. He had difficulty getting it into the grooves, and she could see his aggravation mounting until finally the lid slid into place and he was able to twist it shut with a grunt. His expression shifted to a sort of sad resignation, and she questioned whether he would ever believe in the enoughness of his small triumphs.

"How about a walk outside, man?"

Ray took Claire aside in the front yard as Jackie held Nick's arm and walked with him to the car near the end of the drive. "Nick was pretty restless when he got back from lunch with his grandfather, so we did some stretching and then played checkers, which calmed him." Ray paused, seeming to deliberate his words. "Does he generally get agitated around certain family members?"

"No," Claire responded, somewhat puzzled. "He hasn't seen his grandfather since June, right before he came home from Andover. They live in Boston. Maybe the shift in routine threw him off?"

"I'm sure it's nothing to be concerned about," Ray promised her. "Patients in Nick's stage often get anxious, as you well know. Might've just been seeing him after so long. Are there any other diversionary activities he likes? Mr. Montgomery mentioned the weight room, but that just amped Nick's arousal even more."

"He's a beautiful artist. I just got a call that one of the charcoal drawings he did in his art therapy class at Rancho won a spot in their 'Art of Rancho' showcase book. But he hasn't wanted to draw since that last week I was there with him. Maybe if you worked with him on his dexterity, we might be able to get him to pick up his pencils again. I can get out some of his sketching supplies."

"Perfect. We'll get him back on course, Mrs. M., don't you worry," Ray said with such a twinkle of confidence that Claire had the feeling she'd just sat on Santa's knee.

"And I should probably explain"—Claire lowered her voice— "our situation here at the house. It's a little . . . unconventional at the moment." She imagined questioning Michael when he got home about just how unconventional things had really become.

"Look," Ray said, walking her toward her car, "my job is to help Nick with his daily living skills. We're gonna work on household chores and we're gonna do fun things, maybe some driving, and definitely some art. My goal is to give him opportunities to succeed here so he can take that confidence and apply it outside." He raised his eyebrows, as if to say that he had a firm grip on the less-than-solid situation he'd walked into. "I'll keep him moving forward, Mrs. M, and you can get the situation to wherever it needs to be."

"Thank you, Ray." She placed her hand on his arm, thinking less Santa Claus and more angel.

Nicholas got into the backseat of the Jeep with Jackie, and Claire drove them to the neighborhood park where Nick had played soccer through middle school. They walked along the bike path, Nicholas between them, a head taller and a nearly shoulder's width broader than both of them. From behind, someone might have guessed he was a man in his twenties who'd suffered a bad ski injury and was still trying to work off his limp. It was that soothing magic hour before sundown, and a quiet had settled on the park after a throng of kids had climbed into their mothers' SUVs and headed for violin lessons and homework and dinners.

"Allie and Miranda can't wait to see you, Nick," Jackie said as they rounded the bend near the playground. "We'd love to have you over for pizza this weekend."

Nicholas stopped, then broke from them and walked over to a nearby bench, turning his head away.

"Are you okay?" Claire asked him. "Is this too much on your ankle?

He pretended to shield his eyes from the glare, avoiding both of their gazes. "It's always too much. But I just have to . . . deal it—deal with all of it. Don't I?" His words oozed with the naked emotion he'd been holding back since he'd gotten home. Three teenage boys dodged out onto the field in front of them and began tossing around a Frisbee. Nicholas leaned forward and watched them. "I want to get better, Aunt Jax," he said quietly. "Before I see the girls." He stayed focused on the boys' rapid-fire movements. "I don't want to see *anyone* until I'm . . . better."

Jackie looked to her sister, and Claire signaled for compliance, completely appreciating the idea of hiding from the world until things were looking up.

"We can wait a couple weeks then for dinner, okay? But *I* plan to see you again before that," Jackie said, sitting down and wrapping her arm around his waist.

They watched the game for a while as the sun started to dip. The boys looked to be a couple years younger than Nicholas, and were swift and athletic as he once had been. One of them launched the Frisbee toward his friend near the playground, but it glided south with the wind and landed a few yards away from where they sat. Unexpectedly, Nicholas pushed himself up from the bench and made to run for the disc. Claire stopped herself from trying to steady him before he might fall—not wanting to be one of those helicopters who, out of their fear of recurring bad luck, hover and suck the adventure out of their children's lives.

Nick rolled on his ankle and tumbled to the gravel at the edge of the grass, his hip and palm catching most of the fall. Claire gripped Jackie's wrist, but remained glued to the bench, as she had during hundreds of hockey and lacrosse games, waiting for her son to right himself. He reached out for the Frisbee and got to his knees. One of the boys approached, and Nick tossed it feebly toward him.

"You need some help, dude?" the boy asked, holding out a hand.

Nick pressed himself onto his feet and, once balanced, unfolded to standing. "No," he snapped. The boy shrugged and jogged back to his buddies.

Nick wiped his upper lip with the arm of the new hoodie. A light dusting of gravel fell to the ground. "Let's go home," he said, starting back down the path to the car without turning around.

When they arrived back at the house Michael was working in the study. Nick lowered himself onto the chaise opposite the desk and elevated his leg on one of the pillows, saying nothing to his dad. Michael greeted Claire and Jackie with a distracted hello, and tousled Nick's hair before returning to his chair.

"We had a long walk at the park," Claire said, filling the silence that ensued, and ignoring the same discomfiting nausea she'd felt the last time she'd been in the house. She scanned the room, seeing herself still there in the pictures with Nicholas on the bookshelves and piano, in the fabrics and furniture and artwork she'd chosen—and the stasis somehow surprised her. She would start out gently, she decided.

They discussed the program for Nick's first day at Craig and the schedule with Ray for the week, and all the other appointments and moving pieces that would be the new routine. Nick responded to everything with a series of nods and *whatever*s, the park mishap clearly still bothering him. Michael was only slightly more engaged. And when Berna poked her head in to announce that Nick's dinner was ready anytime he wanted it, he seemed only too happy for an opportunity to escape. Jackie followed him into the kitchen.

"Nick was kind of up and down this afternoon," Claire said, apprising Michael. "This is *not* an easy adjustment, you know. Even if he doesn't complain."

Michael was simultaneously sending a text and checking something on the computer screen. "Yeah," he said, focusing on the computer. "But everyone's doing fine here," he emphasized with a brief glance. "And Ray seems very capable."

"I picked up some new clothes for Nicky today at Neiman's," she said evenly.

His attention had returned to the screen.

"And when I went to pay, they told me the card was no longer valid." She cocked her head and smiled, waiting.

He looked up. "What?"

"My Neiman's card, you've had it . . . closed?"

He typed for a few seconds, clicked the mouse, and came around to her side of the partners' desk. "I don't know. Maybe Dana did." The shadow of his beard and his bloodshot eyes said all-nighter, or tanking deal.

"Hmm."

"I think it had been inactive for a while so she probably just shut it down. She's been streamlining things." He leaned onto the edge of the desk and shrugged.

Okay, Claire thought. Not totally unreasonable.

"So you used the Amex, then?"

She nodded.

"Fine, crisis averted." He walked toward the door, loosening his tie with one hand and monitoring his cell with the other. "Nicky's got a big day tomorrow, and I'm sure Jackie needs to get back to Boulder. Let's call it a night?"

"Sure," she said, while commending herself for not having launched the original nuclear attack she'd composed. And despite her desire to grill him about the exact nature of his intentions and his non-recollection of Taylor, and to find out how many lawyers he'd consulted and how he envisioned the endgame, Claire repeated her new mantra of Sara Lee Clinton and kept her smile plastered in place. Which, as she thought about it, she'd been doing for a very long time. She cut past him and went to the kitchen.

"I've got to get your aunt back to her car," she said to Nick in her ongoing imitation of cheerful. She wasn't sure she'd ever get comfortable with these exits. And she didn't believe that Nick had. "I'll see you in the morning, honey."

"Cool." He flipped through TV channels, barely registering her departure.

"*Cool?* Are you kidding me?" Claire said to Richard's jovial voice later that evening.

"Aw, he's just being stoic. What else is a teenaged boy supposed to do in the face of everything he's dealing with? It's the 'whatever' approach, and he'd probably be slinging it with passionate indifference regardless of the injury."

She had called Richard for a little distraction from all that her mind was spinning, and for a dose of the encouragement he'd always been able to supply. And because she was, at long last, resigned enough to answer his inevitable "how's your marriage?" question. Which came within the first three minutes of the call.

"I think the clarity has come," she responded. "You were right."

"Well, that's one in a row."

"It's finally, sadly, circling the drain. And I'm going to see a lawyer this week."

Loud barking echoed in the background, followed by the sound of some sort of scratching. "Bring it here," Richard said. "No, *here,* buddy. Come! Jagger!"

"Trouble with the help?" Claire asked in her best imitation of her mother-in-law.

"That," he said between a string of new and clearly unanswered, commands, "was the second biggest mistake of my adult life."

"But no less unpredictable than everything else. Right?"

"When you pick out a Lab at the shelter, the only quality you're pretty much guaranteed of is that he'll be dying to play fetch with you, right? But we got Jagger, the Labrador non-retriever. And now *I* have said mutant all to myself."

Claire chuckled, relaxing into her sheets and imagining how perfect it would be to snuggle up to a warm, uncomplicated cyclone of fur. "I see now that there's no going back for us," she said, wanting for some unexpected reason to steer their conversation back to her marriage. "Which seems so strange. This resignation I'm starting to feel, I mean."

"Okay, Smitty. Answer me this. Who's your best friend?"

She could hear Jagger barking. "Curious minds?"

"Humor me."

Without further hesitation she told him that it was Jackie. And Gail and Carolyn, to a lesser degree.

"Your biggest cheerleader, the person who's always got your back, and vice versa?"

"Definitely Jackie," she repeated.

"Well, then I'd say that there's nothing unusual about your resignation."

"Huh?"

"You're not going to lose your best friend, are you?"

She propped herself up against two pillows, contemplating the significance of his question, and her response. "I was thinking more in terms of, you know, *friends,* but—"

"Look, when I realized that Judy wasn't the answer to that question for me," he continued, "I was finally able to see that she was right about ending things. Because, really, shouldn't we hold our best friends closest and not do anything to screw them over? Shouldn't we *care* most about them? I just read somewhere that infidelity doesn't kill a relationship. Indifference does."

"Mm-hmm." Claire knew instinctively that she never could have hurt or been indifferent to her sister. She also knew—or at least wanted to believe—that Michael had once been the answer to that question for her. She recollected how enthusiastically he would trumpet her achievements at Sotheby's and her early fundraising projects, how he once actually looked forward to being her "plus one" at those events, and how he used to seek her impressions of potential investors he'd introduced her to. And how with every decision *she* weighed, Michael had been her first consideration. But those days were ancient history. She drew her knees up to her chest and hugged them tightly. The foggy nightmare of the last seven months, while no less heartrending, was starting to seem a little less illogical in terms of the whys and wherefores of her actions.

"Okay, I can hear your eyes rolling back into your head, Smitty. But sometimes a mulligan isn't the right thing. You know?"

"I guess I do now," she sighed, considering all the things she *didn't* know or innately feel about her husband, and the probable laundry list of things she didn't know that she didn't know. So much had fallen away when it came to the man she should *get* better than anyone. She closed her eyes and tried to visualize a Michael Top 10 list. Squeezing them tighter and trying to push his Best Ofs into sight, she landed on Happiest Day, which she assumed was Nick's birth. But like too many other things, she was no longer certain. She swallowed slowly, acknowledging the strange truth that her husband, with whom she had shared a hundred magic moments, had become a mystery to her.

"You okay?"

"What's your favorite song, Richard?" she asked.

"Easy. Stones, 'You Can't Always Get What You Want.' "

Of course it was. She would have guessed that, if pressed. She also knew that Richard preferred peanut butter to chocolate chip, Mexican to sushi, ellipses to dashes. Inconsequential details, but they made her wonder when she and Michael had stopped noticing their details. "I suppose that should be mine, too," she said, looking out the bedroom window. A full white moon lit the sky, and Claire experienced a fleeting swell of melancholy. "We'd have these moon moments when he was traveling, Michael and I," she said, talking more to the memory than to Richard. "He'd call me from Hong Kong, or wherever he happened to be, and we'd describe the moon. It was . . . reassuring."

"I know it's hard to let go of all that, Smitty. But when your roof seems to be crumbling around you—and I don't mean to sound cheesy—sometimes, for the first time, you can really see the stars."

Though Richard had said the words solemnly and with the insight and candor she had come to admire about him, Claire burst out laughing at the absurdity that yet another greeting card adage could be apropos of her circumstances. She truly had become a cliché. "Well, I hope I can at some point," she said, stifling a snicker.

"As long as I'm entertaining you, let me add this gem to the cheese platter: Falling in love is like falling off a building. It doesn't hurt till the end."

"Thank you, oh, Great Cheese Whiz. You are truly wise and witty, and I'm sorry for acting like a five-year-old."

"You know," he said, not sounding the least bit offended, "I've been thinking that I could use a little time on the slopes. Maybe

I'll head out to Vail next week, and swing through Denver. Can you spare an afternoon for lunch?" Jagger howled mournfully over his words.

"I think your friend will miss you."

"No, he just needs a W-A-L-K."

"And I need sleep," Claire said, feeling relaxed and comforted by their easy rapport. "Call me when you're coming, and I'll take you to my favorite Mexican joint."

Chapter 35

"Let's go," Nicholas said to Claire as he and Ray greeted her at the house the next morning. His voice was ebullient, his energy buzzing, and he was fully dressed with the hood of the new hoodie pulled up around his head and framing his eager smile.

"We talked about some of the folks he'll be meeting at Craig today, and he's pretty psyched about getting started on his new program," Ray told her with a hesitant look.

"I need to catch up on classes . . . senior classes," Nick said. "And then maybe my Stanford application. And APs."

"Hold up there, Flash. Remember, you'll be doing evaluations today so they can set up your training program," Ray said in a calming voice. "The tutor and schoolwork will come a little later."

"I want to start now. Dad mentioned getting a . . . college coach."

"We can talk to your patient counselor about all of your goals," Claire said.

Nick shuffled past them out the front door toward Claire's car. "College. That's my goal."

Before the accident, Nicholas had been on track to have excellent chances for admission to most any school, with his high ACT scores, strong grades, and distinctions in varsity sports and art. But now that an entire semester had passed, along with college deadlines, never mind the study skills he'd have to relearn and all the deficits he still faced, it wasn't likely he could make up five months of school work, much less get any applications in, Claire knew. Then again, she didn't know what his team *could* help him accomplish now. Maybe the fervency of his desire to get up to speed academically would get him through all the sessions with the speech and occupational therapists. If college *was* his new motivation—and not just her own secret desire for him to have a normal future—then why not do everything in her power to help him play catch up?

"I think he sees academic improvement as a more manageable goal than overcoming some of his physical limitations," Ray said softly. "Focusing on the cognitive stuff for a while is fine, but college next fall is pushing it."

"But it's possible, isn't it?"

"Ingrained academic skills are already in the memory bank. But let's not get ahead of ourselves."

The morning was still cold, and Nicholas cranked up the heat inside the car. "Chazz applied early . . . decision at Penn and got in, and Brice is going to Co . . . lumbia," he said with undisguised envy as they pulled out of the driveway.

Claire was surprised to hear Nick bring up the friends he'd been doing his very best to avoid. "Did you talk to them?" she asked.

"Facebook."

"Good for them." She looked over to see him biting his lip. "Did you respond?"

"I will. Soon." He pressed his hooded cheek against the window and stared at the oncoming traffic.

Claire understood that no amount of art or speech therapy would make Nick's lack of relatable, "post-able" accomplishments any less agonizing. In the world of competitive teenagers with type-A parents, it was hard to compare graduation from inpatient to outpatient therapy, to an acceptance to the Ivy League in a Facebook posting. And no amount of arnica would make that psychic bruise heal any faster.

"You'll get there, Nicky, and—"

"I know. I just want to get . . . moving forward."

* * *

Sherry, the new social worker, greeted them inside Craig's skylit waiting area and it was off to the races. They chatted about Nick's desire to focus on a school reentry plan, with the aim of finishing out his senior year locally. There were meetings with recreational, speech, and physical therapists, and in the afternoon, Nick underwent the various functional evaluations that would provide "real life" assessments of his strengths and limitations. And as he pushed through them all, his silent resolve impressed everyone. By the end of the day, with a "nothing's going to stop me" expression of intensity, Nick had established his own new approach. Sherry, who brimmed with all the confidence-building enthusiasm Claire had hoped for, reminded Claire that, like an adrenaline filled come-from-behind victory, today's show wasn't a sustainable high for Nick. There would still be down days, a need to temper expectations. Claire didn't need reminding, but she saw no reason not to celebrate his commitment.

"How about an early dinner at the club?" she asked as they left the facility. "I think a steak's in order after all that hard work."

"Cool," he said with a nod. He stretched and exercised the fingers of his left hand. "But I don't need to be in a . . . hospital anymore."

"You're not, Nicky. The team there is just going to help you get to the best place you can."

"I don't want to keep doing step-ups and chest presses . . . and balance exercises. It's not like that will college—get me into college." The tone of his voice took on a familiar edge. "It's not like lacrosse is going to happen again. Ever."

When they pulled into the country club parking lot, she noticed lights on in the skate house and activity on the rink. She tried to distract Nick from the peewee hockey team on the ice, taking his hand in hers over the armrest. But he pulled away and opened the car door, stretching himself onto the pavement. She could see his face fighting to regain a neutral expression as they walked up the steps to the main entrance.

Inside the dining room Claire scanned the smattering of occupied tables for familiar faces. It was early, and only a few elderly couples were enjoying their evening cocktails. She hoped she and

Nick could be done before the rush of hockey families. The maître d' emerged from the kitchen, and Claire waved to him. He seemed to hesitate for a second before approaching them.

"Good evening, Mrs. Montgomery," he said, guiding her away from Nicholas and toward the reservations desk. "May I have a word?"

"Of course, Eddie. How are you?"

He lowered his eyes and pulled a piece of paper from a leather folder. "I regret to have to say this, but your account is in arrears and we can't allow you to dine until this has been taken care of." He handed her a list of members not in good standing due to unpaid charges, and second from the top was Michael Montgomery. "I've tried to reach your husband about the matter, but I've, uh, not had any success. I'm so sorry, Mrs. Montgomery, I don't want to turn you and your son away, but my hands are tied. Club policy." He looked as mortified as she felt.

Claire faltered slightly, before placing her hand on his arm. "No, no, Eddie, I understand," she said softly, folding the memo in half and handing it back to him. "It isn't your fault. I'm sure there's been some miscommunication. We'll just straighten this out at home."

Lack of lunch, combined with the ever-unfolding series of strange events, left Claire with a sense of hallucinatory wooziness. She didn't understand what this latest surprise meant or how she should handle it, other than to tell Nick that the dining room was reserved for a private party and they could go to Larkburger instead. So she let the Nuggets basketball game on the radio fill the space between them during the drive and just focused on the present, got them to the restaurant, parked the car, and ordered food at the counter and sat down with her son.

"Mom, everyone keeps telling me I had this . . . this drug overdose," Nicholas said, putting down his cheeseburger and making air quotations around the words that continued to confound him. "But I'm fine. I don't need all these . . . people."

And here we go again. "Yes, Nicky, you *did* have an overdose. You snorted some cocaine, you had a brain hemorrhage, and you *do* need these people to help you get better. These people are going to help you get to college. We've talked about this with Dr.

Adamson, and with Sherry," Claire said in an overwrought voice. "Honey, you have to—"

Nicholas pushed his chair back and swept his food onto the floor. "No," he shouted. "It's not true. I don't remember any . . . of that."

Claire cupped her shaking hands over her face. "Oh my God, Nicky, I'm so sorry, I shouldn't have—" Snapping back to time and place, she looked up to see that he was already rushing out the door and into the parking lot. She chased after him, ignoring the stares of the other customers.

Claire found him pacing around the car and blocked him, containing his quaking body in her arms. She could feel his heat and his heart racing against her shoulder, and they nearly fell against the hood with his weight. She balanced her foot on the tire and held him tightly, whispering into his chest. "I know this is still hard to believe or understand. And because of the way our brains work, it may never make sense to you. It was a terrible night, Nicky." She looked into his flushed face. "The most frightening night of my life. But you came through it, thank God, and I will do everything I can to help you get better." She stopped to catch her breath and wipe her eyes.

"Why?" he asked, his body relaxing slightly.

"Because you're the most important thing in the world to me, and I want you to heal and finish school and do everything you want with your life."

"No." His eyes bore into her. "Why did I . . . overdose?"

She fell back against the Jeep. "I—uh—there was someone," she said, her throat catching, her fingers grasping the hood like some tenuous ledge. "A person who came to the house, and he had some cocaine with him. I don't know why he would have brought it, and it must have fallen out of his pocket. And you found it," she went on, hearing the Valium-like lethargy in her own voice. "It was all a terrible mistake. I never should have allowed him to—"

"Who?" he asked, looking desperate and confused. "Was it . . . Taylor?"

Claire shielded her eyes from the headlights of an approaching car. "No, Nicky, I don't know who Taylor is. It was someone you don't know. It was . . . no one," she choked. "All that matters is that you came through and you're getting better."

"I don't get this," he said, balling his fists. "Why I can't . . . remember?" He backed away and opened the passenger door. "I just want to go home."

"Nicky," she said, meeting him inside the car, "we're going to get through this. I don't know exactly what will happen with . . . everything, but you'll get there. We'll get there."

"Yeah." He pulled the hood down over his face. "Right."

Looking up to the moon, Claire searched for that old convincing fiction that everything really could be fine.

Michael had been delayed for about an hour according to Berna, who was standing sentry in the kitchen when they returned to the house. The counters were spotless, but his ever-efficient capo continued to wipe them in spite of Claire's insistence that she would wait for Michael with Nicholas. Berna then began to clean out the refrigerator, checking expiration dates on yogurt and milk cartons, and arranging them like soldiers in rank order. The woman clearly had instructions, and Claire clearly didn't have the authority to override them. She gazed slack-jawed around her kitchen, deciding it wasn't big enough for the two of them.

"Nick, do you want to play some checkers in the study?" she asked, hoping this would have the relaxing effect on him it usually did.

He shook his head. "I'm going to bed."

Claire followed him into his room. They both sat—he at his desk, and she on the bed—with the dog-tired relief of boot campers at lights-out. She wanted to close her eyes and fall asleep right there, but she watched Nick log into Facebook on his computer. He stared at the screen and, as before, skimmed the keyboard but didn't type anything.

"Can I help?" she asked cautiously.

"I don't know what I want to—" Nicholas said before abruptly powering off the computer. "No. Just . . . leave me alone. I'm tired of talking." He didn't turn around when she put her hands on his shoulders, wouldn't look at her when she tried to turn his chin toward her.

"It's been a long day. And I'm sorry for being short. But any-time you do want to talk, Nicky," she said open-endedly, trying to imagine what was really going through his mind, what he was pro-cessing, and what his brain was purposefully keeping in the shad-ows. "I'll be back tomorrow, and we'll think of something fun to do."

"I'm going to the mall with Ray to work on some . . . stuff," he said, taking off his sweatshirt.

Ray had mentioned to Claire that they would be doing an out-ing where he would observe Nick's ability to perform certain tasks and behave appropriately in a public setting. The idea left Claire queasier than she already had been, given the last hour. But she reminded herself that they'd likely be dealing with Nick's confu-sion, disbelief, and outbursts for a good long while. Like their own shadow-filled Groundhog Day.

"Okay, buddy. Why don't you brush your teeth and we can check your blood—"

"I know . . . what to do. I'm taking a shower," he snapped, leaving the room and heading for the bathroom. He dragged his hand against the wall for balance.

Claire wandered into the study and stared at the partners' desk she should have crawled under all those months ago. Sitting down in the Herman Miller desk chair, she wondered how long it would take for Berna to appear and start dusting the bookshelves. But she noticed the light on in the garage beyond the patio, and as-sumed Frau Rommel was now rearranging the soda cans in the garage fridge into alphabetical order. As if on cue, the phone rang, distracting her from an imminent spiral into her mire of "if onlys." She picked it up without thought.

"Mrs. Montgomery?"

"Yes?"

"I need to speak to your husband, please."

"You might try him at his office," she said, annoyed in the role of helpful secretary.

"I've been trying him everywhere." The man's voice was tense and urgent. "Tell him that if I don't receive the Janus information from him this week, things could get *very* serious. We're running out of time. Please." The caller left a name she didn't recognize and hung up.

Claire set the phone down and twisted her wedding band up and down her finger. Where once the ring wouldn't move above her knuckle, now it slid easily back and forth. *Janus? Mac Kessler?* The mysteries of her husband's pursuits, it seemed, were endless. She hit the space bar on the keyboard, waking the computer. And instead of both of their login and password prompts, Michael's desktop appeared—unprotected. Surprised and inspired by this uncharacteristic gap in security, Claire tentatively navigated the mouse around various folders on the screen. Hoping for illumination. "Manhattan Beach Fund," "Rancho Los Amigos," "Net-Jets." Nothing out of the ordinary jumped out at her. She clicked on the e-mail icon and scanned Michael's Inbox for "Janus" or the cryptic Mac Kessler, fighting the sense of utter sliminess such snooping would normally elicit in her. But as she scrolled down the long list of messages going into the previous week with no luck, she abruptly changed tracks. "Taylor," she typed into the search box.

Numerous messages containing that name appeared: from Eric Taylor, a frequent real estate investor; from a Taylor Technologies; from a *Post* story on Steamboat Springs' Taylor Gold bowing out of the Olympic half-pipe; documents To Eric Taylor; trash with various news outlet stories about various Taylors. The list went on extensively and unremarkably, until an older message from Michael's drafts box caught her attention. It was to Nicholas, with a subject line that read "I'm sorry," and dated the day before his accident. Uneasily, she clicked the mouse.

Nick,

I'm sorry I was so hard on you about the choices you made with Chazz's sister last week, in light of the choices I made surrounding Taylor. Very different circumstances, of course, but you were right to be angry and shocked. Obviously I didn't know you'd found out about Taylor, and I just want to tell you again how much I regret not doing the right thing, like I've always encouraged you to do. You are my happiest, proudest accomplishment, and the last thing I want is for you to be disappointed in me. I am devastated more than you know, and I hope you can understand that this situation really is more complicated than what you might have overheard. I trust that we can keep this between us for now, and when I get back from London, let's please

The draft stopped there, unfinished.

Time stopped, and her feelings of deviousness vanished. Claire reread the message, experiencing the visceral sideswipe of her husband's deceit. Suddenly, every extended business trip, every late night at the office and early morning text from the previous year came into a new and disturbing focus. As did Michael's contempt over her transgression with Andrew. Carolyn had been right. He really was having an affair with this Taylor whom he claimed not to know, and Nicholas had found him out. Her gut was telling her this loudly and clearly, there was no denying the message. And she could neither stop herself nor drag herself away from the mess, like the truest of train wrecks. Clearly the marriage was over—evidently for longer than she'd imagined—but to ask their son to keep such a secret *and* to spend the last months punishing her without a hint of remorse? That was beyond hypocritical. Feeling as if she'd just polished off a fifth of vodka, Claire struggled to maintain her focus. *Sara Lee Clinton,* she whispered aloud until she managed to calm down and take a mental step back. *Sara Lee Clinton.* There was so much she didn't know. And knowledge was power.

She took a deep breath and typed "Janus" into the search box—just before the kitchen door slammed open with a sobering thud. Claire could hear either Berna or Michael in there. She glanced back at the screen and saw at least a dozen e-mails in the trash with the subject "Janus," many from Mac Kessler, and most marked urgent, but there was no time to read them. Her mind spun with questions as she quit Michael's e-mail and logged out so he would assume he'd left things inaccessible, as he normally did, the last time he'd sat in that chair. She was on autopilot, her only concern, getting out of there with no one noticing that she'd even been in the study. But as she stood, it hit her that she hadn't checked to see whether Michael might have sent a different version of his note to Nick, whether Nick had actually received any e-mails from his dad before his overdose. Flouting her nerves and better judgment, she typed Michael's password into the log-in prompt. The search would only take another second, and then she would bolt. But the prompt didn't accept Nicky's initials and lacrosse jersey number. She could hear the faucet turn on in the kitchen. Hastily, she reentered what had been Michael's password since Nick started at Andover. But again, the prompt just blinked back at her its silent but clear pronouncement that things were definitely not as they had once been. *You guilty, hypocritical bastard!* She grabbed the piece of paper she'd written Mac Kessler's name on and crumbled it into her pocket.

Peeking her head into Nick's darkened room, Claire listened to the reassuring cadence of his snoring. Berna—and not Michael—appeared in the hallway, much to her relief. The ironies seemed never-ending. "He's gone to sleep," she said protectively, before shutting the bedroom door and slipping past her.

She didn't remember the drive home or the number of times she washed her face before feeling the water on her skin, or taking off her wedding ring and listening to it drop to the bathroom floor and roll into a corner. And only later, upon waking from a sweat-filled dream and staring dead-eyed into the shadows, did she focus on the fact that she had no shot of getting back into Michael's new password-protected files.

CHAPTER 36

"This is unbelievable," Jackie said for the second time, repositioning herself on the couch next to Claire and covering the fringe on the cushion to protect it from the further unraveling her sister's busy hands were trying to inflict. Claire had gathered her support system to the apartment and, driven by an unhealthy amount of caffeine, relayed the previous night's events.

"Nothing surprises me anymore," Carolyn said. "Nuh—thing."

"This is crazy, right? How did I not know this was going on? And what the hell *else* is going on with this Kessler person?"

"Whatever it is, it's not kosher," Gail said, biting into a scone. "What are your instincts saying about all of the financial weirdness?"

Claire fiddled with a Kleenex, tying the tissue into several small knots. "Well, I called Neiman's accounting this morning. Are you ready for this? The account had been shut down not due to disuse, but for nonpayment of an old balance. They're sending it to collections." She looked at the group incredulously. "He leases a jet and we have a charitable trust. And the country club has put us on the shit list and our bills are going to collections? What the *hell?!*"

"Not good," Carolyn sniffed. "The market's bad, but this smells worse."

"All I can guess is that a couple of his deals didn't perform and he's distracted." Claire smirked and stared up at the ceiling, but the dam broke. "Because of his girlfriend, no doubt." The pain of it all was so surprising, so impressive in its heft that it might as well have been physical. "*Taylor's* obviously why he's refused to try to work through our issues, why he was so cut and dried in his decision to separate." She looked from Jackie's grim face to the jaded expressions of her two friends. And as her thoughts careered toward illumination, anger displaced the sadness in her eyes. "Oh my God," she said after a long moment.

"What is it?" Jackie asked.

"What if he's had one foot out the door for . . . however long, and I provided him with the 'convenient' excuse? *I* had the affair. *I* practically killed our son. He's trying to put the failure of our marriage all on me so he can slither out of whatever mess he's made, and into the comforting arms of his girlfriend without blame," Claire said, pulling the tissue knots until they flayed under the pressure and fell like snowflakes into her lap. "Introduce her around as his new companion after the dust settles, and who would possibly blame him?"

"Double fucker," Gail said. "Seriously."

"How could I have been so stupid?"

"Claire, what if that e-mail wasn't referring to an affair?" Jackie intoned in her voice of reason. "Not that I'm trying to protect Michael, because this is monstrous. But what if it was something else?"

"Yeah, well," Carolyn said, sounding all too familiar with the self-protective naïveté of deflecting uncomfortable realities with vague possibilities. "There's far too much smoke for there not to be a fire smoldering somewhere."

"Little white lies, hon," Gail reminded her.

But Claire didn't need reminding. Not this time.

Jackie nodded with a sad groan of acceptance.

"My question, sweetie, is what you plan to do with this knowledge?" Carolyn asked, handing her a glass of ice water.

"I'm going over to the house tonight and I'm going to confront him," she said, the water swishing over the rim of the glass as she gestured with mounting intensity. "I'm going to see what the bastard has to say about all this. And then I'm going to—"

"Whoa, time out, hon. I was hurt, clueless and divorced at twenty-four, and I'm not going to let you make the same mistakes I did during my first rodeo. Have you called Jack yet?"

Claire nodded, composing herself. "I'd almost forgotten. I have an appointment this afternoon. But now I'm not sure of the best way to handle all of this, given these new developments. Do I file for divorce immediately and get the lawyers to sort out whatever is going on with this potentially *serious* Janus issue and all the unpaid bills?" She stood and began pacing, pinching the ache between her eyebrows. "I totally blew it by not printing out those files. I just got so sidetracked and—"

"No," Gail responded, looking as if she were about to dine out on Michael's insides. "Have your preliminary meeting with Jack. Give him his retainer and get him up to speed. And then you're going to do a little Sherlocking before you confront Michael with anything."

Claire's expression was drained of everything except skepticism and misery.

"Hold on," Carolyn said. "She needs to digest this first, take a little breather and get her head screwed back into place. It's going to take more than a new scarf and a competent lawyer to clear things up." Carolyn walked Claire back to the couch and sat her down. "A little away time will keep you from a drape-drawn retreat into bed for a week. *Believe* me."

"She's right," Jackie said. "Go away for a day and channel your energy. You need to come to grips with your own emotions before unleashing them on Michael."

Gail seemed to weigh the options. "Fair enough. Go marinate in some fabulous spa for twenty-four hours. That boutique hotel near Beaver Creek would be perfect. And then when you get back to Denver, you're going to get back into that computer. Something's up, and you need to know what's going on in order to plan your next move."

Claire shook her head. "I can't. I had that one shot when Michael apparently forgot to log out—which he *never* does. It was like there was an angel on my shoulder guiding me to the computer. But unless she comes back and whispers his new password to me, I'm screwed. And isn't that illegal, by the way?"

"Illegal? This is your house and your computer, too, Claire. And if you just happen to stumble onto some information there, then I'm sure Michael will be more than happy to negotiate fairly with you." Gail raised her eyebrows in a mother-knows-best ending to the conversation.

"But I'm still locked out of his desktop without the password."

Claire walked down the portrait-lined corridor to Jack Kaufman's office, willing herself to maintain her fight, and not turn around and head straight for the spa.

"Please, come in," Jack said, stepping into the hallway and reaching a welcoming hand to her just as she had stopped to gather her wits.

"I nearly ran away," she said as he ushered her into his sleek office and offered her a chair. "But Gail thinks the world of you." Claire scanned the well-appointed space, focusing a trained eye on the handwritten lyrics to Bob Dylan's "The Times They Are A-Changin'," which were beautifully framed and hanging above Jack's desk. Her nerves relaxed slightly. The manuscript had probably cost him in the neighborhood of a quarter million at auction. And she wondered how much of that her pal had helped fund. "So here I am. And I thank you for getting me in on such short notice."

"I'm always happy to meet any friend of Gail Harrold," he said, sitting below Dylan's poetic rallying cry and pulling a Montblanc pen from his pocket. "So, how can I help you?" he asked with a kind smile.

Her mind reverted to Michael's computer screen, to Andrew, and once again her ability to speak in coherent sentences all went *pftt.* She tried to start at the beginning, or what she thought was the beginning, but the story kept going farther back in time than the night at The Palm. And the more she strove to organize the story of her marriage and its disintegration, the more disorganized everything sounded. It was like trying to paint a scene from memory, struggling with recreating the exact hues and expressions, only to find that it had never really existed, at least not as she had remembered it. So Jack asked her pointed questions, and slowly she was able to piece it back to life. When finally it was out there in all its blackness and devoid of any stardust, Claire numbly asked what needed to happen next.

"I would not have advised you to move out of the house," he said, running a hand through his wavy hair. A silver wedding band disappeared into the gray at his temples and reappeared against the darker patches at the top. "But what's done is done and we'll work around that. Do you anticipate a custody fight?"

The question threw her. She couldn't imagine Michael going that route. He hadn't been unfair about her time with Nicholas so far. "No, I don't think he would do that. He understands the importance of consistency from both of us for Nicky."

"Well, divorce brings out surprising sides to people, Claire. You need to be prepared for the unexpected."

"Can he fight for sole custody?"

"Judges strive to put the best interests of the minor first, which is typically time with both parents. Assuming there aren't any drug or alcohol issues?"

"No." But a more frightening possibility suddenly hit her. "Could he say that I'm unfit because I, um, allowed Andrew into the house with the cocaine?"

"We'd have a pretty good argument against that, so let's not get ahead of ourselves. What I do advise for now is that we file the divorce petition. I want you to get copies of your financial documents, including bank and brokerage account statements, credit card bills, home loan papers, etc. . . ."

"We don't have a mortgage," Claire said as she fiercely took notes, shoving aside any thought that Michael would try to take custody. She knew he couldn't manage caring for Nicholas without her, nor could she fathom him being that cruel. With one glaring exception, she had always been an excellent parent.

"My paralegal will give you a list. You can take some time to digest everything we've discussed and to gather this information, along with the other information you said you needed to get from your home. But we need to get this done soon in order to establish a clear mark in time of the marital breakdown. The longer we delay, the more time Michael will have to potentially hide or transfer assets, or even run up debt. Did you have a prenup?"

"Yes, but it just covered Michael's trust from his family and future inheritances, which he gets exclusively. He also gets to keep all of his premarriage assets, and I keep mine. I have no problem with the document."

"I'll need a copy of that as well. And I definitely don't like what I'm hearing about unpaid bills and mysterious calls for information. It may be nothing, but I don't think that's what you believe, and in my experience, your first instincts are generally right. We'll get to the bottom of it in discovery, but the more information you can gather in the next three or four days before he knows we're filing, the better."

"I can't believe it's come down to this," she said, looking up from her notepad and feeling parched and lightheaded. "I just never imagined I'd be serving him papers."

"No one ever does when they're saying 'I do,' Claire. But by us filing first, and not Michael, you're going to be demonstrating to him and his team your resourcefulness and determination to get this resolved. On our terms."

She nodded weakly.

Jack finished with the finer points of the divorce process, along with his retainer and other fees, and told Claire that the petition would be prepared and ready to be served to Michael just as soon as she gave him the go-ahead. He took her shoulders in his hands and gave her a gentle, reassuring squeeze. "You're in good hands, Claire."

"Thank you."

"And I'll hold your check for the retainer until after we serve him, so as not to raise any red flags."

"It's from my own account, so no worries."

Claire emerged from Jack's office building and into the bustling parking lot. The glare from the afternoon sun reflected off the eighteen stories of mirrored facade, causing her to wince. She groped for her sunglasses in her quilted leather bag, and hid behind their comforting shelter. In her rattled state she had forgotten where she'd parked her car; she scanned the shiny rows of four-wheel drives and Lexuses, searching for a sign of something familiar. A bicycle courier jumped the curb in front of her and the whoosh of cool air danced over her cheeks. A blond man in an expensive pinstriped suit set the remote alarm to his Mercedes as he moved toward the building entrance. His hair was slicked back with gel in the same fashion Michael wore his. The high-pitched beep of another alarm turned Claire's attention to a younger man. He, too, bore a striking resemblance to Michael, and walked alongside a woman with gorgeous auburn curls. Then another look-alike. The terrible Fellini-esque fantasy closed in on her and she felt her stomach swirl up into her skull.

She hurried up and down rows, searching for the Jeep. When it appeared just a few cars away, she scrambled inside and turned on the ignition. The chill inside was bracing, and she exhaled a cloud of breath as she reached for her cell phone and dialed information. She couldn't escape this town, the proximity of Michael, soon enough.

CHAPTER 37

The mountain hotel was quaint and welcoming with its whimsical eaves and blue-striped awnings. Claire barely recalled the drive, but there she was, mired in fresh turmoil, handing her bag to the bellman and giving herself over, body and soul, to this place of rejuvenation. She hoped it would help.

She checked in and confirmed an appointment for a massage at six o'clock. That left her a little over an hour to relax, but she knew that her mind would not allow her any peace when it was too busy obsessing over what Taylor looked like, and how Michael could have been such a snake. So she put on her favorite 2004 Bolder Boulder 10K T-shirt and, running her fingers over the faded lettering on the shirt, remembered how lovely life had seemed then. Nicholas hadn't yet gotten sick and Michael probably hadn't started cheating on her. As far as she knew. She headed for the gym before the memory sucked her will away. Maybe if she ran long and fast enough, she might find herself in a place with a better view.

After three miles in under thirty minutes, Claire entered the ladies' changing area of the spa, where a young woman gave her a silk-lined terry bathrobe, slippers, and a key. She glanced around the softly lit room where women lolled in nearby hot tubs and uniformed staff delivered herbal teas to the guests as they lingered in this relaxing cocoon. How good it was to be there, she reminded herself, to be shielded, if only temporarily, from the detonation of any more bombs.

The scent of eucalyptus drifted from the steam room across from Claire's locker. She stepped in and the door sealed behind her like a vacuum. Adjusting to the dim light, Claire saw that she was alone in the fog. No unwelcome chitchat, no examining eyes. She laid a towel down on the marble tiled bench, stretched her naked body out along its length, and closed her eyes. But within seconds, unbidden and unwelcome, the vibrancy of distant memories snuck up on her and she saw herself with Michael in the steam room of the Georges V in Paris for their honeymoon, drunk on champagne and making fast, silent love on the slick marble. It was so powerful, this Proustian sensorial moment, that Claire tried to physically expel it. She coughed forcefully and waited for the steam to do its detoxifying best and rid her of the sensation. *Bastard,* came the familiar refrain. Why had she chosen someone with such an inability to be forthcoming and at ease with his life, and her? The fog grew denser. Ten minutes crawled by, and she felt about as soothed as she was going to get.

After showering, she curled into a plush chair in the waiting area, feeling more mired than ever in the noxious soup of anxiety about the future and, now, her husband's extracurriculars. A man called her name softly. Claire looked up through heavy eyes to see a uniformed therapist with dark hair and a sincere face. He greeted her and led her down a moss-colored hallway to her treatment room, where he left her to undress. The room was warm and smelled of vanilla and hot cider. Letting her robe fall to the floor, Claire climbed onto the massage table and covered herself with the sheet.

A moment later a knock came at the door and the massage therapist returned. He dimmed the lights and asked if she had any areas that needed extra attention.

"My psyche," she replied. Catching his raised eyebrows, she tried to steer things back to a more impersonal level. "My neck and shoulders. I tend to carry my stress there. And I've got a bit of a sinus headache as well."

He gently rearranged Claire's hair off of her forehead and neck. "Let's see what we can do to get rid of all this stress." He stood behind her and cupped her head in one palm, and, alternating between firm strokes from her shoulder to her temples and gentle acupressure on her ears and scalp, he began to free the pressure behind her eyes. His fingers and knuckles expertly unleashing endorphins, his hands releasing tightly wound knots. "Just close your eyes and try to relax." Her breath slowed to the pace of his strokes, and Claire focused on the healing energy she felt in his touch. He moved on to her neck, kneading with his elbow and forearm. There was something special about the way he gripped her skin and muscles, so knowing and intense, and yet completely nonthreatening. She drifted into a welcome state of calm as a knot at the base of her neck seemed to unclench like a baby's fist.

He entwined her fingers with his own, and raising her hand upward, massaged her palm, her arm, her armpits. Her flesh prickled as he moved along the side of her rib cage and breast. When he lifted her other arm, she could feel his breath on her skin, could sense his proximity and energy. She let her arm go limp under the strength of his grasp, allowing herself to drift, weightless. And all the anguish she'd been holding on to began to recede. He placed a folded towel over her breasts and slowly inched the massage sheet down so that her stomach was exposed to her hips. The sliding motion of the crisp linen across her torso and the nubbiness of the towel caused her nipples to harden. His fingers touched down on her belly, and her muscles contracted. But he massaged her stomach in a soothing circular motion, causing more layers of tension to evaporate like a fine mist.

Pinning one hand over the sheet on her left hip, he uncovered her left leg with his free hand and tucked the sheet under the length of her right thigh. In shielding her nakedness, he grazed a hair from her untended bikini wax, sending a shiver through her. The alternating sensations of relaxation and stimulation were surprisingly arousing. She pretended she was someone for whom reminders about appropriateness were not legion and ingrained, and further melted into the fantasy that life was wonderful and steady, heartbreak-free. He began massaging the balls of her feet, then the arches, all the right pressure points, slowly and thoroughly.

As Claire reached a new level of surrender, he raised her leg perpendicular to her torso, and with a firm, deep grip worked each muscle group up to her buttocks. He moved to the side of the table and placed her ankle on his shoulder so that her legs rotated away from each other. The cool draft she felt whisk between her legs was in dramatic contrast to the heat she'd felt emanating there just seconds before. And instead of feeling vulnerable in this position, Claire reveled in the liberating freedom of the moment. She let her lips part, wetting them with her tongue. Her body grew warmer and she didn't care that her breathing was perceptible and quick. Gently, the therapist placed her leg back on the table and cloaked it under the sheet.

When he uncovered her right leg, he didn't tuck the sheet under her other thigh as he had done before. Instead he immediately set to work massaging the acupuncture meridians of her feet, then moved slowly upward with long, deliberate strokes. Calf, quadricep, hamstring all releasing. Her skin became one large exposed nerve, charged by the slightest contact. When he lifted her body to reach under her buttocks, his hand lingered for a second, and then worked its way around to her inner thigh. This time he must have felt her growing wetness, heard her soft moan, and he allowed his fingers to wander and explore as she let her knees fall open. And with that tacit permission, the sheet cascaded to the floor where the towel that had covered her breasts already lay.

Claire floated naked in a quiet ecstasy, wondering through closed eyelids what name it was she'd seen embroidered on his polo shirt. But the only name that came to mind, inexplicably, was Richard's. She squeezed her eyes tighter and focused on the improbable thing that was happening to her. He ran his hand down her leg again and then, almost teasingly, stroked her from her ankle back to where she, just as improbably, desired his touch the most. His fingers became Richard's fingers, moving rhythmically around, and then inside her. Faster and more powerfully he stroked her, and she responded with appreciative gasps. She tried to shut out the image of her friend's face and her shocking fantasy. But this man had found her buttons, her cadence. And there, in that room, next to other rooms where facials and sports massages were being given, he brought her to an astounding orgasm. At the height of her climax, she let out a transcendent sigh of satisfaction or, more likely, payback—but most definitely release. After it was over, Claire lay there in the soft light, her forty-three-year-old body and spirit utterly exposed before this intimate stranger. Tears rolled from the corners of her eyes as she exhaled.

"Are you okay?" the therapist asked her after a moment. His voice was kind and gentle, and he rested his hand on her thigh.

Claire kept her eyes closed. "Yes."

Before the moment could become awkward, he asked if she would like to finish the massage on her stomach. She nodded and rolled over, her body still trembling, her brain still playing catch-up with reality. He covered her below her waist with the sheet and began to work on her shoulders. Safe from possible eye contact, Claire finally allowed her eyes to open and look down through the face cradle of the table. He wore white leather tennis shoes and white cotton pants. And a very noticeable erection.

"You know," he said, "you had a black energy field around your head when you first came in. But now your chakra's a beautiful shade of red." She could hear the smile in his voice. "I think you have a very colorful aura when you allow it to shine through."

"Oh," was all she could say. She had no idea how to respond to such New Age earnestness. But in a bizarre way she felt understood by this man, seen. Unblocked. And if he could distinguish colors around her body, then maybe he had helped, strange as it seemed, to strip away some of the layers that had been suffocating her. As Richard had with all of his prescient advice and dependability. "Thank you," she whispered through the hole.

He pulled the sheet up over her shoulders. Claire cleared her throat, swallowing pieces of her disbelief. And when she inhaled, a sense of serenity swathed her.

"I hope you're feeling better now." He ran his fingertips up the length of her body through the sheet. "How are those sinuses?"

"Um, better, thank you."

"I'm glad I could help. I'll leave you to dress and meet you outside." The door clicked shut.

Claire found it difficult to move. Her legs felt like spaghetti, freshly boiled and buttered. She gripped the side of the table to steady herself as she stepped down, laughing at the inconceivability of the whole situation. How would she face him out there? There were no signposts, no protocol. Stunned and still flushed by her unexpected submission, she put on her robe and slippers, and inched out into the hallway where he was waiting for her.

She stepped past him and hesitated, then turned and inclined her head in a gesture of thanks. And again he rescued the moment from silence. Placing his palms together in the sign of prayer, he bowed to Claire, and uttered three words that took her by surprise. "God bless you."

Claire smiled in his direction, and walked away. "No, God bless you," she said to the walls. She felt his gaze on her as she headed to the locker room, but she never looked back, never caught his name.

As the hot water of the shower washed over her, she reached between her legs to touch the traces of her arousal, and she wondered: Did all his female clients receive this treatment? Or just the obviously tormented, black-energied ones? And how did he know she would respond to him so positively? Perhaps she was just special. Claire laughed to herself again, still incredulous, but sensing that he, like Richard, had been placed on her path for a reason. She dried off and checked the mirror for a red halo. What she saw was a sense of relief.

At the spa reception desk she signed the tab for her massage, leaving a fifty percent gratuity.

CHAPTER 38

The next morning, Claire called Ray on her way down from the mountains to check on Nick's schedule for the rest of the day. And there was another matter she could use his help with, she'd mentioned, testing the limits of his willingness to oblige. To her relief, Ray responded with a cheerful *how can I help?* So as nonchalantly as possible, she asked him about the timing of Berna's trips to the grocery store. He told Claire that Berna was putting together Costco and Whole Foods lists for later that afternoon. "She likes to watch *The Doctors,* which is over at two," he'd added.

"You're the best, Ray. I'll come by when you and Nick get back from Craig," she said, running her hastily cobbled plan through her head again, and thinking she might just have a shot at success.

"Well, before you fall in love with me, I need to talk to you about our field trip to the mall earlier."

He proceeded to explain that Nick did fine finding his way to the food court, that his eye contact with the cashier was appropriate, but that he got confused counting out his money to pay for his food, which resulted in a minor outburst. Snow had begun to fall on I-70, and Claire watched for black ice as Ray continued with the short list of Nick's other failed tasks.

"This is not to say that he won't be able to accomplish these things," he added. "We just need to help him build more self-awareness and compensation strategies. I can talk to his team at Craig about this if you'd like."

"Yes. Please," she said. "How frustrated is he?"

"He wasn't very happy with me, but he didn't tell me to take a hike when we got back to the car. Which was nice."

"So you're probably saying we should give up on the idea of college for next year?"

Ray paused before responding. "I still think we need to help Nick readjust some of his goals for the short term."

Claire understood that Ray was also referring to her own goals for Nicky, and Michael's. And she knew that the longer it took for him to feel comfortable with simple tasks, the longer he would put off reconnecting with his friends. Which scared her even more. With everything else about to get less predictable, she had held on to the hope that Nicky would find comfort in his progress, and eventually his friends.

"Do you think bringing in a tutor is a good or bad idea? I've made some preliminary calls, but Michael wasn't impressed with their philosophies. Not aggressive enough."

"I think the right tutor could really help Nick. I know a great woman who works with TBI patients and has had success in helping some kids mainstream."

A knifing wind kicked up on Vail Pass, and Claire finished the call and gave the road her full attention. Which required more effort than usual, given the latest developments. Who else, she wondered, could possibly be going from learning her husband was a deceitful miscreant, to a much-needed (as it turned out) "release" at the hands of a stranger, to the commencement of a domestic espionage operation in the course of two days? The evolving etiquette of her circumstances was getting harder to keep up with by the hour.

Claire idled on the street outside the house, waiting for Ray and Nick to return from his art therapy class, her shoulders inching up her neck as she began to second-guess the whole caper. At

1:30 Claire saw them turn the corner onto the street, and she drove through the gates just ahead of Ray's Honda.

"Hi, Nicky," Claire said as she watched her son get out of the driver's side. "Did you drive all the way from Craig?" She looked quizzically at Ray.

"Yeah. We practiced a bunch this morning. They let me . . . participate in the driving clinic. And then Ray let me drive home." Nick wore a broad grin.

"He did a very nice job. Smooth as silk. We took side streets mostly," Ray said with a thumbs-up.

"Wow, Nicky!"

"It was sweet." Nick handed her a folder and ambled toward the house. "Bathroom," he said, by way of explanation.

Claire opened the folder to find three charcoal drawings. They were all architectural, with precise lines and angles. She could see several jags where his hand must have seized, but the overall quality was excellent, and completely different in style from the interpretive landscapes he'd favored before the accident. "So, he liked the class?"

"He didn't want to leave," Ray responded. "I think he'd been nervous all this time about his abilities."

"These are great. Totally unlike what he used to draw, though."

"That happens. Maybe he's approaching things with new eyes."

Claire stopped to consider this, liking the possibility from all viewpoints. After a distracted moment, she noticed the rear of Berna's station wagon jutting out from the open garage. "Listen, Ray," she said, snapping back to the situation at hand. "I'm hoping Berna's still on schedule to go to Costco?"

"Let's go and find out." He started walking toward the garage.

"If she's still leaving around two-ish, maybe you and Nick could go to the park for some exercise just after that?" Her palms began to sweat and she shoved them into her pockets. "There's a, um, situation that I need to get sorted out, and I could use a little privacy here," she said hopefully.

"Come on," he said.

Claire followed him into the kitchen, where Berna was eating a sandwich in front of the TV. The plastic surgeon from *The Doc-*

tors was discussing a new varicose vein procedure, and she didn't seem to notice them walk in.

"Excuse me, Berna?" Ray said.

She looked up at both of them, and Claire busied herself examining Nick's sketches. Berna carried her plate to the sink. "Can I help you with something?" she responded. Her voice was softer than Claire had remembered it, less severe.

"If you're still going to Costco today, there are a couple things that Nick could use. Can I jot them down for you later?"

She picked up a notepad with a long list already penciled in, and handed it to him. "I'm leaving in fifteen minutes."

"There's no one better than you, Miss B," he said with a wink. Berna gave him a satisfied nod, and he wrote down a couple items before pausing. "You know, they may not have the resistance bands we need at Costco," Ray said, scratching his chin. "If you don't find them there, Sports Authority would definitely carry them. I've written down the exact brand and specifications."

Berna furrowed her brow, ready, it seemed, to balk.

"We've got some evaluations we need to work on this afternoon, and then I promised Mr. Montgomery I'd show him some new exercises with the bands tonight for Nick."

"And you know how disappointed Mr. Montgomery would be if he didn't have the proper equipment," Claire added, crossing her arms across her chest with a commanding smile.

Berna grabbed the list from Ray and walked into the pantry. Claire watched her scan the shelves—either in an effort to see what other items she might have missed on her list or, more likely, to avoid acknowledging her. Claire stepped in behind Berna's thick frame, close enough to smell her no-nonsense antiseptic scent. "You know," she said, picking up a bottle of mustard just out of Berna's reach, "it might be a great exercise for Nick to help you organize all of the soups and sundries in here when you return."

Berna looked over her shoulder, and Claire could see the woman's annoyance fighting a reasonable facsimile of anticipation.

* * *

When the house was finally empty, Claire sat down in front of the computer in the study and pushed up the sleeves of her sweater. *Okay, Sara Lee, let's go.* She hit the space bar on the keyboard and held her breath. The login and password prompts appeared on the screen. She looked for a password hint, but there was none. Unfortunate, but not unexpected. In the past when she'd rolled her eyes at what she'd deemed unwarranted home security protocols, it never occurred to her that they were there to protect more than sensitive investment data. She ran through her hastily scribbled list of likely passwords. She tried "Nicholas" and all variations of his name in combination with other significant numbers and dates, but the obvious, as she suspected, were clearly all too obvious. She searched through the drawers of the desk, checking for sticky notes or other papers that might bear some clue. But the perfectly organized drawers revealed nothing, and Claire racked her brain for the umpteenth time for names or songs or movie titles Michael might have chosen. Scanning the room, she looked for signs in their collected books, photos, and artwork; each failed guess serving only to substantiate her husband's inscrutability. After a handful more of what seemed like clever stabs—Michael's eating club at Princeton, dorms at Andover— her early, albeit meager optimism over her ability to carry out her Operation Mikey-Leaks plan was skidding toward oblivion.

She glanced at her watch and estimated that she had just over an hour left to crack the password and copy the files onto her freshly purchased external drive—no small feat, she fretted, for a neophyte hacker. She opened the French doors to the backyard to hear for any cars pulling up around the front of the house. All was quiet, the breeze from the garden, chilly and damp. And she sensed that the snow would be in Denver soon. Impulsively she grabbed her phone from her purse and Googled "password recovery software." A host of options appeared, all of which would take longer than she had hoped or planned. But she was swinging blindly at a piñata, and getting nothing but air.

As Claire read through the instructions of what looked to be the easiest recovery tool, the possibility that she might disrupt something on the computer, or worse yet, lose data, gave her pause. She sat down and leaned back into the chair, pondering other options. Maybe she could find an IT expert—someone hungry enough to sneak into the house with her under some yet to be determined cover, and hack into the files—which seemed about as practical as any of her present alternatives. She stared at the walls, reminding herself that the whole scheme had been fanciful at best, while still hoping for some kind of illumination.

And by some miracle, she found it. The dial of the antique radio console near the door glowed orange in the waning light of the room, and her thoughts veered to the old-time radio comedy spoof Michael and Nick used to listen to. Something about a private eye. They had loved that show, and imitated the characters and their gumshoe vernacular over the years with howl-inducing accents and embellishments.

The title of the program escaped her, but there was a provocatively named woman—the PI's assistant—whom they just couldn't get enough of and had joked about incessantly. Like Pussy Galore, only with an M. *Margie something? Margie Boobofsky?* She typed both names into the prompt, separately and together. No dice. It was a long shot, she knew, but she tried different spellings, hoping she might be onto something. Still no luck. She tried every M stage name she could think of. *Mercedes, Melon, Maxi,* feeding the monikers into the computer like quarters into a slot machine. And then, amid the reels of misses, it hit her. *Moxie. Moxie Bubofski.* She could hear Michael and Nicky taunting each other with, "I'm looking for Miss Bubofski, Miss Moxie Bubofski." She laughed out loud at the idiocy of men and their obsessions with elementary-school boob humor, as she typed *Moxie* into the login prompt, and watched with astonishment as the screen opened up to her. *Jackpot,* she whispered.

Delighted with her own moxie, she plugged her USB drive into the computer and began the process of copying the hard drive, just as the technician at the computer store had instructed. The room dimmed further as a pall of clouds obscured the sun from the patio. Claire pulled her sweater tight across her chest and said a silent prayer to the gods of good timing as the progress indicator marked the early stages of the transmission. The threat of Berna returning early or, God forbid, Michael, toyed briefly with her composure. But she was feeling the adrenaline rush of the spy game, and felt confident that all would pan out with just a little patience. The insane hailstorm that was her life had suddenly taken on a thrilling twist. She pictured herself later that night with the copied hard drive plugged into Gail's laptop, exposing the mysteries of her husband, and instead of feeling dread at the prospect of more shattered images, Claire felt a sense of power. An intense, internal strength born of all the wreckage, and additionally fueled by the possibility of finally gaining the upper hand. Of finally taking a stand. She perked her ears and listened for cars, voices, or footsteps, and heard only the murmur and hum of the computer spilling its secrets.

After plumping all the pillows in the room and flipping through old *W Magazine*s and *Vanity Fair*s, Claire gave in to her mounting impatience, deciding there was no point in waiting any longer to get to the bottom of those secrets. She opened Michael's e-mail and began a search for all the correspondence relating to Janus. Her hands shook as she typed, and she felt the same clamminess and nausea that had overcome her the last time she'd peered through those particular curtains. She hit the return button. But nothing appeared. Hastily she searched his sent box, his drafts, and then the trash. Her jaw tensed. She typed in "Mac Kessler." And again, no e-mails surfaced. Everything she had glimpsed the other day was . . . gone. Vanished. Her heart sank. She clicked around the toolbar in a panicked search for answers, only to discover that the trash had recently been emptied. And was not recoverable.

With that bit of housekeeping brought to light, Claire knew there was no simple explanation for Mac Kessler or Janus. Or the country club bill, or Neiman's. Operation Mikey-Leaks was turning out to be more like Mission Impossible. But there had to be other important details left in there, she thought, something the data transfer actually *was* capturing. Snow had begun to fall from the leaden sky, and she stepped outside and listened to its lonely whisper, convincing herself that there had to be a few more lulus left on the hard drive, because that's just how things were going in her world. She stretched her arms and shoulders wide, half in anticipation of what new bombshells awaited.

Back inside, Claire checked her own e-mails on her phone. Amid alerts from Barnes & Noble, *The Post,* and Bergdorf, there was a message from Richard. Her posture softened at the sight of his name, while her cheeks heated up. She did not allow her brain to wander back to the spa.

Smitty—skiing Vail next week with some of my old paper buddies, and coming through Denver Monday. Lunch, noonish?

With the impending cache of new reading material, in addition to all of the documents she needed to sort through for Jack, the timing wasn't ideal. On the other hand, she had no doubt she would be in the advice market again by then.

Sure, she typed. *Things have gotten a little thorny here. I may need some more of your expert counsel. Call me when you land.*

She pushed send, and pulled open the file drawer in the desk. Michael kept both of their brokerage account statements at his office, along with all documents relating to the house and insurance policies. But she thumbed through the files and grabbed those for their joint Amex card, her Visa card, and her own bank account. And after some digging, she also found the old attorney file with their prenup. The rest, Michael would have to provide to the attorneys.

Claire slipped the files into her bag, and as she closed the French doors there was the sound of crunching gravel from the driveway. She prayed it was Ray. But he always parked in the porte cochere, and she couldn't see his car there from the patio. She raced back to the computer, where the progress indicator showed about four more minutes to completion. And she was not about to acknowledge defeat, not after venturing this far across the line. There would be no second chance. She tidied up the desk, pushed Michael's chair back into place and slung her bag over her shoulder, prepared to sprint the second the transfer was done. The kitchen door opened with the same noisy bang against the wall from the other night. *The woman has no respect for hand-troweled wall finishes,* Claire thought as she circled the desk impatiently and counted down the time. She couldn't afford for Berna to find her in the house with Ray and Nicky gone.

"Halloo?" Berna's yodel echoed in the hallway. Claire was almost certain she could hear her sensible shoes squeaking on the kitchen floor.

After another tidying pass around the desk and two failed attempts at a hair knot, the indicator flashed that the job was complete. Claire popped the flash drive out of the port and into her bag and logged out, before closing the French doors behind her and disappearing into the gathering white.

"Oh, hello, Berna," Claire said, surprising the housekeeper from behind as she was unloading the groceries from her car in the garage.

Berna spun around. "Where did you come from? I saw your Jeep and—"

"I just love walking in the snow, so I did a nice loop around the neighborhood," Claire said, wiping the dampness from her hair. "Looks like you could use a little help with the bags." She took the smallest bag from the hatch and marched past Berna and into her kitchen, where she put the kettle on to boil.

A few minutes later, Nick breezed through the mudroom door and threw his parka and hat onto the chair next to where Claire was sipping her tea. "It's freezing out there and this guy's . . . making me do the . . . climbing bars at the park."

"But you did great, *and* you got to drive, didn't you?"

Nick nodded and took out his glucose monitor.

"I'm proud of you, Nicky," Claire said, kissing a cold ear.

Nick rubbed his hands together and pricked his finger, placing a small droplet of blood onto the test strip. Claire watched him. Only two months before, he didn't have the dexterity to manage this on his own.

Berna brought in the last of the groceries and the therapy bands, and announced to Nick that she had a pantry project for him. The cozy group nodded then resumed their business, at which point the visibly miffed housekeeper made herself scarce.

"How 'bout some sugar-free hot chocolate?" Claire asked with a satisfied grin.

"I'm low. I get the real stuff."

"How low? Let me get you some juice before—"

Ray inserted himself between Claire and the refrigerator. "What do *you* need to do, bro?" he asked Nick.

Nick got a bottle of orange juice and was able to unscrew the top, pour himself a glass, and drink it down before the shakes set in. "I'm good," he said after a second glassful.

And Claire felt even more grateful for Ray and all that he, as a nonparent, could push Nick to do without the usual pushback. She mouthed a silent thank-you to him as she spread Nick's sketches out on the breakfast table. "So, I love these sketches, Nicky. The detail work is fantastic."

"They're cool, I guess."

"What do you think about your new art class?"

He didn't look her in the eye or answer, and instead ran his fingers over the drawings, back and forth, tracing the figures. It was hard to gauge his emotions, so Claire just waited. One of the building's columns smudged under his finger, and when Nick noticed what he'd done, he abruptly swept all of the sketches onto the floor with the back of his hand. His face reddened and he kicked the leg of the table. "Damn it," he shouted, kicking twice more. "I'm retarded. Everything was fine before, but now . . . I'm retarded." His body shook as he repeated the phrase, seemingly powerless against the siren song of what had been. "I don't know . . . why this happened," he cried, tearing the drawings with the heels of his boot, "but I can't . . . do anything now."

Ray helped restrain Nick's thrashing arms and got him into one of the chairs while Claire reminded him that the smudge was a simple mistake, and that he could do some more sketches with pencil, if he preferred, and that he was doing beautiful work. And that there was nothing retarded about him. The teakettle started to boil again, its piercing whistle heightening, and then ultimately diffusing, Nick's outburst. When he was done, he sat breathing heavily, clasping and unclasping his fingers.

"Sometimes it's hard when things don't go exactly the way we expect them," Ray said, kneeling in front of Nick. "But we learn to roll with that, right, man?"

Nicholas lowered his eyes.

"Do you want me to grab your art supplies?" Claire asked in a soothing voice. A strip of sunlight reflected off the snow through the picture window behind the breakfast table. "You could work on some more sketches in here."

"Whatever," he muttered.

"That's a great idea, Nick. How about getting your sketchpad from your room? You can do that, can't you?"

Nicholas grudgingly picked up the torn drawings from the floor and threw them into the trash, and sulked down the hall to his room.

"Is it ever not going to be like this?" Claire asked.

"Maybe," Ray answered. "But he's feeling disconnected right now. He's not living with people who struggle with the same things he does anymore, and my guess is that as much as he wants to be on his own and be out of the hospital setting, he misses that comfort zone and camaraderie."

"There's just no winning, is there? What do we do?"

"Exactly what we're doing. We keep promoting his independence through classes and activities outside of class. We provide him with opportunities to be successful. And we don't let him sink into depression or the lure of the past, if we can help it."

"Piece of cake," she said, tossing that challenge in with all of the other hurdles on the horizon, and wondering how shatterproof she and Nick really were.

Ray handed her a piece of paper. "Here's Andrea's info. The tutor I mentioned."

Claire forced a smile and took the note. "I'll set up a meeting. And maybe you could casually float the idea to Michael? He's more receptive to suggestions when they come from professionals." She had no desire to debate Michael on the merits of a tutor over a college counselor. She could barely stomach the thought of sitting in the same room with him. She rubbed her hands along her jeans, recalling a painfully accurate comment about ex-husbands and cellulite being forever. Michael would be part of their future no matter how much she spent on lawyers and vanishing creams. And she would need to keep her composure through it all, for Nicky's sake.

Ray nodded and leaned in over the table and asked her in a low voice how everything had gone while he and Nick were at the park.

"It was one step forward," Claire said, just as Nicholas padded up the hall with his sketchpad. "How about a study of the Aspen trees in the yard?" she asked, while Nick set out his pencils on the breakfast table.

He sat down and stared out the window at the trees. After a few moments he began to draw. He wore an expression of intensity as he sketched, but there was a lightness, too, in the rhythm his hand took on. Claire watched him, her sometimes broken boy, transforming the blank pad with purpose and passion. He took his time with his rendering of proportion and detail, which were good by any standard. And when he stopped to assess his progress, Claire could see his satisfaction. It was as if in creating images, Nick was connecting to who he was, when nothing else was making sense in his world. The drawing was a likeness of Ray's car in front of the porte cochere, the naked branches of the tree bowing to the hood. "I'm liking this," he said softly, as he shaded the driveway.

Claire watched as he finished the sketch in silence, wishing she could save him the trouble of rose-tinting his memories of life before. Overcoming distorted perspectives was no easy task. That much she knew.

She dialed Andrea's office as she pulled out of the driveway, and left a message about Nick and her hope that they could meet.

CHAPTER 39

With the flash drive still warm and burning a proverbial hole, Claire got to work as soon as she returned to the apartment. She promised herself not to get sidetracked by Taylor—at least not after checking for any further correspondence from Michael to Nicholas about her. And when she couldn't find any, it came as a relief. He had been smart enough not to actually e-mail anything so incendiary. A piling-on of excuses and apologies from London about his mistress would only have made Nicky more miserable. Then again, she thought sadly, Nick had already been miserable enough to try and obliterate the memory of both of his parents' bad behavior with the cocaine. She sighed and redirected her search for any messages between her husband and his mystery woman. But Michael's meticulousness in covering up his duplicity only served to blunt Claire's pain, and kindle her indignation. Jackie was right. It would not be so difficult to put the past aside and put up the good fight. Lies crush love. Deceit eclipses nostalgia. Betrayal cuts deep. Rock, paper, scissors.

With Michael's e-mail trash emptied of Mac Kessler and Janus messages, Claire decided on a macro approach of looking through anything that didn't seem familiar, even if it took all night. She scanned messages about investment deals. There were requests for capital calls, questions from investors, valuations and numerous spreadsheets. The meaningless names and numbers bled together like an unfathomable abstract canvas—right up to the moment she found herself in messages from the previous July, and staring at an e-mail to Andrew Bricker. Seeing Andrew's name backlit and in bold was like a visual bucket of ice over her head. Claire took a second to catch her breath before opening it. It was a forwarded message that Michael had originally sent to a Jeff Sidon.

Jeff, I've had great respect for your firm over the years, but you should be aware that when discussing your HariMed deal out here in Denver, Andrew Bricker engaged in some extremely unprincipled activity which impacted my family. Given the sensitive nature of this, I would be willing to speak with you in more detail, but clearly I will not be investing in this deal, or in any future deals so long as Mr. Bricker is in Silverthorne Capital's employ. And it would be unfortunate for you to lose other investors and potential opportunities because you've chosen to retain someone of such questionable character.

She looked in Michael's inbox for a response. There was just one.

Michael, again please accept my sincerest apologies and best wishes for your son. You can rest assured that your concerns have been addressed and that our phone conversation will remain in confidence. I look forward to seeing you on your next trip to New York.

Claire stared at the screen and wondered if Andrew had felt helpless that morning, seeing his future snatched out from under him with the push of a send button. She knew he'd be un-hirable anywhere on the East Coast with a Montgomery blackball on his name. And she almost admired the tidiness of Michael's retribution, were it not for its inherent hypocrisy. He was hardly in a position to cast stones at anyone's character. But still, the thought that Andrew had been made to pay in some small way left Claire with a sense of satisfaction, bittersweet and petty though it was. In this horrible zero-sum game, was this the karma she had been looking for?

Closing her eyes and taking several moments to slow her hummingbird pulse, Claire returned to Michael's business files. Most of the LLC and partnership folders were names she recognized, though still nothing appeared for Janus. She skimmed financial statements and operating results. And while she couldn't make sense of *all* the numbers, what became increasingly clear was that nearly all of his real estate and green-tech venture deals had booked stunning losses in the last year. She went back to the e-mails associated with the biggest underperformers. One deal in particular, a condo development outside of San Diego, had inspired a large amount of angry investor communication over the last four months. Claire sat back in her chair reading through the messages and attempting to digest the big picture. Which, by her own inexperienced calculations, left Michael on the line for millions to salvage this one investment alone. And given the dreary state of the financials she'd scanned before, there were likely other deals in similarly bleak straits.

This wouldn't have been overly worrisome under normal circumstances. There would be enough cash somewhere to plug the dam until things turned around. But with the recession, it had been a rough year for even the most seasoned financiers, and Michael's investors looked to be especially hard hit by negative returns. Was there enough for Michael to cover their shortfalls, too? Claire speculated that Mac Kessler might be one of these desperate partners, looking for information that would provide the solution to whatever this Janus deal might be up against. But the fact that Michael had deleted those particular e-mails still troubled Claire. Had the golden boy lost his famous touch and credibility? And just what kind of alchemy was he practicing to get it back? She also began to wonder how deep the losses had hit them personally.

She made a pot of coffee, determined to understand what were still *her* finances, too, and what she might be facing. Forty-five minutes of fishing around, however, provided little further enlightenment, apart from the fact that there were indeed more deals underwater, and that Michael was short on life preservers. And then Claire stumbled across a QuickBooks icon buried in an applications folder. She opened the accounting program and took a sip of the coffee. Michael's personal and corporate bank account registers appeared, along with their brokerage account statements.

She scrolled back to the previous January in his personal check register and scanned the payments and deposits. Credit cards, insurance, utilities—all of these payments showed up with regularity, along with their other routine expenditures and charitable contributions. On the deposits side were occasional dividend checks and the monthly salary he took out of New Haven Investments, his holding company. She continued rolling slowly through the entries, the unremarkable numbers resuming their abstract blur, until she came across a five-hundred-and-thirty-thousand-dollar deposit from their Schwab account in June—half of which appeared to be transferred to New Haven that same month. She began taking notes on the curious details and figures. There were the monthly checks to her, but as she continued through the summer months, Claire also noticed Michael's salary deposits diminishing, until there were none at all for September forward, as well as smaller than normal credit card payments. She wiped her eyes and finished her coffee.

Pushing on, she located their online brokerage statements from Schwab, which revealed that she and Michael had taken a bigger hit in the market than she had realized. When they last discussed their portfolio over a year before, it was a discussion of "paper losses" and no real cause for concern given that most of the companies in their portfolio were long-term holds. But Michael apparently had other ideas come that June, and had cashed out two of their larger positions. Glancing at the clock, Claire tried to dispel a growing sense of foreboding. It was getting late, and her hope for straightforward answers was thinning.

Uneasily, she opened Michael's corporate ledger. There were tabs for each of his investment deals, in addition to checking and money market accounts for New Haven. The books looked bleak—very few deposits, and lots of money going out for payroll, overhead expenses, capital calls, and operating fees for his use of the plane (which in light of the circumstances seemed absurd, but inspiring confidence in his investors with the appearance of success was something on which she knew Michael placed a premium). There *were* a couple investment distributions in the first quarter, but then nothing until the Schwab transfer in June, which was practically depleted by early fall. *Jesus.* The business was running on fumes. The unpaid country club bill, the credit cards, Michael's volatility and visible stress—it was all starting to add up. Claire looked from her notes to the computer screen, feeling her nerves collide with a simmering headache. How the hell was he keeping it all afloat? And how was she going to come up with a clear game plan for her future when there was nothing clear about the game?

Scrolling down through the months, Claire found a vague answer to her first question. In September there was a deposit for two million dollars from Wells Fargo, followed by a "loan payment" of ten thousand dollars to Wells the next month. She slumped back in her chair, running scenarios through her head, and growing increasingly ambivalent about her cockeyed attempt at sleuthing. She worked the tightness in her forehead, reevaluating her commitment to the Gail Harrold school of marital detective work. The forensic accountants could sort through the disorder far more methodically, while sparing her the mind-game spiral. Maybe she should just tell Jack to serve the divorce papers and subpoena Michael's records, and officially move on with the business of moving on.

Claire dragged the mouse across the screen, fairly resigned to let the professionals handle things. But just as she was about to close out QuickBooks, the driving mystery behind the entire Mikey-Leaks operation practically leapt up and announced itself to her. She froze, staring at the first entry for the month of November—a deposit for 3.2 million dollars wired from Janus Capital. She swallowed slowly, and moved forward through the month. There was a 4.8-million-dollar check to the San Diego condo LLC, a two-hundred-thousand-dollar check to a Wincor Technologies, and another loan payment to Wells Fargo. She reread the information, feeling foolish for assuming that Janus had been some real estate deal, and clicked on various subheadings looking for a brokerage account statement from the investment firm. But there was none.

With her eyes burning and brain at capacity, Claire went into the bathroom and splashed cold water on her face, trying to recall any discussion of an account at Janus. But she knew *they* didn't have one. Had he been accumulating assets in a hidden account, as the Hamster Wheel book had warned? And why was this Mac person asking for information? The whole picture seemed even murkier than before. But what *was* imminently clear was that their extremely comfortable life had become a house of cards. And that Michael really couldn't be trusted. She pressed a hand towel to her face, exhausted by all that he had been hiding. A week ago she would have wondered if her involvement with Andrew had pushed Michael into silence about the state of their financial affairs. But Claire now understood that silence and secrecy had long been his true MO. She walked back into the kitchen and stared at the USB drive, thinking of crystal balls and all the inconvenient secrets they held.

"It's a mess, is what I'm saying. A huge, convoluted mess between the affair and the financial disarray. And what I really need right now is some distraction. Tell me something good, Mother. Please. I just want to turn my brain off until tomorrow." Claire lay in her bed fully aware of the irony that she was curled in the fetal position and looking to her mother for a few moments of grace.

"Okay." Cora paused before softly continuing. "Remember when you were a little girl and Daddy would take you out for malted milkshakes and hot dogs for breakfast on Sunday mornings?"

Claire warmed at the memory, missing her adventures with her father and the confidences she could always discuss with him.

"I got you all to myself during the week after Jackie was big enough for school, but I knew how special your weekend time was with him."

"I miss him so much." Claire closed her eyes remembering her father's strong hands wiping mustard from her chin, his upbeat voice suggesting a trip to the record store with the friend she'd accidentally angered.

"So do I, honey. And if Daddy were here, he'd do everything he could to help his little girl out of trouble, and to make that cheating BASTARD pay for what he's done." Cora's voice shook with anger and loud, clear regret.

"Mother, I don't believe I've ever heard you swear." Claire stretched her legs out under the covers and put her free hand on her belly, feeling it rise and fall.

"I just may call him worse," she seethed. "I can't even begin to comprehend why he would run around with some . . . *woman* when he had you."

Claire found a strange comfort in Cora's fury, while wondering just how much presence and comfort Taylor had provided her husband.

"And I certainly don't understand why, with all the money his family has, Michael's gotten himself into this financial pickle, whatever it is. Paul and Margot could give him a loan until everything gets—"

"Michael would never ask them for money." Claire reiterated the Montgomery philosophy of not spoiling the children with anything so gauche as cash or, God forbid, emotional support. And how, for the most part, it had worked beautifully. "All the boys have been wildly successful. Screwed up and dysfunctional, but very rich. I thought Michael had dodged that bullet, but apparently not."

"They'd always seemed like such lovely people."

"Well, they've been good to Nicholas. And to me, before the accident. Michael just preferred to keep some emotional distance. Goes back to the lack of cozy memories."

"Oh," Cora said softly.

"Paul would invest in his deals, but it was always business between the two of them. No friends-and-family favors. In fact, Paul is one of the investors on the San Diego deal I mentioned, and I suspect Michael's desperate to turn that one around for more than just the sake of his equity. There's nothing he loves more than sending daddy a nice fat profit check. A negative return would not go over well."

"So Michael's up against the wall and he's cashing out everything you have to salvage his deals. I'm not condoning his behavior, but I can see how—"

"Mother, don't," Claire said, sensing the inevitable slide into plotting mode. Her head throbbed. "There's no excuse for what he's been doing, not to mention the fact that it looks like he may be hiding assets."

"No, of course not. This so-called husband of yours is full of CRAP, and I'm sorry. And I want you to know that if you need any money for lawyers, or anything, I can send you a check. I can come out there to be with you, too, Claire, to help. Whatever you need, sweetheart."

Cora's supportive words pushed Claire past her capacity for surprises, and she started sobbing full stop into her pillow, while the unsinkable Cora Dunn continued to swathe her in memories of warm Ovaltine in bed and the news from Burlingame. No rationalizations, no outlandish schemes. Just the protective and unflinching support of a mother. Claire closed her eyes with the phone cradled between her ear and shoulder.

"You know," Cora said, "now that I think about it, maybe you should come out here for a weekend visit instead. A little dose of your city by the bay would be such good medicine, dear."

"That's a lovely idea," Claire whispered, teetering on unconsciousness. "I love you, Mama," she said, meaning it. "And I'll figure it all out somehow."

"Can't you goggle that man, or whatever it is you do on the Internet?"

"What man?" Claire said, through a yawn.

"The man who called about Janus."

Claire opened her eyes, annoyed at her own negligence. "I am such an idiot."

CHAPTER 40

"God, I think my vagina's broken," Gail said as she pushed past Claire with a slight hitch in her step, and placed a portable printer on Claire's kitchen table.

Carolyn followed close behind with a fruit tray and began untangling and plugging in cords. "Miss Pilates Thighs couldn't hold the stud at bay with her quads?" she asked with barely concealed jealousy.

Claire watched the scene in her bathrobe, confused and still groggy from sleep and two Advil PMs.

"Jackie called early this morning with some concerns from your mother," Gail explained. "Most notably that there's so much crap—and *crap* was the word Mama apparently repeated with such frequency and venom in her voice that your sister is ready to get her a T-shirt with the word emblazoned on it. Anyway, she was worried that Michael's shit trail was overwhelming you, and that you could use some help. She couldn't get out of school, so here we are."

"Crap triage, at your service." Carolyn took a ream of printer paper out of her Chanel satchel and loaded it into the printer tray. "We'll help you print and organize all the data for Jack, so he can prepare for the forthcoming . . . what was it?"

"*Legal crapendectomy,* I believe," Gail said, taking Claire's hand and walking her over to the table. "I had no idea Cora had such a wonderful way with words."

"Neither did I." Claire checked her cell and found three worried text messages from Jackie. She wiped the sleep from her eyes and wrote back to thank her for sending in the cavalry, noting that it really wasn't necessary. There was also a voice mail from Andrea announcing an opening at 4:00. "I need to call Nicky and get cleaned up a bit before we . . . do anything," she announced to the chipper posse.

"This is a sweatpants and dirty-hair day, sweetie. Don't waste your time on a shower," Carolyn said, pointing to her ponytail and cashmere tracksuit with fur-trimmed hood.

Claire excused herself to the bedroom, and reached Nicholas on his cell phone. He and Ray had plans to work out with the new therapy bands and do laundry. He sounded tired and unenthused, but perked up when he remembered that he was also driving downtown with Ray to meet Michael for lunch.

"That should be nice," Claire said, straining to keep the acrimony from oozing through her words. "And then maybe you can drive us to an appointment we have later this afternoon with a tutor?"

"Okaay."

She hated trying to discern Nick's temperament and expressions through the phone, and hated that she had to spend her morning sorting through the fallout of his father's lies. But she sent a message to Michael about the appointment, asked Nick's social worker at Craig to forward copies of his files to Andrea, and got dressed.

"So, Ashton's back in town?" Claire asked, helping herself to some kiwi, and dreading any sort of rehash about what she'd discovered in Michael's files. She appreciated her friends' concern and willingness to jump right into the muck with her—loved it, in fact—but still, she wondered if any possible financial improprieties were best kept private. At least until she fully understood them.

"Yes, *Austin* was in town for the night, and I couldn't resist the call. It's pitiful, I know. He still wears his boarding school T-shirt and ball cap, but the boy's got a tireless tongue, God love him."

"Ugh, you're killing me," Carolyn said, curling up into the club chair. "I can barely remember the last time Robert and I even had sex, much less when there was any tongue involved. Not that he would be my first choice. And *you* get to have your pick between Pool Boy and the Hedge Funder?" She kowtowed with one hand toward Gail. "You've made a superb comeback since the last divorce."

Claire sat down in front of the computer, pleased that they had gotten lost in the detour. She typed "Mac Kessler" into Google.

Gail sat down, too, but quickly stood and began stretching her lower back. "I've gotten married and unmarried so many times, I'm perpetually in comeback mode."

"Well, you seem to have mastered it. And I'm beginning to think I should jump on that train."

"Oh, hon, my not-so-lasting loves are hardly the answer. The Hedge Funder is very mediocre at foreplay." She folded herself into a downward dog, the diamonds on her watch flashing morning light across the room. "But he *is* excellent at jewelry, I have to admit. Which basically gets me to the same place. Anyway, the point is," she said through her legs, "that it's never perfect."

"I guess we can all vouch for that." Carolyn looked over at Claire. "You okay, sweetie?"

Claire was reading the screen intently. "Mm-hmm. Just give me a sec."

"In fact," Gail continued, reverting to upright and studying Claire's face, "I think I'm finally swearing off marriage. You know the old saying about fish and bicycles."

"Uh, sometimes a fish *does* need a bicycle," Carolyn said, chewing on a cuticle. "And not the battery-powered kind."

"Or maybe the perfect massage," Claire mumbled, envisioning a pastiche of her therapist and Richard, and just as quickly dismissing the thought. She had found Mac Kessler at a Boulder business called Flat Irons Consulting, which advertised itself as a pension plan administration firm. Mac specialized in third party pension administration for small businesses. Like Michael's.

"My God, what I wouldn't give for a nice long bicycle ride," came the sigh from the chair.

Gail retrieved a container and silverware from a small bag and handed it to Carolyn. "Here, hon, try this. It's Eric's bread pudding with caramel sauce, and it's sex in a spoon. I've already eaten about a gallon of it."

Carolyn skipped the spoon altogether and dipped her finger in, several times. "Oh my God, that's . . . orgasmic," she moaned. "You have to taste this, Claire." She brought the dessert to the table, dipped the spoon in the sauce and held it to Claire's lips.

Claire took the spoon and sucked on it mindlessly as she read about the various administrative services Flat Irons provided for its clients: record keeping to maintain plan compliance with IRS requirements, filing of government reports, distribution of participant statements.

"Okay, hon, what's going on?" Gail asked. "You look even more stressed than you did the last time we were here." She came up behind Claire and started rubbing her shoulders.

Claire quickly closed the laptop and leaned into Gail's hands. "I'm concerned about both of your vaginas. And I need to get reading glasses."

"Seriously," Carolyn said, kneeling next to her. "What are you looking at?"

Claire ladled the spoon through the caramel and began eating it like soup as she moved the Janus puzzle pieces around in her head. "What do you know about pension plans?" she finally asked, more as a stalling tactic than a question.

"Don't have one," Gail said. "But Warren did. It was pretty healthy, as I recall. Why?"

"I'm not sure exactly. Michael may . . . have some kind of trouble with his company's plan."

"Well, Robert didn't like how ours was performing, so I remember him moving it to some new fund last year. I don't remember the details, but I can ask."

"No," Claire panicked. "I don't want to arouse any—wait, you haven't said—"

"Of course not, sweetie," she said, taking back the spoon. "Don't worry. Robert has no clue how I spend my days." Her tone was surprisingly benign.

"Hello?!" Gail shouted. "From what Jackie mentioned, Michael's business is in the crapper, he's got deals and creditors screaming for cash, he's likely squirreling away assets in some mystery account—all unbeknownst to you. And now you think there's a problem with his corporate pension, never mind the mysterious caller and the bimbo? Rats bite, Claire. It's time to lay some traps."

Claire closed her eyes, knowing she needed to get to the bottom of whatever Michael was doing. There was no point in arguing or postponing the inevitable. So she reopened the computer and searched Michael's documents for the word *pension*. Seconds later the three women were reading a letter from Michael to someone's assistant at Janus Capital in Denver, dated November 5 of the previous year.

As trustee for New Haven Investments' employee pension plan, I will be making a change in the disposition of the plan assets. Please liquidate positions today, and upon settlement, wire transfer the funds at your earliest convenience to the account below. It was Michael's business checking account.

As the printer surged to life and spat out more hard truths, another revelation-soaked morning slogged toward afternoon.

Nicholas drove them to Andrea's office just a few miles away, earnestly observing stop signs and speed limits, and asking for directions only once. Claire watched him in profile, trying to remember when the last remnants of baby fat had disappeared from his face, leaving him with the angular jawline of a man. The accident had stolen much of his boyishness over the last months to be sure, but the young man she was looking at now exuded a nascent maturity, a lifetime away, it seemed, from the boy who had struggled so mightily with his toothbrush. Nick cranked the radio version of Cee Lo Green's "Forget You" and began singing the unsanitized lyrics. And for the first time since his hospitalization, his *fuck you*s were joyful and not personal. She smiled in approval of his skills, and car danced to the groove the way they used to when his favorite songs would come on, while all thoughts of treachery—financial and otherwise—floated away on the lightness of the mood. He pulled up to the converted Denver Square office building just as the song ended, and glanced sidelong at her. And for an instant Claire saw the old familiar flashes of her father, not just in his sparkling quarter moon grin, but in the way he cocked his head and seemed to read her thoughts.

"You're not gonna dance inside, are you?" he asked with a time-honored eye roll.

The absolute *typical teenager-ness* of the interaction washed over Claire, and she closed her eyes and savored this blast from their playful past. "Maybe," she said.

"Please . . . don't."

They found Andrea's office on the second floor. Nick had gripped the banister and taken the stairs two at a time. His forehead was shiny and his mood still ebullient as they sat down in the waiting room and talked about his PT group's ski trip on Monday. A few minutes later Claire heard a voice in the hall, and she felt her serenity fade. Michael walked in, putting his phone in his pocket, and sat down across from them.

"Sorry I'm late," he said. His left knee bounced rapid-fire, like a child who had to go to the bathroom.

Claire painted her Sara Lee smile back in place and greeted him impassively.

"Jeez, Dad. You look like . . . you just ate Grandmother's . . . liver sauté thing."

"Busy day, pal. No worries."

No worries, really? She clenched her teeth.

Nick studied both of them carefully. "What's with the two of you? I'm the one with—with the brain . . . damage. Just . . . get the divorce already." His tone was composed, and he smirked, as if conveying the obvious to the ignorant. "I'll survive."

Claire swallowed her shock and gaped at Michael, her eyes asking, "Now what?" Michael pinched his lips between his fingers, looking equally stunned and miserably faking the cool veneer she'd completely lost. She could almost hear him say, "Punt." But he remained silent.

Andrea cleared her throat from the doorway. "So, would you all like to come in?" she asked in a voice that was both upbeat and calming. She was a petite woman with a soft round face and long dark untamed curls and, except for her striped tights, was dressed in full black.

Nick pushed himself up from the love seat and walked over to her. "I'm Nick Montgomery," he said, shaking her hand, as they had always taught him. "Nice to meet you."

"Well, hello, Nick Montgomery. I'm Andrea Anspaugh. It's very nice to meet you, too. You can call me Andi." The tiny diamond stud in her nose enhanced her aura of cool authority. "Please." She indicated her office beyond the door, and waited for Claire and Michael to unglue themselves from their seats. Nick disappeared into the room.

"I'm so sorry," Claire said, standing. "I don't even know what to—"

"It's just that we're in somewhat of a . . . transition at the moment," Michael interrupted, his face looking even more waxen than when he'd walked in. "And Nicholas sometimes has difficulty controlling his emotions."

"Don't apologize. I've been doing this for almost twenty years, and I'm very comfortable with raw emotions. Just as long as I don't have to put anyone in a headlock."

For a second Claire imagined the diminutive woman pinning Michael on the floor from behind, and laughed without really meaning to. Michael stared at her.

"It's happened," Andi assured them matter-of-factly. "But usually only with kids who have significant frontal lobe deficits. And from the hospital and rehab reports I've skimmed, I don't anticipate those issues with Nick," she said, tucking her hair behind her ears with turquoise- and silver-jeweled fingers. "He's made tremendous strides, and I'm already very impressed with his progress."

"We are as well," Claire said, her expression hovering somewhere between pride and still-stunned.

"Can you help him with his educational goals?" Michael asked point-blank.

"Let's find out."

They followed her into her office, which resembled a loft with exposed brick walls, cozy furniture, and canvases of varying sizes hanging from picture wire. Nicholas stood in front of an acrylic portrait of Kurt Cobain.

"Did you do these?" Claire asked, scanning the other musicians on display.

"I did."

"Ray told me you teach . . . some classes at the Art Institute," Nick said, turning around. His spirits appeared intact, elevated even.

"Yes." Andi offered them seats on maroon velvet couches. "Just a couple intro and human form classes."

Claire sat down next to Nicky, and Michael chose the adjoining sofa. "Your Jim Morrison is wonderful. Incredible likeness."

As Andi reviewed Nick's history with them, Claire watched Nicky's eyes travel from canvas to canvas with obvious admiration. *Clever man, that Ray.* Nick spoke openly with her about his speech and memory challenges, and his desire to work through them. Michael was not as easy to read.

"I don't remember the . . . drug overdose," Nick said, making his air quotes around the offending event. "But I guess I can't . . . anything—do anything about that. I just want to finish school." He looked at Andi as if she were the only person in the room, determined, focused. Resolute.

Claire relaxed into the couch. Nick was clearly making more than just physical progress at Craig, and with Ray. Michael's knee started up again.

"You absolutely can reach your potential, in spite of your injury, Nick. Your brain is just functioning differently than it once did." Andi leaned in toward him. Her earrings swayed hypnotically against her cheeks. "I'm guessing you can probably blow right through a calculus problem, but maybe you have a hard time making change for a dollar?"

Nick nodded.

"Totally normal after a TBI. It takes time for the brain to rewire itself, so you're just going to need some special strategies. Got a smart phone?"

"Yeah." He took his phone from the pocket of his hoodie.

"Ever use the calendar function?"

"Not really."

"I'd like you to enter basic things into the calendar like breakfast, shower, workout—your everyday tasks—with times and alarm reminders when you get home today. Organization and planning are crucial for school, and I want you to get used to scheduling everything with an alarm so you can increase your follow-through and independence. You should use a planner, too, for assignment due dates."

Nick started typing into the phone.

"You could put blood tests in there also," Claire suggested. "And your classes at Craig."

"What about school?" Michael asked. His posture was perfectly still and erect now. "*Can* he finish senior year and get his diploma?"

Andi walked over to her desk and returned with a folder. "I like to look at short-term goals, say four to six weeks at a time, since Nick's needs and abilities are evolving. But in terms of school, I think he would do great at East. That's your district high school, right?"

"Yes," Nick answered, looking up from his phone.

"I work with several students there. The teachers and class options are excellent. We can get him registered and can get an individualized education plan in place to give Nick some time accommodations and other help." She handed Nick a course catalog. "I think you'd like the art department there as well." Their faces radiated an obvious simpatico. They were partners in his future already, Claire could see.

"What about tutoring him privately, rather than public school?" Michael asked in a reedy tone, as if the thought had just suddenly occurred to him. "So that he could, maybe, meet graduation requirements at Andover?"

"Dad!" Nick fixed a defiant stare on Michael. "I'm not graduating from Andover. I'm *not* . . . going back there," he snarled, clutching the catalog with both hands. "And I'm obviously not Princeton—not going to Princeton." The face-off shifted to mute, the two of them engaged in the intractable power struggle between fathers and sons.

Attaboy, Nicky. Claire studied Michael's neck, the involuntary bob of his Adam's apple above his straight-point collar, and wanted to strangle him, almost as much as she wanted to give her son a standing ovation.

Kurt Cobain's piercing eyes seemed to look down over Nick's shoulders at Michael, too. The intense blue was almost an exact match to Nick's, she noticed. But while Kurt's exuded pain, Nick's unwaveringly said: "My will is strong." And like the whisper of a brush through hair, Claire heard the subtle rustling of a defining moment. She laced her fingers and smiled.

Andi came around the table and sat down next to Michael, and for an instant Claire panicked that she would put her hand on his knee or make some other ingratiating gesture that would completely offend Michael's sense of the professional. Instead Andi handed him a report. "In my experience," she said in the confident manner of an expert, "patients have a better shot at reaching their goals in real-life settings. Being in class with other students, getting where they need to be on schedule, socializing—these are all challenging situations, but also good opportunities to build the skills they need for success moving forward." She paused, assessing her audience. Michael scanned the information, while Nicholas moved closer to the edge of the couch. "Of course these situations will be frustrating at times. For all of you." She and Claire locked eyes this time, like coconspirators. "But as you can see," she said, pointing out the relevant figures, "the odds for an improved outcome for patients with Nick's abilities increase dramatically with school reintegration, and combined with intervention by strong advocates, like you two"—she smiled reassuringly at Michael and Claire—"and with a specialist, a tutor, like me, if you're so inclined."

Claire felt certain that this was how Nick would find the keys to move forward. "What do you think, Nicky?" she asked.

"I want to go there . . . to East," he said without hesitation. "I just want to finish." He wiped a tear from the corner of his eye, but he didn't break down.

Their focus shifted to Michael, who placed the report on the coffee table and appeared to compose his thoughts. After an excruciating pause in the proceedings, he finally responded. "Well, sport, it sounds like Andi's got a good program in mind." He reached out and enveloped Nick in an embrace. "I know you can make it work. And then we'll just see what comes next. You know, in terms of college."

Michael's phone vibrated loudly from his pocket. He pulled away from Nick to read the text. And in what amounted to a thirty-second fire drill, his eyebrows migrated nervously around his forehead as he apologized for having to duck out, thanked Andrea for her time, and asked Claire to make arrangements with her for school registration and a tutoring schedule.

Which was the ideal conclusion in Claire's estimation.

"I would've . . . punched him if he said no."

You and me both. "C'mon, Nick, you're far more resourceful than that," Claire said as they gathered his ski clothes and gear from the basement for his group trip.

"So, when's it . . . happening?"

"Well, I'll download the paperwork tonight and go over to school Monday morning with Andi and get you registered."

"No," he said, "the divorce."

Claire stepped out of the storage closet and leaned on Nick's ski pole. "Oh."

"Is it because of my . . . accident?" His surprising vulnerability transformed his features. Behind the action-hero jaw and dogged stoicism, her little boy reemerged, exposed and in need of the same reassurance every child in limbo craves. Despite earlier statements to the contrary.

"Nicky, your dad and I—we have our problems. But they're just that, *ours*. Don't for one second think you've done anything to cause them."

Claire turned on the fireplace and sat him down on the floor. And huddling there with Nick in front of the hearth, she laid out the simple, unfortunate truth that life takes left turns at the most inconvenient times, but that her devotion to him—along with his dad's—ran to the moon and back. Always had and always would. She apologized and told him that things might get tricky for a while, but that his best interest was always their number one priority. The flames reflected in his pupils, and she could see him fighting some deep, painful emotions. She knew this was the moment of reckoning. But she was also afraid to elaborate on his parents' mistakes, because in spite of her desire to finally be frank and truthful with Nick, she never wanted him to feel that as equal parts them, he was also equally stupid and selfish.

"Nicky, the cocaine from your overdose," she said in a trembling voice. "It came from that man I invited to the house. He was a business associate of your dad's. I didn't know him well . . . and that was my mistake." She swiped at the tears that fell from her eyes.

"Then why did he come?"

She swallowed hard. "Because he seemed like an . . . interesting person. And I thought—I thought his business proposal was promising, so I wanted to spend some more time with him." It was a cop-out, she knew, but the psychologist had told her to not to get too deep into the particulars unless Nick asked specific questions.

"Why did he bring . . . coke?"

"I guess it was something he liked to do. But after I saw it, I asked him to leave." She looked away for a second, debating. "I should have made him go sooner. But I didn't. And he must have dropped it," she said, reaching out for him. "Inviting him over in the first place is the biggest regret of my life, and I would give anything to change that, honey. I'm so incredibly sorry."

Nick pushed back, eyes narrowed, as if considering the veracity of her story. And Claire sat there, holding her breath, waiting for him to pronounce the fate of their relationship, and suddenly nervous that he would bring up Taylor again. That was Michael's story to explain, and she doubted she could fake uncertainty about it this time. She needed to keep her cool.

"And Dad blames you for . . ." His voice trailed off.

"Yes." She exhaled. "And I . . . can understand that." There was still no erasing the painful truth that, in spite of Nick's discovery about his father's dalliance and the anger it had clearly inspired in him before the accident, they would not be sitting in this place were it not for her choices.

He turned to Claire with an expression that conveyed both sudden insight and long-term resignation. "I still can't remember that . . . night. But it was obvious for, like, *ever,* that you and Dad weren't . . . that happy anymore. I get that much." His voice was quiet and sad, and so sure.

Claire sat dumbstruck as Nick stood up and began stuffing his ski clothes into a duffel bag, his back intentionally to her. Her gauzy portrait of the past, it seemed, had not been so puzzling a picture for their son. "I love you so much, Nicky," she said after a beat.

"I know."

Later that evening over her last quarter bottle of sauv blanc, Claire checked in with Jackie and shared her strangely illuminating discussion with Nicholas, along with her optimism over his new academic path. And just like during their teenage assessments of the latest *Seventeen* magazine, Jackie waxed poetic on the intelligence of sensitive, creative boys, and wholeheartedly endorsed Andi's East High game plan.

Switching gears, they tossed around Claire's options with Michael in light of recent revelations: Dig deeper into the pension mystery, or give it all up to Jack and his legal eagles to handle, and file the papers ASAP. Jackie voted for Plan B. Claire was getting sick of Plan Bs, but held off on any concrete decisions until she understood more.

And then without planning to, Claire blurted out the story of her massage. The memory, which continued to bubble up and alternately shock and comfort her, was too uncontainable, too good a story not to share with *someone*.

"Oh my God," Jackie shrieked through the phone. "He totally took advantage of your vulnerability."

"What? No, not at all," Claire said, not at all expecting that response from her sister. "It was . . . therapeutic. It was *good*."

"Therapeutic? Are you kidding? This seems like something you'd be *so* not comfortable with."

"That's just it. I felt so weirdly at ease. Well, and maybe not a little pissed at my philandering husband, and I just went with his efforts to release all the blackness, so to speak." They both dissolved into hysterics. "Seriously," she said, trying to be. "It wasn't at all sexual. This man *saw* something in me, Jax." She left out the part of seeing Richard in the man. "And he helped me step out of my misery."

"Well, that must have been one hell of an orgasm. So, good for you, I guess."

"Yeah." Claire stared guiltily at her empty bottle of Groth. "As long as we're analyzing my louche behavior, do you think I'm drinking too much?" she asked.

"You're asking a woman who, at this very moment, is wearing a T-shirt that says 'Wine Makes Mommy Smarter.' Carpe vino."

CHAPTER 41

"Smitty!" Richard stepped into the grotto-like lower level of the restaurant and waved to Claire, backlit by stained glass saloon doors. If he had doffed a cowboy hat and flung it onto the nearby cactus, no one would have thought it odd. "Great joint," he said, wrapping her in a fleece hug.

"Best guacamole in town." Claire stood back and studied him with a reflective smile. He looked tanner and more rested than he had at Rancho, or possibly it was his haircut—all of which made him appear younger. He wore a Pebble Beach turtleneck under his jacket, baggy jeans, and what looked like bowling shoes.

"You're digging the sartorial pizzazz, aren't you?

She hugged him again, fighting back an unexpected avalanche of emotion. "Did you leave your loafers at the bowling alley?"

"These are some of the finest golf shoes my buddy at the pro shop could sneak out the back door, I'll have you know."

They sat down on opposite sides of the rough-hewn table as the avalanche gathered speed, and broke free. "I thought you were here to ski," she feebly choked out.

"Hey," he said, reaching across to her. "What's going on? I usually don't inspire tears."

"Sorry. And I'm usually not such a puddle. It's just that since we last talked, things have gotten . . . complicated. It's a Grand

Canyon–sized mess, and I just don't want to do anything stupid. Again." She wiped mascara from her cheeks and readjusted her posture, hoping her mood would follow suit.

The dimples that framed Richard's mouth conveyed the cheerful optimism Claire had tried, but failed, to muster. "First things first," he said, signaling to the waiter who had been hovering close by. "Señor, you've got some thirsty customers here. How 'bout a vat of margaritas, Smitty?"

"Hmm." While her pre-five o'clock protocol said no, her willpower bent. And swiftly snapped. "Maybe just a pint of tequila. And a chaser of salt for my wounds."

He gave her a look that said *Oy*. "We'll have a pitcher, please. And keep the chips and guac coming."

For the next half hour, Claire brought Richard up to speed on her discovery of Michael's extracurricular and apparent financial waywardness, as well as Nick's progress—which somewhat tempered the bleakness of the situation.

"So," Richard asked, scrunching his nose and looking vaguely alarmed, "what do you think is going on with this pension stuff?"

"I was hoping you could tell *me*. It looks like he may have borrowed the funds to prop up some of his deals, but I can't be sure."

"Claire, that money belongs to his employees. And the fact that Janus just sent him the funds doesn't smell right. That money needs to be transferred directly to another pension account. Which is probably what this Kessler guy has his pants on fire about."

She nodded and poured each of them another glass from the pitcher. "I don't know what to do next."

"One of my colleagues did a story not too long ago about a fund manager who went to jail for something similar. This could be serious, Smitty." The optimism had totally left his face. "You're not an officer of the company, are you?"

"No."

"Okay, good." He leaned back, tilting his chair on two legs. "If you'd like, I can make a few calls to make sure you've got no liability here. And I know the business writer for the *Boulder Daily Camera*. Maybe she can get us a little more information about Mr. Kessler's clients."

The reassurance she had been hoping for from Richard was woefully lacking, and she found herself slouching deeper into her angst. "I don't want to tip anyone off to . . . anything, though."

"It would be good to connect the dots on that one, just to make sure Michael really is one of his clients. But we journalists can be clever, despite our occasional missteps in footwear." He clinked her glass and winked. "Don't worry."

"This is giving me an acute case of indigestion."

"How 'bout I look through the info you've got at home after lunch? Maybe with a better sense of the big picture, I can come up with some suggestions."

"I was hoping you'd tell me that I may have misread things and that it'll all be just peachy. But, yes, I'd appreciate your business expertise. There's a lot I could use help deciphering." She pushed her glass and chips away. "If it's not too inconvenient."

Richard waved off her concerns and took out his cell phone to call his friend at the Boulder paper. And as Claire listened to him restate the basic facts—confidentially and in the dispassionate manner of a reporter—it became painfully obvious to her that there was no rearranging them into a less ugly design. Richard then conferred with someone named Hilly in the legal department before signing off with a genial, "Owe you one, pal."

"Okay," he said, taking a hearty swig of his drink. "The good news is that Meg will get back to me by the end of the day on Kessler's client list. And the other positive is that legal's pretty sure someone in your hypothetical situation would have no personal liability if Michael turns out to be a crook. Although Hilly suggested getting with a lawyer and untying the knot in the very near term."

"That's on my short list."

"This is never easy, Smitty. Especially when you're dealing with someone playing close to the edge."

Claire's right eye twitched as if irritated by some invisible, unreachable eyelash. "I just want to minimize the trauma to Nicholas, and get out with my sanity and my own bank account intact. You managed that, right?"

He cocked his head and thought for a moment. "I guess we did. The only nice part about not having a lot of dough is that there's less to fight over. I basically got Jagger, and Judy got the house and the goldfish. But goldfish get suicidal around me, so that was a no-brainer." He was trying hard, Claire could tell, to cheer her up. "Lauren was going off to college, which we'd fortunately planned well for. So now we split holidays with her, and she's doing great. Kids are resilient, Smitty. And they do want to see their parents happy."

"Right." The restaurant music abruptly switched from brassy mariachi to Elvis Costello. She hummed along softly.

"But I don't want to gild the lily. The financial negotiations were about as fun as a colonoscopy. Fortunately you get amnesia about it all. Eventually."

"Ugh. You're giving my indigestion whiplash," she said, folding her head into her hands.

"Sorry. Let's change tracks for a momento and assume that Michael has some decency and will want to do right by you and Nick. He may not be able to salvage his holdings, and he may even be in a legal stew, but a guy with his connections and family money is bound to be able to pull something off, no?"

"Look," she said, unfolding. "We were merely wealthy, and not obscenely rich like his family is. Note the use of the past tense," she added with particular emphasis. "But in Michael's defense, he's not someone who'd magically found himself on third base and thought he'd hit a triple. His dad's extremely allergic to handouts. And scandal. Michael has *never* relied on his family."

"Huh, intriguing. The elusive Paul Montgomery's a cold fish."

"You know Paul?" Claire asked, taking fresh and suspicious notice of the journalist across from her.

"Noo. I've had colleagues repeatedly shut out by him, but I've got no professional interest in your father-in-law. Cross my heart," he promised. "My aim is just to make sure you're okay." He reached out and wiped the hair from her eyes. "My aim is true."

She couldn't help smiling, and her nerves gradually subsided over what turned out to be a shared appreciation for the clever lyrics of the man on the speakers, particularly as they related to relationships and heartbreak. They had both been Costello groupies in their college days, they discovered, never imagining that their own dreamboats would also turn out to be the footnotes they had sung along to.

"C'mon," Richard said, taking out his credit card. "Let's blow this joint and go see if we can't find something helpful in all that dirty laundry."

Claire followed him out into the bright afternoon and to their cars, and he followed her to the apartment. She squinted through the drive, hoping her pal could just find the right approach for her. Because she still didn't trust her own instincts.

Gail and Carolyn had helped her organize Michael's printed documents into a triptych: Michael's draft e-mail to Nicky, investment deals, and the QuickBooks logs. She offered Richard a bottle of water and the second two piles with profuse gratitude.

"Making sense of dirt and questionable business practices is right in my wheelhouse, Smitty." He slipped on tortoiseshell reading glasses and settled into the couch. And for nearly two hours he read everything she'd given him, in addition to files and e-mails on the computer when he needed supplemental information. Claire answered his infrequent questions for clarification, but generally left him to his digging and note taking, which were peppered with vociferous grunts and mutterings. Mostly, though, he looked as troubled about what he was seeing as Claire felt. She tried to busy herself cleaning her clean kitchen and texting Nicky—who was loving the powder at Winter Park, and hating that he was barely skiing blues. And as she reminded herself to be grateful that her son was back on the mountain and poised to start school again soon, Richard's cell phone erupted into the dueling banjos from *Deliverance*.

"Whatcha got for me, Meg?" he answered, pushing his glasses onto his head.

Claire sat down next to him and listened to him confirm that New Haven Investments was indeed a client of Flat Irons Consulting, and that Mac Kessler was a well-respected consultant who had joined the firm five months ago.

"And one more thing. Can you get me some background on a

Kimberly Erickson at Janus in Denver . . . ? You're the greatest, Meggy. Give that daughter of yours a big hug from me." He set down the phone and rubbed his bloodshot eyes.

"So?" Claire asked, impatient for the postmortem.

He exhaled deeply. "I think you're dealing with someone who's never found himself striking out, to use your baseball analogy. Guys like this—charming, smart, masters-of-the-universe types— they have enough ego to believe that certain rules don't apply, and that they can always turn things around and get right back on top with just a few sleights of hand." He shook his head incredulously. "And the screwing around fits right into the profile. I see this all the time, Smitty. They play fast and loose with everything until—" Richard stopped and stared at Claire's wilting expression.

"Until what?"

"You know." He made a soft exploding sound.

She could almost feel the bomb in her head. "God, he's such an arrogant . . . ass," she said, sulking into the kitchen. She picked up a dish towel and twisted it into a tight knot.

"I'm really sorry, Smitty. I wish I had better news for you."

"Were you able to make any more sense of this?" she asked, reappearing and flicking the towel at the mess of papers on the couch.

He nodded somberly, his puffed-up cheeks making him look like a despondent beagle, and he explained that, according to a marketing report to the investors in the San Diego project, construction on the high-rise had been completed, but due to the collapse of the local real estate market, the units were priced at forty percent above market and all the buyers of their presold units were walking away from their contracts. The bank was calling for an eight-million-dollar capital infusion to avoid foreclosure. As a result, Michael had issued a capital call to the three other investors in the deal for 1.6 million dollars each, in addition to the 3.2 million he would be responsible for as the majority partner.

"He can save the deal, then?" she asked with a twinge of hope.

"Theoretically he could pay down principal with the cash from the capital call, service the bank debt, generate additional operating funds to rent up the building to eventually sell it, and preserve their original equity. But one of the investors has done nothing but hedge on sending the one-point-six, Paul is questioning the financials, and the third investor declared bankruptcy and is totally out."

"So that leaves Michael holding the bag for how much?"

"About four-point-eight million, *if* the two others don't bail."

"There's no way he'd let the deal tank with his father involved," she said, trying to process the information. "He won't disappoint him. And four-point-eight million, he could get that in a heartbeat."

"Seems there's other deals in need of cash, too, but it looks like San Diego and a venture called Wincor Tech were what pushed him to the dark side." Richard pulled his glasses back onto his nose and took out his notes and launched into an analysis of what he saw as Michael's Tour de Desperation. On top of having to pony up for his bankrupt partner and cover his own share of the capital call, he explained, Michael had personally guaranteed the bank loan on San Diego for forty-eight million. So not only was he at risk for losing the partnership's equity in the deal if they didn't put up the eight million dollars, he *could* be liable for a whole lot more.

Claire started pacing in front of Richard.

"Sit, Smitty. There's more," he said, patting the couch.

She looked at him uneasily before curling into the couch and listening to him detail the Wincor Technologies saga, which for a minute sounded like it held the answer to Michael's cash-flow problems.

Michael had been the sole angel investor in the fledgling energy company over the previous two years, and he'd made a deal with a group to come in and buy his majority stake in the company for what amounted to five times his investment. However, a condition of the sale was that Wincor complete the patent process for its proprietary technology. And unfortunately, it seems Wincor's lawyers ran into a licensing problem with the owner of a small but essential working part of their solar panels, and needed to pay the owner a two-hundred-thousand-dollar licensing fee. Without this license, the patent could not be issued, and the sale would not go through. And additional funds were needed to pay salaries and legal fees while they completed the patent process.

Claire raised her head, waiting for the next blow.

"It looks like Michael fought any further investment. But, really, he couldn't afford *not* to fund Wincor, given that it had been his baby all along, and given the likelihood of a windfall—which he desperately needs—with its sale." Richard showed Claire the relevant legal messages from the attorney on the deal, which only made her feel more nauseous.

"God, it's like once I started pulling the thread of his secrets, the whole sweater came undone," she said in a parched voice.

He handed her his water bottle and gently brushed a piece of towel fuzz from her nose. "The grammar lapses alone on some of his e-mails are grounds for divorce."

She laughed a little and rested her head on his shoulders, the scent of his cologne reminding her of licorice. "Okay, you may as well hit me with the rest. What does this dark side amount to?"

"Well, it was a perfect storm of crappy markets and unfortunate timing. And without much liquidity from what I can see, he had to go somewhere for a quick five mil plus."

"The pension?"

"Yep. *And* your house."

"What?" Her body stiffened. "I saw a loan from Wells Fargo for two million—"

"Yeah. He mortgaged most of your house for that, Smitty. And what's troubling—apart from the pension improprieties—is how he could manage that without you signing any loan documents."

Silently Claire added up her own mistakes against Michael's and cursed her inexperience. "He paid cash for it all those years ago, and he probably put the house in his name," she said, feeling doubly foolish. "I never thought to ask to see a *deed.*"

Richard consoled her with the benefits of community property law, which only worsened her mood. Not wishing to be tied to any part of a two-million-dollar mortgage, and exasperated by the financial morass Michael had sucked them both into, Claire asked him for some good news.

He nodded halfheartedly. "It looks like the Wincor buyer is still anxious to close the deal. But the patent timing is unpredictable at best." Richard's cell phone vibrated with an incoming text, which he paused to read. He looked back up. "Bad news is that the assistant at Janus who liquidated the pension funds and wired them to Michael was, not surprisingly, a newbie. And Ms. Erickson will probably be finding herself in some serious hot water."

"Nice," Claire whispered.

"It's one flimsy scheme, Smitty. I'm sure he's banking on the Wincor sale so he can return the pension funds before tax season. But it's ballsy, and unlikely he can put Kessler off much longer on the records from Janus. I don't know how he plans to pass this off, 'cause it definitely ain't kosher."

Claire stood and resumed her pacing. "What the hell do I do now?"

"You've got plenty of information to give to your lawyer."

"But that amounts to turning him in, doesn't it?"

Richard looked at her, confused. "Well, I can check with my pal Phil who did the piece on the pension raider and see what Michael might be up against if this thing blows."

"I don't want it to blow, Richard," she said, staring at the carpet and chewing on the future. "That's just it. As much as I hate him right now, I certainly don't want him to go to jail." She imagined Michael in a prison-issue orange jumpsuit and felt a brief flash of satisfaction. "Nicky needs a dad. Especially now."

"Right. I hear that. And frankly, I don't understand why he'd be pushing for a divorce in the middle of all this. His malfeasance would come out in the discovery process. Unless he's even slicker than we think."

"Actually," she said, "he's been backpedaling, or at least seems in less of a rush to formalize things legally. *No need to get a bunch of lawyers involved.* Which makes sense now. He's stalling until he can pay off the debts."

Richard advised her to go straight to her lawyer with everything and let him make the call. But still shading in her confusion, Claire wanted to know what Michael's legal issues might be. Richard made the call to his pal at the WSJ. And the news he got was not inspiring: Michael, as trustee for his corporate pension, had the authority to invest the funds as he saw fit, but zero authority to distribute the funds for his personal use. And doing so amounted to embezzlement, which was a federal crime. Phil suggested that paying restitution would be a start, but no guarantee of avoiding prosecution by the Department of Labor. Much would depend on lawyers, reputations, and other intangibles.

Claire understood that to a certain degree, her choices would determine Michael's fate. If she went to her lawyer with the evidence of his actions, Jack would be obligated to turn the case over to the authorities. But if she went to Michael first, providing him the opportunity to somehow get the cash together and return the funds, and then turn himself in, things might turn out much better for him. For all of them. Still, she fretted about how he would get the cash together in a hurry if he hadn't been able to already.

"That's not your problem, Smitty. You're giving him the chance to fix things. That's far more generous than he's been with you," he said pointedly.

"I know," she said, fighting the feeling she'd been appointed head of some sinister cabal, and wanting to block the whole mess from her mind. "And I really appreciate everything you've done."

"All in a day's work," he declared with a hopeful smile. "Though I much prefer the company here to my usual associates."

"I'd offer to cook you dinner, but . . ." She walked into the kitchen, wanting really to just disappear on the spot. She opened the refrigerator door to reveal a bachelor's minimum.

"No worries," he said, studying the red toes that peeked out from her tailored jeans. "I'll take my fee in salsa."

Claire looked from the refrigerator to Richard. "But I don't have any."

"Dancing, Smitty. One of my favorite Denver joints has killer steaks and a great salsa band on tonight. And we're going."

Richard's haunt on the west side was right out of Cuba, circa Marlon Brando in *Guys and Dolls,* its walls dotted with black-and-white photos of salsa kings and tango queens, and still redolent of a smoky past. Claire slid into the vibe much quicker than she'd imagined, appreciating the steak and Malbec, and the general diversion of eating a proper dinner in a restaurant with another human being. But the specter of her future never lurked too far, so she attempted to focus on Richard's past.

"We were like Fox News and MSNBC, Judy and I. And the hot-and-cold running squabbles got less entertaining over time," he told her, sounding jolly and regret-free, and like everything Claire wanted to be. "It was an unnecessarily drawn-out death, and one of us should've pulled the plug years ago. But I'm sure I don't need to point out that your situation's a little more urgent."

Claire surreptitiously chewed on a hangnail she had picked loose during the ceviche course. She imagined throwing back a cocktail and dancing herself into a blinding haze, but her back remained firmly glued to the wooden chair, and her hot meter registered a bland two or three at best.

"Listen, after a certain point, you have to accept that there's really nothing left you can say or do. But if it's any consolation, you do get to a place of détente with your partner." Richard ordered a round of mojitos. "And with yourself."

"I think it's different for a woman. I'm sure you never worried about starting over at forty-three. Or being a single parent and rebooting a dormant career."

"Is that why you've hung in for so long?"

Claire shrugged. "Maybe. I just wasn't unhappy enough to get out. Christ," she said, restating the still strange truth, "I didn't even know I *was* unhappy. And, yes, it's all very daunting."

"Depends how you look at it." He leaned in over the table with the fiery enthusiasm of the recently transformed. "Instead of living in some kind of netherworld, what about the chance to really squeeze the marrow out of life?"

"I suppose . . ."

"And maybe even test drive some new cars along the way?"

"Are you talking about dating now?"

His expression shifted to a goofy grin.

"The idea of dating is about as appealing as that colonoscopy. Never mind the odds that I'd make a huge mess of it." She cut a piece of steak, but left it on her plate. "This whole thing has left my soul with a unsettling case of ADD."

Richard stood and took her hand. "Smitty, your soul's in need of a little smack. It's time to go blow off some serious . . . whatever it is you've got going on in your head."

The driving beat of the trombones and timbales combined

with Richard's grip to leave her with little choice. Which made her almost happy. She took a quick gulp of courage with her free hand and followed him toward the dance floor. The two couples already there moved seamlessly through turns and pretzels and sexy body rolls, while Claire did her best not to trip over Richard's feet. They hadn't exactly taught merengue in cotillion, but she was grateful for the ingrained lesson of following a lead. She let her hips and shoulders sync to the music and fudged her way through two songs, as promised. When the band broke for beers, she led him back to their table.

"Well, that was fun for a few minutes," she said, wiping the dampness from her temples and leaning back into the chair. She tapped her feet under the table, feeling the exhilaration of the adrenaline rush begin to recede. "Did I hurt you?"

"Not too badly. Fortunately the shoes are bulletproof."

"God, I'm sorry. But you can't say I didn't warn you. I just had no idea you were such a Renaissance man."

"I took a few lessons. But you've got some moves, too, when you let go."

Her body prickled for an instant at those haunting words, but she smiled at his very genuine attempt to reengage her in something outside her present reality. "I guess that was just the shot of Cholula I needed. So, muchas gracias, señor."

They walked out to the parking lot making plans to get together soon, possibly in San Francisco when she visited Cora. Richard spun her to the music that had started up again inside, and they laughed as the starlit night and distant sirens swirled around them. On the downbeat he pulled her body toward him and tilted her chin up.

Claire's feelings of temporary abandon and pleasure vanished. "No," she yelped, quickly disengaging. "I don't want to risk our friendship with some haphazard . . . thing. I'm a wreck right now, and you're too important to me."

Richard stared into her eyes for a long moment, reading her with a sad but accepting expression. "Well, that was a very thoughtful delay of game," he finally said. "And I'm sorry. I didn't mean to complicate things. Rewind?"

As she looked back into the generous sparkle of this man who had given her so much, she thought of the fantasies he'd inspired, and she worked hard to reconjugate their relationship in her mind. But circumstances were circumstances, and she knew that arm's length really was all she was equipped to handle. She reached her hand across the darkness to him. "As long as we can agree on the rules."

He paused. "BFFs?"

CHAPTER 42

With Michael on business in San Diego—scraping the barrel, Claire hoped, for some sort of salvation—Claire and Andi accompanied Nicholas to his first day at East. Nicky pulsed with nervous excitement as they walked into the counseling office at seven a.m., where Mr. Doyle had miraculously assembled the school psychologist, the school nurse, and most of Nick's new teachers for a brief introduction. Claire's nerves were more maternal in nature. It was like the first day of preschool, except that she had the bittersweet sense that she was witnessing the last gasps of her son's youth.

While Andi got everyone up to speed on Nick's background and laid the groundwork for the academic accommodations and individualized plan he'd need in place, Nick responded to their various questions with dogged thoughtfulness. With his backpack on his shoulders, he entered notes into his phone and appeared battle-ready and confident. And when it came time for him to go to his first class, Claire took her cue to let him find his own way. "I've got it, Mom," he said as they were swallowed into a sea of rushing students outside the office.

Claire had made plans to meet Jackie and Carolyn at Gail's house later that morning for breakfast. She arrived before the others, and while she'd learned to expect the unusual when she visited her pal—be it the chance arrival of a minor Scandinavian royal for tea, or a well-defined male model posing nude in the sunroom for a sketch in charcoal—finding Gail standing in the vestibule, rather than of one the uniformed staff, with a cigarette in her mouth was Claire's surprise du jour. They kissed hello, and Claire took in Gail's cheetah-print Cavalli jeans, her wet hair pulled back into a ponytail, and her lack of makeup, and tried to imagine just what, exactly, was going on at the Harrold household on this day. Harry Winston, Gail's new white powder-puff bichon, circled her bare feet, stopping intermittently to lick and bark at the sparkle of Gail's tiny diamond toe ring.

"Okay, I give up." Claire raised her hands in mock exasperation. "Why are you standing here, and when did you start smoking?"

"Ugh, come with me." Gail took Claire's wrist, stepped over the frenetic activity at her ankles, and led her into the kitchen. She spoke in a throaty voice as they walked. "I'm practicing being alone. I gave everyone the day off. Everyone. I've been cleaning out my closets, I've deep-conditioned my hair, and I'm in the process of reorganizing my files. And if I smoke, I don't eat." She sat down on one of the cushioned bar chairs at the center island and took a long drag on the cigarette. Then she dropped it into the sink.

"So, how's that working out for you?"

They stared at each other for a second until Gail burst out into raspy hoots. "It sucks. This house is too big to rattle around in alone. And I'm just not good at it. I don't know what I was thinking, except that I was worrying that I was turning into my mother."

"They can certainly do a number, can't they?"

"Bloody Mary?" she asked, already making herself one.

"I can't. I'm picking Nick up after school and taking him to the shelter to drop some things off."

"First day back to school—very exciting!"

"I know. I was anxious, but *he* seemed perfectly fine walking into a strange new environment and playing catch-up. The kid amazes me every day."

"Hon, it'll be his turf, his place to make whatever mark he wants to. I think this will be a huge boost for him."

"Your mouth to God's ears."

"And I'm glad to see that the mother-son shelter trip lives on."

"Well, it's good to keep up the familiar routines. I had Nicky grab some outgrown clothes and old games at the house, and I put together a bag of food. And we'll make our delivery."

"That's lovely. I always write checks, honey. But most of the time it's just better to do." Gail walked over to the enormous butler's pantry. "So, how 'bout I put together another bag of food for you to take with you?"

"That would be delightful."

"And I've got a bunch of clothes I could give you as well."

Gail disappeared into the pantry, and Claire's thoughts drifted to the night before and Richard's knowing eyes, to Michael's dark secrets, and to the idea that she'd be living the discount version of Gail's lonely life all too soon. The dog began licking her shoe, and Claire picked him up and placed him in her lap. "So, talk to me, Harry Winston," she said into his pink-rimmed eyes. "What's it like being unattached and clueless?" He licked her neck and hopped down just as Gail emerged from the pantry with a collection of food. Claire got up and scanned the contents of the bag. "Adriatic fig spread, imported caper berries, and jalapeño jam." She looked up at Gail. "What? No water crackers or crostini? No tapenade?"

Gail curled her nose and pillowy lips into a crinkle. "I guess those weren't ideal choices. I'm a little off my game at the moment."

Claire went into the enormous venetian-plastered pantry to search for some more suitable items. A second later she returned empty-handed. "Is there no can of soup or tuna fish in this godforsaken kitchen?"

"You know Eric. He makes everything from scratch, and I'm pretty much helpless without him, aren't I?"

"Um, I thought we were having breakfast here," she said, noticing the barren glass breakfast-room table.

"Shit. I completely forgot to pick up the quiche." Gail pulled her hair out of the ponytail and let it fall into her eyes. "I broke up with the Hedge Funder last night, and I gave Austin his walking papers again this morning, and then I got so caught up in my purging exercise that I—"

"No worries. I'll just put on the coffee, and we can have the fig spread on some toast."

"God, I'm Zsa Zsa Gabor two-point-oh," Gail sighed, dramatically draping her legs over the armrests of the bar chair.

"Well, if it makes you feel any better," Claire said, pouring some Italian roast into the Gaggia, "I can raise your pair of breakups with an embezzled pension fund *and* a leveraged house and portfolio. To the tune of well over five million. Plus a mountain of other potential debt." There was no point in holding back facts anymore. What she needed was a plan architect and field marshals.

Jackie and Carolyn walked into the kitchen.

"Okay, I fold," Gail replied wide-eyed. "You win."

Looking into her friends' flabbergasted faces, Claire decided to take them on the full Tour de Desperation, stopping at the more scenic points for them to vent. And the more she told, the more incredible it sounded to her that she had been so oblivious to Michael's activities. "I knew there was something he'd been holding back all this time. I just never registered the significance of certain . . . signs. But there you have it," she said, glancing at the over-mature rose in the bud vase by the sink, "my hopeless mess in all its glory. Not only is the marriage bankrupt, we just might be, too."

Jackie came around the center island and sat down next to her. "This situation is not hopeless, and you are not helpless."

Claire shot her a muted stink eye. "Um, no matter how I slice it, we all lose. If I go to Jack with all the evidence, Michael will likely be facing some pretty serious consequences, which won't be good for Nicky. And if I go to Michael first, his chances of quickly securing the cash won't be any less bleak, never mind that he'll probably want to kill me on the spot. Which, again, is bad for all of us."

Gail swung her feet to the floor with barely disguised irritation. "My dear, sweet friend. Do you need a Miracle Ear or what?" she growled into her face. "Michael has been playing three-card monte with your life. There's a PRICE for that, father of your child or not."

Jackie nodded. "He's going to have to pay this bill one way or another."

"And *that*," Carolyn added in a voice delicious with possibility, "could be your angle."

Claire cocked her head, uncertain about what, precisely, this Machiavellian observation meant.

Carolyn poured a dollop of milk into her espresso. "You could hit him with some serious leverage of your own, Claire, and make whatever demands you want."

"I like what I'm hearing," Gail said, leaning in. "Go on."

Carolyn fixed a deadly serious gaze on Claire. "How dirty do you want to play?"

CHAPTER 43

"Wish me luck, Mother."

"Just keep thinking about your future, dear, and everything on that checklist of yours."

Claire eyed the notes she'd taken from her last conversations with Richard and Gail, arranging them in her memory in specific order. "It's a little unnerving, to say the least," she said, rolling her shoulders. The scent of Chanel and bananas hung heavily in the apartment air, and she fought a serious case of stage fright.

"Hold your ground, and you will be brilliant. I know you will. Tell me about Nicky's week before you go. I'm so proud of him, I can't stand it."

The distraction wasn't unwelcome, and Claire happily recounted their trip to the shelter, where Nick had spent several hours doing art projects with the kids in the therapeutic preschool program, as well as the reports she'd gotten from Nicholas and Andi about his return to school. Nick was integrating into his classes well and socializing with kids, which had the very noticeable effect of improving his moods. Being with new peers in the "real world," especially kids who had no preconceived notions of him, Claire realized, was doing more to boost his confidence and outlook than fifty successful swats at a balloon. The routine and structure of his new schedule seemed to provide a sense of comfort as well, while the adjustment to entering nearly every facet of his life into his phone and planners, along with the other adaptive skills he was learning to employ, challenged him. He had missed handing in several assignments on time and still had difficulty shifting from one task to another. Which was to be expected, according to Andi. But he loved his drawing class, and overall was displaying an unceasing desire to thrive.

"Dear, that's so wonderful. Maybe Nicky *can* apply to college."

"We're taking things slowly, Mother. But I suspect that may be a possibility at some point—just not in the traditional way his father expects."

"What do you mean?"

"Possibly art school." The notion seemed logical and reassuring to Claire. But she would sit back and let Nick drive that bus, if that was the route he chose. And Michael would have to ride along.

"Well, who do you know at the top schools? Maybe we should start making—"

The eagerness in Cora's voice would have been endearing if it weren't so historically lethal. "Mother, how 'bout we just let things unfold naturally for once. Hmm?" Claire looked out the living room window toward her old house and downtown, scanning the area just between the two.

There was silence, followed by a brief and remarkably unphlegmy cough. "I'll just button my tongue for now. But," she said, not missing a beat, "I have to ask how the house hunting is going. That's not overstepping, is it?"

"No, and I think I've found the perfect option. Jean showed me a darling cottage in North Country Club that's been completely renovated, with the original woodwork and moldings. It's close to school, and I wouldn't have to do a thing except paint Nick's room, which is currently pink. It's got great light and a nice alcove for a studio." Claire picked up the property brochure from the pile on her dining table and stuck it in the folder in her purse.

"That sounds lovely, dear."

"It is, and it's going to go fast if I don't move on it." She put on some lipstick in the hallway mirror and tucked another item into the folder. "So send some serious positive thoughts."

* * *

The sun was preparing to set as Claire pulled into the driveway. She had just under an hour before Andi would drop Nicholas off at the house after their tutoring session. There was no time to waffle or stew any further, so she marched straight to the front portico, unlocked the door with the new key Michael had finally given her, and moved deliberately through the house, taking in the antiques and oriental rugs, all those pieces she'd lovingly selected and arranged over the years. But the happy memories of their origins had been so marred by the truth that her home appeared to her now as merely a collection of "stuff," devoid of any sentimentality or meaning. She closed her eyes and pictured the cottage she'd returned to three times that week, pictured Nick there with her. And she visualized the bullet points on her checklist one last time, before proceeding down the hall.

Shielding her unease behind her best poker face, Claire cleared her throat from the doorway of the study and studied her husband. An odd sensation struck her when their eyes met—odd that he was her husband, and even odder that he wouldn't be for much longer. His haggard face told her that he was still not sleeping. And that the San Diego trip had been less than successful. If she didn't know better, she might have thought he'd been on some kind of bender.

"What are you doing here?" he asked with undisguised frustration.

So much for any attempt at casual bonhomie, she thought. "I'll get to the point." Claire approached the desk, took a CD case from her folder, and placed it just out of his reach. She paused for a second, noticing the text message that lit up the inside of her shoulder bag. *Go tell him how it's gonna be, Smitty. You can do this!* Adrenaline flooded her chest. "I know who you are," she said in a strong, even voice, belying her emotions. "And I know what you've been doing." She glared at his face, containing eighteen years of misplaced trust and politeness with a firm stance.

Michael's cheek twitched, and Claire watched his irritation turn to nervousness under her scrutiny.

"Do you have *anything* to say?" she pushed, after a long stretch of quiet.

He fixed on the CD case and reached to pick it up. "What's this?"

"*That?* That's the very unfortunate truth. All of it."

He turned it over in his hands, which appeared to have developed a slight tremor. "What are you talking about? You march in here like some bad Broadway detective with some kind of evidence of *the truth*? I don't have time for theatrics, Claire. I've got a lot of work to do here."

"Yes, I'd say you do. But," she said, sitting down in the other partner's chair and reflexively flicking the heel of her ballet flat off and on, "I'm going to help you."

His lips moved, as if trying to compose the correct response, but all he managed was a dull "Huh?" His hands still gripped the CD.

"You've been very busy this last year—and then some, I'm sure—with your girlfriend and—"

"Girlfriend? Seriously?" He tossed the CD into the trash. "You've got a lot of guts accusing me of whatever it is you think I'm guilty of after the mess your little . . . diversion caused." He picked up the desk photo of Nick and turned it toward her, something fierce flashing in his pupils.

She caught a retort between her teeth, and held it. "Let's be clear about something, Michael," Claire said. "You've been making me out to be the wicked whore of the west, leaving me to drown in my guilt, and all the while you've been playing a much more wicked game with our lives." *No,* she thought to herself, *nothing golden remained.* "There are consequences for our decisions. I know this better than anyone. And now it's your turn to face them."

"What the hell are you talking about?"

"I'm talking about San Diego and the mortgage on the house and our Schwab holdings. I'm talking about Mac Kessler and the company pension you used as your own personal bank account." She watched Michael's face blanch as she continued. "I could forgive you for *Taylor*"—she practically spat out the name—"but this," she said, retrieving the CD from the trash, "makes everything easier for me. Because now I know that it wasn't just one unfortunate lapse in judgment. It's an epic string of lies and cheating, and complete disregard for me and for Nicholas. And I won't suck that up."

"Taylor," he whispered, looking confused. "You know about . . . Taylor?" He ran both of his hands through his hair, rocking back and forth in his chair and revealing circles of perspiration in the creases of his Turnbull & Asser bespoke shirt. "How?"

She eyed the disc. "That's hardly the issue, Michael. What *is* at issue are the many lines you've crossed, both legally and ethically. And to coin a choice phrase of yours—it stinks. It stinks to high heaven."

Michael's eyes darted around the room, the desperation of his reaction accentuated by the dark half-moons above his cheeks. There was a time bomb between them, Claire felt. And it was ticking off the seconds before one of them blew. She took a mental step back, digging deep through the recesses of her memory. Michael's defensiveness, the fear, the indignant responses—they really had been a pattern for some time, along with the detachment and apparent insomnia. A pattern, she thought, of a guilt-ridden soul challenging the elasticity of its integrity. God only knew what other secrets he harbored, and that she had failed to connect the dots on. But this time, she reminded herself—as had Richard, and the girls and Cora—she had all the tools and ammunition she needed. And she could finally stop pretending. She exhaled her own indignation and smiled sweet as Sara Lee. "There are a couple ways I can choose to handle the information I have. But like I said, I'm willing to help you out."

Michael shifted in his chair. "You're going to help solve a— a—" His voice took on the familiar mumbling tic of the dysarthria patients in Nick's speech classes. "A complex real estate and financial market . . . problem? Enlighten me. Please."

"The complex problem is not about markets at all. It's about embezzlement, and how you're going to make things right."

"Embezzlement? All of a sudden you're some kind of expert on embezzlement? You know nothing about the intricacies—"

"I wouldn't underestimate what I've become an expert on," Claire said, interrupting him and checking her watch. "Here's the deal, Michael. You took three-point-two million dollars from your company pension and used it to fund business deals. That's not your money to spend. Theft from an employee benefit plan is a federal crime, and you will undoubtedly have some legal issues. But if you return that money immediately, and volunteer to the authorities to pay whatever interest and fines they slap on this, you will hopefully ingratiate yourself and not go to prison."

He gaped at her, his hands shaking on top of the desk. "Well, since you appear to have all the details, you know that the bank account's a little anemic at the moment. I'm working my ass off to secure some new funding. So stop this ridiculous charade and go take care of Nicholas, would you? Aren't you supposed to be picking him up?"

Just as her veneer was cracking, another alarm sounded in Claire's head. Michael was like a cornered animal, and he was lashing out. And she understood that she had to make him see the logic of her plan without lashing back at *him* and further arousing his fears and insecurities. "Michael," she restarted as calmly as she could, "I'm well aware that you've depleted much of our joint brokerage account, in addition to mortgaging our house. All without consulting me." She watched him fumble with a pencil. "But I'll put that aside for now, in light of your need to make restitution on the pension. Immediately. And it seems that your only option for quick cash is your father. He could help you make this all go away, or at least improve your—"

"My father? Are you nuts?" He launched out of his chair, sending it crashing into the bookshelf behind him. He turned and kicked the casters, knocking over a dish of pistachios in the process and sending them raining onto the floor, all the while muttering to himself and incubating . . . something. After an agitated bout of pacing, he turned to her, his face a riot of red splotches. "I have a reasonable expectation of privacy, so don't think for one minute that my lawyers won't nail you to the wall for breaking into my computer, which is obviously what you've done here," he shouted. "I'll give you the fight of your—"

"I don't think so," she said, cutting him off. But instead of a swell of self-assurance as she was about to take her folder dramatically from her purse and give him the "when you play, you pay" line she'd rehearsed, her voice froze in her throat. Her body shuddered and her eyes blurred. She sunk back into the chair, over-come. "Shit. Shit! What are we doing?" She looked at Michael, at the landscape of their history all around them, those happy mo-ments frozen in the picture frames insinuating themselves where, just a second before, outrage boiled. "What the hell are we doing? This isn't *us,*" she cried. She bent her head into her hands. "It's not me."

The guttural sound that erupted and echoed through the room startled Claire, and she looked up to see Michael's rage dissolving under his own squall of tears. Slowly he groped for his chair and lowered his body into it with uncharacteristic submission, then braced his hands on the desk as he rolled forward, the drone of the furnace a mournful accompaniment to his visible anguish. For a long while they both sat steeping in their grief. And in his raw, hiccupping exhales Michael was transformed to Claire from the two-dimensional villain of her outrage into a flawed human being.

"How did we get here?" she asked miserably.

There was no answer in his gaze, only the strain of the last min-utes, and months.

"I had what amounted to a one-night stand with the most hor-rific consequences," she said, wiping her tears. "And you've ap-parently been having a long-term affair, and now you've almost literally robbed Peter to pay Paul? My God, Michael, how did we make such a mess of things?"

He blinked repeatedly, as if some convoluted details were fi-nally registering. "I wasn't having an affair. There was never any-one else. You think Taylor was . . . some woman I was sleeping with?"

Claire felt her anger reignite. "You apologized to Nick for the situation with her. I *saw* the e-mail. Or more accurately, you were sorry Nick apparently overheard some conversation and found out about her. How can you keep on denying what you've—"

"Claire," Michael said, looking more desolate than she'd ever remembered seeing him, "Taylor was a boy I knew in Belmont Hill when I was a teenager. And he died." He cupped his face in his hands as he continued. "He killed himself because he was gay. Because I—we . . . hazed him. We were just kids—three stupid, cocky seventeen-year-olds—and we didn't think about consequences. Christ," he moaned, his eyes once again distant and focused on that faraway time and place. "He was a nice kid, a pool boy at the country club. And we just got swept up in all of the . . . the one-upping that goes on with teenagers. And then one day, in the middle of the summer, he hanged himself. In his parents' shed."

Claire's mouth went slack as she tried to digest this particularly unexpected and tragic secret. "Oh my God, why didn't you ever tell me? This is so—"

"Horrible? Devastating? Yeah, it was all of those things, multiplied by a factor you could never comprehend. No one could. We made stupid choices in our immaturity, and a life was lost. An innocent, struggling boy. There had been a note, no names mentioned, but our taunts were spelled out in it. My parents, they helped Taylor's family afterward. Financially." Michael's body seemed to have folded in on itself in the chair. "And none of us ever spoke about it again. I couldn't do anything to change what had happened other than to—to move forward and try to be a better man, to live a life with a higher purpose. But I failed miserably," he murmured in a small, broken voice. "I failed."

"Michael," Claire intoned. She followed with a flood of questions, which he went on to answer with weary resignation. He explained that Nicky had found out about Taylor at Paul and Margot's house just before coming home from Andover. They had asked him at dinner, as was their custom, what his proudest accomplishment had been at school. He had gotten an A, he had told them, on a speech about Tyler Clementi, the gay student who killed himself after his roommate webcammed him. Hate crime legislation was the final topic in speech and debate class, and his speech had gone over so well that he was going to use it for tournaments next year. Apparently things got very uncomfortable and weird at the table after that. And Nicky apparently did some listening at their door later.

"That's what you two were discussing in the study before you left for London, wasn't it?" Claire asked, still stunned by the turn of events.

Michael bowed his chin. "He told me I was a hypocrite for not standing up to my friends and doing the right thing like I'd always hammered him to do. That I had no right to get on his case about not calling Chazz's sister after taking her out once—which is a whole separate story—given the much more *damaging* choices I had made at his age." *Hypocrite,* Michael repeated despondently. "And he asked me if I regretted letting my father buy me out of the whole mess and make it all disappear. He didn't buy me out of anything, Claire," Michael said, shaking his head, his swollen blue eyes focusing on her. "It was a different time. People weren't as open and accepting, and families liked to keep things like this private. So Paul did the only thing he could do under the circumstances, and Taylor's parents were grateful for the . . . help. I told Nicky that I regretted my actions every day of my life, but all he could see was cowardice and a failure in character. I mean, how do you tell your kid you were just clueless and immature, when you ask him to be so much more?" He shook his head again and turned away from her.

But for Claire, it was as if the drapes suddenly had been drawn open on their marriage, and for the first time her view was unobstructed. Her husband's secrets and motivations were not those of the unfaithful, deceitful man she had come there to condemn, but of a haunted and conflicted man who had spent his life in flight from himself and his failures, trying to right an unrightable deed by stacking up accomplishments and money and good works, and hoping to win back the respect of the man he had least wanted to disappoint. And by pressing their son to live up to the high family standards he had long ago failed to uphold. *Seventeen already, Jesus,* she could hear Michael uttering. *On the verge of everything promising.* The promise of doing better than he had. And the fading promise, Claire thought, that Michael might, at least, have the respect and admiration of his son. That Nick had discovered his father's secret at that very same age when the hubris and naïveté of adolescence often collide—and that once again the results had been ill-fated—was almost too sad an irony for Claire to bear. And as she imagined how scarred Michael must be, she also considered how much those scars should count toward excusing his inability to forgive her and commiserate over their mistakes. After all, it was their *compounded* carelessness, though from different decades, that had come home to roost.

"I'm sorry you've been living with all of this," she said, meaning it. "But your behavior toward me since the accident—all of this makes it doubly irrational. Why were you so callous, so unwilling to try and work through everything?"

He chewed on his lip for a long moment. "I don't know," he said feebly. "I thought I was losing Nicky. He's everything to me, the best thing I've ever been part of. And I couldn't believe that life and death could so easily be . . . intersecting for a kid again, my kid. Maybe it just made everything more manageable if I could blame someone else. I don't know." He avoided Claire's eyes as he continued. "And then the portfolio problems, everything was imploding. The pension money was supposed to be a one-week float at the most. But there were complications. So many fucking complications." He paused, exhaling somberly. "But the bigger truth is, our marriage wasn't working anymore. It hadn't been for a while, Claire. You had to have seen that."

Claire shook her head slowly.

"Not because of what *either* of us did." He looked her in the eye now, his grief clearly mirroring her own. "Just . . . because. Life sometimes happens that way, you know? And I'm sorry. For everything. I just kept thinking I could somehow get out from under all of it." A glimmer of sun hovered on the horizon, framing him in a burnt-umber glow.

She was surprised by the lack of anger she felt with his explanation. Mostly, though, she felt sad that they had both been lost and living with their own bad decisions for far too long. "I thought we'd built something good for the longest time, Michael. And then I guess we just stopped paying attention. I'm sorry I didn't pay better attention."

He wiped his face with the back of his hand. "And I thought for the longest time that staying together was the right thing for Nicky. But I guess I was just distracting myself from being responsible for another terrible disappointment. I couldn't be . . . responsible again." The sharp contours of Michael's habitually squared jaw were gone. "Another failure wasn't an option. Well, until it . . . was."

Claire pondered this uncharacteristic show of honesty and emotion. There was something so unexpectedly vulnerable, so Nick-like in his face. The furnace clicked off, and she steadied a hand on the desk as she stood, processing her own truth that as hurt as she was, it wasn't the shattering hurt of lost love. But the final, undeniable shattering of the illusion. They *had* loved each other once. Just not in a timeless love-story sort of way. And for the sake of that once-lovely truth, and the gift of their son, she made a choice.

"We need to put an end to this quickly, Michael. So we don't continue to hurt each other, or hurt Nicky," she said, taking the folder from her purse and picking up the CD. They were just two parents now. "I came here to force your hand. I was going to insist that you go to Paul tomorrow and ask him for the three-point-two million to repay the pension, or I would give this information to my attorney—who would be compelled to report everything to the authorities. And I was going to have you ask Paul for additional funds to be wired to me, so that, among other things, I can buy this house." She removed a Coldwell Banker brochure from the folder and pushed it across the desk. "But," she said, knowing that it really wasn't her nature to live life through a lens of darkness or revenge—and banking that it really wasn't Michael's either, "I'm hoping that you'll come to your own conclusions about the right way to handle all of this."

Michael took the brochure and read through it, looking up at her every few seconds, as if to remind himself that it was Claire sitting across from him. "It's a nice house," he said. "But I'm not going to my father." He untwisted a paper clip into a jagged hook. "You should know that better than anyone."

She did know now—how desperate he had been to rehabilitate himself in the eyes of the man who had rescued him once before, and what a *Sophie's Choice* it would be to ask for his help again. "What I know is that he's your best option, your *only* option, if you want to minimize the extent of your problems. It's difficult, I get that. But pension fraud is serious business, Michael, and I don't want you to go to prison. You need to get that paid back immediately."

"I can't do it."

"Think about Nicky's best interests. Is your pride more important than being around to help raise your son?" She could hear him breathing, could see his chest actually heaving. "I know your parents would not want to see you in this position. You've proven yourself enough to them over the years. And you know how they feel about Nicky." She didn't bring up the potential for an embarrassing scandal that *couldn't* be kept under wraps if he didn't make an effort to resolve things quickly. Or that she would go to Paul if she had to. "Call him, Michael," she urged. "The longer you wait, the trickier things are going to get with the Department of Labor."

With their house of cards collapsed and splayed around them, it amazed her, the amount of urging it took. But if not for his hubris and her years of standing quietly, blindly by, she recognized that they wouldn't have found themselves wading through such wreckage. And so she reiterated her case, in addition to clarifying her wishes on the issues of an educational and medical trust for Nicky, a lump-sum divorce settlement, and all of the other financial imperatives she'd gone over with Gail.

"I'd like to be able to restart my life with a nice home for Nicky. So if you'll get the loan from your father and forward the funds for me to buy the house next week, I'll walk away with the number we discussed," Claire said, trying to ignore the heartrending sense of disbelief that it had all come down to this. "I don't want to fight or drag things out unnecessarily. We've already done enough damage."

Michael's stared numbly at her, and she could see that he had expended the extent of his emotional capital for one afternoon.

"Just toss it around—with or without your lawyers. It's fair. And if nothing else, we owe each other that." Claire looked at him with regret and gathered her things. "Good-bye, Michael," she said softly. "Call me by noon tomorrow and let me know where we are."

She counted the steps to the door as she walked out, willing herself not to look back. She had been squeezing into the role of guilt-ridden partner for so long, that in peeling it off like a too-tight pair of jeans, she could breathe again. It felt almost euphoric, until she began to hyperventilate.

And in her wired, uncertain state, she didn't hear Nicholas quietly shut the door to his bedroom behind the study, didn't hear him tear the sheets from his bed.

CHAPTER 44

"Oh, hon, you didn't ask for nearly enough. You're holding all the cards now, and Paul Montgomery could write you a check for a couple million every year until he croaks and still never spend half his money."

Claire, Gail, Jackie, and Carolyn sat at the back of DJ's, an out of the way café in the Highlands, filling the hours until noon and buffering Claire's tenterhooks.

"I didn't want to give the old man a stroke," Claire said over her plate of uneaten eggs Benedict. "And I don't want to be beholden to them. I just want to be able to walk away from this as honorably and as quickly as I can. And not be financially tied to Michael's choices anymore."

"You did good, Claire," Jackie said. "You and Nicky will have a great place to live, he'll be taken care of financially, *and* you'll have a nice cushion to start over with."

"It's all still a big 'if.' I couldn't get a good read on Michael when I left. And I honestly don't know what's more frightening to him—going to Paul with the truth and asking for his help, or dragging this Wincor thing out to the bitter end and risking prison." She didn't tell them about Taylor, except that to say that *she* was a *he,* an old friend with no impact on the present situation. The rest would remain Michael's secret, his story to explain, or not, to Nicholas.

"Sweetie," Carolyn assured, "Michael will do everything in his power to keep his ass *and* his reputation pristine, if you know what I'm saying. And if that means requesting a little cash from Daddy, you can bet he will. Never mind that you've given him a head start with the authorities *and* offered him the deal of the century. I wouldn't have been so generous to the lying bastard."

"And never mind that our attorney is going to need a therapist when you tell him what you've offered without his advice," Gail said.

Claire looked at her watch nervously.

"Michael's just digesting things," Jackie reassured her, glancing at Claire's iPhone, which was propped against the bread basket. "And I'm sure that's requiring more than the usual amount of Pepto."

"I don't know. It's eleven thirty, and still nothing." She could feel her optimism for a simple resolution waning with the morning. "I wish I could just push a button and have this all behind us."

"Isn't there an app for that?" Gail asked, reaching her fork across the table to Jackie's French toast.

"Gail," Carolyn said, "you know better than anyone that this is not going to be simple."

"I know. But I also believe that Michael and Paul will come through. It's far too good a deal for them not to," she said to Claire, shaking her head. "Paul is a smart man."

"I have to agree that you've made things far easier than they ought to be, sweetie. That money will be gone quicker than you think. And I'm feeling incredibly concerned about your future."

Claire felt every last bit of mileage she'd put under her belt in the last few weeks. "I appreciate that. But I'm coming from a slightly less elevated rung on the financial ladder than you and Gail, and I'm fine with what I offered. I'd rather walk away with a smaller amount now than wait for all of Michael's deals to stabilize and start cash flowing again, and be dependent on a monthly check. However, given that I haven't been able to sleep for more than two hours at night, I *have* spent considerable time thinking about my own future cash flow. And," Claire said, amazing herself with a smile, "I've come up with a plan I'm actually excited about."

The women put down their coffees and put on their reading glasses, and focused as Claire expounded on the business proposal she placed in the center of the table. "I've made some calls and reconnected with my mentor and old colleagues in New York and London, and my plan is to do private art consulting." Her as yet unnamed advisory service, she explained, would help clients identify onetime purchases or long-term collecting strategies, as well as source and acquire works. "I'm thinking about doing a private tour to Art Basel in December. Miami's on fire now. I can also advise on framing, placement, and installation, too." Her voice rose in excitement. "Hell, I'll do it myself. And given the economy, I anticipate a brisk business in selling off single pieces, and liquidating entire collections, too."

Jackie shot her a knowing smile. "I'm proud of you," she whispered.

"Sign me up as your first client," Carolyn said ecstatically. "Now that the collection's in my name, you will be my go-to person for all acquisitions and sales. I also need to have a few pieces independently appraised, *and* I've been wanting to shift everything around on the main level. But I just can't get the vision right. So," she said with a flourish of her checkbook wallet, "you're hired!"

With all the enthusiasm and light bubbling up around her, Claire felt as if she were taking the first steps out through the shadows. "Oh, let's not worry about fees. I'll come over and we can spend a morning creating a new vision for the space. And I can bring my appraiser, too."

Carolyn leaned back into her chair, obviously pleased with the prospect.

"You know," Gail said, pouring more syrup onto Jackie's French toast, "Zibby's been very tied in with the San Francisco art scene ever since she bought her little pied-à-terre there. And she just adores you, so I'm sure she'd be happy to make some introductions."

"Thank you."

"By the way, hon, what are you going to call this fab new brain-child?"

Claire relaxed slightly. "Well, my first thought was 'Nothing Toulouse,' but I'll probably need to go with something a little more refined." She laughed.

"How about Renaissance?" Jackie suggested after some consideration.

Claire rolled the idea around. "Renaissance Fine Arts Consulting," she repeated, envisioning logos and business cards, and warming to this idea of her future. "That's not bad." Just then her cell phone vibrated and lit up with Michael's name. It was 12:00. Claire looked from the phone into her cheerleader's faces. "I guess this is it," she whispered.

"No," Jackie firmly stated. "*This* is it." She pointed to the business plan. "Everything else is just details."

"Hello," Claire said with a small pit in her stomach.

The call lasted a mere two minutes. As Claire listened, her expression shifted from one of hope to devastation. When it was over, she set the phone down and wiped her mouth with her napkin.

"Sweetie?" Carolyn asked after a stunned silence. "What happened?"

Claire took a sip of water and gathered herself. "He called Paul."

"So, he accepted your proposal?" Jackie asked

"Yes."

"Then why so downbeat, hon? This is what you wanted, right?"

"Apparently Nicky came home early and overheard me make my demands. And he confronted Michael about the pension fraud after I left. Nick got very agitated and threatened to call Paul himself, if Michael didn't. He's terrified of his dad going to jail, and he's devastated by the whole mess," she explained, feeling no elation in what should have been a small victory. "I guess it was a very long night. And Michael's apoplectic."

"Shit," Jackie said, summarizing Claire's mood.

"But he's following through on what you asked?" Gail pushed. "The restitution and the money for you?"

"Yes. Both Paul's and Michael's attorneys will be contacting Jack on Monday," she said, distractedly.

"Then it looks like Nicky helped to make your offer one that Michael couldn't refuse. Which is good for both of them in the long run."

"But drawing Nick into everything was not my plan. He's suffered enough collateral damage already. This is his father, and he really didn't need to hear about all the financial crap." She closed her eyes and tried to imagine what it must have been like for a kid to learn—for the second time—that his boyhood hero was anything but super.

CHAPTER 45

The following week evolved into a flurry of lawyer and realtor meetings, offers and counteroffers between all involved parties. Michael and Paul attempted a re-trade with Claire for less money, while Jack encouraged them not to play cheap in the face of what could be. His client was, after all, sparing Michael weeks with the forensic accountants, and far worse. Their lawyers relented after expensive hours of posturing and Jack's added, nonnegotiable provision that Michael would also be responsible for all legal fees. The initial wire transfer for the house arrived shortly thereafter. The remaining funds would follow over the next two weeks, during which time all other formal joint custody, property, and financial matters would be formalized. Michael's team of lawyers notified them that the 3.2 million for the pension had been placed in an escrow account, and that they were in meetings with Mac Kessler. On the real estate front, the house in North Country Club had attracted another bidder, forcing Claire into an unanticipated full-price offer—but thus sealing that deal.

And then there was Nicholas.

"I want to drive," he'd demanded in the school parking lot the Monday after his unintended earful. His expression was urgent and he knocked on Claire's car window until she got out and moved to the passenger seat. He had not responded to her calls and texts over the weekend. And not wishing to add tension to trauma, Claire had given her son his space.

But she studied him then as he threw the car into reverse, desperate to understand how this news had affected him. The exhaustion and stress she saw in his face recalled the early Rancho days—telegraphing his renewed angst, and confirming her worst fears.

"Dad's kind of a mess, and I don't really want . . . to go to the house now," he said as he pulled out of the lot. His nervousness was undisguised.

"We're not actually going back to the house now, honey," she said, placing her hand on his bicep, and wishing somehow to erase the memory of what he had heard pass between his parents. "I'm sorry you had to hear what you did. That was never my intention, and—"

"Um, where *are* we going?" he interrupted. "I'm holding . . . traffic."

She saw the cars bunch up behind them and reminded herself that he needed to concentrate on the task at hand. "I'm sorry," she said again. "Take a left at the light and I'll show you where to go."

Their silent drive to the cottage took just under ten minutes from school, which made what had seemed like a harried leap into new home ownership feel slightly less so. When they pulled up in front of the charming yellow house with the "Under Contract" sign on the lawn, Nicholas turned to her, perplexed. Jean, the realtor, was waiting for them on the covered front porch.

"So, you've obviously gathered that . . . that we're moving ahead with the divorce," Claire began, winging the whole speech since everything she had rehearsed had vaporized under the pressure of the moment. "No matter how badly Dad and I may have screwed things up, we're doing what we think is best for all of us now. Our lives will be different than what we might have imagined, but . . . I guess that's part of the journey," she said, praying with all her might they could both find some goodness in that. "And I promise you that along the way, no one will have your best interests at heart more than I will."

Nicholas studied his Nikes. There were a thousand thoughts

and words simmering behind his pursed lips and strained façade, but Claire could see that they still weren't ready to be spoken. She squeezed his palm reassuringly, hoping that one day those words would come. He was a teenager, plagued by uncertainty and cloaked in cool—the total adolescent dichotomy. And she would wait. "Yeah," he finally whispered, squeezing back.

Claire pointed out the window with her free hand. "So *that*," she said, exhaling at least a month's worth of anxiety, "is going to be our new house."

A light rain had begun to trickle down over the well-tended block, and mist rose into the afternoon air. Even in winter, the front yards along the street were neat and pruned. Nick's body uncoiled and he rolled down the window, filling the car with the scent of damp concrete.

She had his attention. "I know this is sudden, Nick. But we need our own home, a place where you have your own bedroom, just like you do at our—at Dad's."

He cocked his head left and right out the window, seemingly taking in the picture from different perspectives. "Are we going in?" he asked after a moment.

Jean showed them into the house and gave Claire a stack of documents to sign. The closing was set for three weeks, she mentioned, before leaving them to explore. Claire led Nicholas through the family room to the kitchen and breakfast nook. The aroma of cinnamon combined with the pine floors to give the home a cozy feel. Nicholas looked out the picture window to the back-yard. There was an arbor, and a cobblestone terrace surrounding a shaded garden.

"This looks . . . like you," he said.

Claire was grateful that he didn't seem angry she'd made such a major decision without him. But, still, she couldn't discern any interest on his part. "And how 'bout you, buddy? What do you think?"

He looked around some more, running his hand along the cabinets, doors, and walls as he made his way to the center hall. His gait seemed shakier than usual, but it also could have been his billowy sweatpants lending the illusion of fragility. "It's . . . cool. No upstairs?"

"No, but there's a basement, and a great alcove attached to your room that we can make into a studio if you want."

He followed her to the bedroom and gave the space a serious inspection—the closet, the bathroom, the photos and dolls on the bookshelves, the alcove that was presently serving as a playroom, the view from the window, which he opened—nothing escaped his scrutiny. After a good five minutes of pacing and eyebrow furrowing, his posture seemed to droop under the weight of some silent dissatisfaction.

"Nicky?" she asked nervously.

No response.

"I needed to jump on this before someone else snapped it up. Maybe we could have Chazz come out for a long weekend and—"

"No!" he shouted, tripping on the pastel flower-bouquet rug in the center of the room. His eyes looked as if they would suddenly spill buckets.

She took a step toward him, but he backed away. "What's going on, honey? I know this is unfamiliar, and a little unexpected. I just thought that Chazz might help—"

"I told Dad. I'm done with . . . Andover. I . . . have new friends here," he shouted even louder. "I hate this." He tried kicking the rug back into place, but it just twisted under his foot, causing him to crumble into a heap on a bed of woven tulips.

Claire knelt down next to him. "I'm sorry, Nicky. Is it the house you hate? Or something . . . else?"

He remained quiet for some time. A cold wind blew in from the window, and he pulled his hoodie over his head. "I can't count on . . . my brain," he whispered from inside the fleece.

Gingerly she took this opening and walked with him through the many fears he'd been harboring, which the prospect of moving had clearly stirred up. There was the lingering fear of never measuring up to his past and to the memories of those who knew him then. There was his embarrassment over the bumpiness of his speech, the lost words and all the other things he could not remember. Being the new kid with no baseline or history made it easier to blend in, but blending in, while comforting, was not something he was used to either. And then there were all the coping skills he needed to develop for this latest shift in his routine. The challenges were epic and paralyzing.

"I was good at so much," he said, staring up at the framed beach landscape on the wall.

She nodded, following his gaze.

"I'm not . . . good at anything anymore."

Her heart splintered for the umpteenth time. "Oh, honey. You are. It's just difficult to lose abilities and to remember how much better we used to be at certain things. Adults deal with this all the time. And I get that it's harder for someone your age," she said, while reproaching herself for throwing him into the spin cycle without so much as a warning. "But the abilities you've cultivated are beyond impressive, and your dad and I are so proud of you."

Nicholas peered out from the side of the hood deliberately, like a tortoise. "What if Dad goes . . . to jail . . . for what he did?"

The comment caught Claire unprepared and she turned his chin toward her, studying him, stalling for time. His color was off and his face was taut. Anxiety about the future *and* the past—no wonder he seemed so contorted. A snapshot of Stretch Armstrong, the action doll from her childhood, flashed to mind, and she wished Nicholas could somehow see himself in the way she did: as a boy who was stretching the limits of what was possible, and not merely as being deformed and broken. She wrapped her arm around him, still searching for an answer that would lessen his strain. "Dad and your grandfather have excellent lawyers," she tried. "If he does things right, I imagine he'll have to pay some fines. And hopefully that will be it." She braced for him to ask about Taylor again, but that subject did not appear to be plaguing him.

His breathing slowed. "Okay," he said, fluffing his hair and pushing up from the floor.

She wondered how he felt about all that he had overheard in the study, but for the present, all that really mattered was that he felt safe.

"When do I have to move?"

"It should be about three weeks, honey, but we're doing this together. And I promise to make it as easy as possible," she said, intending to enlist Andi and Ray throughout the transition.

Nick resumed his inspection of the room.

"You can count on me, Nicky," she said, hoping to convince him at least of that, and convince herself that she'd be able to help him salvage his confidence. Claire glanced at the collection of snow globes and Madame Alexander dolls on the shelves, and pictured a polite and optimistic girl packing up her things for her next great adventure.

"Pink?" Nicholas said, sharply turning from the alcove and fixing a scowl on her. "You expect me to live in a . . . pink bedroom?"

It was like aspirin kicking in after a long battle with midnight. The scowl, now tipping up at the sides, was bogus and ironic. She stood up, smiling. "I share your concern," she said, taking a Benjamin Moore color deck from her purse and handing it to him. "Pick one, kiddo. We can paint the room any shade you like." She wanted the idea of a fresh palette to become much more than just a metaphor.

Nicholas fanned it out and considered the spectrum of choices, laughing softly as he did. It was the first time she had heard him laugh in over six months.

As they drove off, Claire looked over her shoulder, and framed within the soggy halo of the rear wipers, their new cottage—the last stop, Claire hoped, in their year of living precariously—receded into a light fog.

CHAPTER 46

Claire phoned Cora from the SFO baggage carousel. "I'm just heading to get the rental car, so I can be in the City in about half an hour. Do you want to meet for lunch at the Fairmont?"

"I'm so excited you're here, dear, but I completely forgot about my meeting with Martha Van Deegan about the debutante committee. This quitting smoking has left me positively batty. I need to be in Pacific Heights at noon." Her voice rang with excitement. "Isn't that just fabulous?"

Claire hoisted her garment bag onto the cart with one hand. "Just fabulous, Mother." *Just so fabulously Cora.* "So, what time would you like to meet? I have a cocktail party at seven thirty."

"How about tea instead? Say two thirty?"

"Fine," she said, thinking the trip was shaping up to be much more relaxing than she'd originally imagined. "Call my cell when you're leaving Mrs. Van Deegan's delightful manse, just to make sure we're still on schedule."

"Okay, sweetie. Toodleloo," Cora chirped, not even asking whose cocktail party was on the docket.

Claire remembered Mrs. Van Deegen from her own deb days, and she'd likely be seeing her that evening at Letty Rusalka's, along with enough of San Francisco's social doyennes and their art patron husbands to knock Cora completely out of her tree with excitement—all thanks to Zibby Harrold's graciously procured invitation. Zibby had the apartment below Letty's, and wouldn't hear of Claire not staying at her place and attending the party in her stead, since she had commitments in New York. Claire had met Victor and Letty Rusalka at various auctions and receptions over the years, and had always admired Victor's impeccable eye for new artists, and Letty's outspoken support of the arts, and she had been saddened to learn of Victor's death the previous winter. Theirs had been a devoted and enviable marriage of over fifty years—the kind that Claire had long ago hoped she and Michael might grow into. So the chance to reconnect with the venerable Mrs. Rusalka amid her extremely notable private collection, coupled with the opportunity to spend one glorious night in Zibby's marble and taffeta pied-à-terre before heading down to her girlhood room in Burlingame, was too good to pass up. The fact that Richard was driving in to be her escort was an added bonus.

Claire strolled out to the curb feeling unbound. The weather was overcast, but mild and warm. She tied her sweater around her shoulders and boarded the rental-car bus. Fifteen minutes later, she was in a Ford Taurus driving north on the 101, putting some much-needed physical and emotional distance between herself and Michael and the lawyers, and the draining march toward divorce. Clouds veiled the colorful row houses of Daly City, but as Claire rounded the curve that opened San Francisco to her view—a sight that never failed to take her breath away—the sun broke through, draping the glass and steel skyline in diamonds. She cruised toward the city, and away from the disarray of the previous weeks.

Off the highway, the streets rolled past her, hilly and angular and gray, and in no time, wet. A profusion of striped and floral umbrellas blossomed up outside the boutiques and cafés. At a stop sign, a man dashed in front of Claire's car, holding a newspaper over his head with one hand and a steaming coffee cup in the other. He licked his wrist and made for cover under the awning of a gallery. As Claire drove past, she saw him fold the paper into neat fourths and begin to read as he sipped. The familiarity of the act struck her—transported her, really, to a hundred

Sunday mornings in Burlingame. And instead of making the turn toward the Fairmont, she found herself heading downtown to the financial district. After a brief scuffle with traffic, she pulled over and looked up to see a grand pyramid flooded with light. Slowly the letters of the familiar insignia emerged from the receding mist. The building seemed even larger to Claire than she remembered from her childhood—her father's place of business, the Transamerica Building—towering above her and glistening through the rain. She killed the engine and leaned her seat back.

"I was charmed by a silly illusion, Dad," she whispered, still missing him with all her heart and wishing for just a slice of clarity and confidence he'd always been able to help her find. "Bamboozled and blinded. And now I'm picking up the pieces on forever." She had been dreaming of him lately when she did sleep, and she closed her eyes, recalling her weekend visits to the office with him, their lunchtime walks through the emptied streets, hot dogs in hand and the seemingly insurmountable issues of the moment up for examination and, almost always, resolution. She wanted the beautiful forever he had always promised to start now.

Claire studied the bronze reliefs on the massive main doors of Grace Cathedral, recognizing them as replicas of Ghiberti's *Gates of Paradise* from the Duomo in Florence. Her right hand went to her chest, and she stepped back to take in the beauty before her. The rain had ceased, and the Gothic arches of the cathedral had carried her in the direction of the church from the Fairmont valet. She had another hour before meeting Cora.

Venturing inside, she needed a moment to adjust to the mystical dimness. Ahead and above her rose the high arched ceiling, dark and ornate in its detail, and contrasted by the dazzling beauty of numerous stained glass windows. On the floor she saw a sprawling maze etched into the stone just before the nave. A sign announced the "Interfaith Labyrinth," and she then understood why she had been drawn to this place of spiritual growth and healing. Several people were making their journey to the path's center, and she watched these "pilgrims" for a moment, so deep in their meditations. She felt her body tremble and she looked up, wondering if Someone was doubting her ability to find such visible peace. There was another labyrinth, she read, just outside and adjacent to the church plaza. Something about that option felt right.

Claire walked through the door beyond the sign, and into a courtyard overlooking Nob Hill. She took in the Zen-like arrangement of trees and plants there, and glimpsed a speck of dew reflecting off a spider web. It shone like spun iridescence, and she marveled at this bridging of two azalea branches with nature's glue. A hummingbird fluttered above the low branch of a flowering plum tree to her right. Such an extraordinary painting, she thought. Only it was real. At the center of the courtyard was the labyrinth—eleven winding circuits paved in white and gray terrazzo. Alone in the space, Claire faced its starting point and considered the symbolic journey before her, to one's spiritual center, as the sign had explained. *Who couldn't use a little centering,* she thought.

She began the serpentine path with tentative footsteps, her feet never falling outside the marble lines that delineated the sharp curves and switchbacks. As she ventured toward the elusive center, she had to pay close attention to her balance while navigating the turns so she wouldn't step outside the path. What would happen, she wondered, if she just cruised through the labyrinth, letting her feet fall where they may, and disregarding the rules and boundaries she believed to exist there? What if she skipped or danced her way to the center, singing as she did? She made the next hairpin turn without regard to the path lines her feet were crossing, but just that small adjustment was noticeable and unnerving. She had to force herself to move more freely and not walk as though she were walking down the aisle at her wedding, one foot forward and then the other catching up to pause at its side for a beat, then moving on. And this absurd contest to be less constrained prompted a sudden rush of tears from a very deep place. There was nothing at stake here, she had to remind herself, no need to be impeccable. Reflexively, Claire looked around to be sure there was still no one there to see her. But it was just her, the birds, the occasional car horn and trolley bell, and what seemed like fifty more turns to reach that mystical center.

She let the tears flow until she regained her composure, and with each successive step she began to release the distractions of protocol and uncertainty, her body finding the pace it wanted, her mind quieting. The noises of the city around her fell away. Soon she had the sensation of floating in a tank, hearing the power of her heartbeat and her breath, as questions lined themselves up for inspection.

As Claire proceeded, she imagined her life in the context of a path. *Maybe we inadvertently cast ourselves to sea in search of . . . different horizons? Necessary vicissitudes?* The scent of orange blossom filled her head, along with the rapid fire fanning of hummingbird wings. It was as if the volume of her senses had suddenly been turned to high, and things were coming into a brighter focus. *But what about Nicky's journey, where would he find himself?* She continued winding forward, the turns reminding her of the inevitable changes in life, the unpredictability. *Maybe a little ambiguity and imperfection isn't so awful. Maybe there's growth to be found in that.* With each one hundred eighty degree change in direction, it was almost as if she could feel her awareness shifting between her right brain and left brain, her movement becoming effortless, her mind more balanced and attentive to her intuition. *Get comfortable with the asymmetry,* she found herself chanting. *Find the beauty in the scars and the uncertainty and the possibilities. Don't be paralyzed.* There was a sacred sort of wisdom bubbling up, something that seemed to know what she needed. When Claire looked down after some indeterminate time frame, she was in the center of the labyrinth. A peaceful energy coursed through her. She opened her mouth and took a hungry sip of air, feeling as if she'd just broken the surface of a cool, deep lake. Pausing for several moments in that serenity-filled space, she drank in the healing forces at work, releasing angst and guilt, and receiving the permission she needed for things to be just as they were.

She walked out of the labyrinth in the same direction she entered it. Looking skyward, she smiled before sitting down on a shaded stone bench to meditate. *You are on a path, exactly where you are meant to be. You are okay.* Surrendering to possibility, her soul felt stretched, her body revitalized. After a few moments

Claire was tipped from her reverie by the vibration of her cell phone. "Hello, Mother," she murmured into the phone. "I'm at Grace Cathedral, meet me inside the entrance."

Twenty minutes later, and seemingly forty pounds lighter, Claire reentered the cathedral to find her mother. And there, at the back of the nave, stood Cora, hatted, with her coordinating navy bag and pumps, and dark round sunglasses clutched in her hand—her best imitation of Jackie O. If Jackie had had a perm and recently quit chain-smoking Kool Lites. Claire kissed her mother warmly and guided her toward the cathedral doors. "Shall we take a little walk?"

"That sounds lovely."

They emerged, blinking, into the sunlight, and Claire took her mother's hand. "I've just found my way through an extraordinary labyrinth." She looked out across the city, and the sky was a blue she hadn't seen before.

"Are you all right, dear?" Cora said, sizing her up and reaching into her pocketbook. "Here, take my hanky."

Claire took the handkerchief and just held it, feeling an overwhelming need to talk. "Mother, I don't know how to convey what I've been going through since the accident. It's been ungodly painful but, I think, somehow . . . necessary."

Cora looked at her skeptically as they walked down the great church steps and onto California Street.

"I was in hell. Lived there for quite some time, actually," she continued. "But it's helped me to see things more clearly. It only took me forty-three years, the near death of my child, and the breakup of my marriage to wake up."

"This is so dismal, dear. How can you seem so . . ." Cora focused her tractor beam on Claire. "So fine with it?"

"Because I can finally breathe. Because I'm not underwater anymore." She held her shoulders back and spoke with a renewed dignity. "And because I'm going to stop waiting for life to come to me."

All around them, view-seeking tourists pointed their cameras toward the bay or the three gilded Grande Dame hotels at the top of the hill. But for Claire and Cora, the scenery melted into the distance. "Claire, I'm so sorry. I only ever wanted the best of everything for you, and I was so grateful that Michael seemed to be able to give those things to you when your father and I couldn't."

"You and Daddy did give me the best. We all make our own choices and decisions, Mother. My life was laid out in front of me like this beautiful magic carpet, and I just hopped on without checking underneath for dust and pretenses and all the other things we hide under our rugs. You know? And I just kept shoving more stuff under it. I couldn't reconcile the flaws—" She looked back at the cathedral. "With my reality."

Cora made a sad, tight *o* with her lips, holding back some soothing response, Claire was certain, while attacking a piece of Nicorette through its foil blister pack. She put the gum in her mouth with a satisfying-sounding crunch and breathed a sigh of relief. "What are you saying, dear?"

"I was always chasing the perfect. Or," she said, searching for the right words, "at least trying to capture all these perfect moments like a photograph. When things were ugly, I shoved the ugly away. Which doesn't encourage much growth or depth, does it? And I'm afraid we pushed Nicky into this unreasonable striving for perfection, too." Their pace slowed as they climbed the hilly street and digested Claire's theory. "And look where that led us."

"Claire, you may be right about your own experience, but in my humble opinion, that pushing business with Nicky was Michael's crap, not yours. Just another item on that bastard's list of . . . crap." She had been like a preschooler for the past weeks, playing with a dirty word and relishing the danger of it.

"We both contributed. That's what parents do, for better and for worse." She didn't expect Cora to hear any accusation in her statement. It was a universal truth, at least in her humble opinion.

"Well, if he doesn't do the right thing by you, he'll have me to deal with. He's a pusher and a—"

"Mother, can you say anything nice about him?" Claire asked jokingly, trying to avoid any more trips to the dark side.

Cora placed two fingers against her lips as if holding a cigarette, and seriously considered the question. "He wears a suit well," she finally said.

"He does, indeed."

Cora took back the handkerchief and dabbed her forehead. "What's happening with the pension?"

"Well, because he made restitution so quickly—"

"Thanks to you, dear."

"Several people helped him see the light. And it looks like he's just going to have to pay some stiff penalties and interest. No jail time. The boys from Skadden, Arps are working overtime to make this disappear. My guess is that the legal fees are going to be far steeper than the fines. But that's not my problem."

"Couldn't happen to a nicer guy," she said with a satisfied sniff. "Especially after piling all that blame and guilt on you without any consideration for your pain."

"It was his way of coping, I suppose. It wasn't about me, not really." Claire no longer felt the need to share her mother's resentment about Michael. That well of bitterness and anger, she noticed, was newly filled with a sense of peace. And a delightful absence of headaches. A cable car approached, and they stopped walking to watch a young man and his three-legged collie chase after it at. The man waved at the conductor to stop. And the dog, a lopsided whirl of slobber and barking, wagged his tail and smiled a carefree doggy smile as he tried to keep pace with his master. The man hopped onto the platform and shouted for the dog to "Leap, buddy!" The collie struggled stalwartly to make the leap and then to climb into his master's lap, reaching his mark just as the bell clanked and the cable car resumed its journey. Claire stared as the car continued up the street, the melancholy beauty of the scene piercing her. In her periphery she could see her mother wiping her eyes behind her sunglasses.

"You know, dear," Cora said, linking her arm inside Claire's, "sometimes things unspool for a reason, to help us become who we are meant to become."

CHAPTER 47

As Claire and Richard stepped out of the elevator and onto the chevron parquet floors of Letty Rusalka's beaux arts co-op, she promised they would only stay for an hour.

"Hey, I'm in for the long haul, Smitty. I've got the new threads and my curfew's not till midnight." In his houndstooth blazer with red pocket square, and new glasses, Richard looked hipper than she remembered, and most definitely festive. "Besides, your pickings here will be prime for new business contacts."

Claire rolled her eyes and smoothed the Donna Karan draped-front cocktail dress she'd retrieved from her old closet. The crowd of sparkling guests was already thick in the salon, and Richard gave her a little push forward. Within seconds, Letty was approaching them, with her jewel-tipped cane clearing the way of inconveniently placed loafers and Weitzmans, and her deep green brocade turban and jade earrings marking a stunning contrast to her legendary porcelain skin.

"Claire Montgomery, I am so delighted you came! You know, I'll never forget the lovely condolence note you sent after I lost Victor. I was very touched."

Claire smiled softly. "It's wonderful to see you again. Thank you very much for having us." She turned to Richard. "This is my good friend Richard Elliot. He's up from Los Angeles visiting his daughter at Berkeley."

Letty cocked her head. "Are you the writer from the *Journal*?"

"Guilty."

"My husband enjoyed your column. Most weeks," she said with a twinkle.

It had never dawned on her that Richard was somewhat of a celebrity in the newspaper world, and she felt stupid for having been too wrapped up in her own mess to learn more about his professional life.

"Well, I'm honored. Your husband was a true visionary, and his involvement, along with your own, with the California Arts Council has had a tremendous impact. I'm a big fan. But not as big as Claire." He took off his glasses and winked at Claire from the side. "She's a great admirer of your support of young artists."

"Is that so, my dear?"

"Well, yes," Claire said, trying to contain her surprise. "You've always had such fantastic foresight in terms of the artists you've promoted, and I've long admired your interest in collecting an eclectic mix—the things that have really grabbed you. I'm not a big fan of collecting art just because it complements the couch."

"Ah, you *understand*." Letty's dark, curious eyes glowed, and she handed her cane to Richard and took both of their arms. "I'll give you the tour," she said, leading them away from the salon and toward a grand hallway. "Zibby just adores you, and she told me about your recent difficulties. You know, I've always thought Margot Montgomery was a colossal pain in the neck. And of course the apple never falls far from the tree, does it?" She gave Claire a knowing look as they passed through a frosted glass door. "But *you,* my dear, are going to be just fine. I've heard all about your consulting business, and there are some artists here I want you to meet."

"Smart cookie, this one," Richard whispered behind Letty's turban.

Claire eked out a grateful thank-you, and was immediately lost in the sleek perfection of the Rusalkas' private gallery. It was a stunning marriage of antique and new, the up-and-coming next to the established. From the Murano-glass chandeliers to Ed Ruscha's

Burning Gas Station, from the Moroccan antique ceramics to the sheet metal alphabet sculpture, every piece seemed to vibrate with light and meaning. She and Richard wandered the room, admiring the mix of media on display. "The California Arts Council?" she whispered. "Very impressive. Where did *that* come from?"

"I research for a living, did you forget? And I always like to be a helpful date." He put his hand at the small of her back as they stopped in front of an Asian grouping.

"These vases and block prints are from our stint in Japan," Letty explained. "And over there, by the Steichen photographs, are some of our favorite art students' pieces."

A visually explosive abstract canvas stopped Claire mid-approach, giving her that breathtaking heart wobble she felt when she first saw Renato's drawings, and she asked Letty about the artist. The doyenne's slow nod and satisfied smile seemed to convey her approval of Claire's eye.

"Her name is Marietta. She goes only by her first name, and she's a graduate of the San Francisco Art Institute. And I suggest that you follow her career."

"I'd like to see more of her work," Claire said, feeling possibilities.

"I believe she's coming tonight, so I will make sure she finds you."

"Thank you, Letty. I'd be grateful. And it's truly a privilege to see what you and Victor have curated here. This room is so alive and inspiring."

"Yes, this was our life together, our experiences. It enriched our world so," she said with a widow's wistfulness. "I'll loan the collection out one day, but I'm not ready to part with it just yet. In the meantime, I want you to meet Georgine Gray tonight, too. She recently cashed out her husband's Microsoft options and needs help with a collecting strategy. Gorgeous home in the Marina, taste in her behind."

"Sounds like the perfect client," Richard quipped.

They followed Letty back through the frosted door toward the party. A butler stopped with a tray of martinis, and Letty picked up two and handed them to Claire. "Here," she said, "bring these along to Georgine, she'll be much more agreeable."

Claire handed one to Richard and they walked with their hostess across the lavish salon, its floor-to-ceiling windows and expansive views of the Golden Gate bathing the room in a sexy glow and, it appeared, the usual shellacking of foreheads. The female guests, mostly in their fifties and north, all seemed to be pulled or injected to within an inch of their thirties. Georgine, no exception, stood by a marble column, a vision of buttery confection in a flouncy number reminiscent of a Barbie gown, but with enough serious jewels to lend the overall picture gravitas. Letty made the introduction and was then called away to her kitchen. Claire offered Georgine one of the martinis, and they were off to an enthusiastic start.

"I'm in the market for some unique artwork, and Letty tells me you can help me create an artistic vision for my home." She spoke with wild flourishes of her hands, but somehow managed to keep the gin from jumping the rim of her glass. "I honestly don't know anything about the finer points of collecting, other than to say that I don't want another impressionistic bridge in France, and blah, blah, blah. I want *statement* art," she said, finishing off the martini with a lick of her lips. "I want it to speak to me, and to everyone."

Claire felt a familiar bubbling inside her. Something concurrently exciting and doubt-inducing. *Just leap,* she reminded herself. "Well, I can certainly help you identify artists and works that would complement your goals. In fact, I've a few in mind that I think you'd like. And then we can design an acquisitions plan."

"Yes," Richard said, replacing Georgine's empty glass with a fresh one, "Claire is dynamite at unearthing impressive finds for her clients and creating collections with serious flair."

"That's *exactly* what I want."

Claire removed a newly minted business card from her minaudière. "It would be great fun to work with you, Georgine."

On their way back to the bar Claire pinched Richard and thanked him for the unsolicited endorsement. They took their drinks to a cabaret table.

"Here's to you and your newest client," Richard toasted. "You were marvelous, Smitty."

The champagne did little to calm her revving nerves, but it

tasted heavenly. And when Richard questioned her expression, she launched into the multitude of emotions her journey through the labyrinth had stirred up, as well as the moving image of the collie that kept limping back into her consciousness. She wondered aloud if life would always be so full of opposition—the excitement of possibility tempered by her lurking fears about Nicholas.

"All you can do is encourage Nick not to let the past hold him back. And that even with imperfection, life can be pretty damn great."

"I know," she agreed, taking another heady sip. "But do you think I'm wrong to jump into this consulting thing so soon? While he's still figuring everything out? I never want him to feel that he's second fiddle, you know?"

"Listen, Claire," he said in a serious and commanding tone, "the accident doesn't erase the fact that you are an excellent mother. You will be setting a great example for him by moving forward and doing something you love."

She nodded.

"Maybe this left turn will turn out to be a road that gets you both to somewhere great. To where you belong."

And with those familiar words, Richard had wrapped her worries in something warm and safe. She pictured Cora at the cable car stop, impressing upon her the same message. And she hoped, once again, that clichés really could be prophetic. She squeezed his forearm just as Letty called her party guests to attention from the center of a winding staircase at the corner of the salon. The hum of conversation and background music ceased.

"I'd like to bring awareness to a new organization here in the city. It's an arts program for primary school children—and as you all know, I'm passionate about exposing youth to the arts from an early age." Letty spoke with an air of discernment and devotion that she wore as effortlessly as her turban, and Claire could feel her fire. "For many of these kids, it will be the one thing that will make their hearts sing. I'm not asking you to take out your wallets, but rather to volunteer some time if you're so inclined. You'll find information about the program scattered about tables, along with the New Year's resolutions and artwork by some of the youngsters in the program." She signaled with her cane for the butlers to pass more champagne. "Enjoy the rest of the evening."

Claire and Richard accepted more Moët, and simultaneously noticed a note card sitting under the watch of the single, fragrant white rose on the cabaret table. They both strained to see the words and accompanying pictures by candlelight. Richard handed her his glasses, and Claire laughed aloud as she read the first line written in purple crayon. It was genius in its simplicity. *Eat more elk jerky!—Amos Dugan, age 7.* Above the other expected decrees of *Listen to my Mom; Be nicer to my brother; Clean my room when Dad says so,* this kid had gotten it right. He was going to do what brought him joy, even if it was not the expected, appropriate choice. Maybe especially because it wasn't.

"Where did a seven-year-old get to be so goddamned smart?" Richard asked, heisting an opened bottle of bubbly from the passing staff, and refilling their glasses.

"To Amos!" she said as they drank to the young sage.

"You know, sometimes you have to take advice from unlikely sources."

"Do I look elk deficient?" she joked.

"No, Smitty, you look radiant." He took her hand, grabbing her attention away from the unexpected compliment. "Maybe it's time to stop overthinking things and just take life as it comes."

"I agree," she said, clinking his glass. She imagined herself looking at limitations as potential agents of change. She imagined embracing life again, crappy moments and all, and finding that fire she'd lost along the way. "You can be my plus-one anytime, Mr. Elliot," she said.

"I'll go anywhere with you."

A willowy young woman with raven hair and angular features approached their table. "You two look like you've just solved the Middle East crisis, so I'm very sorry to interrupt. But Mrs. Rusalka insisted that I come introduce myself. I'm Marietta." She shook Claire's hand and gave Richard a shy wave. Her fingernails were short and painted deep purple, and were she not an artist, she could have easily been an Anthropologie model.

"We were admiring your work inside the inner sanctum," Richard said. "Killer lines."

"Well, thank you. I think."

"He's a business writer," Claire defended. "And Letty certainly can't say enough great things about you and your future. In fact, I believe she used the term 'embryonic superstar.' "

Marietta smiled coyly. "Mrs. R has been a great champion of my work. And she tells me you are someone I need to know. You're an art consultant?"

"Not *just* an art consultant. She's the tops," Richard began singing in an endearingly off-key falsetto. "She's the Louvre museum." He swallowed the last of his champagne and tipped an imaginary hat. "And with that, ladies, I'm going to excuse myself to the gents' so you can talk some shop." He danced across the parquet corridor and disappeared into the crowd.

"Your husband?" Marietta asked.

"Nope. Just a very sweet friend," she said with a laugh. "But let's discuss your latest work. I'm dying to see more."

Marietta talked about her studio and some of her recent exhibitions in the city, and then took out her iPhone and scrolled through images of canvases and panels, explaining the different series she'd completed over the last year. Many shared an early abstract-expressionist feel, but with a revitalized edge, and Claire was wowed. She asked about her sales and pricing structure—which she felt could be enhanced—as she browsed the striking pieces. And one in particular, a small acrylic with symphonic bursts of color, prompted Claire to slide the phone from Marietta's elegant hand.

"What's this one titled?"

"That's from the *Kindness* series. I called it *Support*."

Claire smiled. "I love the palette and geometry of it. And I have a buyer," she said without hesitation.

"Who?!" Marietta made no effort to conceal her elation.

"Me. There's someone I'd like to give it to." Claire took out her own phone, looked up Richard's address, and forwarded it to Marietta. "I'll come by the studio tomorrow with a check, and if you'd make arrangements to have the piece shipped, we'll be off to a wonderful beginning."

"Thank you so much, Claire. Mrs. R was certainly right."

"Yes, she was. You've got a tremendous future ahead of you.

And I'd like to show your work to several people, before the crowds come calling. Then you need to start thinking about art fairs—Basel, Frieze. The throngs are flocking there in search of the next big thing to invest in, and there's no reason it shouldn't be you." She gave Marietta one of her cards, cupping her hands around the artist's, both of them practically vibrating with possibility.

A Cole Porter trio started up in the salon, spurring a few toes to tap amidst the clusters of politically and sartorially aligned guests. The din of their conversations rose above the music to the high ceilings, filling the apartment with the cacophonous buzz of a Turkish bazaar. Claire looked up and scanned the room until she saw Richard, who, though smiling in the direction of the two St. John–clad women in front of him, had his eyes glued to her.

"I think I'll let you two say your good nights," Marietta demurred, her own gaze volleying between them. "I'm really looking forward to tomorrow." She excused herself with profound thanks and retreated to a circle of other artists.

Claire looked back at the crowd of burnished faces, and there, still watching, was Richard. She thought of her father, and how like him it was to focus in on one thing—a book, the news, her—and shut out the crush around him. Richard raised his chin and winked at her. She didn't want to talk art or the future anymore, or even Nicholas. She wanted levity and normal, and space to assimilate her thoughts and plans. She smiled back and they made their way toward each other like two refugees, eyes locked across a sea of bodies swaying in splendor.

At the elevator they stood facing each other, drunk. The most perfect, swoony champagne drunk.

Richard took her hand and kissed it tenderly.

"Didn't you say you had to get back to Berkeley at a reasonable hour?" She stared at his lips on her skin and backed away.

He glanced up from her wrist. "Yeah. I promised Lauren a beer and a game of Scrabble before she crashes."

"You're a good man, Charlie Brown," she said.

"A kiss on the hand isn't a contract, Smitty. We don't have to define any of this right now. Okay?"

She was embarrassed at his ability to read her so well. "But what about our rules?" she asked, laughing.

"We can always make new ones." He stepped into the elevator, and she watched the door close slowly across his reassuring smile.

Just after midnight Claire's cell phone rang, rousing her from a deep sleep.

"Hey, Smitty," Richard's wide-awake voice said. "Look outside."

She slipped out of bed and drowsily padded over to Zibby's bedroom window, and drew open the triple silk drapes. A massive yellow orb hung over the bay. She gazed out at the water shimmering in the moon's reflection, and the city illuminated beyond the bridge. A hundred winking stars emblazoned the picture in her mind's eye. And for a moment, all of her hopes and uncertainties and everything else were a distant flicker.

"Thank you," she said.

"For what, exactly?"

"For reminding me what's out there."

INTERNET RESOURCES

If you are interested in learning more or contributing to a charity related to some of the themes in this book, please consider donating to:

The Children's Diabetes Foundation at Denver (childrensdiabetes foundation.org), which was established by Mr. and Mrs. Marvin Davis in 1977 in Denver to support research in childhood diabetes and to provide the best possible clinical and educational programs for children with the disease. The Foundation's mission is to raise funds to support the Barbara Davis Center for Childhood Diabetes, where more than 6,000 children and young adults from all over the world receive the finest diabetes care available.

The Craig Hospital Foundation (craighospital.org/foundation) which raises funds and dedicates its resources to further advance the needs of the Craig Hospital family and its mission to advocate for and provide exemplary rehabilitation care to people affected by spinal cord and traumatic brain injury so that they can achieve optimal health, independence, and life quality.

Rancho Los Amigos Foundation (ranchofoundation.org), which raises funds for programs, services, and equipment for Rancho patients and their families. It is the mission of the Foundation to help pediatric and adult patients, whose lives have been forever changed through disabling injuries or illnesses, experience the restoration of health, the rebuilding of lives, and the revitalization of hope.

The National Center for Bullying Prevention (pacer.org/bullying), which helps to promote awareness and teach effective ways to respond to bullying.

SURFACE

Stacy Robinson

ABOUT THIS GUIDE

The suggested questions are included
to enhance your group's reading
of Stacy Robinson's *Surface*.

DISCUSSION QUESTIONS

1. What is the significance of the novel's title? Talk about the imagery of "surface" and "surfacing," and how this is represented throughout the story.

2. How do you think Michael's and Claire's descriptions of their marriage might have differed before Nick's accident? What exactly is a beautiful/good marriage? Is fidelity essential to this?

3. How do you imagine that Claire's upbringing affected her life choices?

4. *Surface* explores the consequences of flawed choices that any of us might be tempted to make. Have you ever made a choice that had implications far beyond what you could have imagined?

5. As a woman finally coming to terms with the fact that her "beautiful" life really wasn't the life she'd wanted, Claire struggles mightily with all that has brought her to this realization. Denial is a theme that runs through *Surface,* as does the idea that what seems beautiful on the surface isn't always so. Did Claire need a cataclysmic event to shake her out of her denial?

6. Of the four main female characters, Claire, Jackie, Gail, and Carolyn, to whom do you most relate?

7. Some readers may view Michael as a jerk, while others may be moved by his humanity. How do you see him? How does Michael change, if at all, over the course of the novel?

8. The themes of betrayal (of others and oneself) and forgiveness loom large in this story. Talk about Claire and Nick's journey toward forgiveness/new beginnings.

9. Despite the disastrous aftermath of Claire's indiscretion, do you think she, Nicholas, and Michael are better off for it at the end of the story? Do you believe that there sometimes are blessings to be found in tragedy?

10. What role does the motif of art play in the book? Discuss the idea of getting "comfortable with the asymmetry" and finding "beauty in the scars," as Claire chants in the labyrinth.

11. How does Claire's journey through the labyrinth transform her views about moving forward? What greater meaning did this experience hold for her?

12. When Claire launches her art consulting business, she finds new purpose and energy—the beginnings of a second act. How do you see Nick adjusting to a potential second act? Michael? Where do you see each of these characters in ten years?